DEADLY STORMS

Bring It Up Series

Deadly Treasure
Deadly Rivers
Deadly Currents
Deadly Storms
Deadly Darkness
Deadly Cold
Deadly Enemies
Deadly Discoveries

DEADLY STORMS

A DEADLY WASHINGTON TRIO UNCOVERED

WILLIAM W. BENNETT

Auctorem House
276 5th Ave, Ste 704-2591
New York, NY 10001
www.auctoremhouse.com
Phone: 1 888-332-7718

Published by Auctorem House: 09/12/2025

ISBN: 978-1-968059-10-1(sc)
ISBN: 978-1-968059-11-8(e)

Library of Congress Control Number: 2025920933

To my children: Jeremy, Jeff, and Serena

Special thanks to my beloved wife, Cathy

When I pondered to understand this, it was troublesome in my sight until I came into the sanctuary of God; then I perceived their end. Surely You set them in slippery places; You cast them down to destruction. How they are destroyed in a moment. They are utterly swept away by sudden terrors! Like a dream when one awakes, O Lord, when aroused, You will despise their form.

—Psalm 73:16–20 (NASB)

CHAPTER 1

Favgnana

Her body aching from keeping still, Penelope Perill watched the battle unfolding between the deep ocean tug and the smaller boat. Whoever commanded *Bring It Up Coral* designed a perfect takedown plan. Men who were obviously crack military troops fired down into the smaller vessel from the deck of the tug, while others came up out of the water undetected, taking the boat quickly.

Moving with precision and speed, the battle was over in minutes, and a single prisoner was escorted onto *Bring It Up Coral*. That rocked her. She hadn't known she wasn't alone, watching, and later she found the guard who was supposed to watch the one prisoner's back. He was dead, his neck snapped. *If they knew someone was there, did they know I was there? No! No one made a move against me. How had they known the prisoner was there when I missed him? These guys are good!*

After that, crew members took the wounded from the smaller boat up, probably to tend to their wounds. Other bodies were checked and left where they lay, obviously dead. Those on the boat that were alive were questioned and herded into the tug's interior, probably to the sick bay. Everything had been handled with absolute military precision. Two hours later, the wounded were transferred back to their boat, now minus the machine gun, and one of the mercenaries not too badly wounded took the wheel and slowly moved away. On the deck of the tug, activity was at a peak, and soon the crane was erected and Kalil shackled to its structure.

Finally, when she was sure no one was watching the shore, she moved from her cramped position. A determined look filled her eyes and changed her facial features, and with a frown, she moved away. Knowing where they would take the sunken vessel, she made arrangements to travel there.

Three days passed while she waited for her turn to examine the contents of the ship and make her report to Sir Edward. During that time, she studied the exploits of *Bring It Up Coral*. Her agile mind connected the dots easily, and though there was no evidence they had anything whatsoever to do with the capture of the Committee of Five, she guessed they were behind it. It was more of an intuitive idea than anything based on actual evidence. Yes, the crew had been in France when the Committee of Five were taken, but there was no evidence they were involved. Nothing. It frustrated her.

Two days later, she sat down in front of Sir Edward's desk and presented her report to her director of operations. He gave nothing away as he read through the pages. She waited patiently, knowing that one could not read this man. Finally, he looked up at her, sliding the report to one side of his desk, his eyes boring into hers. Preparing herself for another mission, she simply sat and waited, watching him.

Sir Edward knew that Penelope Perill was the very best agent he had in MI6. Struggling against her gender and her name, she had risen in the ranks and overcome all obstacles, driven to rise to the top. And, against all odds, she had done just that. Women were jealous because she was lovely, and men constantly underestimated her because she was a beautiful female. Yes, she was quite lovely, a strength she used often in the field, causing men to be distracted. He smiled at her as he organized his thoughts.

"What's your assessment of this outfit *Bring It Up*?" he asked.

"Jim Shepherd and Chance Edwards occupied a room in the Hotel Sofitel Bordeaux Aquitania across the hall from the activist Mike MacCaully. MacCaully missed two of his speeches and claims he was drugged. No trace evidence was discovered in his room, and his medical tests proved negative on anything in his blood. However, he did miss seventy-two hours of the conference that he cannot explain.

"The Committee of Five and Piaf's goons were taken down in the hotel by GIGN. Francois Beaumont of GIGN is credited with the takedown, though the prisoners have not surfaced. Rumor has it they were turned over to Ira Lehman on a ship in international waters. I know for a fact that Kalil was also turned over to Ira Lehman, who collected the man personally from the deck of *Bring It Up Coral*. Moreover, Kalil was roughed up, and he was trained by Chu. Someone on that boat is very skilled in martial arts.

"Captain Shepherd has an international group of soldiers numbering twenty-four, including men from Australia's SAS and possibly British SAS. When they took Kalil's boat, they acted in teams of eight with amazing precision and skill using military tactics and weapons, yet when their ship was searched on several occasions, no such weapons were found.

"My personal assessment is that they are a black ops group of some kind working outside of regular channels. Effective and highly motivated, they have a bona fide cover of being treasure hunters and a legitimate search-and-rescue operation. In my research, I discovered that General March personally released Oxton, Brown, Edwards, and Eustus, and since then they have dropped off the map. Rumor is they all left the service, but I recognized Oxton and Eustus on that crew!

"There is presently no evidence whatsoever connecting these men to several incidents in various parts of the world. I doubt that one analyst would look at the information I gathered and make a connection. However, I am convinced that Captain Shepherd is much more than a simple businessman!"

"Yet you have no evidence," Sir Edward stated flatly.

"None, sir," she replied without rancor.

"So why are you bringing this to me?" he asked, already knowing the answer. He kept the smile off his face.

"If my guess is correct, there is a group of men wandering about the world applying the military solution to various problems without proper oversight. Since you released some of those men, I believe that you at least know about them and what they do. If I can uncover this connection, someone else may! For some strange reason, I don't think that would please you." Penelope sat back and studied her commander.

Sir Edward certainly was not nervous or upset that she had made these connections. If anything, he seemed amused. His reactions puzzled her, but she was determined to get to the bottom of this problem. Something was out of line here, and her fierce loyalty to Great Britain insisted she find the answer, even if she didn't like what she found. In her work, that was often the case. Finally, he leaned forward. His next words surprised her.

"Captain Shepherd has agreed to look into the disappearance of the Minister of International Finance. From time to time, I find that Captain Shepherd can uncover things we cannot through regular channels. Since you are so interested in his crew and what he does, I'm going to assign you to assist him in his investigation. You will report directly to me, and to me alone. While on his boat, you will treat his men and Captain Shepherd with utmost respect and withhold judgment until you have all the facts. I'll ask him to give you all the facts," he added.

She raised an eyebrow at that, now sure he knew much more.

"I want the perpetrators of this heinous crime uncovered and brought to justice. If necessary, I will get sanctions and you will carry out the assignment. Learn everything you can from Captain Shepherd and his crew. They are the very best in what they do. Questions?" He watched with that knowing smile playing at the corners of his mouth, knowing she was assimilating the information, aware that she would be thorough and probably end up working with them.

"I doubt he'll accept a female on his crew applying for a job. Do you have any suggestions?" she replied after a moment of thought.

"I'll call him. Rosa Calienté is flying out to meet them. I'll arrange for you to fly with her," Sir Edward said.

"Just like that?" Penelope asked, her surprise showing in a slight widening of her eyes.

"Just like that," he replied. "Pack your bags. You leave tomorrow.

I'll send the information to your apartment. Good work, Ms. Perill," Sir Edward added.

She didn't like it. Sir Edward, whom she highly respected, knew more about this crew and its operations than she realized. His connection to them suggested that he not only knew about the black operation but that he condoned it. Military units did not operate without oversight, but she was certain that Jim Shepherd's crew did. *What's changed to allow this?*

Rum Cay

Esteban Lorenz remembered the shot that nearly took his life. He remembered it every day for Esteban had only one eye. Over the empty space where his other eye should have been, he wore a leather patch. The missing eye still burned and itched, phantom pain, something he learned to live with. Dreaming about it was another thing. Sleep may elude him and vengeance be denied, but he was driven by one hope, one desire, and today his desire would be realized. On this rainy Rum Cay Island day in the Caribbean, he could see the outline of six divers in the water around the yacht. His stomach churned as he thought of what was to come in only moments, but he was resolved.

Juan Carastino considered himself a modern-day pirate. He hadn't always been a pirate. Once he was one of Castro's pet terrorists. His cell was known for its success, careful planning, and complete anarchy. Then one day they failed, and Juan knew what the consequences would be. True to form, Castro sent in a kill squad to eliminate the entire terrorist cell and their families. Carastino escaped, leaving his comrades to die. It wasn't difficult to find a new money source. He sold his services to one of the less known smaller drug cartels of Colombia, and they were eager to use his talents.

Seizing through piracy at sea luxury yachts for his bosses to use for smuggling their drugs into various countries was child's play. On the side he made a good income by selling the women and children from the yachts into slavery. The men he killed outright because

Carastino was first and foremost a coward. Self-preservation was important, and unknown factors, such as the men who owned and piloted the yachts he pirated, were a source of danger to him. Also, he admitted to himself that he liked the killing. It effectively terrorized the women and children he kidnapped. Once they had seen their loved ones die, he knew they would fear him. At first, they would loathe him, but after watching one of them being repeatedly raped by him and his crew, tortured and beaten until her spirit was completely broken, until they witnessed her change from horror to anticipation at the coming of his men, they would fear him. They would fear him because they would know he could do the same to them. He loved the power that gave him.

His choice of today's yacht had nothing to do with who owned it, but rather from whence it came. It was a beautiful seventy-five-foot yacht, old enough to have a wooden hull and ripe for the taking. She was registered in Plymouth, which meant she came from Great Britain, and time would pass before anyone started looking for her. Looking up from beneath the surface of the clear waters, he could see that both screws were well maintained and that the hull was relatively free from the typical creatures that tended to encrust wooden vessels.

He surfaced, his men coming up with him, as silently as ghosts. It was early morning, and the family was having breakfast on the upper deck. Carefully the divers climbed on board and split up. Two of them went below and brought up every person they found beneath the decks. Two of them went to the bridge to take care of the captain and any of his crew there. Moving quickly and with precision, the pirates went about their tasks. Juan took his friend Carlos with him to the deck where the family was eating breakfast.

A man, curious about the sudden movement of the yacht, rose from his seat and looked over the railing. Carastino fired one shot, and the man fell back, the bullet entering beneath his sternum, punching through his lung and entering his heart through the inferior vena cava and punching out the top, tearing the pulmonary valve and bringing instant death.

Screaming erupted, and suddenly the occupants of the yacht

found themselves facing men with silenced weapons. All the men were herded to the deck where the people were separated, women and children on one side, men on the other. The crew joined the captain of the yacht, huddling together, unsure what was happening, staring at the dead body of a very important man. Juan walked to the center of the deck, turned, and with his silenced Heckler and Koch MP5, opened fire on the men, literally mowing them down.

Some fell overboard, others collapsed on the deck. When they were all down, he drew out a Ruger .22 silenced pistol and shot every man on the deck twice in the head and then nodded to Carlos and the others to throw them over the side. In the bloody water below, bull sharks appeared, and a feeding frenzy thrashed the water. Juan dragged the owner's wife over to watch, forcing her to look. She fainted and vomited on his leg on the way down. Laughing callously, he kicked her aside and gave orders to wash the deck and get moving. Finally, after boarding his own vessel, he turned and looked carefully at the island.

He stared balefully at the hillside of Rum Cay. Behind the leafy foliage, Esteban Lorenz froze. Movement might be seen from the rusty ship, and he wanted to be undetected. Satisfied finally, Juan turned and headed for the bridge. Moments later, the yacht set off for its destination. The women and children were herded into one of the holds on that ship, where they were shackled to the walls and left in the dark. As the second ship finally moved off, Esteban relaxed for the first time that morning. Near the end of his plan for revenge, he allowed himself a small smile. He had his film. Evidence!

Carefully wrapping it in a special envelope, he went home, looked up the address of the British consulate in the Bahamas, and sent the package there. Once that was done, he went about his usual routine of going out fishing, returning to sell his catch to the hotels on the islands, and then drinking his memories into oblivion until he dragged himself home to sleep it off and do it all again the following day.

Carastino's men pulled the yacht into a small boatyard on the Colombian coast, where it would be significantly altered in looks, given a new name and registration, and then put at the disposal of his bosses. Carastino was not far behind, and his ship dropped anchor in the bay. He was handsomely paid for the yacht, and feeling good about his haul, he went below to visit his new slaves. Only after questioning them did he begin to worry. The yacht belonged to Sir Henry Crowell, the minister of finance of England!

He swore and slapped Mrs. Crowell, beat her mercilessly for a few minutes, and then, securing her in a terrible device, brutally raped her. She was still young enough to enjoy, so he allowed his crew to rape her as well, making sure that the prisoners watched the entire grisly scene. Helpless, she screamed until she could scream no more.

Only then, while the poor woman was savaged by the crew before a traumatized audience of family and friends, did he decide that his best move was to eliminate all the evidence. An hour later, he returned to the hold where the woman still lay where he left her, bound cruelly to that horrible device, still in shock, too hurt to do more than breathe, and that shallowly and painfully. Enjoying her horrified stare, he shot each person in the head twice, saving her for last.

The bodies were wrapped in chains and dumped far out at sea, and the denizens of that realm soon reduced them to bones lying scattered along the bottom. For twenty-one days, Carastino hid and waited for an outcry, but none came. No news broke over the disappearance. Nothing was said anywhere. Police or other agents did not pour into the area looking for the yacht or its passengers. Thinking himself safe, he returned to the sea to look for another yacht to steal.

CHAPTER 2

Sixteen days after the murder of Sir Henry Crowell, *Bring It Up Coral* dropped anchor near Miami. People on the shore watched as the ship's high-speed boat was lowered into the water. Two men in uniform climbed down into the sleek craft and the engines roared to life. As the boat sped away, the rest of the crew continued working. Work on board a seagoing vessel never ceased.

Jim and John Shepherd were in the high-speed boat, now cruising at a respectable sixty knots, the throttles pushed to two-thirds power. Correct Craft boat company designed and built the HSB especially for *Bring It Up SAR*. Two turbo-boosted Chevy 350 cu. in. engines powered the thirty-foot craft, giving plenty of power to move at up to ninety knots if necessary. At that moment, Jim and John were having a great time skimming over the waves. Both felt the power of the boat beneath them and the sense of freedom as the air whistled past them.

Wearing their dress uniforms for the occasion, the two men looked immaculate, because the uniforms fitted both their rank and their responsibilities, and somehow even their inner character. They were meeting eight new members and knew the importance of making the right first impression. The uniforms were newly designed with their new insignia and, though expensive, well worth the price.

The eagles on Jim's collar were not the typical silver eagles of the military and maritime companies all over the world. A talented silversmith fashioned his eagle, brown feathered, with a white head and red legs. Only the claws of the feet, spread for attack, were silver. The same eagle was sewn onto the first strip of his four-striped epaulets. *Bring It Up SAR* was written in bright gold thread, with four gold stars above the words between the bright brass button and the first stripe. His blue dress coat had four double strands of golden rope forming four stripes on his sleeves and had been tailored to fit his physique.

John wore the insignia of commander on his coat, the eagle above the three stripes of his epaulets. On his collar, he wore the traditional silver oak leaf signifying his rank as second in command of the ship. Crisp white shirts and matching white pants with a blue stripe outlined in gold twill ran down the outside of both legs. They looked resplendent in their uniforms, though neither would have described themselves that way.

Jim paid for a berth at the marina while John docked the boat and tied her off. He pocketed the key with a whistle on his lips and a spring in his step as he moved to join his older brother. Jim was just ten months older than John, and because of that, they grew up together, going to the same classes through every grade in school. John was an inch taller than Jim, heavier by twenty-five pounds due to bone structure and muscle development.

Jim was six feet two inches tall and weighed two hundred and five pounds. He was broad in the shoulder and narrow in the hip and waist. There was something in the way both men walked that made other men step clear, even though they couldn't have expressed why. Twice on their trip to the gate of the marina, John stopped to talk to a pretty girl. Jim stood by with a taciturn expression on his face, somewhat amused by his brother's antics. Like most brothers, they were quite different in personality, but appreciated the differences rather than resenting them.

They caught a cab to the hotel where their eight new crew members waited patiently for their arrival. All eight were housed at a Courtyard by Marriott hotel near the beach. When the cab dropped them at the front door, Jim paid the driver and gave him a generous tip. They walked into the cool lobby of the hotel and found all eight men seated together in one corner where two couches and several chairs formed a square around a glass table with no discernable purpose other than to occupy space.

They rose as one and saluted when Jim and John approached. Both returned the salute. Jim waved them to sit back down and walked around the group, followed by John, greeting each man and shaking hands. He had memorized their names and knew a great deal about them already.

Calvin Weston led the former SAS group. His accent was standard BBC English. Jim knew he was five years younger than he, but the man had the maturity that comes from five years of military service. Paul Donnelly was a huge bear of a man with a surprising soft deep voice and a very cultured Oxford accent. David Carr and Matthew Banks were slender men with whipcord strength. Men like these not only had the credentials but also possessed an aura that told the captain much. Jim welcomed each one to his team.

The marines recognized two other marines immediately. Exchanges of "semper fi" and "ooh-rah" echoed in the lobby. Bill Dodge, who led this small team, was the same height as Jim, but he must have weighed a good fifteen pounds more. Roger Corrigan and Jim could easily exchange clothing, so close were they in size and weight. Jim liked Corrigan's quiet ways and evaluating brown eyes immediately. Sam Colt looked like the perfect marine in build, certainly projecting that image somehow in his demeanor and body language. Sid Barrett was slender with steady eyes and hands. Barrett possessed an aura of patience about him that Jim sensed immediately, an important virtue in a sniper.

Weston's assessment of these two men was favorable. He'd read about their exploits in both the military and civilian life and was impressed. Looking over their uniforms and the way the two men moved, he decided that though they were a civilian outfit now, the two men were both keeping their military skills honed. There was that indefinable something about both that radiated a deadliness Weston knew and warmed to.

Handshakes tell a lot about a man. There are those who must impress by squeezing hard and those who want to intimidate that lean forward with the handshake and invade personal space. Others were unsure of themselves, and still others intimidated by the presence of a uniform or soldier's prowess. Jim's handshake was solid and friendly and told Weston the man was sure of himself, and even eager to meet him.Dodge, on the other hand, already knew the reputation of both Shepherds and had worked with both on occasion. Marines are a breed apart, and not just because marine boot camp is the most difficult of all the services. They are a breed apart because they had what it took to get through the training, the subsequent training, and the subsequent battles. Hardened to a keen, sharp edge these soldiers knew their measure. It would be an honor to serve under Jim and John Shepherd.

For a moment, Jim looked the men over, sitting there in a group, wearing their new uniforms with a sense of expectation and anticipation that was almost palpable. Again, he felt the pride that comes from command of such men. Each one was, he knew, the best of the best in his particular field and a dedicated and successful soldier. He smiled at them.

"I hope you had a pleasant stay," Jim said to them. There were nods, smiles, and some verbal offers of thanks. "If you'll get your gear, we'll take you to your new home on the water."

Checked out early, they stood as one, each man with a large duffel bag that he hefted easily, and followed the two officers out of the lobby. Military men could fit most of what they owned or needed in such bags, for military life was a Spartan existence. The weapons they'd each requested were already on board the ship.

Outside the hotel, Jim gave instructions to the men which marina address to provide for the cabdriver and took the first cab in the line, piling in with John, Bill Dodge, and Calvin Weston. John sat in the front seat with the driver. No one said much of anything during the short ride to the marina. Jim paid each cab as it arrived and then followed the men out to the boat.

Calvin Weston looked at the boat with respect. It was painted a pearl white with burgundy and aqua blue trim. Experienced eyes picked out the military features of the boat quickly. He hopped aboard, stowed his duffel bag where it would be out from underfoot, and caught the other three bags his men threw on board. Weston saw that Sam Colt was doing the same for his team. Bill Dodge was making his way to his side.

"I think I'm going to like working for this company," he said with a tight grin. They'd introduced themselves at the hotel and liked each other immediately. Both teams spent the two days of R&R at the hotel together, and the men were already bonding. Weston liked Dodge and knew enough about his career to respect the man. Calvin grinned back.

"Never saw transportation like this in the UK," he admitted easily as he stowed the last bag.

The roar of the motors drowned out any other conversation, and John backed the boat out of the slip and then headed her out into the bay. Once past the buoys, he opened her up to sixty knots, and the boat leaped out of the water, heading for the ship. John always enjoyed driving the boat and took full advantage of the opportunity to take it through its paces.

Curious, the new recruits looked at the ship as they neared. Crew began to appear at the rails as the boat approached. Weston and Dodge looked them over critically and decided they were in the presence of soldiers of their own kind. It was obvious in the way they moved, the comments they made as the boat drew to the gangplank lowered to receive them. They grinned at each other.

Dodge had been on navy ships much of his military career at one time or another, and this one was immaculate. He'd read his contract and knew that he and his men would be responsible to keep it that way, and he understood the necessity. The color of the ship was appealing to the eyes, and it gleamed in the Florida sunlight. There was about the whole ship a panache he hadn't seen elsewhere.

On the deck, the CH53D Sea Stallion, with rotors folded, looked resplendent. Beside it, on a stand, sat the submersible, and the new recruits saw the Rigid Raider, also on a stand. An empty cradle stood ready to receive the HSB. As they climbed on board, their eyes weighed the other men on the crew, and each man came to realize he was part of something very special.

Jim introduced them personally to each crew member on the deck and told them that later they would meet everyone in the dining room. One thing that told them volumes about these men was the easy way in which they spoke together and greeted their captain. Only one man snapped to attention and saluted the captain, a lieutenant junior grade that didn't fit the physical features of the rest of the men. Weston decided he was probably an administrative assistant and bean counter of the ilk he disliked and wondered at the man's presence. Such men were, he knew, necessary, but somewhat of a surprise with this crew.

Dodge and his team pounded three other marines they obviously knew well. Wade Adams, Clancy Franklin, and Vince Hall were bumping shoulders and wrestling in a friendly way with the four of them as they exchanged typical greetings. It was, Weston decided, a glorious day full of all the promise of new beginnings.

CHAPTER 3

Later that evening, they made their way down to the dining room. Still in a daze over the weapons room and the accommodations, Calvin tried to fit everything into context. Weston shared a room with his three team members, but it was unlike any room they'd ever been assigned. The beds were comfortable, bunk beds on each side of the room. There were four desks and on each desk, a new MacBook Air. They had their own bathroom to share and comfortable chairs for relaxation. There was even a game table in the room.

Access to the Internet was high speed, and he had a book full of passwords to access military information he'd never had the occasion to visit before. If he wanted to, he could access Interpol! Familiar with the Macintosh operating system, he'd tried out his new laptop with pleasure, and even sent off an email to a girl he knew in the UK. Judging from her response, she was happy to hear from him, despite his news that he would be TDY for some time.

His mind dwelt on that hidden bulkhead in the hold that housed the weapons room. Every weapon he'd requested was there, along with a few he hadn't thought to add. The Kevlar protection these men wore when they went into battle was amazing, and though uncomfortable and heavy, it would give each man an added security.

When one faced heavy fire, it was nice to know a stray bullet couldn't reach vital organs!

In the dining room, they met the entire crew. Jim introduced them and then made the announcement that Lee Roy Brown, Chance Edwards, Phillip Eustus, C. G. Franklin, and Vince Hall were all being promoted to petty officer third class (PO3). Weston and Dodge were pleased that they were now lieutenants on board the ship, and their own teams were also earning a company PO3 pay grade, much higher than they would be earning in the military. Still shocked at the partnership and potential earnings, they grinned at their teammates as the announcements were made.

However, it was not until the following day that both new teams fully realized that they were now in a different dimension of military service. Most of them were convinced that they were on the cutting edge of training, the best of the best in what they did, and unrivaled in skills and physical conditioning. Once they realized that there were men on this team who were steps ahead, they settled down to serious training and the competition every soldier is familiar with. Each man was determined to catch up quickly, and Jim suspected that they would. Motivation exuded from each one.

Jim rode them hard because hurricane season was almost upon them. He needed every member of the crew to be at his or her own personal best. Bill Dodge, who carefully researched the exploits of Jim Shepherd, knew he was in the presence of a military genius and vowed secretly to himself that he would learn everything he could from this man. Watching Jim in the hand-to-hand combat training sessions, and actually sparring with him, convinced him that he had a way to go to match that skill. All that combined made him very optimistic about his future with this company and its ability to deal with any terrorist threat.

Toward the end of three-week training, Jim watched the crew with a deep sense pleasure. Bonding into one cohesive group was complete. His new recruits were better than he expected. It aggravated him that the military could produce soldiers of this caliber but refused to allow them to advance and even use their skills on the level they sought. Military paradigms should have been more flexible, accepting necessary changes and seeing the benefits of those changes. Surely on his team they would be able to do that and more.

Weston already had a nickname everybody picked up immediately. He became Hobbs to everyone on the ship. Donnelly was nicknamed Bear when sparring with John. John, in a clutch with Donnelly, failed to move him, listening to the comments and laughter around him, and tried again unsuccessfully and then replied to the renewed laughter.

"Would somebody move this circus bear out of my way, please?" Everyone enjoyed the moment, as often happened with John's antics, but from that day on Donnelly answered to Bear. For Sam Colt the name came easily. Zeke started that the first day.

"Colt, as in Colt .45?" he asked. It stuck, and Colt became simply 45 and seemed to like it. Roger Corrigan and David Carr became RC and DC because of their initials. Bill Dodge was already nicknamed Viper after the infamous snake and famous car, both of which he facetiously claimed were named after him. Sid Barrett asked for a different scope for his Barrett M82A1, and FM handed him a bottle of Scope mouthwash. After that everyone began to call him Scope. He got even with FM by pouring several bottles of Aqua Velva aftershave into FM's Scope bottle.

Matthew Banks chose the Walther PPK as his favorite pistol and was immediately nicknamed Bond, after the infamous James Bond. The men teased him by saying in a phony British accent, "My name is Bond, Bank Bond!"

Jim watched them all now working hand in hand with the others on a rescue drill and sighed again with pleasure. Each had not only caught up, but now challenged some of his former team. It was indeed an honor to lead such men. He was in command of an amazing group of men, and he gave a silent prayer of thanks.

A small hand wormed its way into his, slender, cold to the touch, seeking the warmth only he could give. Jim looked down at Cecilia with a real smile of delight that changed his stormy green eyes in a way that she loved. He was getting used to her wanting to share his touch, holding hands, and with a twinkle in his sea-green eyes, he leaned down and kissed her. Her kiss was warm, passionate, and stirred within him feelings he had often thought he would never enjoy. She leaned her head against his chest and sighed with pleasure. That too he accepted with equal pleasure.

"I'm not sure that's a proper greeting from a captain to an ensign!" FM said, gliding past them carrying an emergency medical bag. He winked at both of them as he passed. It was a constant teasing they both enjoyed from the rest of the crew.

"I happen to be the captain's favorite ensign!" Cecilia said, her hazel eyes full of laughter, a slight blush on her cheeks.

"Oh yeah! I forgot!" FM said over his shoulder as he hurried on his way.

"You were very quiet at breakfast this morning," Cecilia said to Jim, turning so that she could look up into his eyes. She loved this man to distraction. Remembering the first time she saw him, she shivered a little. There had been something in his eyes, something that even then thrilled her. His feelings went deep and were not easily shown. He was, in many ways, a hard and ruthless man, yet he was a good man with a good heart. The antinomy of his character often amused her. Today, she was worried.

"Tomorrow we become the bait for Carastino," he said simply, his face changing little. Only his eyes grew harder as he spoke. In that expression she saw a very dangerous man, but there was no danger for her. She shivered again, then a thought struck her, and she smiled. Looking up into his eyes once more, a giggle escaped her pretty lips before she spoke.

"I've never heard of bait that ate the fish before!" she said, swaying back and forth, her eyes twinkling with mischief. Jim heard the humor in her voice.

"Yes, well!" Jim said quietly. "Not all this bait is as deadly as I'd like!" he said. Sighing, he looked out to sea. The clear waters of the Caribbean always impressed him. He sighed again.

"Andrea and Rosa can take care of themselves," she said softly.

"And you?" he asked with a smile.

"Three years ago, I would have been an easy victim. I am, whether you like it or not, a warrior now. I fight back!" she said, suddenly kicking at him. It was a classic karate kick, designed to take his head off if it connected. She knew it would not. Her husband, she knew, had almost inhuman speed. He easily blocked the kick, shaking out his hand and wrist afterward with a rueful grin.

"Ow! You kicked me!" he complained, laughing at her. "Is that any way to treat your captain?" He was aware that others had watched the interchange and were grinning at the pair.

"You shouldn't have kissed her, boss!" FM said, passing by at that moment, having finished his part of the drill. He was returning the medical gear. Chance and PU were behind him, and they laughed.

"Looked like gross insubordination and striking a superior officer to me!" DC said, joining in the fun.

"Not superior, merely higher ranking," Cecilia commented demurely.

"She's quick!" DC laughed.

"You have no idea!" Jim said with a huge sigh.

"You two done playing yet?" a voice asked from above.

Jim looked up at his uncle Andrea and responded with a quick smile. Andrea spent his entire life on the sea, and he looked the part. Though Italian by birth, he looked more like a Greek. His rugged face was cracked into a smile. He had a big face, a big nose, a wide generous mouth, a cleft in his chin, and was as brown as a nut from constant exposure to the sun.

"We have a plane to meet," Andrea reminded them with some excitement in his voice. "I do not wish to be late, nephew! And I'm sure you are anxious for your appointment?"

"And an informant to debrief!" Jim added. "We're on our way."

Jim was wearing his dress uniform. The uniforms were new, and he liked the way Cecilia's looked. The Mandarin collar on her coat accented her slender neck. The gold bar on either side of the collar stood out against the bright white material. Tailored to fit her perfectly, the coat accented her feminine figure from every angle. Her white pants, with a wide black stripe and a gold braided cord running down the center of the stripe, looked sharp. Simple white tennis shoes with special rubber soles adorned her tiny feet.

His own coat was white, and he knew, from looking in the mirror, that the eagles on his collar were not at all the traditional silver eagles of a captain. They were the adopted rendition that appeared on every insignia of the company. The eagle was descending on its prey, ready to make the kill, talons outstretched, eyes red with the desire and joy of the kill. The bird had a deadly look to it, and Jim enjoyed the pins that adorned his collar. Brown feathers, red legs, silver talons, white head, and red eyes looked quite impressive. Somehow the bird seemed to perfectly depict the nature of his mission.

Around the sleeve of his coat were four double strands of golden cord, signifying his rank as captain. Four golden strips on a black background signified his rank on his epaulets. The eagle was sewn into the fourth stripe, and between the brass button and the stripes were the words, in gold, *Bring It Up SAR* in a bold Rosewood standard font. Several of the men were responsible for the design, and they wore it proudly. So did he, for that matter, because the uniform and insignia represented the service. Uniforms served an important purpose, and though these were more expensive than any before, he felt the cost well worth the product.

His pants too boasted the wide black stripe and gold cord running down the center. His shoes were black canvas shoes with special rubber soles for slippery decks, and even they had the eagle sewn on the outside of each shoe. Cecilia thought the tailoring of Jim's uniform accented his broad shoulders and narrow hips in a most pleasing way. He looked, she decided, the very person he was, a successful and respected captain of his vessel.

Andrea's uniform was less formal in that he did not wear a coat. His white shirt was open at the collar, showing the crisp white ironed T-shirt beneath. On each sleeve he wore three inverted red chevrons, with one half-circle stripe connecting to the top chevron. Beneath this half circle the eagle insignia was sewn, and above the stripe three red stars, indicating his rank as master chief petty officer. Between the stars and stripe was the logo of the ship, written in white, all set on a black background. Using the insignia design and rank of naval officers seemed appropriate to the unit.

On each shirt collar, he wore a white pin with three red chevrons, the eagle, and perched above, in a triangle, three red stars. Jim thought it the best collar pin he had ever seen for that rank. Andrea's shirt was short sleeved. On the long-sleeved version, he would have four red stripes to indicate the years he had served on the crew. On this shirt, that patch was sewn onto the back between his shoulder blades. He looked, Jim decided, like the professional officer he was.

Andrea's pants did not have the gold braid down the center of the black stripe, but a white braid instead. Like Jim, he wore black canvas shoes with the eagles on the outside of each one. Andrea was still in pretty good shape for a man of his age, and he looked a solid professional in his uniform, a man who knew his way around a ship and on the ocean.

The helicopter was ready for them. Their CH53D Sea Stallion gleamed in the morning sunlight, the seventy-nine-foot rotor picking up speed, creating a downwash that the passengers hunched forward against as they passed beneath. Inside, at the controls, Dorf, Mark, Smitty, Sparks, Hobbs, and DC each sat at a station. Dorf was the pilot, Mark the copilot. As soon as the door was closed and latched by DC, Dorf increased the rotor speed to prepare to lift off.

Cecilia, Jim, and Andrea all took comfortable seats, borrowed from the first-class passenger cabin of a 747, with a table between their four seats. Andrea was flushed and excited because they were going to the airport to meet Rosa. Rosa, flying in from Italy, ran the winery Andrea now owned. Jim didn't have a chance to tease him because as soon as they were moving toward the Miami shore, Sparks called him to the communications center of the aircraft. Ever vigilant, his men often discovered more than anyone would suspect.

"You have a phone call from Dr. Persons in California, boss," Sparks announced, handing over the headphones. Jim bent down, put the phones on his head, and adjusted them, and then pressed the talk button.

"Hey, Dick! How in the world are you?" he said with real pleasure.

Dr. Persons was a friend, met through Dr. Alistair Gregg of the Cairo Museum of Antiquities. Dr. Richard Persons taught archaeology at the University of California, presently at Berkeley.

"I'm good. I'm better than good," Dr. Persons said. He'd never lost his midwest accent, and he looked more like a farmer than a university professor. His doctorate degrees were all in the areas of archaeology. Jim smiled at the memories of working with the man. He also guessed accurately the reason for the call. "I've found information on a ship, and I think you will be interested in this one!" Dr. Persons ploughed in.

"What ship, and why the interest?" Jim queried.

"The *Estelle*. She was built in Chester, Pennsylvania, in 1959. Her length is four hundred and eighty-three feet six inches, and she's a steam turbine–driven beauty. She went down without a trace somewhere in what is known as the Bermuda Triangle. What makes her interesting is that she was owned by a French shipping concern and was carrying a fortune in precious gemstones from Chile, Sonora and Zacatecas, Mexico, Gerais, Peru, Bahai, Brazil, and San Luis Potosí, also of Mexico who bankrolled the entire venture. At least that's what the records say. A group of very wealthy gem merchants seem to have been part of the banking as well. She was also far off course with no explanation and went down without a trace, as often happens in that part of the world. The guys who bankrolled this venture spent a fortune trying to find her!"

"What do you have in the way of research?" Jim asked, his interest piqued.

"Can't say on an unsecured line. We need to meet," Dick replied quickly.

"Okay, Doc," Jim agreed seriously. "I'm going to Miami airport to meet someone. I'll purchase a first-class ticket for you on the first flight out tomorrow. See you then. Bring a digital copy of your research for Zeke with you please. It will be great to work together again. Over and out," Jim said. He smiled as Dr. Persons replied.

"Wow! I'll be packed and ready to go, Jim. You won't regret this one!" Dick said with enthusiasm.

Jim gave the headphones back to Sparks and headed back to his seat. Walking in a helicopter wasn't as easy as walking in an airliner, but he made it without any mishaps. He immediately put on the intercom headphones that connected him to everyone on the chopper and indicated that Andrea and Cecilia should do the same. It was really the only way one could talk in the chopper without yelling. As soon as everyone had earphones in place, he spoke.

"Listen up, everybody. I just talked to Dr. Richard Persons. He's on to a sunken treasure ship called the *Estelle*. I'm bringing him out tomorrow. All I know is that her cargo is precious gemstones and a half dozen of Europe's richest gem merchants who bankrolled the venture. She went down in the triangle," he added with a wan smile.

"Cool!" Dorf responded, voicing everyone's feelings on the subject. "Now everyone quiet while I contact the airport tower!" he added. Everyone immediately stopped talking.

They listened to the chatter between Dorf and the tower and watched through the windows as the huge helicopter came to rest near a hangar at the edge of the airfield. Although used to the technical jargon in such an interchange over the radio, it was still interesting, and each person translated the degrees of the compass into a direction easily. Attention turned to the field as the rotors slowed and stopped. A stretch limousine waited there.

On the way to the terminals, Andrea leaned forward to look around Cecilia at Jim. "I meant to tell you the riverboats have arrived in Key West. They have been placed in storage until we need them. Why did you order them shipped down, by the way?"

"We may need them to run down our pirates or their bosses," Jim answered. "We won't really know until I've questioned Esteban Lorenz," he added.

"Also, Calvin Beardsley called. The sportfisherman didn't work out, so he sold it for a profit and bought a one-hundred-eighteen-foot Gulf Cruiser Majesty Liner. She's outfitted and will arrive tomorrow sometime in the afternoon. He's bringing her over himself," Andrea said. "According to his account, she is a fine ship that will please us much better than the sportfisherman."

At that moment, they arrived at the terminal, went through a gate, and drove right out onto the runway to meet a Learjet that just landed. Rosa Calienté walked majestically down the steps to the tarmac as Andrea leaped from the limousine to meet her. Their embrace was warm, and Cecilia sighed, her head resting on Jim's shoulder as they stood together waiting for the two to join them at the car.

"Isn't love great?" Cecilia was enjoying Rosa's chase and Andrea's attempts to avoid the ultimate commitment. Andrea, she knew, was afraid that having been unmarried all these years, he would be a difficult partner for any woman. He was set in his ways, and he loved the sea. No woman would want a man who was gone months at a time. But Rosa had plans for Andrea, and she obviously set her heart on winning him. Cecilia knew that she would eventually succeed.

Jim didn't reply, disappointing Cecilia slightly. His nature was to hold his emotions in check, and often he seemed almost afraid of emotions. He hated emotionalism and dramatics with a passion. With her he had opened up considerably but still had a way to go. She smiled up at him, and he smiled back. At least where they were concerned, he thought love was great. They stepped forward together to greet Rosa.

CHAPTER 4

A very beautiful young woman walked down the steps of the jet behind Rosa and stood aside as the friends met. Then she stepped forward and introduced herself.

"I'm Penelope Perill," she said, extending her hand in an aggressive manner. Jim smiled at her.

"Sir Edward told us you would be joining us. He didn't mention that you would be quite so ravishing, though."

Penelope raised an eyebrow. Often people laughed at her name or made comments about her being a woman. This man had done neither. He seemed to accept her as the professional she was and constantly fought to have others recognize. She smiled, and when she did, her whole face changed. Maybe working with this man would not be as difficult as she had thought. Still, she was prepared to fight for recognition of her incredible skills and abilities. Cecilia was smiling at her. She shook hands.

"My husband is very astute, you'll discover quickly," she commented. "You've come highly recommended, and we trust Sir Edward completely. I'm certainly glad you're joining us."

Sir Edward had indeed warned them about the chip Penelope carried on her shoulder and her distrust of Jim's unit. Her name was against her, and she was a beautiful woman. She wanted to be the best agent MI6 ever produced, and she was fighting an uphill battle to be recognized as what she was. Sir Edward was convinced that she was indeed second to none in his agency. He hoped very much that she would shine on this mission.

They climbed into the limousine for the trip to the end of the field, where they found the CH53D already revved and ready to go. As Penelope entered the interior of the helicopter, she did a double take. It was unlike any CH53D upon which she'd ever flown. The interior had been redesigned and refitted with more comfortable seating and separated by a folding wall; the cargo area was presently closed to eliminate as much noise as possible. Seats, though from a 747, were covered in vinyl, making them waterproof, a necessity at sea. Each seat was accompanied by a set of headphones for communication during flight.

One of the tallest men she had ever seen was waiting to welcome them. The two stripes on his epaulets and connected pair of silver bars on his collar identified him as a lieutenant. He bowed over her hand and kissed her knuckles lightly, and then surprised her by punching her on the shoulder in a friendly way.

"Zowie! I've heard a lot about you, Pen. You don't mind if I call you Pen?" His eyebrows were raised in question, and she shook her head, her dimples showing with her smile. Few men had ever punched her like that, like she was one of the guys, and she felt an instant liking for this giant. "And I hope you don't mind if I beg you to take this guy down a peg or two on the mat during training!" he added, stepping aside to allow Mark Drumheiser to greet her.

"Don't mind him!" Mark said with a grin. "He hates the fact that a little guy like me can kick his great big muscular rear end around the mat. I won't go easy on you!" he added, shaking her hand, seeming to sense her strength.

"Nor will I," she replied lightly.

"I'm Mark Drumheiser," he introduced himself, turning away. He was wearing the insignia of a lieutenant junior grade, one pay grade lower than his giant friend. She watched the two of them move into the flight deck and joined the captain and his wife.

Andrea and Rosa were huddled close together in a pair of seats behind the captain. Penelope sat across from the captain and made a mental note to thank Sir Edward. She'd read the jacket for this man, and his exploits for the marines, navy, and now in his own company were legendary. He was, she knew, perhaps the most formidable man in antiterrorism forces anywhere in the world, even if she did disagree with his methods. After watching him move, she had no doubts about his physical prowess either. Deciding she could learn from him and remembering Sir Edward's command to withhold judgment, she settled in to observe and learn.

Jim, in turn, studied Penelope carefully. She was as tall as Cecilia, perhaps a quarter of an inch taller. Blessed with a nice figure, she was a striking woman with pretty blonde hair tightly pulled back into a ponytail. Her eyes were strikingly blue, and she had a straight nose, turned up slightly, and lips that formed a pert cupid's bow when she was relaxed. Her ears were small and lay close to her head. She did not look at all like a deadly adversary, which was all to her advantage.

Introducing her to the rest of the crew was fun. She obviously enjoyed the attention of the men. Jim noted that she paused noticeably when he introduced her to Weston and his crew and Dodge and his three men. *What does she know about them? The presence of Weston certainly caused a reaction!*

That afternoon she trained with them and proved her worthiness quickly. To her surprise, however, she was no match for Mark or Jim. Her respect for the little man everyone called Mad Mark grew quickly as they sparred on the mat. Mark was fast, confident, and skilled enough to make defending himself against her look easy. Picking herself off the mat for the third time, she grinned at him. He'd used her own aggression against her. Instead of chastising her, he simply gave her a high five and nodded toward Jim.

Jim Shepherd was a different story altogether. At no time before had she had to work to stay balanced and concentrate so that her speed did not work against her. Shepherd was balance! The man seemed to flow from form to form with a speed that was truly frightening. Twice he stopped short of a killing blow, not so much to prove he was better, but because it was part of his style. She noted with some relief that he was no easier on his wife. Cecilia grinned at her as she picked herself up off the mat. She smiled back.

John Shepherd wasn't quite as good as his brother, but he was very close and vastly different in his style. He was a match for her, neither gaining the advantage, much like her battle with Drumheiser. She liked his smile and easy manner, though, and was somehow moved by him. Up until this moment, no man had ever moved her in any way, and it gave her a moment of alarm.

After the hand-to-hand combat training, she was introduced to the war room and given a locker and weapons. At least now she realized why no one ever found the weapons they sought. The design of the bulkhead and room was genius!

Every weapon she'd requested was there and in perfect working order. Following the men to the shooting gallery set up in a hold beneath the rear deck, she watched with growing appreciation as they demonstrated both terrifying speed and awesome marksmanship. It was an eye-opening experience to witness the skill of the shooters at the range. None of them were mavericks or showed signs of the Wyatt Earp syndrome. They were serious soldiers, every one.

In the dining room, she met the kitchen crew and Sturdy, who was even taller than Dorf, and even more impressively built! His huge hand engulfed hers in a gentle handshake. Abe, equally impressive with his body-builder physique, welcomed her just as gently. Looking over the other three crew members in the kitchen, she decided all of them were former military, much to the delight of Windy. The food was excellent, designed for an active military unit, but much better than anything she'd ever been offered in such a setting.

During dinner, Jim, at Sir Edward's urging, explained the purpose of the company and their clandestine activities. She listened as he explained the advantages of a paramilitary operation unhindered by bureaucratic oversight. Agreeing with him secretly, she raised the question of vigilantism. Without hesitating a tic, Jim answered her.

"What we do is neither vengeance nor vigilantism. President Royce, Admiral Runion, Ira Lehman, Sir Edward Marsh, Petros

Kladas, and General James March all know what we are going to do before we do it. Their votes are added to those of the team, and unless the vote is unanimous, we don't do it." He watched her as he spoke. A moment passed as she thought about what he said, and he decided she would always carefully consider the words of others. Understanding her hesitation, he waited patiently.

"That's what Sir Edward told me, probably to allay my own fears of working with you. Still, you have a lot of freedom. Dangerous freedom that in the past has proved too difficult for some men to handle!" she pointed out after organizing her thoughts.

"That's *why* we are effective. We have the freedom we need to act. So far, we've managed to avoid letting that freedom go to our heads," Jim said.

"You're talking about the military solution," she pointed out, one eyebrow raised slightly.

"With extreme prejudice," Jim replied, his eyes suddenly hard. She thought about his answers, sorting through them, remembering the honesty with which he'd answered and the amount of information he'd allowed. She decided that she could trust this man, and that came as a surprise to her.

"Do I take my orders from you, then?" she asked.

"Only if you want to. Technically you don't work for me. You work for Sir Edward. You'll have to decide that for yourself. I respect your position and will do my utmost to involve you in all decision-making. If you were part of this unit, you would be considered an equal. We use rank here to define responsibility, not for authority. Is that satisfactory?" Jim answered.

"Thank you, Captain. It is," she replied.

"You'll find out very quickly that rank doesn't mean that much in this outfit. Feel free to call me Jim, or Shep if you want to. We're all professionals, equal in intelligence and skill for the most part. I respect that. A unit like this develops a character all its own, which is for the best," Jim said with an easy smile.

She thought about that, nodding slowly, and looked around the table at the others to see that they were all in accord.

"Yeah! He's a great captain!" FM piped up with a wicked grin. "I've personally seen him kiss an ensign!"

"That ensign happens to be my wife!" Jim retorted, putting his arm around Cecilia protectively. "And I like kissing her!" To emphasize his words, he kissed her. Just to make his point, he made sure the kiss lasted a long time. Everyone laughed at the diversion.

Later that night, settled into her guest room accommodation, Pen thought about her day and decided that working with this team would be a very positive experience. In a way she secretly wished she could join them, because she often wished for the freedom they seemed to have. Yet the freedom also frightened her and made her uneasy. *Are these men of strong enough character to escape the temptation to misuse the freedom for their own ends?* Sighing, she gave up the thoughts and relaxed. Sleep came easily as the boat rocked gently in the swells.

Activity outside her door woke her at 4:30 in the morning. She rose, showered, and dressed in her tan work uniform, provided by the company. Her rank, she saw, was that of an ensign. The work uniforms did not show rank except for the hats. Her tan hat had the gold bar of her rank sewn onto the front. The company logo with the eagle was sewn onto the bill of the hat. Like the rest of the uniforms, hers had been tailored to fit comfortably.

Making her way down to the galley, she found herself in the middle of a group of crew members with the same idea. Breakfast, she saw, came early on *Bring It Up Coral*. Buffet tables lined one side of the dining area. Eggs, bacon, fruit, and yogurt were available. At one end of the buffet, she found pancakes, syrup, muffins, toast, and butter. Helping herself to eggs, bacon, fruit, and a glass of milk, she sat down at the nearest table already occupied by five men. As she approached, they all stood and waited until she was seated before joining her. She was impressed.

Two of the men were from Australia by their accents, and they introduced themselves as Ox, a medical officer, and PU, pronounced *Pew* like the bench in a church. Two others were obviously American. They introduced themselves as Viper and 45. She knew the other gentleman at the table, Calvin Weston, British SAS legend. For some reason, the men all called him Hobbs, though he introduced himself as Calvin. She put it together quickly and nearly choked with laughter. He was as unlike Hobbs as anyone could be.

She introduced herself by her full name and got no reaction. These men went up in her estimation. Most people teased her about her name. It was inevitably Viper who gave Pen the nickname she would carry the rest of her career. Calvin spoke.

"We'll have to call you something other than Pen. I know! Pipi, as in Pippi Longstocking! Also, your name is two Ps, so it works!" He looked around for the men to agree, and they all nodded. "There's definitely a bit of that troublemaker, for sure!" Hobbs added, wiping his mouth with his napkin so she couldn't tell if he was smiling or not.

"It just seems to fit with the initials PP," Viper repeated, hoping Penelope would not become angry.

Far from angry, she thought about it for a few minutes and then nodded. "Good enough by me!" she announced, nodding emphatically. "I like it."

And she did! Without knowing it, these men had inducted her into their inner circle by giving her a nickname. That was something she had never experienced before, and it gave her a deep sense of satisfaction to know that she was accepted as one of them. Keeping her pleasure hidden, she listened to the conversation at the table and ate a delicious breakfast.

CHAPTER 5

At midmorning, the CH53D took off again for the airport to collect Dr. Persons. Jim and Cecilia went as a courtesy to the good doctor. While they were gone, Pen was introduced to the CIC. Her duties, she learned, involved working with Zeke in gathering intelligence. Stepping into the cool interior of the CIC, she paused to take it all in again. The technology in this room alone was almost mind-numbing.

Zeke did not get up when she came in, hardly even glanced her way. He was working at three different stations, almost at once, the information he sought flashing on six different screens around him. He nodded sideways at a chair next to him.

"Plant yourself, Pipi!" he said with a grin. "We've got work to do!"

Sitting demurely, she watched him for a few seconds and began to take in what he was doing. His speed was inspiring. Without being told, she began to gather the printouts and separate them into three different piles. He nodded, almost absently.

"I didn't think you were watching," she said, looking at him.

"Uncle Zeke is always watching!" he said.

"Uncle Zeke. That's your nickname, isn't it?" she asked.

"Yup. Gave it to myself," he added with some pride.

Lunch hour came, and the crew stopped what they were doing,

and everyone headed down to the dining room. At any time, there were fruit drinks, sports drinks, water, flavored water, and various types of soda available. Meals were taken at mealtime, and so far, she had seen no one eating anything between meals or after dinner. The discipline impressed her.

Cold cuts, cheeses, various types of breads and buns, salads, lettuce and tomato for the sandwiches, pickles, olives, radishes, and fruit were abundant. Most of the men avoided bread at lunch, eating mostly high protein foods. Those who had no weight issues took bread, but most didn't. She followed suit. Physical fitness was important to her.

Penelope was secretly pleased when John Shepherd and his wide-shouldered friend Wade came over and sat on either side of her. Although she listened mostly to Wade explaining the construction of the bulkhead wall that hid the war room, she was most aware of John sitting quietly next to her, shoving food into his mouth as though he had to finish eating in seconds. She noticed that Wade ate the same way, very quickly, even though he was talking. They were not alone in eating as if it was the last time they might for some period. Whenever John injected a remark, it was funny and brought real laughter to her lips.

Soon after lunch, they went through another two hours of physical training. Today they were zip-lining from the helicopter to the deck. Each team of four worked closely together, seeming to drop at the same instant and land together. She was part of Zeke's team, with Jim Shepherd leading, FM and Smitty dropping on either side of her. Concentrating on skills she hadn't often used, she landed easily with the men, never missing a beat in timing.

When the exercise ended, they went into the deepest hold and climbed thirty feet of rope. Most of the men did it in the pike position, and they did it fast. She was disappointed to find herself seconds behind the slowest climber and chided herself. To her surprise, Jim said nothing about her performance. It was Cecilia who spoke as Pen watched Jim walk away.

"He knows you'll do your best to catch up. He knows all of his crew are committed." She smiled as she said it. "These guys do this every day, so he didn't expect you to be where you want to be."

Pen thought about that, and she realized that Cecilia knew she wanted to be the very best, to push herself to excel. Smiling easily at Cecilia, she allowed herself a moment to chide herself for not being as fast as the men who did this every day.

Just before dinner, a yacht half the length of their ship appeared beside them, her diesel horns hooting twice as she dropped anchor less than fifty yards distance. Pen watched as the crew lowered the HSB into the water and Driver took it over to collect the four men on the yacht. Calvin Beardsley and two of his team were dressed in Hawaiian print shirts over grimy blue jeans that hadn't seen a washing machine in several days. Beardsley had a reputation, and she appreciated that this company sought out what she considered the best shipwright in the business. The other man was obviously an islander, very nervous, and showed all the signs of a man who abused alcohol.

Nulli Secundum lay proudly at anchor. She was a Gulf Cruiser Majesty Liner, one hundred and eighteen feet in overall length. At the waterline she was ninety-four feet two inches in overall length. Her beam was nearly twenty-five feet, and she had a fairly shallow draft of five and a half feet. For long trips across the water, she could carry up to fifty-five hundred gallons of diesel fuel and over a thousand gallons of water. Displacing 110 tons, she boasted ten berths, five cabins, seven bathrooms, a crew berth for three, and a bathroom for the crew. As a luxury yacht, this beauty lived up to her reputation.

Beneath her fiberglass hull, she was powered by two CAT C30 1,550 hp engines. Beardsley had modified those engines, the shafts, hull, and screws so that instead of the originally designed twenty-two knot speed, she could now do thirty knots across the waves. Inside each berth was a secret compartment for the storage of weapons and other gear. In the main saloon, the entertainment center actually turned one hundred and eighty degrees to hide a weapons store behind.

From her fly bridge, main deck, and down to the lower deck,

she was everything anyone could wish for in luxury appointments. Every technology possible was included in her design, including some extras Smitty and Zeke thought necessary. Few would imagine what type of advanced equipment this ship possessed, or why it was there. Jim allowed the crew ample time to go over the yacht before calling a team meeting in the conference room.

With everyone crowded into the room, it seemed cramped, and Jim decided it was time to talk to Calvin Beardsley about redesigning the ship to accommodate the number of people now crowding the ship to near capacity. No one complained about the lack of space or having to move around people with whispered apologies as they helped serve the men around the table. Quiet settled over the room as Jim sat down. Penelope was impressed with the respect this man received from his men. Having come up in the royal navy herself, she knew this was rare indeed.

For an hour, he questioned Esteban Lorenz about the video he'd provided to the British Consulate. Lorenz was glad to talk, and as he watched the men around him, he decided that perhaps he would see his revenge finally on the man who had killed his best friend and left him for dead in a sea full of angry sharks. The man knew that his falling overboard was what saved him from that final shot to the head, guaranteeing death. After the debriefing, he was escorted off the ship onto his own boat, towed by the yacht, and left. What he thought he kept to himself, never speaking of his visit to the ship to anyone, even when in a drunken stupor.

"We're going to try to lure a pirate to take the yacht," Jim said quietly when Lorenz was gone and the escorts returned. "You've all been briefed on the background of Juan Carastino. Our plan is simple. Cecilia and I, Andrea and Rosa, FM and Pen will occupy the yacht. Banks, Boswell, and Drumheiser, you're elected as crew." Jim grinned at the three men. "You get to drive, cook, clean, and serve us rich folks as we luxuriate!" he added, mimicking a hillbilly accent.

"I get shotgun!" Mark said.

"You get KP!" Jim replied. "Banks serves, Driver drives!"

"Slave driver!" Mark's comment was served with mock surprise and facetiousness.

"*Bring It Up Coral* shadows us, never more than thirty minutes helicopter flight time from our position," Jim continued. "We are on yellow alert. Commander Shepherd is in charge here. Andrea is in charge on the yacht. We'll be in constant contact, and I know Uncle Zeke will be watching," Jim added with a smile.

"Half an hour, boss?" FM said. "Can't we keep them any closer?"

"We'll take down the pirates. Their MO seems to involve the takedown and then an eighteen-minute window before their ship arrives to offload the slaves. That gives everyone time to get to us before the main ship arrives. I want the guns on the CH53D locked and loaded. Anyone breathes wrong on that ship, and I want it hit hard! Any questions?" He waited as the men thought the plan over.

"How are you going to take down the bad guys?" Windy asked. He'd missed that part of the earlier meeting.

"The women will all be armed. When the pirates come on board, we'll provide cover, and they'll draw their weapons and take care of the pirates," Jim replied.

"Yes, we will shoot them, just a little bit!" Rosa said proudly.

Everyone laughed, and FM spoke into the laughter, "Just exactly how do you shoot someone just a little bit?"

"She means we wound them," Andrea said, wiping tears from his eyes. Rosa did not look at all flustered.

"My English, it is not always correct in the things I say, no?" she said haughtily into the quiet that settled over the room. "But my aim is always correct!" she boasted. No one questioned that. They were all familiar with her skill with a pistol.

"Taken out by women! Now that's poetic justice!" Inchworm said from the side of the room.

Early the next morning Jim, Cecilia, Andrea, Rosa, FM, and Pen climbed on board *Nulli Secundum*. The name meant "second to none." Mark, Driver, and Bond were already on board in their uniforms of service for the journey. Driver was resplendent in a captain's cap, shirt, and white short pants, white shoes, white socks. Bond wore the white uniform of a waiter, and Mark the white uniform of the cook. As he welcomed the others aboard, he looked down at his uniform with a frown.

"If anybody I know sees me in this getup, I'm poisoning your breakfast," Mark said with a grin. Everyone was sitting around the table waiting for breakfast to be served at the very late hour of seven o'clock.

"We'll have to learn to stay up late, rise late, and pretend convincingly to be lazy," Jim said, stretching as if already weary. "Is one of our biblical characters about to serve breakfast?" he added peevishly.

"Biblical characters?" Pen queried, laughing despite her attempts to keep a straight face.

"You know, Matthew, Mark, and Jack," Jim said lightly.

"I don't remember Jack in the Bible, honey," Cecelia said with smile.

"The beanstalk guy! I'm sure he's in there somewhere. Doesn't it say in Genesis 6 that there were giants in the land?" Jim asked innocently. He looked around the table with such a comical expression that everyone broke into gales of laughter.

"You know, boss, there's a special place in hell for guys like you," FM said, and everyone broke up laughing again.

At least we're beginning a dangerous mission on a light note! Jim looked around as the group finally gained control of themselves. Bond put the food on the table, then took a plate up to Driver. Mark and Bond would eat in the crew's mess. It was separate from the dining room, separated by a door, so they were within easy earshot.

Jim discovered very quickly that acting lazy was not easy. He chaffed at the inactivity. Twice daily he went into the workout room to jump rope and lift weights. The rest of the time he sat on one of the cushioned seats on the fly deck with Cecilia next to him reading. He liked to read, but he hated to sit still for hours. To keep him sane, Driver stopped the yacht occasionally so they could swim about in the crystal clear water.

Jim wore nothing but swim shorts thereafter. Cecilia wore a black one-piece, and Pen wore a bright red bikini. FM took to wearing just his swimsuit, like Jim, while Andrea and Rosa dressed casually and changed each time they swam. After four days, Jim began to enjoy the leisure. His tan grew to match his arms and legs, and Cecilia thought that he looked impressive in his white trunks, with his tanned hard body, gleaming white teeth, and his shining green eyes from his darkening face.

They enjoyed swimming among coral reefs. Jim often held Cecilia's hand as they leisurely kicked their fins in tandem. She could tell that he watched her when she swam to the surface and began wearing her white bikini for his benefit. He touched her more often when she wore that bathing apparel, another reason to wear it most often. Jim decided he liked watching her swim, especially in that bikini, because it accented the beautiful lines of her body as she moved in the water. Beneath the surface of the water, she was graceful in her motions and a strong swimmer.

Pipi began to loosen up as well. All her life she had worked to be accepted for what she was, and everyone on this crew fulfilled that dream. Most of the men on the crew looked upon her as an equal, while the others seemed almost afraid to speak to her, perhaps because she was a beautiful woman. Jim especially sought her advice often and seemed to enjoy her expertise as an asset.

After passing through customs at Bimini Blue Water and Marina, where they dropped anchor for that purpose, they lunched at the Sea Crest Hotel before departing. Swimming became their favorite pastime during the next days. Yet even while they swam and frolicked, they paused often to scan the horizon while on the boat and to scan the surrounding waters when they were beneath the surface.

To keep up their cover, they never used diving equipment, and they didn't have any on board the ship. When they came to an island, they put into shore and spent money at the casinos, dined at the best restaurants, and bought the finest wines to take on board the boat. Purchasing groceries always included the very best cuts of meats and most expensive fruits and vegetables. At the casinos, they won more often than they lost and always quit while still ahead, much to the dismay of the owners.

When gambling, they never dropped more than five thousand dollars total when they didn't come away winners. Anyone watching would recognize the pattern of the ultra rich clientele that visited the islands on a regular basis. The women bought expensive outfits in the high-end stores, sometimes dropping more than they did gambling! At each stop they also did research, walking through bookstores, visiting museums, spending hours in the libraries.

This was a part of his life Jim had only enjoyed once so far, and he was enjoying again exploring new places and discovering stories and facts about lost ships and treasure. He and Andrea spent hours in the libraries and bookstores at each island. From the Bimini Islands, they traveled north to Grand Bahama and the Abacos.

At Club Soleil Resort and Marina, Jim picked up on their tail the first time. There was nothing specific that drew his attention to the man, but once his attention was drawn, the man's body language told him he didn't want to be seen or identified. Rosa made sure they dined at the finest restaurants, bought the finest wines, visited the museum and bookstores, and then took the ladies shopping while the men pored over the books and charts. Everything they did identified them as rich tourists. Twice during the day, Jim spotted their tail, but he made sure the man wouldn't know he'd been spotted. Andrea had become so adept at this skill that he too could describe their shadow down to the shape of his ears.

For Pen this was an adventure she had been denied for many years. Concentrating on her career in MI6, she had not allowed herself to be a woman, and she was finding the transition difficult. Cecilia saw what was happening and seemed to know just the right thing to say at the proper time to help her along. Very quickly the two young women became close friends.

This was also something new to Penelope. Up until this venture, she had never taken the time to make friends. Her work kept her occupied, and she knew the dangers of any entanglements during a mission. Nor had she worked with a team enough times to form close relationships. Now, however, she was spending weeks with one group of people, one team, and discovering that having a female friend like Cecilia was a positive experience. That came as a surprise to her, for she had never considered her need for such a relationship.

From Great Abaco, they traveled south to Dunmore Town on Eleuthera Island. There were six marinas on that island, and they visited each one, staying around the island for six days. Each day Jim saw the tail at least once and, at Hatchet Bay Marina, got a good look at his boat.

After visiting Davis Harbor Marina, they headed west to Nassau, putting in at Lyford Cay Club and Marina for two days to spend nearly one hundred thousand dollars. Pen was shocked by the largess until Jim let her in on the true state of their combined wealth. A hundred thousand dollars was a drop in the bucket and good seed money to spread the rumor of wealth throughout the islands. Providing the essential picture in a perfect cover seemed to come second nature to Jim. Pen appreciated that. She also realized that his wealth would allow him to do things working for a government denied. Ms. Perill was able to laugh at herself for her instant jealousy.

CHAPTER 6

They cruised along the Great Exuma Islands but to demonstrate that they were traveling at their own leisure, did not put in at any ports. Instead, they went snorkeling along the coral reefs. At one of the more spectacular reefs, they came upon a research crew studying the coral beds. They were from Norfolk, Virginia, and belonged to the Old Dominion Center for Coastal Physical Oceanography. In visiting with the captain of the ship, they learned that the tour might be cut short because of a lack of funds. Dr. Henry Booker, who was leading the expedition, heard the captain and sadly shook his head.

He walked over to Jim and Cecilia and introduced himself. Jim liked him immediately. Almost painfully thin and nearing sixty-five, this would be his last visit with the school. He had intense pale blue eyes, a long beak of a nose, and an engaging smile. Dr. Booker was most concerned for the coral reefs in this area because they were being so badly damaged by tourism, sewage, and waste disposal problems in the islands, along with other natural factors.

Dr. Booker also talked quite freely about God's magnificent creations. That, in itself, was unusual in this day and age and only endeared him further to the members of Jim's unit. For several minutes, they shared their faith with each other, unashamed. Jim was pleased to hear Pen share her own faith, which seemed quite deep.

She too was pleased that the crew with which she served seemed to be following Christ. Often, she saw that dedication to the Lord in the crew, seeing it for what it was and appreciating it. Even when the men fought and argued, they were quick to admit wrong, ask forgiveness, and the injured party seemed ready to reconcile quickly.

Watching the college students on deck, and later beneath the waves, Jim decided he would do something to help. He found Dr. Booker working in one of the labs and approached him with a wide smile. Dr. Booker wept tears of joy when Jim handed him two bound stacks of cash amounting to fifty thousand dollars.

"Doc, it's for *you* to decide how to use it! It's not a gift to the college or the center but to *you* personally. I know you'll use it wisely," Jim said, receiving a firm hug, almost embarrassed by the show of emotion. It was quite obvious that the good doctor had been deeply touched by Jim's generosity. He held Jim's hands and prayed a prayer of thanksgiving for God's provision that touched Jim's heart.

"We'll be able to stay our whole tour with this!" Henry said through his tears.

"Good for you. Tell these kids they're doing a fine job. What they are discovering here will affect how people treat our oceans in the future, and that's important. I'm just glad they have a teacher who knows and appreciates the creative genius of our God!" Jim shared, shaking hands and escaping to his own yacht finally. Cecilia remained quiet until they were on their way again. She put her hand lightly on his forearm, standing over him for a moment.

"That was a wonderful thing and very unselfish. You can't even claim that for taxes!" she said, bending down to kiss him.

"What did you do?" Andrea asked.

"I gave the professor fifty thousand to keep his studies going," Jim admitted. "Cash gift, straight to him for his use. I think it surprised him!" Jim shrugged as if it were nothing.

The company, he knew, gave donations to worthy causes, and not just for tax purposes. In his newfound faith, Jim realized that his wealth was a gift from God and that he needed to view it that way. All the partners felt strongly about that, and gifts were given regularly. Giving Dr. Booker the money had been the first impulsive response to God's prodding he could remember, and somehow it felt wonderful to have been able to respond in that way. However, his feelings of euphoria soon wore off as the grim reality of the future came back full force.

It was at Rum Cay that Jim decided the pirates would make their move. He and Cecilia bought an entire island through a realtor on Rum Cay and paid cash for the land. Eventually he would call Ken Worthington to arrange for a resort hotel and other buildings to be built there, and perhaps a research center. As they walked out of the realtor's office Jim saw the tail talking earnestly on a pay phone across the street.

They anchored the yacht near the Chimney, a vertical tunnel that descends from 50 to 100 feet. It leads to a coral cavern. Coral heads rise from the floor, and there are encrusted forms along the sides. From the cavern, a ravine leads to a drop-off at 130 feet. It wasn't as popular a spot as Snowfields, but still well known. It was near this spot that the British minister of finance was killed.

At dinner, Jack stayed at the wheel, watching the underwater monitors so he could warn the crew and passengers when the divers arrived. Jim called *Bring It Up Coral* before they left Rum Cay, and he knew the ship was ten miles away, on the other side of the island. John was following a grid pattern, as if searching for something. So far only one boat had checked them out, a small ship that John recognized as the pirate ship. It was staying on that side of the island too. The helicopter was already sitting on the ground on the Rum Cay airstrip with two teams hidden inside, armed and ready to attack. Until then it had made two runs for supplies, so this was not unusual.

"Jim, we have divers in the water thirty feet away. I'm coming down to the kitchen so we're all together," Driver said into his headset. He appeared a moment later with a grim smile.

Pen checked her H&K Mark 23, made sure the safety was off, and slid it down the back of her bikini pants. Cecilia did the same with hers. They grinned at each other, one nervous, one a professional who was used to this. Pen saw the signs and nodded slightly to let Cecilia know everything would be okay. Rosa chose an FN Five-seveN for her weapon and tucked it in her handbag. It was the only thing in the bag. Smiling at Andrea, she patted the bag.

Driver came down, helped himself to some bread, and watched as Mark and Matthew took up their places. Less than a minute later, the divers showed up, shouting in Spanish, brandishing their AK-47s menacingly, herding everyone together. The men did exactly what was expected. They formed a curtain of protection for the women, and unseen behind them, the women drew their weapons. Carastino was entering the room to separate the men from the women, quite sure he had the upper hand, carelessly holding his AK-47.

Six divers crowded into the dining room when Jim suddenly and unexpectedly dropped to his knees, and the other men did the same, their hands laced behind their heads. Each woman took two targets. Pen shot Carastino's thumb off, the bullet taking the AK-47 out of his hand. Her second shot killed the man next to him, the bullet entering beneath the right eye, close to the nose. He had been too close to firing at them with that deadly automatic rifle to take any other shot. Cecilia and Rosa aimed for knees, each hitting their mark. The deafening echo of gunfire ceased as suddenly as it began.

Carastino held his bleeding stump tightly and looked with dismay at his men. Not one shot had been fired by the pirates! Then something exploded against the side of his head, and he dropped to the floor.

"Take the boat!" Jim commanded into his headset, which he quickly put on after the first shots were fired. He nodded at Mark, who stood over Carastino. Mark had knocked the pirate out cold.

Cecilia and Pen cauterized Carastino's thumb by the simple expedient of using a lighter fluid–type fire starter that lay in a box next to the propane fireplace in the grand saloon. If the smell of burning flesh affected either of them, it didn't show. They wanted to get the task done before he became conscious. Having his hands tied tightly together with restraint ties made the task easier. Both knew the burn would make Carastino howl.

Jim was listening to his headset, one hand pressed to his left ear, his head bent forward, his chin thrust out as though to better his hearing. The attack was well planned. While the helicopter held the attention of the men on the ship, John brought the remaining team on the Rigid Raider right onto the boat unnoticed. A short firefight ensued. Quickly now he helped the other men stem the bleeding and truss the pirates left alive on his own boat. After a wait of twenty minutes, Jim heard John's tired voice on the headset.

"Jim, do you copy?" John's voice said.

"Loud and clear, JR. Give me a quick sit rep!" Jim's answer was cryptic.

"We have taken the ship, repeat, we have taken the ship. Four casualties for the pirates, probably a dozen wounded too. Doc and Ox are working on them now. Doc thinks two more may die before the night is over. Vince is our only wounded soldier. He took one in the vest and went over backwards. The back of his head is cut open, and he broke a thumb in the fall. He's up and around now, helping with the cleanup," John finished his report. "What about you. Anybody hurt?" His voice was concerned.

"Just our pride," Jim admitted with a tight grin. "We had to let the ladies take them down for us. I was on my knees when it happened. The girls did us proud!" he added with a smile.

"Do you have casualties or wounded?" John asked. "We're not far from you now, probably five minutes out."

"One dead among the pirates. Five wounded. They were sure of themselves and careless. All of them underestimated our response, which was a deadly mistake. Pen shot Carastino's thumb off. They're cauterizing it now," Jim replied.

"Good! I hope it bloody hurts!" A new voice came in on the headset. That was Calvin Weston. "I've seen the hold of this tub, Captain. It ain't pretty! There are shackles for little children down there and a contraption I don't ever want to see again!"

"It will hurt when he wakes up. Mark put him in dreamland so he couldn't contact his ship." Jim chuckled. "I heard you about the hold. Slavers are the scum of the earth!"

"Yeah, boss, well, these blokes are still wonderin' what happened," Weston said gruffly. Jim could hear the edge of rage in Weston's voice and understood. He dismissed it for the moment, knowing it for what it was, trusting that Weston would keep it together. Thoughts raging, he considered all he'd heard and reached a quick decision.

"Listen, John!" Jim said. "I don't want any of the pirates to know what happened to Carastino. Let's turn the ones on the boat over to the coast guard. We keep Carastino a secret until the coast guard is gone. Also, I want full forensics in the hold. Get the team on that. My guess is there aren't any records but look close."

"Done!" John replied quickly. "We're just coming alongside now. Tell Driver not to scratch my boat with that fiberglass monstrosity he's piloting," John added.

"Monstrosity!" Driver's voice sounded loudly. "You keep that tin can you're driving away from the paint job. Who's letting some crazy marine pilot a ship anyway?"

Jim grinned at the interplay. The men were relieved, the battle was over, and they had the victory. Most of them were safe, and no one had been seriously wounded. It had been close, though. Without the Kevlar vest, Vince might be dead! Jim breathed a prayer of thanks for God's mercy to his men. Picking up his satellite phone Jim, dialed Admiral Ashley's private secure line.

"Admiral Ashley, it's good to hear your voice," Jim said when the admiral answered. "We have the pirate Carastino and his ship. We're turning all the pirates except Carastino over to the coast guard. Can you arrange that? We're just north of Rum Cay Island. The coast guard can process the pirate's vessel as well. There's plenty of evidence on board. If what one of my men says is there, DNA evidence will tie them to the most recent victims. He claims the area hasn't been sterilized. My men are doing a full forensics investigation as well."

"How much information do you think you can get out of Carastino?" Admiral Ashley asked.

"Everything we need," Jim replied quietly.

"Remember, he's a murderer and he's KGB trained as a special terrorist. Castro hated losing that one," Admiral Ashley said. "Carry on, Captain. Carastino is a sanctioned kill," he finished.

The pirates were carried off the yacht onto *Bring It Up Coral*, where they were all handcuffed to the railings on the observation deck. Those who were unable to sit up were put in sick bay under heavy guard. Each prisoner on the deck sat with his hands handcuffed together above the top rail. They could stand or sit, but they could not move more than a few feet.

Driver took the yacht south, past Long Island, and then east to some of the smaller islands, uninhabited, mostly part of a long sandbar thrust up above the surface of the sea. They dropped anchor at the easternmost island. There was no one around. Driver made sure the second anchor was secure before leaving the bridge. It felt good to be at this juncture in their mission. Success was sweet. He knew that the hard part lay ahead.

That evening they sat around the dining room table and ate fresh crab cakes that Jim cooked. He'd learned the recipe from Abe and was anxious to try it. Cecilia helped him with the meal, and they all enjoyed the repast. Everyone asked for seconds, so Jim decided he'd followed the recipe and done a good job. Cecilia had concocted a delicious shrimp salad and cooked sugar snap peas and red potatoes to go along with the crab cakes, turning it into a sumptuous feast. After the battle, it felt good to relax and enjoy good food.

Andrea broke out a bottle of white wine, a perfect complement to their dinner. As he inserted the corkscrew, he looked around the table where everyone was poised to begin eating. "This wine comes from the V. Sattui Winery in St. Helena, California. It is a Johannisberg White Riesling, very dry, very demanding, and will awaken your taste buds like nothing you've had before!" he instructed. "Rosa insisted we buy it in case we eat anything like this on the trip, so after you develop a taste for it, you can thank her."

"A California wine? How is it that an Italian will even consider such a thing?" Cecilia asked, laughing.

"Johannisberg Riesling is a grape variety that originated in Germany. There the climate is cooler than in California. But in California it does extremely well, especially in the Napa Valley where the richer soil and abundant sun help produce fruity, floral, pleasing wines of the highest quality," Rosa informed them, speaking as a teacher now. She was holding her glass and breathing in the fragrance of the wine. Everyone could hear the passion for wine in her voice. For a moment, she studied the wine in her glass as one might look at a favorite collector's item. Her eyes were bright with appreciation for the color and bouquet of the drink.

"V. Sattui knew that Rieslings are made in a range of styles, from bone-dry and lower-alcohol to sweeter late-harvest and high-octane wines," she continued and paused while FM laughed.

"High-octane?" Jim asked with his eyebrow raised. Rosa ignored him with a smile and wink.

"Sattui's winery produced two Rieslings in the lower middle of that range because they cover the widest span of food-friendly styles. This is one of their finer triumphs," she finished with real appreciation, sipping a little of the wine.

Jim led in saying grace, and before they ate, he lifted his wineglass, looking at the pale vintage sparkling in the evening sunlight streaming in through a west-facing port. "May I offer up this toast to Rosa and our other two ravishing beauties?" he inquired.

The men nodded, and the women blushed becomingly. "Then, to these lovely ladies, may you find peace and beauty in the midst of this world of woe and love to warm your hearts and keep you on your way." For Jim it was an unusual speech.

Jim leaned over and kissed Cecilia, then lifted his glass and drank a sip of his wine. He let it travel around his gums and beneath his tongue. It was dry, and at first, he didn't like it. But as the meal progressed, he found himself enjoying the wine more and more. By the time he had emptied his glass, he was tempted to have more. He declined on the basis of habit, nothing more. He never had more than one glass of wine for any reason. He supposed, now that Andrea owned his own vineyard, that might change in the future. He noted that only Rosa poured a second glass, and that only half full. Still, between the nine of them, they emptied the bottle and half of another. Rosa told them they should drink it by the next day at the latest or it would begin to change.

"I think we'll have seafood again tomorrow!" Jim mentioned, putting his glass down with a sigh of pleasure.

"Why was Mother so against drinking wine?" he asked Andrea. Since he was her brother, he should know.

Andrea smiled as he wiped his mouth with his fine napkin. He dropped it on the table and thought about his answer.

"Your mother was raised in a home where wine was for communion and weddings. Stronger drink ruined it, I think, for your mother. One of our uncles was constantly in trouble because he drank too much. Our priest was very much against using wine for anything else too. I caught him finishing off a bottle after communion one day. He said that since it had been blessed it could not be thrown away. I believed it then." Andrea chuckled at that memory. "Later I realized he always blessed far more bottles than we would ever use."

Jim nodded. He remembered his mother talking about that uncle and the pain he caused his family. It was good to remember family history, to know the struggles your family faced. It gave one hope that the struggles of today could be met and overcome. The uncle in question eventually beat his alcoholism and distinguished himself as a poet.

Once dinner was complete, they worked in companionable silence cleaning up the yacht one final time. With nine of them, it didn't take long, and Jim nodded his approval as he put his dishtowel in the hamper with the rest of the towels. He had taken upon himself the chore of cleaning out the dishwasher and stove.

John arrived with the crew shortly after they finished. Calvin Beardsley and his men came on board to take the yacht back to Florida, where she would be berthed until Jim needed her again. He thanked Calvin profusely and sent him on his way with many wishes for a safe trip back to England.

Dragging a resisting and cursing Juan Carastino, he crossed over to his own ship with a sigh of contentment. *Bring It Up Coral* was his home now.

CHAPTER 7

Carastino became quiet when Dorf stepped forward. Dorf was wearing just a white T-shirt, his muscles bulging beneath the fabric, his face set in a hard and dangerous look. He took Juan by his ponytail and hauled him down to the brig, pushed him roughly inside the door, and hit the switch to lock the prisoner in. Carastino staggered to the first set of bunks, wearily sat down, and looked around his prison. His hands were still tied behind him, and he wondered why.

This was no ordinary brig. The walls were steel, the ventilation ducts long and narrow, so narrow he wouldn't be able to fit more than a hand inside. A lidless toilet in one corner was stainless steel, with an automatic flush mechanism. Next to the toilet was a stainless-steel sink, also with an automatic water system. There were four bunks in the cramped space and absolutely no privacy. Instead of bars, the entire eight-foot stretch of front wall was thick glass. He could see men working in the kitchen, and as he studied them, he caught his breath.

Sturdy walked through, a man even taller and stronger than the giant who had escorted him here. Behind him a shorter man with massive physical features stalked past. Abe was an impressive figure of a man, and he could probably win a Mr. Universe contest if he ever chose to enter. Carastino shook his head and scooted onto the mattress to lay down. He desperately needed rest.

In the conference room, Jim met with the teams and in conference with those on land. There was a vote to take regarding Carastino, and it unfolded in much the way Jim thought it might. Unanimously the group passed a death sentence on the pirate. How was another matter, and Jim asked the men to think about it and share ideas. In the morning, perhaps they would decide.

Pen noted that Sir Edward took part in the vote, as did the other men of the committee, including Jack Royce. Even Pen agreed with the sentence and felt that justice had been served, for more than twelve men and women formed the ad-hoc jury. She was slightly surprised to note that the kitchen crew, mechanics, electricians, and medical crew were permitted to voice their opinions and cast a vote.

Jim reminded them all, before the vote, that if one person objected to the death penalty, it would not be carried out. Zeke took over at that point and presented the evidence that they had to date. Questions were encouraged and clarification asked for and given. By the end of Zeke's presentation of the evidence against Carastino, the vote had been unanimous. Pen was surprised that Jim included her in the vote.

She was an unknown, and she might very well have objected to Jim's team carrying out the sentence. However, Carastino was a sanctioned kill, and when she saw and heard the evidence, she was more than willing to participate in the trial and cast her vote. Perhaps for the first time, she realized that the men of *Bring It Up* did not take this responsibility lightly.

There had been no quick vote. Several of the people in that room had taken nearly half an hour to deliberate. Every question was pointed and appropriate. Jim Shepherd's vote had been the last checked and put in the box. Pen did not miss the look of deep sadness that he experienced in that vote, and her estimation of the man rose another notch.

When Juan Carastino awoke, it was dark, and men were opening the door of his prison. Stiff and cramped, he struggled to a sitting position, the sour taste in his mouth telling him he had slept for several hours. Shaking his head was a mistake. He moaned in pain, and his thumb hurt and throbbed terribly.

"Get up!" a voice ordered. The English accent surprised him. He looked up into a pair of icy blue eyes. Calvin Weston was dressed in his battle gear, black boots, pants, shirt, vest, and a thin balaclava covering his head and face. Only his eyes and mouth showed. The H&K MP5SD in his hands was held professionally, and Carastino saw that the safety was off. He complied.

Behind Weston stood Banks and Carr, and in the rear, Paul Donnelly towered above them. Carastino looked at him closely. This was not the man who brought him down, nor the giant in the kitchen. *How many giants work on this boat?* Rising slowly, he tested his legs and then walked toward the man with the gun. His hands were still tied cruelly tight behind him, cutting into his flesh.

"Turn around," Weston ordered.

When Carastino was turned around, Weston cut the ties that held his arms. He motioned with his head for Carastino to move out of the cell. Banks and Carr took the lead, then Juan, behind him Weston and the giant Donnelly. Carastino felt small in the middle of these men. He was only five foot three, and the shortest was the man before him, David Carr, who stood five feet ten inches in height. Unlike Juan, Carr was wide in the shoulders, strongly built, obviously a formidable soldier.

He looked with curiosity as they escorted him through the empty kitchen and dining room, down a narrow corridor, up steps, down another corridor, and up another flight of steps to the rear deck. They led him right to the stern, where a larger version of a Rigid Raider was being hoisted over the railing so it could be lowered into the sea. Two men worked the cables fastened to the boat, while another operated the crane. No one else was visible. The men working did not even glance his way in curiosity.

When the boat was in the water, Banks and Carr stepped onto a platform that could be raised and lowered, acting as a dive platform. He followed, the other two men crowding on behind. Banks reached for the control box, pushed the down button, and the platform took them down to the boat. Again, Banks led, Carr next, Carastino, Weston, and finally Donnelly. Not one of the men spoke. Weston nodded his head, and Banks took the wheel of the boat, started the powerful outboard engines, which were amazingly quiet, and headed in toward a sandy shore. Carastino wondered vaguely what they were going to do, but he was not overly concerned. He was in civilized hands. Tonight, he would not die!

It was low tide, Carastino realized, as the boat gently grounded on the soft white sand. Donnelly stepped out and simply dropped an anchor on the sand and mashed it in with his boot. Banks and Carr joined him, all three carrying shovels. *What are the shovels for?* Carastino shivered.

With his hands free, he could drive the boat away, but when he looked, the key in the ignition was gone. Banks had taken it with him. He saw one of the emergency paddles and pulled it quietly to his side. It was a weapon. Convinced that this was some ploy to frighten him, he felt better with the weapon at his side and watched and listened, pondering if he could hotwire the ignition and escape. The wires were in a dark steel box that was screwed tightly shut.

He listened to them talk as they dug quickly. All four men who had him were English. *Are they SAS or something else?* Their conversation told him nothing. In less than half an hour, they were done. When they turned, Carastino saw three pistols pointed at him. Wisely, he left the paddle where it lay.

The big one took a length of nylon cord, looped it around Carastino's chest, and pulled it tight, pinning his arms. He wrapped it around and around until Juan was trussed completely, unable to move his arms. Only his hands could move.

"I think this is cutting off the circulation," he said in English.

"That's the least of your worries." That was Weston speaking. He nodded, and Donnelley picked Carastino up easily, deposited him in the hole on his knees, and the men began to fill it around him. When he was buried up to his neck in the soft wet and heavy sand, they pulled the boat over and sat on the seats, talking quietly, paying no attention to him. He stared out to sea and watched the water slowly move toward him. Behind him was the island, and he knew that when the tide was all the way in, his head would be three feet below the surface! It didn't take long for his mind to connect the dots. With a shake of his head for their stupidity, he remained silent. *Surely these buffoons do not believe that I will crack with this empty threat!* Watching the water didn't help, and his head faced the open sea so he could see the implacable movement of the tide.

They want to frighten me. I will remain strong! Civilized men do not kill prisoners. Watching the inevitable march of the ocean toward him, he began to sweat profusely. The first wave reached him, washing up to his chin. No one said anything. They weren't even looking at him! He tried to watch them, but his eyes were drawn back to the water. It rushed in, this time covering his mouth and nose for about ten seconds, before the water was sucked out. He glanced over at them, but the water came again, up to his eyes.

"What do you want?" he panted.

"Who hired you? Who gets the yachts? Who do you sell your slaves to? Where do you take them? The lot, mate," Calvin answered. "Talk fast. I want the information before you drown."

"I can't tell you that!" Carastino sputtered, spitting out some saltwater and blinking his eyes.

Weston turned away from him! The next wave covered his head and lasted for twenty seconds before it swept out. Coughing and spitting, he barely had time to breathe before the next wave came. They were going to wait until he drowned! He screamed, "I'll talk! I'll talk! Please!"

Donnelley slapped down half a fifty-gallon drum with both ends open, pushed it down into the sand, and checked to make sure Carastino's mouth was above the water. If he tilted his head back, he could talk.

"Start talking!" Weston ordered. They weren't going to pull him out!

"Get me out of here!" Carastino yelled with vile curses.

"Pull it," Weston commanded, nodding to Donnelley. The can went up, and Carastino was buried beneath the water again. Donnelley put the drum back and with a small cup, bailed enough water out so that Carastino could breathe again. His wild eyes saw only the night sky above.

"You were saying, Juan?" Weston queried.

"The Santa Marta Cartel!" he gasped, spitting water out with each sentence. "There are three bosses in the cartel. They pay me to steal the yachts. They use them to ship their drugs different places in the United States and Canada mostly. There is always a need for yachts. Most authorities do not expect an expensive yacht to be transporting drugs.

"I sell the slaves in Cúcuta! Gregorio Vásquez buys them. They work in the mines. Francisco Valdez is the colonel in the army who protects the cartel and Cúcuta. The bosses are named José Rivera, Garcia Márquez, and Antonio Caro. Caro is the powerful one of the three. Now, please, get me out of here!"

"What happened to Sir Henry Crowell's family?" Weston asked. "Did you sell them?"

"I killed them! I didn't know he was a minister. When I found out I knew, I couldn't sell them," Juan answered. He was now gasping for air. Donnelley bailed a little more water out.

"Tell me how you did it," Weston ordered. Carastino did not wish to confess, but he was terrified now beyond endurance. It all came pouring out after the drum was removed once more and almost a minute passed before he could gasp a short breath. Panic tore at his very sanity!

"I raped the children's mother after beating her and then allowed my crew to rape her repeatedly. I made the women and children watch and then shot them all in the head and dumped their bodies in the ocean. Mrs. Crowell, I killed last. I made her watch me kill the women and children before I killed her!" Carastino sputtered through the water. "Please, you have to let me out!" Water was covering his nose now, and he was finding it difficult to catch a breath.

Weston nodded to Donnelley, and the can was lifted. Carastino had only enough time for a tiny breath, and the water rushed in over his head. He could see that it was up to Donnelley's knees. It took forever for it to sweep out so he could catch a breath, and then it came in again. He realized then that they were not going to let him out, and he screamed in impotent fury. Donnelley's legs disappeared. The last sound Carastino registered was the outboards starting up. Then there was nothing. Deep enough now the tide did not uncover his head again.

Each man in the Raider took off his mask and wiped the sweat from his face. They looked at each other, their expressions hard, eyes still filled with anger and revulsion at Carastino's confession. Weston had seen the torturous contraption in the hold where they'd raped the women. He felt an impotent fury inside that he could not rescue them from such horror, but that was the way of life sometimes. It gave him only some consolation that Carastino would never do it again. He tried to hold on to that.

"The bastard made them suffer!" Banks said, spitting out the words with revulsion. "We should have found a slower way to kill him."

"There ain't a way slow enough for that!" DC said, shaking his head.

"What do you think the boss will say?" Banks asked no one in particular.

Back on the ship, they stood at attention and gave their report to Jim and the rest of the team in the conference room. It was one of the few times that no one outside the military unit was permitted to join in the discussion. Only the team sat around the table. Jim listened to their story carefully and then nodded his head at their seats, telling them they could sit.

"Sit down, men," he invited. "We don't stand on that kind of formality here unless we're in public." He watched as the men sat down. They were nervous, and he knew why. Carefully he studied their eyes and decided they hadn't taken any serious hurt from this experience. Still, he was concerned for them, because he knew what it did to a man to kill another in this manner.

"We tasked you with the responsibility of getting the information any way you could. We also told you to act according to the information.

I'd say, all things considered, that you showed incredible restraint. Personally, I'd have hauled him out of that water, skinned him alive, and stretched him out in the sun to die slowly!" Jim's voice was hard as he spoke.

All four men visibly relaxed. Calvin looked a Jim with new respect. *This guy didn't stand on tradition. He would be a good bloke to work for.*

"Zeke," Jim said, looking over at his trusted intelligence man. "Let's run these names and see what Langley has, and check Interpol too. Then see what you can find through local police forces, FBI, and DEA. I want everything we can get as quickly as possible.

"Let's meet back here at four and see what we have for information and ideas. We have the rest of the day off. We're going to anchor off the Snowfields. Anyone who wants to dive is welcome," Jim announced, nodding to the men as he rose. He knew they hadn't expected that and gave a small smile of pleasure in doing so.

Weston's team remained seated as the other men passed out. Several of the others clapped them on the shoulders and complimented them on their work. Those who didn't make physical contact or say anything nodded in approval as they filed past. Every man on the team had cast a vote for this, and they shared in the responsibility. The entire episode was more than revealing to Hobbs and his team. When the last one filed out, Weston looked at his men.

"This bloke is serious about applying the military solution to terrorism!" Calvin said quietly. "That's the first time I got a pat on the back for doing my job!" he added with a grin. "Now I wish we'd planned a more fitting end!" He paused for a moment, his eyes hard. "He should have died as hard as those he tortured and killed!"

"Best pay we've ever been offered too!" Banks offered with an answering grin.

"You did your jobs well this morning. Thanks," Weston mentioned, nodding at each man. They got up and filed out. Weston remained sitting at his chair and heard the door open. He looked up to see Jim coming in.

"Are you and your team okay with this?" Jim asked quietly, sitting down next to Weston and propping his feet on the table.

"Dead right we are!" Calvin said. "I had my doubts when we signed up, but you just took care of all of that. We're in all the way, Shep," It was the first time Calvin called the captain by his nickname, and Jim smiled slightly.

"Damn glad to have you!" Jim said, shaking Calvin's hand vigorously. "Now let's put this behind us and have some fun!" he added, getting up. They walked companionably to the dining room for breakfast.

CHAPTER 8

Pen sat down at Jim's table, having walked down with Cecilia and followed her through the breakfast buffet. On her way, she glanced over at the brig, behind the kitchen, and saw that it was empty. She put her plates down, returned to the drinks bar for milk and orange juice, and slowly made her way to her seat. Jim was busy eating scrambled eggs and bacon. He stood with the rest of the men as she sat down and nodded to her before returning to his breakfast. She smiled at the gesture of decorum. It was highly unusual in her world.

"Where's Carastino?" she asked before picking up her fork.

"Took a long walk off a short pier," Calvin Weston said lightly. Perhaps it was the way he said it that tipped her off that something had happened.

"What is that supposed to mean?" she asked. There was something in the way Weston said it that warned her to ask respectfully.

"He's bloody dead, Ms. Perill!" Weston said, pausing before putting his forkful of eggs into his mouth. "Sorry for the bad language," he apologized sincerely just before the fork reached his lips.

Jim watched her. For a moment, her eyes narrowed, then she relaxed. She looked across the table at Jim and saw him watching.

"A sanctioned killing," she spoke quietly. She had been in the meeting in the conference room when sentence passed and had voted for the death sentence. That the sentence was carried out so quickly really was no surprise.

Jim nodded. "Once Hobbs discovered all the information we needed, and he learned exactly how Carastino killed the Crowell women and children, he thought it prudent to terminate the life of a murderer without burdening whatever local judicial system might be involved."

"Will you tell me about it?" she asked.

"Not at breakfast," he replied. She nodded, satisfied. Cecilia who watched the whole interchange, winked at Pen to let her know everything was going to be all right. Pen gave only a slight nod in response. This was something she knew about, but the experience left her full of doubts.

She looked over at Hobbs, eating as though unconcerned, but she also noted the sadness in his eyes and the slightly haunted expression they conveyed. The confession must have been very bad to affect him so. Giving him a nod of approval, she concentrated on her own meal.

Jim invited her into his office after breakfast, but before he told her everything, he ordered the ship to weigh anchor and move to the Snowfields site. When he was finished with that order, he sat down across from her. She waited patiently, not fidgeting in her chair, as he gathered his thoughts. Captain Shepherd would always gather his thoughts before he spoke.

"Carastino beat and raped Mrs. Crowell, while the children watched, and then shot them and dumped their bodies over the side. He was afraid, when he learned that the yacht he stole came from Sir Henry Crowell, the UK's minister of finance. He sells the women and children to a slaver who works a mine. Those unfortunate enough to be enslaved probably live an average of two years.

"He also gave us five names. Three cartel bosses named José Rivera, Garcia Márquez, and Antonio Caro. Caro is the most powerful member of that trio. Francisco Valdez is a colonel who provides them with military protection. The slaves are all sold to a Gregorio Vásquez. He works them in his mines." Jim paused, watching her reactions. She kept her cool very well.

"Okay. I agree. He had to die," she said after a moment of thought. "I'm okay with sanctioned killings," she added. "Why didn't you tell me what you were going to do?" she asked suddenly.

"Low tide was at two thirty-eight this morning. Calvin came up with the idea and volunteered to take care of it with his team. He woke me up to tell me his plan, and I didn't feel like waking anyone else up," Jim answered honestly. He told her how they got the information and how Carastino died. Pen nodded, noting the sadness in his eyes once again.

"Thanks," she said, standing up and leaving the office. Cecilia walked in as she left, leaned down, and kissed her husband.

"She'll be just fine," Cecilia said.

Just then Finn came in, saw them together, and paused just a moment. When they parted, he continued to the desk.

"Is it true we all have a day off, sir?" he asked.

"Absolutely, Lieutenant," Jim said with a grin. "I'm just going to change into my swim trunks. We're diving on Snowfields today."

"Uh, thank you, sir," Finn said, as Jim got up and wandered away with Cecilia. It was obvious that Marvin Finn thought a day off frivolous and a waste of time. Jim sighed and then gave it no more thought. He knew he wasn't going to change Marvin Finn's nature and was willing to accept that.

By midmorning, most of the crew was below the surface, cruising through the water, looking at the white coral and the abundant life surrounding it. This was not the first time the entire crew had a day to enjoy doing something like this, but days like this were few enough and far enough in between to make them special. They swam around coral heads laced with delicate white formations brimming with life. Visibility was excellent, helping the divers spot some of the smaller, more reclusive reef dwellers. The white Staghorn coral was amazing, and in the cool aqua waters of the Caribbean, life flourished on the reef dam.

Everyone was in a better frame of mind when they gathered in the conference room later that afternoon. Pen came in beside John, the two obviously having enjoyed each other's company, and they sat together as if it were the most natural thing in the world. Some of the men smiled at the couple. John didn't seem to mind. When Jim arrived with Zeke, the last two to enter, the room became silent immediately. Jim took his seat and waited until Zeke had set up the computers at each station before he began talking.

"As you can see, the Santa Marta Cartel gets far less attention than the Medellin Cartel. There's a very good reason for that. For one thing, the amount of drugs they ship out is far less than that of the Medellin group. Antonio Caro seems to have arrived at the idea that wading in blood is not good for business, and he has managed to use bribery to keep his cartel out of national news. He's still ruthless and kills easily. He's adopted the Mafia tradition of making examples. 'Make an example of one, teach a hundred' seems to be his motto.

"Francisco Valdez has been on our radar a time or two in naval intelligence. He controls the Caribbean coast to international waters and inland about a hundred miles. He's too greedy to use money to keep his men in line. Whole families have been sold into slavery to Gregorio Vásquez. That seems to be the connection between Carastino and Vásquez. Valdez is a sadistic killer, a man who uses his military rank and position for his own gain. Zeke will tell you the rest," Jim finished, sitting back in his leather chair.

"I won't bore you by going over the reports you have in your computers. I did some digging and discovered a money trail from Carastino to Vásquez. Gregorio and his cousin Valdez have been protecting the cartel and Carastino's operation. I've also traced the cartel's money operations. They keep their money in flux, so it's difficult to track. I'm telling you this so you appreciate my genius," he added.

There were catcalls and other comments that Zeke pretended to ignore, polishing his fingernails and studying them as if bored. Jim grinned at the interchange. Zeke continued after raising a hand to silence the comments.

"Large amounts of the money are always moving. Caro came up with the plan some time ago, and so far, it's worked for them. However, Caro has some interesting stuff on his office computer and on his laptop! I think we can interrupt about seventy percent of his cartel's cash flow anytime we want to!" Zeke beamed at them all with this last tidbit of information. "That ought to get his attention and take the wind out of his sails!"

"How much money are we talking about?" Pen asked.

"Three billion dollars and some change," Zeke replied.

A collective silence settled over the room as the men thought about the sum. That any one organization could make that kind of money in the drug trade seemed preposterous, yet it happened on a regular basis. Pen broke the silence. "Who gets the money if we take it?"

"Actually, we won't take it. Sir Edward will have to arrange that, as the bank it will pass through is on British territory," Zeke replied, not looking at her. He looked up suddenly. "You'll have to take the information to him and supervise the operation. We'll keep your spot warm until you return," he added, looking back down at his computer screen.

"What makes you think I'll return?" she asked, somewhat amused.

"You have to see this thing all the way through!" Zeke said. He was right, of course, and Pen smiled. She did indeed have to see this venture all the way through. *And then what*?

"I'll be ready to go in an hour," she replied.

"So our next project is to think about taking down this cartel. Team leaders, get your boys together and start brainstorming. I want some ideas by tomorrow morning. Pen, please get back as quickly as you can," Jim added, looking directly at her.

"You don't mind having an interloper looking over your shoulder?" she asked with a small smile.

"I don't mind having a true professional to help," Jim corrected matter-of-factly. "I've never met a better intelligence officer," he added seriously.

"Thank you," Pen said, simply. Secretly pleased by this announcement, she looked over at John, who raised both thumbs to signify he agreed with Jim.

"Okay, let's get some rest. We'll anchor over the Chimney tonight and dive on that tomorrow after our meeting," Jim said.

"Another day off, sir?" Finn asked.

"Shut your hole, you finicky little bleeder!" Weston snapped.

"I beg your pardon, sir," Finn said, his face flushing.

"You heard me! Shut it. All work and no play makes Sharky a dull boy. Unbend a little, live a little," Weston replied seriously. Jim didn't say anything. He knew that Finn had been rubbing Weston the wrong way. Finn would rub everyone the wrong way, no matter what anyone said. Jim also knew Finn would take the rebuke because Weston outranked him. Sighing as the scene unfolded before him, he watched quietly.

"You're extremely rude this morning, sir," Marvin said. "No disrespect intended, *sir*," he emphasized the last word.

"Where did you ever dig up this bean-counting bleeder?" Weston asked Jim. Finn had pushed all the wrong buttons, unfortunately.

"Moderate your language in front of the ladies, please," Jim said quietly.

"My apologies, ladies," Calvin apologized quickly, chagrinned. "I just don't think of you as women." Several of the men burst out laughing, and Pen looked at him with one eyebrow raised. It was Cecilia who came to the rescue.

"Poor man!" she said lightly. "Too much work and exhaustion has scattered his wits to the wind and made his mind stop working. Dear, you have to stop working the men quite so hard. Who ever heard of a sailor who couldn't recognize a woman?"

"I said I was sorry!" Hobbs said, laughing with the rest.

"Yes, you are!" Pen replied.

"Okay, let's break this up and get with your teams," Jim said, his smile leaving his face. As one the group rose and filed out of the room.

Jim went up to the bridge to take the ship the short distance to the Chimney. He didn't get to pilot the ship much anymore, and this was an opportunity to enjoy his moment behind the wheel. Cecilia followed him up, and the two of them stood in the bridge for a moment looking around them. Then Jim ordered the anchor raised and waited until he received confirmation that it was raised and locked in place. He pushed the throttles forward and took the wheel with both hands, checking his heading, running at about eight knots. Beneath his feet the engine rumbled, and he smiled.

Andrea and Rosa passed the windows, heading up to the observation deck. They were holding hands, something that Jim saw more and more when they were together. Over eighty percent of communication is body language, and he smiled as he read both of them accurately. Rosa was in her element, Andrea was a little reserved, still fighting the inevitable. Cecilia sighed when they passed, put her arms around Jim's left arm, and rested her head on his shoulder. It was a posture she often took.

"This is certainly a beautiful part of the world," she said.

"Wait until the hurricanes start," Jim said with a chuckle. "This ocean can change from a millpond to a raging torrent in seconds flat!"

"Will we have to wait them out?" Cecilia said.

"No, honey. This fine gentleman is equipped to tow a full oil tanker through whatever Mother Nature wants to throw at us. We have all the power we need to tough it out. Most likely, we'll be needed for rescue during the hurricanes. Some of us will get sick, but most of the men are up for it," Jim added. "It's the lubbers in their yachts that will be the real problem!" He frowned. "Some of them don't even listen to their radios or check on the weather. That's a recipe for disaster!"

"Not the women?" she asked, looking up at him and tightening her hold on his arm.

"I remember you and Aunt Millie got sick last time we were getting tossed around," Jim reminded her.

"Heavens yes! That was horrible. It really gave us both a fright," Cecilia responded.

"What, getting sick?" Jim asked.

"No, silly. Having the boat rock three different ways at once! Every single rivet in the walls seemed to be trying to pop! We were never sure which direction we would be thrown next! It was quite frightening," she answered.

"He can take it," Jim said, patting the instrument panel affectionately.

"He?" Cecilia said.

"Too tough to be a she," Jim joked, winking at her. She slapped his arm and then shook out her hand.

"Ow! You're still too hard to slap! Why is it that every man has to think with the hair on his chest? Too tough indeed! Try having a baby sometime and we'll see how tough you are!" She stamped her foot, something that always made him laugh when she was angry.

"What are you laughing at?" she asked dangerously.

"Those tiny little feet stamping the floor always make me laugh," he admitted.

"I can stamp with the best of them!" she said haughtily.

"I'll sponsor a contest between you and Sturdy immediately," Jim said. He reached for the phone. Hastily she grabbed his hand to stop him.

"Don't you touch that!" she said, slapping his hand. She was laughing and trying to look fierce at the same time, something he loved.

"You said you could stamp with the best of them!" Jim argued, putting his hand back on the wheel. "And may I remind you that striking a superior officer is considered mutiny on the seas?" he added.

"Pish posh!" she said, stamping her foot again. He laughed with her.

Arriving above the Chimney, Jim checked the depth finder and picked a good place to anchor. He ordered the anchor dropped and listened as the huge chain rattled and clanked through the mechanism. It was with a deep sense of regret that he released the wheel. The ship drifted until the anchor chain was taut.

Andrea appeared at the door, Rosa close behind him, their hands still clasped. He was smiling slightly as Cecilia disengaged her arm from her husband. Jim looked at him with an answering smile.

"I have the watch," Andrea said.

"All yours, Papa!" Jim said, using Andrea's nickname.

"And do I get a nickname?" Rosa asked impishly.

"Perhaps Mrs. Papa?" Jim said, half in question, half in jest.

"Perhaps," she said mysteriously.

"Go to bed!" Andrea said with disgust.

"Yes, Papa," Cecilia said, reaching up to kiss his weathered cheek. She and Jim walked hand in hand down the steps.

CHAPTER 9

Cecilia went off to their stateroom, but Jim had a meeting to attend first. He walked pensively down to the dining room, where he knew the teams would be gathered at the tables, drinking their favorite drinks, discussing the mission before them earnestly, oblivious to the surrounding teams. As Jim entered, Marvin Finn, who had been sitting alone in a corner, leaped to his feet and saluted.

"Officer on the deck!" he said loudly. Jim sighed inwardly and walked to his team, giving a half-hearted salute to his lieutenant. Finn was livid when no one even paid any attention to him.

"I said, officer on deck!" he said, almost shouting.

"Yeah, we heard you, you wanker! Shut it!" That was Lee Roy Brown speaking.

Finn shook with rage, his fists clenching at his sides. He hurried over to Lunch Box to administer discipline. Jim sat so his back was to the unfolding scene. Frank Miller grinned at him from the other side.

"Chicken!" he said.

"I'll have to say something if I can see it," Jim said, smiling at FM, Zeke, and Smitty in turn.

Finn reached the table, and Lunch Box stood up. At six feet and two hundred pounds, Lee Roy was only two inches taller than Finn, but he outweighed him by a good forty pounds. All forty pounds of that was hard-packed muscle. Marvin swallowed nervously.

"We have work to do, Mr. Finn. You're getting in the way of that. Anything you want to say right now will get you tossed over the side," Lunch Box said, his eyes menacing, his shoulders bunched and ready for action.

"I'll see you in my office tomorrow, PO3 Brown!" Marvin hissed. Without a second's hesitation, Lunch Box struck, knocking Finn silly, then lifted him and carried him to the rear deck, where he unceremoniously dumped him in the drink. Without a word, he turned around and headed back to the dining room.

Five minutes later, Finn appeared, dripping wet, and walked over to Jim's table. Zeke had his computer out, and on the screen, he saw the letters SMESSCS running down the side of the open page. It was a typical military acronym for situation, mission, equipment, service, support, communication, and signal. Half the screen was already full of notes, and the four men were deep in discussion. Taking his courage in his hands, he drew in a breath and spoke.

"Excuse me, sir," Finn said softly.

"Go change, take a shower, go to bed, Lieutenant. This can't wait," Jim said without turning around.

"Yes, sir, but—"

"Now, Lieutenant!" Jim's voice was hard.

Finn spun around and left the dining room expecting to hear laughter. No one even looked up at him. *Maybe what they're doing is more important. The captain will hear about this. This crew is completely out of hand! Surely, he must see that! Military discipline needs to be applied here!*

At one o'clock, the kitchen crew shut off the lights and went to bed. At two o'clock, most of the teams were clear on what they thought would work. Jim's team, because he was the last to arrive, finished last. Jim sat up, stretched, yawned, and noticed that the room was empty. FM sat with his head in his hands, Smitty with his chin in one hand, and Zeke was staring blankly at his computer.

"Okay, guys. That's enough. Let's hit the sack," Jim said, yawning in the middle of it. FM yawned widely.

"Jeez, boss. Don't get me started." He grinned, yawning again, and pushed himself up.

Pen's absence the next morning was almost tangible. John sat at the breakfast table, his eyes looking off in some inner place, feeling strangely empty. His friends and family surrounded him, yet he missed Pen terribly. Cecilia saw his distraction and smiled to herself. It was quite obvious that her brother-in-law was smitten by the love bug.

"Hast thou been smitten, my errant knight?" she asked with a twinkle in her eye.

"Lover boy here?" C. G. quipped, sitting down and smiling at Cecilia. "He's beyond smitten. He's in deep, he's in deep, well, he's in deep…smit!" C. G. finished lamely.

"I'm still a better shot than you," John threatened, suddenly back with them, his face flushed.

"Only if Pen's not there to watch," C. G. said. "Hey, boss!"

"Yes, C. G.?" Jim said, looking up.

"No more women on the boat, man. We brought two women on board, and they both took down a marine!" C. G. said his hands spread.

"What are we talking about?" Jim asked. Cecilia laughed and patted his hand.

"Never interrupt a marine when he's eating," she said to C. G. Jim went back to eating in his usual style, and the men laughed.

After breakfast, everyone expected another meeting, but Jim surprised them with another day of rest. Marvin stalked out of the dining room, furious. His fury grew when Jim did not appear in his office. They were still anchored off the Chimney, so he gave orders to weigh anchor and head for Dynamite Wall. He wanted to dive again, just for pleasure, and he wanted to give Pen the chance to decide to return. He thought she would.

When they dropped anchor off Dynamite Wall, Jim gathered the divers around an NOS chart. NOS is an acronym for the National Ocean Service, an agency of the National Oceanic and atmospheric

Administration (NOAA). They produced nautical charts for all navigable US coastal waters, the Great Lakes, and US Possessions.

Dynamite Wall is an amazing example of the dividable tunnels that cut deep into the reef walls of Rum Cay. Diving in tunnels involved reasonable risk for an experienced diver. Jim made sure each diver had a buddy, and in one case two buddies to make a threesome. After studying the chart, they decided on their starting point and began checking their dive gear.

This part of the job may have been routine, but every diver was careful to make sure every piece of his or her gear was operating properly and in perfect condition. Jim checked Cecilia's gear as well as his own. Cecilia knew it wasn't because he didn't trust her to do a good job; it was because he wanted to be sure she was perfectly safe. She watched him with a small smile on her lips.

"Everything good to go, Captain?" she asked, reaching up to kiss him lightly when he was done. He blushed and smiled. To her delight, he bent down, put his hand behind her head, and soundly kissed her again. When he stood up straight, she smiled at him.

"Everything good to go, Captain?" Bear said, kissing Jim's other cheek. There followed the usual tussle between the two while the crew laughed. In wrestling, Bear was an even match for Jim, and neither man gained any advantage, laughing together as they tussled.

"Boys!" Cecilia said when the fun ended.

Climbing down to the dive platform, Bear, Wade, and Dorf lifted down the gear. Most of the men chose to dive off the rear deck. It wasn't very high off the water. They dove in, swam to the platform, collected and donned their own gear, as their weight belts slowly pulled them beneath the surface. Jim dove off, but Cecilia decided to climb down the ladder to the platform. When they were ready, they too dipped beneath the clear waters.

Staghorn, elkhorn, and lettuce coral grew in abundance, the colors stunning, the reef life thriving. A small school of spotted dolphins played around the divers all morning, making their dive an extraordinary experience. Side by side, Jim and Cecilia explored tunnels cut into the reef wall, pointing to various forms, fascinated by the beauty surrounding them.

Jim kept a wary eye on his dive watch and gauges. Eventually the time came for them to surface for the last time that morning. Lazily they swam toward the stern of the ship and were delighted when the dolphins performed an aquatic ballet around them. Jim took his mask off, after signaling Cecilia to do the same, and they swam arm in arm to the surface kissing, while the dolphins danced and chattered at them in happy fashion.

Their heads broke the surface, and for a moment, they just kicked their fins enough to stay there, their kiss passionate. When they parted, those on the dive platform and on deck applauded. Jim, in an unusual demonstration of flamboyance, bowed, and then held Cecilia's hand up, and they bowed together. It was one of those rare moments he would remember his entire life. The dolphins, as if they sensed their part in the show, rose above the surface using their tails to dance backward away from the ship, chittering as they went.

At lunch, the tables were littered with photographs taken below, including one of Jim and Cecilia heading for the surface locked in their embrace with the dolphins dancing around them, sunlight making the water around them sparkle. It was an amazing photograph, and Jim suspected it would bring a fair price if sold on the Internet. He asked who took it.

"Bear took it," DC said. "He's a fair photographer."

"He is that and more." Jim's voice was full of praise. "Let's get this one copyrighted in his name. Any others you think we should sell like that, let Zeke know," Jim added. He grinned at the men, knowing they'd expected him to name Marvin Finn. Some of the men, he knew, were thinking about what Jim had just given to Bear in the way of financial gain. Generous to a fault, the captain always looked out for the best for his team.

Jim entered his office in the early afternoon, and Finn was at his desk, standing at attention, before he'd completely settled. He looked at Finn and motioned a seat. Marvin sat down and cleared his throat.

"Sir, about PO3 Brown," he began.

Jim held up a hand, his green eyes suddenly locked onto Marvin's. Finn hated that kind of eye contact. He shuddered and looked away, then was embarrassed and looked back.

"On this ship, rank is secondary at best, Mr. Finn. We hold rank to enhance our organization and define our duties, not to separate us. You use your rank to separate yourself from everyone. One of these days, you're going to push one of these men too far, and you'll end up in the medical wing. If you continue using your rank the way you do, you will earn every bruise, broken bone, and pain. In this company, we are all equals, including me. Get that through your thick skull, Finn! Your rank defines your responsibilities, not your authority!" Jim continued to keep eye contact with Finn.

"Sir, the discipline on this ship is deplorable!" Finn said, mustering his courage.

"This ain't the navy, Lieutenant. And I haven't noticed any laxity in discipline. You're the only one with problems in that area."

"Yes, but…" Finn stopped at the look in Jim's eye. "Me?"

"You're a good administrative assistant, Marvin. You're not a good team person yet. Please work at getting this through your thick skull. We are all equals in this business, and rank refers to responsibilities, not authority on this ship. Now get back to work. Try not to get yourself killed by your fellow associates." Jim waved him off, and Finn stood up, his face pinched and angry, and stalked off into his office.

Cecilia peeked around her office door to make sure Finn couldn't see her and gave Jim a thumbs-up. He grinned at her and sighed as he looked at the stack of papers requiring his attention. The afternoon dragged on while he worked until a call came to his desk.

"Captain Shepherd," he said into the phone.

"Pen's on her way back," Zeke stated. "ETA ninety-six minutes. Also, we've got a tropical storm brewing. You might want to drag your numb butt up here to take a look. I know how you love all that administrative stuff. This one looks like it might get nasty real quick. Smitty wants you to see what he's tracking."

"Bright Eyes is with you, isn't she?" Jim said with a grin.

"Caught! I'm supposed to be the one with the all-seeing eye!" Zeke laughed into the receiver.

"I have two more reports to read and sign and I'll be up," Jim promised.

He read through the reports quickly, signed them, and then picked up the stack and went into Finn's office. Marvin was furiously typing on his computer keyboard, but he looked up as Jim entered.

"Like I said, you are a very good administrative assistant. I'm going up to the CIC," he added, waving a half-hearted salute at Finn. The man was still moody. Shaking his head, Jim made his way up to the CIC.

"Hi, honey!" Cecilia said when he came in. Jim bent down and kissed her on the lips.

"Hi, honey!" Zeke said mockingly. In an uncharacteristic display, Jim made as though he was going to bend down and kiss Zeke. Zeke reared back and fended him off. Cecilia laughed.

"What did I miss?" Smitty said, ducking his head through the door, a wide grin on his face.

"He tried to kiss me!" Zeke said.

"Well, you're always complaining that I don't treat all my ensigns the same way," Jim said, laughing.

"You want to look at our storm?" Smitty asked through his laughter.

CHAPTER 10

Jim nodded and followed him out to the compass deck. A satellite dish provided US television coverage of the weather channel on one screen and some of the news channels on the other. Jim glanced up at them. Then Smitty pulled up the computer screen that showed the tropical storm building.

"Where's this picture coming from?" Jim asked.

"Weather satellite just to the south of us that orbits the earth at the equator," Smitty answered.

"How bad do you think it will be?" Jim asked. His eyes studied the patterns, and he thought it was building up to be a bad one. It had all the signs of building strength very quickly.

"Bad," Smitty admitted simply, confirming Jim's guess but not looking up from his work on a chart. He was drawing some lines from the epicenter of the storm. His eyes were intent on his work and his hands graceful as he drew.

"It's gonna follow a northerly course and sweep through here like a banshee," Smitty said, standing up and pointing at his notations. Jim looked.

"When?" Jim asked.

"Two days, maybe three. We'll start feeling the effects tomorrow in the afternoon." John Smith looked up at his captain with a grin of anticipation. "We stayin' out?" he asked.

"How could one resist?" Jim replied, laughing.

Pen arrived at the airport and hurried to the *Bring It Up* CH53D Sea Stallion, rotors turning, waiting near her landed plane. The Rum Cay airstrip was getting a lot of use today. Her eyes took in each plane and jet sitting there. Automatically she memorized the registration numbers, filing them away. Zeke could check each one. Pausing for only a moment to look again, she wondered why all her instincts were telling her trouble lay on the horizon.

John gave her a hand up, and for a moment, they locked eyes. She felt her own quick intake of breath, her heart fluttering in her chest as those gray eyes seemed to sink into her soul. He smiled at her, and without really thinking about it, she took his face in her hands and kissed him soundly on the mouth. They were both surprised.

"Now I know I'm in the navy!" C. G. jested, shaking his head. "We got two commanders kissin' each other!" The other men laughed, and Pen walked over to C. G. with a twinkle in her eye and a look of mischief on her face. John grinned, watching what would happen next.

Pen reached up, kissed Clancy on the cheek, and then patted the cheek she'd kissed. "There are worse things!" she said lightly, laughing when C. G. put his hand to the cheek she'd kissed.

"You saw Caro's jet?" John asked as the two took their seats. She waited until they were seated and had their headgear on so she wouldn't have to shout above the sound of the rotors. Even the earphones were comfortable on this aircraft.

"I felt like I was being watched with malice," she said into her microphone.

"Probably the seedy-looking character standing next to the blue-and-white Piper," John nodded. "He seems very interested in us, our helicopter, and then, of course, you."

Pen stared at John. "How did you know?" she asked.

"We had a few minutes. I called Zeke with all the registration numbers. The seedy-looking character is a professional. He had the mechanics uniform, the toolbox, and a tiny little camera he could use to photograph you and your plane and our chopper. We think Caro's looking for Carastino," he finished.

"Very resourceful, John," she said, nodding. As she spoke his name, his eyes dilated, as if he liked the sound of that. Finding herself short of breath again, she wondered how one man could affect her so.

"We have a monster of a storm coming in. The next few days should be interesting," John informed her. "I'm glad you came back."

"How bad is the storm?" she asked, smiling at his last words.

"Deadly," he said simply.

"And why are you glad I'm back?" she asked.

"Saved me the trouble of having to come and get you," he said the words almost casually, but she heard the steel beneath. He would come to get her, she suddenly knew, and she also knew she had wanted him to feel that way. The realization came as a shock to her, and for a few moments, she tried to sort through her raging emotions.

"Are we in love, John?" she asked. The question just slipped out, and she couldn't and didn't want to retract it.

"We're going to have to talk about that," he said with a grin. "I'm certainly in love with you, and I will chase you until you catch me!"

She laughed and reached out a hand, taking his, and they sat that way in silence for the rest of the flight. Those who heard every word, because the communication headphones were linked, said nothing. Dorf, flying the chopper, looked over at Mark and grinned. C. G. and Vince gave each other a high five across the deck.

Getting back to the ship was indeed an adventure. Winds whipped at the huge helicopter, and rain seemed to burst from the sky, drenching everything in a sudden fierce downpour. Thunder roared, and lightning flashed in the sky. But the CH53D Sea Stallion was designed for flight in the worst conditions. Bouncing around in the suddenly frenzied skies, Dorf continued toward the ship unconcerned.

His experienced hands manipulated the stick deftly as he turned into the wind and set the skids down on the deck just at the apex of a wave, shutting down everything very quickly, as the deck fell away with the chopper now securely settled. FM, Loony, and Inchworm dove on the skids, hooking the chains over them quickly so the chopper would not slide. When everything was tied down, the crew jumped down into the unfriendly weather. They were drenched between the chopper and the superstructure.

Pen was first through the hatch, laughing as she wiped water from her face and tried to smooth her soaked hair. John wore his hair in the typical marine cut of the day, and he shook himself like some great hairy animal might. She smiled at him. *Okay, I'm in love with this man. I wasn't expecting this, but I can deal with it. Can I?* John walked her to her quarters and then made his way to his own to dry off and change into his working gear.

"We're being watched," John said, walking into Jim's office without knocking.

"Caro's bunch?" Jim asked, looking up.

"Are you clairvoyant?" Pen asked, coming in behind John.

"Stands to reason," Jim said. "Carastino disappears, Caro sends out his agents, they spot us, a military-looking crew, military-looking ship, in the area when their boy disappeared, and hey presto! They now have suspects."

"They'll send somebody snooping around the ship," John said, as if musing to himself. "And they'll check out our credentials. This might be fun! It might just turn out that we'll get some more information on these bad guys too. Besides, with Pen gone, things got boring. Our guys need some excitement!"

"Men!" Pen said, tossing her head but smiling at John. Jim read her body language correctly and kept the smile off his face. He could tell John felt the same way about her. But then, he'd known that for some time. Just when the realization came, he couldn't quite place, but he did know his brother.

"Let's make sure whoever they send on board gets caught but not thrown over the side. Let's hope the silly bugger doesn't fall overboard on his own," Jim added.

Just then the Klaxon sounded the emergency rescue code. Racing to the bridge, they arrived to find Andrea at the wheel and Rosa strapped in, hanging on to the railings, looking very excited. Jim smiled at her as he passed and went into the CIC, clapping Andrea on the shoulder.

"Distress call from the *Lady Francis*. She's the weekly mail boat for the islands. We've seen her several times over the past weeks playing around in this area. Everybody on the islands is worried and listening in. Her engines failed, and she's adrift," Zeke announced. Jim nodded and headed next into the compass deck. Smitty would have an estimated time of arrival.

"Ten minutes!" Smitty said without looking up from his chart. Jim pushed the talk button on his headset.

"All hands to their emergency stations. Lifelines, ladies and gentlemen." He took his hand away and headed out to make his way to the rear deck. Outside the wind howled, flattening his clothes to him and flapping any loose fabric wildly. He clipped his lifeline to the rail as he went down, using both hands to keep from being thrown over the railing as the ship fought the ocean.

The ocean threw itself into an all-out attack on the ship, slamming down on the hull with powerful blows. *Bring It Up Coral* went toe to toe with Mother Nature, giving as good as he got, taking the punishment and shrugging it off as if dodging knockout blows. It seemed as though she was intent on driving the boat under, but he stood up to her blows, rising ponderously from the depths and shedding water to take the next hit.

Lady Francis was in deep trouble. Drifting she was at the mercy of the storm, and already she was beginning to sink. Twice she had nearly rolled over. Her crew, a mere handful of natives, clung to the railings and searched the sea for their rescue. It was no surprise that Smitty, on *Bring It Up Coral*, saw her first. His radar and sonar were working correctly, and he knew where to look. As soon as the crew saw the tug, they began to wave frantically.

"She's awash, Captain," Smitty said into his headset. "We're just in time. Looks like the crew is just about all in and desperately in need of a timely rescue. We'll need a pumping crew and everyone else on the bollard pull."

Everyone heard his commentary on the headsets, steeling

themselves for the battle to come. There were many who exchanged wild grins of excitement.

"Roger that, Smitty," Jim said. He issued the appropriate orders, and as *Bring It Up Coral* came alongside, some of the men made the dangerous leap onto her decks. Jim was one of them, landing lightly on his feet, grabbing the nearest line to steady himself as a huge wave broke over the vessel, threatening to tear him away. When he could breathe again, he made his way to the bow, and the line snaked out over his head. Snagging it with his left hand, he held on desperately with his right.

Strong arms reached around him as the wave broke over the vessel again. It was Dorf, who knew that Jim needed to hold that line and could not hold on one handed. After the wave cleared, he and the others began to pull the cable over. It took a few minutes to get it properly attached, but when they were satisfied, the diesel engines of *Bring It Up Coral* roared and drove the ship into the storm. Slowly the line stretched out, and the floundering boat began to move.

Making their way back toward the ship's bridge, Jim could see broken glass in her front windshield. The white paint was peeling, and the ship had rust everywhere. Jim hated it when people didn't take proper care of their vessels. He found the captain, steering now, some blood running down his face from imbedded glass.

"Ya come ta save the day, Captain. Aye a lie." That's what it sounded like. Jim sketched him a wave.

"We have a pumping crew coming on board to help," he yelled above the storm.

"Aye. The boys'll jine ya, den!" The man grinned, his teeth white in his black face.

Getting the pumping crew aboard in the increasing waves took some time, but at last everyone was working, and the *Lady Francis* began to rise out of the water as thousands of gallons of water were pumped over the side. Mark sounded her hull and found it in good condition.

Andrea headed for Hawk's Nest Resort and Marina on Cat Island, because it was the closest where the *Lady Francis* could wait out the storm and repair her engines. New Bight offered some help to the stranded ship and her crew. By the time they arrived, her own pumps could keep up, and with hearty thanks, the crew saw the men from *Bring It Up Coral* back to their ship with backslapping and many thanks.

Jim saw a small man in a rubber raft climb onto the anchor and then slip over the side of his ship as they were saying goodbye to the crew of the *Lady Francis*. It was a dangerous move, and twice the man nearly fell into the water, but finally he was safely aboard. When everyone was transferred and the equipment cleaned and stored, they headed back out to sea.

"Anybody see our guest?" Jim asked into his headset as he headed up to the bridge.

"He's in number one hold now, Shep," Inchworm said. "He's mighty curious about everything we have. He's takin' his time lookin' through everything."

"Don't discourage him. Make sure someone follows to be sure he doesn't steal anything or leave a mess," Jim said, smiling.

"Roger that, Shep. I'm on it," Inchworm replied.

Whoever this man was, he was thorough. He checked everything in the holds. When it was far into the night, he crept from his hiding place, still sure he was undetected, and began to carefully move about the ship. He looked into the berths shared by the crew. There were four to a room, most of them sleeping quietly in their bunks. It would have frightened him to know that the moment the doors open, every man of Omega Force was awake, feigning sleep, ready to defend themselves should he decide to try to kill a few. He looked through the papers on the captain's desk and then through the papers on Finn's desk.

As careful as he was, it was doubtful with his attention divided, he would hear the arrival of PU, who leaned nonchalantly against the doorpost, his arms crossed.

CHAPTER 11

"**F**ind what you want, mate?" an Australian voice said from behind him. Ernesto spun to find himself facing a powerfully built man. The man didn't have a gun and was not standing in a threatening way. Ernesto relaxed and pulled his hand out of his pocket, the switchblade remaining hidden against his pant leg.

"You work on this boat, senor?" Ernesto asked.

"Really? That's your first question? Yeah! I'm a petty officer, third class. We call it PO3 to make it easy. What the hell are you doing in Sharky's office?" the man said.

"My name is Ernesto. I work for Hefé Antonio Caro. He asked me to search this vessel. Please understand that I mean no harm to you, and I do not steal anything. My hefé is curious. I am paid mucho dinero for doing this," Ernesto explained.

"Well, Ernesto, I don't know any Antonio Caro, and I don't care why you're here. The bottom line is you're a stowaway, and I'm taking you to the captain. You can tell him your story," Phillip Eustus stepped aside and motioned for Ernesto to proceed him.

Ernesto waited until he was beside PU before lunging at him with his knife. Phil grabbed the stabbing wrist in an iron grip, stopping it well short. He squeezed a little harder, and the knife came away and dropped to the floor. Slowly Ernesto found himself being lifted off the floor, that hand still tightly gripping his wrist and the other holding his throat.

"PO3 Eustus! What is going on?"

Ernesto opened his eyes to see a giant behind the man holding him. PU slowly lowered him to the floor and finally released his neck and arm.

"Wanker tried to stab me with this," he said, picking up the knife. "Guess I got a little carried away in all the excitement! Pelican was going through Sharky's desk."

"You are very strong and very quick, senor," Ernesto rasped, rubbing his throat. "You are a soldier, no?"

"Yeah, I *was* a soldier. I'm a civilian now, and I work on this boat, and I don't have to play by the rules anymore. Get it, Pedro?" PU said, slapping Ernesto on the back of the head hard enough to send him staggering a few steps. He rubbed the back of his head and glared at PU. Things were not going at all how he had planned them, and he tried to think quickly. To bide his time, he asked the obvious question.

"What is meant by not playing the rules?" Ernesto asked, looking up at Dorf towering over him.

"Out here on the ocean, if we want to, we can drop you off the bow and watch your mutilated remains wash out through the props. Maritime law allows us to repel boarders with extreme prejudice. Who are you, and what are you doing on this ship?"

Ernesto saw the look in Dorf's eyes and decided to cooperate.

"My name is Ernesto. I am employee of Hefé Antonio Caro. He pays me mucho dinero to search this vessel and report to him. If you harm me, he will be very angry." He looked at both men to gauge the response and realized they were not impressed.

"Good for him. Up those steps. We're going to see the captain," Dorf commanded, pointing.

Ernesto walked up the steps. Even two steps in front of the giant, the man still towered over him. PU followed. Ernesto found himself in the bridge. A man with four stripes on his epaulets signifying he was the captain turned.

"Ah. Our guest has arrived," Jim said. Speaking fluent Spanish, he looked at Ernesto. For a moment, Ernesto was taken aback. The man spoke as though he was born in Colombia!

"It was very foolish to sneak onto this vessel. You have searched our holds and gone through my papers and the papers of my administrative assistant. I wish to know why," he stated.

Ernesto was impressed with the man's flawless Spanish. He answered in the same language. "I am Ernesto. I work for Hefé Antonio Caro. He pays me to look at your vessel. He is a very powerful man, senor."

"Anybody here know somebody named Antonio Caro?" Jim asked. His men shook their heads. It was a convincing performance, and Ernesto bought it.

"Well, whoever the hell he is, tell him to ask us next time. We'll be glad to give him a tour of the ship. In fact, Lieutenant, why don't you give him the rest of the tour he missed?" Jim turned away.

Ernesto was escorted to the CIC first. There was an ensign seated at a chair, just watching the computer screens. They were all showing various aspects of the storm upon them at the moment. He looked up as they entered, nodded, and went back to studying the information. In the compass deck, another ensign leaned over a chart, making notations. He didn't even look up as they passed through.

Ernesto felt small walking next to Dorf, but when they reached the kitchen, he gasped. A man even taller than Dorf stood there to greet them. *Is this a ship of giants?* Sturdy was a weightlifter. He looked the part, his shoulders impossibly wide, his bulging arms and legs impossibly huge. Ernesto swallowed. He watched the kitchen crew busy preparing the morning meal. These men all reminded him of soldiers.

"We've got a guest for breakfast," Dorf announced. The men turned to look, waved, and went back to work. Then another man came out of the walk-in freezer, another body builder. Ernesto was impressed with his build. The man could have won the Mr. Universe contest. Abe grinned at him as he passed. Obviously in charge, he began giving instructions to the crew.

Dorf led Ernesto down into the engine room. Inchworm was on

duty, sitting before a console of instruments and gauges, watching the engines to be sure nothing was going wrong. On the table in front of him, he was cleaning an engine part. His hands were greasy. He looked up with a greasy rag in one hand and looked at Dorf with one eyebrow raised comically.

"So our wandering friend has been found!" Inchworm said. "I'd shake hands, but they're a little dirty. Hey, Dorf, can I borrow your shirt? I need to wipe them."

"Hey! Inchworm! Can I borrow your body? I need it to wipe the floor!" Dorf retorted without a moment's hesitation. They grinned at one another.

"You outrank him, but he does not call you sir," Ernesto said.

Both men threw back their heads and laughed. "We don't count rank for much on this boat, buddy," Inchworm said. "Rank is a means of determining responsibilities. We're all owners in this venture, so we're equals. Works out pretty good." Inchworm went back to work cleaning the engine part.

They did not venture out on deck. The storm was raging outside, and it would have been dangerous. Instead, Dorf took Ernesto up to the inside observation deck, and they held on to the bars beneath the windows to look out.

"We can attach a ten-ton capacity crane on that deck. The grid is fitted with one-inch bolt receptacles spaced twenty-four inches apart. We can bolt down a wide variety of portable equipment. We also have two GPH fire pumps supplying three fire monitors with up to 2,200 gallons of foam per minute. And see that deep submersible module attached to the cradle? We use that for salvage," Dorf shouted over the fury of the storm.

"Are you not afraid of the storm?" Ernesto asked.

"This baby can pull a full container ship through force six, son," Dorf replied boastfully.

Ernesto didn't know what he was talking about but was hardly interested in the technical details. He noticed Dorf's hands for the first time. They were big hands, rough and weathered from working in the sea air. This was a working boat, nothing else. Ernesto sighed.

His boss was hoping for more. Still, Ernesto brightened at the thought that he would be paid, regardless of the outcome.

Ernesto watched people come into the dining room. There were three women wearing civilian clothing. That told Ernesto this was not a military ship. The men too came in, some wearing their work uniform, others just jeans and T-shirts. True, the men were all physically fit, even the older men. Many claimed to have been soldiers, and that explained their fitness and discipline. This captain had done a fine job picking his men.

Breakfast was nearly over when a Klaxon sounded throughout the ship. Everyone hustled to put their plates and utensils in the bins and then sped out of the room, leaving Ernesto alone. He walked up to the bridge to see what was going on. No one seemed to mind that he was there.

"We've got a container ship taking on water. One of her containers went overboard and then she ran over it. According to them, it punched a hole in the hull. They're in the eye of the storm now," Zeke said.

"How far are we from their position?" Jim asked.

"In this weather, at least twenty-five minutes," Smitty said.

"Anybody else closer?" Jim asked.

"Coast guard is heading their way, but they're an hour from us," Wade said.

"Okay. Contact the ship and see who is insuring them. Then get on the horn with that insurer and ask them if they want us to save the ship." Jim straightened and looked around the CIC. "Everybody knows what to do. Somebody get Ernesto a waterproof suit. Dorf, you can use him. Make sure his lifelines are attached at all times."

"Aye, Captain," the men said, snapping a salute.

"Come on, Ernesto, time to earn your keep," Dorf said.

"I am not being paid to work for you!" Ernesto protested.

"You came on this boat and ate our food. Now you're going to earn your keep. Get going," Dorf grabbed him and hauled him down the steeply slanting steps as they rode up one wave. Ernesto was helpless in his grasp.

Dorf threw him a suit that would fit him, made sure his lifeline was fastened properly, and took him out to the rear deck, where he attached the line to the cable provided for that purpose in such storms. Ernesto was still frightened by the savagery of the storm.

"You can't go over the side either way. Follow me!" Dorf yelled, and fought his way to the rear to make sure the bollard pull was ready to operate. Ernesto followed, hanging desperately to the lifeline, fearful for his life as waves washed over the low rear deck, sweeping him from his feet. At the bollard pull, Dorf explained how they would attach the huge cable by winch to the stranded container ship. Ernesto understood about half of it. Despite his reluctance to participate, he was fascinated both by the storm and the way the men dealt with it.

Slowly the storm seemed to die away, though the seas were still high. They were in the eye. Wiping saltwater from his eyes, Ernesto looked forward to see the huge container ship listing to one side. As they approached, the ship seemed to grow until it filled all his vision, towering impossibly above them.

C. G., Vince, Wade, and JR appeared on the deck with strange-looking guns in their hands. They aimed upward, fired the projectiles, trailing ropes, and Ernesto saw four grappling hooks flying through the air. All of them hooked their target. Handles on either side of the gun were grasped firmly, and the four bodies were jerked into the air as the lines were retracted into the cannon body. As they approached the end of their lifelines, they unclipped them.

Ernesto marveled at the strength of the men as they hung on, were pulled to the top, and easily lifted themselves over. Moments later, another line snaked down, and Mark, Jack, and Sparks attached the winch. While they did that, Dorf instructed Ernesto to help drag the feed line to the winch. When that was attached, one of the men pressed something on his face and spoke. Ernesto thought it was a microphone of some kind. The winch and line began to rise.

The other teams were on the deck, erecting the crane so that the heavy pumping gear could be transferred to the crippled ship. They did it quickly, obviously used to this work. Ernesto now knew that these men actually did salvage work. Experience showed in every motion. They knew exactly what to do, when to do it, and moved with the sureness of men familiar with the work. Movement of the ship on the choppy waters hardly deterred their work, and not one staggered as Ernesto did many times. These were men of the sea.

Master Chief Warner took the crane controls, and Inchworm directed the crew in loading the pumps. Each pump rose to the deck of the damaged ship, with four men hanging on to the sides. With crew and equipment aboard the container ship, the crane was shut down and quickly dismantled, stowed away properly, and all tools cleaned and put away with care. Slowly the men made their way inside, until only Ernesto and Dorf remained.

The line played out, and the huge cable was lifted until it could be attached. As the cable fed out, *Bring It Up Coral* moved forward slowly until sixty yards of cable stretched between the ship and the tug. Slowly the huge container ship turned and began to follow behind the ocean tug. Once Dorf was satisfied that the brake was set properly, he motioned for Ernesto to precede him into the safety of the superstructure.

"Nice work out there for a novice," Dorf said, clapping Ernesto on the back and nearly sending him to the floor.

"I did not do much," Ernesto said.

"You helped. That's what counts. Thanks," Dorf replied, hanging his waterproof coverall on a plastic hanger and then placing it on a line with others, dripping on the floor. Ernesto followed suit and was amazed that his clothes were relatively dry. Most of the day, Ernesto spent following Dorf around the ship, doing odd jobs, kept busy and amazed by the myriad of responsibilities of a full lieutenant. One thing he knew, his boss would be pleased to know that this crew was bona fide search-and-rescue and nothing more. More than that, it was an amazing crew, and those with rank certainly did not give orders like the military.

Dorf never gave a direct order. He asked people to do things, did many himself that seemed beneath the station of his rank, and was well liked and respected by his colleagues. Having visited naval vessels in the past, he was curious. Ernesto asked about it while Dorf made a minor repair to a hatch.

"Rank doesn't mean anything on this ship," Dorf said. "We're all equal partners. All rank does is define certain responsibilities. It gives no one authority above those responsibilities."

"That is surely odd for a military operation, is it not?" Ernesto asked.

"For a military operation yes. For us, no! We're a business venture, pure and simple. We do this when the insurance pays, and we look for lost ships. That's why we're here in this part of the world. We're after a French vessel that sank with precious stones as her cargo. If we find her, the cargo is ours." Dorf shrugged, made the final twist with the wrench, and put the tool back in the box at his feet. He picked up the box and returned it to a metal cabinet marked "tools." Ernesto noted that everything on the ship was in its proper place.

"I have been on many vessels, senor, but none other than military vessels that are so tidy and well cared for," Ernesto said, watching Dorf wipe his hands clean and dispose of the hand-cleaning cloth in the appropriate container. Everything on this ship was neat and orderly and pristine.

"We all own this ship, buddy," Dorf said. "We're all ex-military, mostly navy. Upkeep is paramount to our continued success. Besides, we all like it when this baby is shipshape. Keeping it that way is second nature to us," he added unnecessarily.

Dorf went all the way up to the bridge, where he took a pair of Zhumell 10×42 waterproof binoculars and took a long look at the ship they were towing. In the rain, and tossing of the ship, Ernesto could see little, except that the ship no longer listed. Turning to the older gentleman at the wheel, Dorf spoke.

"The line looks good, Papa," he said with a grin, looking down at Andrea.

"Mark is up top keeping an eye on things. He'll let me know if there's a problem," Andrea replied, keeping his eyes roving between the compass, radar, sonar, and the sea before him. If the tossing of the ship affected him at all, Ernesto could not see it.

Dorf nodded and led Ernesto down to the galley for a cool drink. Sturdy came over to stand beside Dorf, and Ernesto suddenly felt tiny. Sturdy was two inches taller and pounds heavier than Dorf. Between the two men, he felt insignificant and somehow threatened. The feeling was not one he felt often, and he didn't like it one bit but had to bear it.

"Everything going well?" Sturdy asked, riding a particularly difficult roll using his balance and feet alone. Ernesto had to grab for a railing. Dorf had not moved his hands.

"Yeah. The pumping crew is keeping ahead of the water. We should be able to dump this tub in about four hours," Dorf said. He sipped from a glass of iced tea. Sturdy looked down at Ernesto with a friendly look in his eyes. It looked odd in that scarred face, and Ernesto didn't feel relaxed.

"What would you like?" he asked. Even his voice was big, deep, resonant, almost frightening coming from that huge head. Ernesto swallowed.

"A lemonade?" Ernesto's voice was tentative.

"Be right back," Sturdy promised, and stalked off on his long legs, rolling with the ship, returning quickly with a full glass of lemonade, never spilling a drop. He handed it to Ernesto with a smile. Ernesto took a sip and sighed with pleasure. One thing this crew had was a talented kitchen staff. The drink in his hand was delicious. Tart and sweet, tantalizing his taste buds, the drink was perfect after his work. Using the glass in his hand as a cover, he covertly, or at least he thought he was being covert, studied the surrounding area and men working. One of the reasons Caro hired him was because he missed little.

"So what does your boss do, Ernesto?" Sturdy asked. Abe came up to stand in the only open space, and suddenly Ernesto felt even more hemmed in. He had no way of knowing if this was intended or accidental.

"That I cannot say," he suggested ominously. "If I did, I might find my tongue hanging from his wall!"

"Sounds like a real jerk," Abe said, his voice as deep as Sturdy's.

"He pays well," Ernesto said.

"We don't like people looking over our shoulders, especially when we're looking for a treasure ship," Dorf said, almost conversationally. Ernesto caught on quickly and was quick to reassure Dorf.

"He has no interest in your search for treasure," Ernesto lied. He couldn't wait to tell el hefé of the possible treasure.

"Ernesto, you're a lousy liar," Sturdy said with a laugh, clapping a huge hand on his shoulder. That massive hand covered his shoulder from neck to arm and felt very heavy. "Either of you comes looking for trouble here, it will be the last time."

Ernesto just smiled. *Hefé Caro had an army, and what he wanted he took.* It would take an army to take this ship, but then Antonio Caro didn't care about casualties, just results.

CHAPTER 12

Spirits were high in the conference room later that evening. The hurricane was moving north, and by morning they would be in calmer weather. Insurance on the container ship included a ten percent of value bonus for the tug that rescued her. Already the costs for the entire year were met. Jim entered the room, and silence fell.

"First, I'd like to congratulate every one of you on a job well done," he said, taking his seat. "Ernesto is on his way to Caro. Caro, bless his black heart, is making plans to watch our ship and when we bring up the treasure, to attack with a large force. That may complicate things some as we go in to take him out."

"Why don't we just fake pulling a treasure off the ocean floor? He could come right to us," FM said.

"We're too vulnerable on the ocean, especially in these waters. He could use air support and then we'd be in real trouble," Jim replied.

"On the ground we could be vastly outnumbered too, Shep," Ox said, leaning forward. "Francisco Valdez has an army he can put into the field against us."

"We'll use the satellite system to monitor what's going on around us. That system is amazing!" Jim waved a hand as he spoke. "If Valdez moves his men, we'll know far enough in advance."

"So we will have eyes on the entire time?" Pen asked.

"Uncle Zeke is always watching," Zeke intoned without looking up from his computer.

"Depending on when he makes his move, if indeed he does, we could be caught in a deadly firestorm," Dorf said quietly.

"We know the situation. Our mission is clear. Every piece of equipment we need is on this ship. Each team will service cover fire for another team and will work in tandem. Support will come from each other. Communications are tested and tried in the field, so we will be in contact with one another at all times. Let's get our signals straight." Jim looked around the table, noting that each man, even the ones who voiced concerns, stood with him. That kind of trust filled him with both pride and dread.

"Team 1 is Red. Team 2 is Alpha. Team 3 is Zulu. Team 4 is Blue. Team 5 is Firefox. Team 6 is Raider. Pen will join Alpha so Zeke can concentrate on his equipment and keep us all informed. Red, Alpha work in tandem. Firefox, Zulu work in tandem. Blue, Raider work in tandem."

"Red Alpha will take the Orinoco River. Firefox Zulu will take the Guaviare River, and Blue Raider will take the Inirida River. Those two are tributaries to the Orinoco and are navigable for miles. I want full intel. Our cover is cartography. We're mapping the changes in those tributaries and in the Orinoco itself for two reasons. One is to help trace *Estelle*. Believe it or not, a grant is paying for the other reason, which is to actually determine how flooding during the rainy season affects water flow in those areas.

"Zeke has already plotted all the maps up to and including a hundred years ago, so the maps will unfold as you travel. If anyone asks, you'll have plenty of plotter paper to show what you've accomplished. Dr. Persons is on a bona fide mission for this grant and has government approval through Berkeley University." Jim smiled.

"We'll keep all weapons locked down and be prepared for searches along the way. Caro and Valdez will be suspicious. Dr. Persons will travel with Red Alpha. He has the appropriate government permits for this study. Each of the other boats will carry a copy with a letter from the university and from the Brazilian and Colombian governments.

Our studies will lead us to the Magdalena River in search of new sources for gem mines. Any questions?"

"We do the survey as cover for our recon," John said slowly. "Then, when we know the score, we meet and plan our offensive. With the maps and studies, we'll know the area better than anyone, giving us another advantage." He nodded to everyone. "Sound strategy, Shep. Let's do it!"

"Sir, what about the rest of us?" Finn asked.

"You drop anchor off Barranquilla and wait for us. You react to any unauthorized boarders as you see fit. We will be in contact at all times," Jim said. "Andrea has the command in our absence," he added.

"But, sir! I outrank Master Chief Orvieto!" Finn said with some heat.

"You're an administrative assistant, Marvin. Command is not about rank. It's about experience and ability. Andrea has the experience, and his word is final on this ship in my absence. Remember, it is not about rank but about responsibility. Is that clear to everyone?" Jim asked.

There were nods and words of assent. Finn, crestfallen, assented also. Dr. Wozniac patted Finn on the shoulder and whispered in his ear, "I outrank you, and I wasn't chosen either. The captain knows what he's doing. I feel quite confident knowing that Andrea has command."

Finn listened and then nodded. Captain Shepherd was aware of the interplay between the doctor and Finn and felt some relief in the doctor's support and sage advice to his administrative assistant. He wondered if Finn would ever get it.

"No one should wear a uniform while I'm gone," Jim said after a moment of silence. "Casual work clothes should do the trick. We want our enemies to forget about our military background and the military nature of our crew. Shore leave will happen in small parties of no less than four at a time and for no longer than daylight hours. Understood?"

Again, there were nods and words of agreement to this wise and obvious advice. Jim sighed and looked around the room. Once again, he was leading his crew into the unknown and into danger. His face was serious when he continued his orders.

"We are all going into harm's way. Our training will give us only a slight edge. Let's remember the basics and all come back alive." He looked around the table and saw that his troops were with him. Their eyes had grown hard, in the way they often did when it was time to go into battle. They were ready. "We depart at dawn," he added, standing up as he spoke.

In the morning, before sunrise, the anchor dropped at the Port of Spain, near the mouth of the Orinoco River. As per instructions, the riverboats had been shuttled there and were ready for their journey. Dr. Persons joined them in Port of Spain, having arrived a day earlier. Under cover of darkness and with utmost secrecy and care, weapons, gear, and explosives were loaded onto the boats and locked away in each cabin.

So cleverly designed were the secret holds in the boats that Jim was confident no one would find them. No plans existed that showed what and where they were. Only the hunting rifles and shotguns locked away behind waterproof doors on the bridge were visible. Dr. Persons arrived just before dawn and hurried on board. It didn't take long for the crew to get everything ready. Then, as the gray light of dawn separated the surface of the earth from the far distant night sky, the six boats set out.

Dr. Persons was in his element, despite the humidity and heat, spending the entire first week on the upper deck with his binoculars up one minute, then down while he wrote on his notes. Jim and Cecilia spent time with him, poring over their notes, fascinated with the changes only a hundred year's passage of time indicated in the river's course. For much of the rest of their day, the explorers sat on the front veranda of the boat, surrounded by mosquito netting screens, discussing the voyages of other traders up and down this mighty river.

A great deal of research had gone into that particular study, and Dr. Persons had detailed notes from many of the explorers and members of their teams for the past hundred years. These the men pored over with great interest, seeing through the eyes of men who had gone before them, the beauty and dangers of this part of the world.

Out of necessity, the names of the boats had been changed. They were going to Colombia again, and the boats had already been on a mission there. *Alpha 1* was printed on the stern of Jim's boat. *Red Eagle* was printed on the stern of Dorf's boat. John was in charge of *Zulu Explorer* and Bill Dodge captained *Firefox*. Sean had command on *Blue Explorer*, and Calvin Weston had command of *River Raider*. Colors had been changed to help identify them as company boats.

Each boat had the *Bring It Up* colors of pearl white, aqua blue, and burgundy as well as the logo posted on the prow of each vessel. They looked sharp chugging up the river together. There was nothing covert about them except perhaps the silence of their hydraulic thrusters. Only the sounds from the jungle, villages, towns, and river traffic could be heard over the soft swishing of water flowing beneath the pontoons.

On *Firefox*, the men sat quietly on the bow observation deck discussing the nature of their work. They liked the fact that these boats were equipped with air-conditioning systems and all the best amenities for river travel. The fact that they were being paid to sit idle had its merits too. Also, Abe had packed a cooler full of their favorite beers and sodas. It was much like a vacation for them, because they weren't doing any of the actual plotting.

Some of the men fished, others took photographs, and still others studied the shoreline and jungle with binoculars to see the myriad of creatures filling the area with calls, roars, and screams. Frogs chirped and hummed from the shoreline, and the insects swarmed over the water. Amazingly colorful butterflies and birds were everywhere. Bright-colored amphibian creatures were everywhere, as were a myriad of reptilian creatures for them to observe. Hardly a moment went by without someone commenting on the teeming life around them.

River Raider's crew was much the same, making a trip like this for the first time. The boat was fabulous. They enjoyed the wild scenery around them as if they were on vacation. Yet they were vigilant, being the rear boat, keeping an eye on anyone following them while they tried to take in everything around them as well. No one was bored.

Passing from the Delta del Orinoco section of the river into the Bajo Orinoco section brought them into the most developed and populated segment. Oil exploration and industrialization brought about important cities and population growth. There were more islands in the river, many of which served as a measurement tool for the rise and fall of the river.

The rainy season was three months into its cycle, nearing its end, so travel on the river was somewhat dangerous, and currents were powerful and difficult to properly gauge. Constant vigilance had to be kept for floating debris, and sonar kept a watch for any sunken objects. They came at last to the place where four of the boats would leave the Orinoco. For a short part of the journey, they would travel together, but then the *Blue Explorer* and *River Raider* would break south on the Inirida while *Zulu* and *Firefox* followed the Guaviare.

It was here that officials boarded them for the first time. Papers were carefully studied and their work to date scanned. When the officials were satisfied that they were doing exactly what they were supposed to be doing, they allowed them to pass. The fact that none of the passengers were the least bit concerned about being searched and questioned seemed to provide an ironclad alibi for their presence. The latter was commented upon by all those in authority who were involved in the actual interrogation of the teams. Equipment and work already accomplished was proof enough that they were fulfilling their mission of study.

Satellite images and some infrared images pinpointed areas where drugs were being manufactured. It galled them to leave those sites alone, to raise no suspicions as the days passed into a month, and then six weeks. Still, they had a job to do, and no one chafed at the inactivity of the moment. Water levels slowly dropped to normal, giving them more information for their maps. Soon the space was filled with rolled maps of amazing cartography carefully recorded. Mission success depended on them being bone fide.

Two weeks passed, filled with inactivity for the most part, though

Dr. Persons continued to teach and record, and Jim, Cecilia, and Pen enjoyed working with him. However, soon the work for this part of the mission was finished. All studies were completed, and the boats returned to the Orinoco, met up with Jim's team, and made their journey back to the Port of Spain.

Obtaining permission from the Colombian government for a survey of the Magdalena River involved some payments to certain officials, but eventually they procured the legal certified permits. It helped that Berkeley University was behind the study, much to Jim's amusement, because the college was considered a liberal, almost communist stronghold on American soil, and in this part of the country, that was a bonus. Enough information had been gathered that by the time they returned to *Bring It Up Coral*, they had a plan for operations.

Pen was impressed with the precision with which these men planned as well as the resources they had at their command. Much of that was due to Zeke's skill in tapping into systems he wasn't supposed to be able to access. She was pleased to be involved in a mission of this type and to work with men of this caliber. This would give her a chance to use her skills in the hardest test of all, actual infiltration.

The ship dropped anchor at Barranquilla, the delta of the Magdalena River beckoning, with the riverboats in tow. Once the officials had been satisfied with their paperwork, along with a few more bribes, they were permitted to undertake their survey. The papers included a tributary that flowed down from Pico Christôbal Colôa through the villages of Fundaciôn, Pivijay, El Piñón, to Campo de la Cruz.

It was along this waterway that most of the Santa Marta, or Santa Maria cartel, did their work and moved their drugs. Caro had his house on the slopes of Pico Christôbal Colôa at nearly five thousand feet elevation. It was a fortress. That was common with cartel leaders. Each leader of this cartel had a small army to protect them and to enforce their rule. José Rivera lived near Campo de la Cruz, and the Garcia Márquez compound was near Fundaciôn.

At Campo de la Cruz, they met Francisco Valdez in person. He met them with a contingent of fifty soldiers. Jim stood on the boat near the gangplank and looked at them with interest. Many of them were nothing more than thugs with guns, their macho charisma flowing outward in evil disdain for life and a lust for violence. Only a few were trained soldiers who found themselves surrounded by evil men and did what they were told to do because it was better than the alternative. Yet he knew beyond a shadow of a doubt that these men would fight to the death.

Colonel Valdez wore his dress uniform with ribbons bedecking his chest, many of which he had awarded himself, and introduced himself in fluent Spanish. Jim answered in the same language. Valdez measured the men he saw and was instantly very suspicious. He knew military men when he saw them, and most of these men looked like the kind of specialists he feared most would one day invade his area.

"Permission to come aboard, Captain Shepherd," Valdez asked. It was a request, but one that the colonel expected to be granted.

"You are welcome, Colonel," Jim replied.

Valdez nodded to two of his most evil-looking thugs. As they came up the gangplank, Jim stepped in front of the colonel. Valdez stopped, surprised.

"You may bring these men aboard, Colonel. There are women on this boat. If they step out of line, I will personally escort them to shore." Jim watched both men as he made his statement and saw them leering at him. The colonel, however, recognized all the danger signals. This was not a man to trifle with. He turned to his men and told them to wait on shore. They were surprised but did as commanded, even with bad grace.

"Sometimes in the military such men are necessary, no?" Valdez commented, shrugging his shoulders. Jim said nothing, stepped back, and permitted the colonel to step onto the boat. His tour of the boat was thorough. Watching Zeke at his computer center seemed to fascinate him. Zeke, of course, was showing Dr. Persons the various changes in the river system over the past hundred years. Every screen was filled with pictures and satellite images, and the two were deep in conversation, hardly paying any attention to their visitor. Valdez was surprised at the thoroughness of the study.

Frank Miller was in the engine room, his hands greasy, his T-shirt grimy, working on the diesel engine. It was routine maintenance Frank was performing, more for show than any other reason. He nodded to Jim as they passed through but continued his work. Colonel Valdez smiled at the lack of military discipline on the ship. No one saluted the captain. Smitty was on the bridge plotting their course. He spoke to the colonel at length about the river ahead.

Penn and Cecilia were sitting on the front observation deck sipping lemonade, which they offered the colonel when he introduced himself. Both spoke fluent Spanish. Pen, of course, was traveling under another name and with a legal passport provided by her government. She was, the passport said, a cartographer and geologist from Eton College. The maps spread out on her table upon which she had made notations and calculations spoke of her expertise in her field. Cecilia, of course, was the captain's wife, who had invited her friend from England on the trip. Nothing that he saw raised any other flags, and he thanked the ladies for the drink. Still, he was not convinced. There was about this crew something he could not quite identify, and he didn't like not knowing.

Colonel Valdez visited each boat and carefully searched them. Finding nothing suspicious, he finally left the *River Raider* with a wave to Captain Shepherd, who was making his way back to his own lead boat. In the back of his mind, Colonel Valdez was mulling over the men he had seen. They were all military men, though they were no longer in actual service. That made him wary of this group.

However, the presence of Pen and Cecilia, as well as Dr. Persons, who was obviously not a military man, made him cautious in his judgment. He decided that he would keep tabs on this group for a few days to make sure they were doing what the paperwork permitted. Always suspicious of Americans and Western Europeans, he felt no compulsion to be diplomatic with them. If they proved to be anything other than what they claimed, he would kill them all.

That made him smile. If that became necessary, the two women would provide some sport for he and his men before they had to be eliminated.

CHAPTER 13

At El Piñón, they tied their boats up and marched into the dense jungle to trace the old route of the river. Trekking through the deciduous jungle, they camped at regular intervals, making their way all the way back to within a mile of Campo de la Cruz. The two scouts Colonel Valdez assigned to follow them reported to him that they were indeed following the old river route. He also learned from his scouts that they were tracing some gem traders who had passed through that area buying precious stones. *Estelle* disappeared in the Bermuda Triangle, he knew. Along the old River route, the traders had indeed purchased large quantities of precious stones.

Neither of the scouts saw C. G. Franklin and Vince Hall slip out of camp to study the compound of José Rivera. Shadows among the shadows, they walked the perimeter of the compound, took hundreds of photographs, some from the trees looking down, most from the ground, showing troops, movement, and points of entry. They slipped back into camp as quietly as they left.

Returning to the riverboats, they took up their journey again. This time they stopped at Pivijay and worked both sides of the river, looking for signs of changes. Colonel Valdez decided to pull his scouts at that point, as the group from *Bring It Up* seemed intent on their search for the gem merchants' past adventures in this part of the country.

At Fundación, aware that scouts no longer followed them, they continued their secondary objective, while C. G. and Vince once again slipped off to study the Márquez compound. Here they would leave their boats and travel on foot up the mountain, following the tributary to its head. According to their itinerary, the purpose for this part of the trip was to study the effect of floodwaters not only on the river's changes, but also upon changes to water flow from the springs that fed the river. A study of this nature would give them ample excuse to move off the trail and deep into the surrounding jungle.

Jim hired local fishermen to keep an eye on his boats, and he paid them well. Each time the teams left the boats, they were open to anyone who wanted to move through them, and Jim was sure they had been carefully searched while his teams were away exploring. He expected nothing less and hoped that none of their expensive equipment would be stolen. Before making the trip, he'd made sure that everything was insured for that very reason. As it turned out, he needn't have worried, because Colonel Valdez wanted to make sure the Americans had nothing to complain about to their government.

Their pace was slow as they moved through the jungle, but not because Dr. Persons was along and would be hard-pressed to keep up if they needed to move fast. They moved slowly because they were entering enemy territory, and Jim knew that here the danger was greatest. Caro's men would consider them a danger because they were Americans, and they were in his personal territory. Obviously, he would know about the purpose of their visit, but would he allow the study, or interfere? No one knew, and no one ventured a guess, content to wait and see.

Point duties fell mainly to Zulu, Firefox, and Raider, while Blue team and Red team shared the duties of bringing up the rear. Moving through the jungle with care, they slowly moved onto higher ground. At times they remained hidden for hours while a military unit put peasants to work manufacturing the drugs. Each of the work sites was marked carefully on a map for their return journey.

Pen found the bulletproof vest heavy and hot. She was sure the others felt the same. Dr. Persons was having no difficulty keeping up because they were moving so cautiously. He adjusted his vest several times during the day but understood the need for it and was not interested in removing it.

Jim was sorry they couldn't wear their full battle gear. It gave them a lot more protection. That was one of the reasons they were being so cautious. Anyone who saw them would know a military unit was in the area. They were all heavily armed. Everyone wore camouflage clothing now that they were well hidden. Everything about the unit shouted military to any, even a casual observer.

Firefox had point, and Bill Dodge was at least two hundred yards ahead of Sid Barrett. For the sake of safety, they were traveling during the night now, and Viper had his night vision goggles on, scanning the area ahead of his feet, then looking up and around for any movement. The quiet of the night was suddenly torn by a terrified scream. Viper turned to his right and moved that way as silently as a shadow.

A young woman was fighting desperately against a man not much larger than herself. He wrestled her to the ground, sat on her chest, and pinned her arms down with his knees. With an evil laugh, he jerked a length of cord from his pocket and quickly tied one of her hands to a young tree. He tied the other wrist, then got up and pulled her arms tightly, tying that one off to another tree.

Viper rose up from the ground behind him as he contemplated his prize and with a quick movement, snapped the man's neck. The girl screamed again as the spectral apparition stepped around the dead body of her attacker. Viper put a finger to his lips to signal that she should be quiet and quickly cut her free. He pressed the talk button on his headset.

"Got a situation here. Hunker down," he said. Then he turned to the girl who was sitting, rubbing her wrists. He spoke to her in Spanish.

"Are you all right, miss?" he asked in a whisper.

"I speak English," she said, whispering back. "My father was a missionary here. Some of Caro's men killed him this morning, because he was teaching the peasants they didn't have to serve this way." She began to cry softly.

Dodge cursed himself. He'd given away his American identity by the way he phrased his question. That had been careless, or the girl was extremely quick. Viper didn't know what to do, but Jim was suddenly beside him, startling him.

"Shep! Don't do that! I nearly messed myself!" he said sheepishly, shoving his sidearm back in the holster.

"I heard what she said. See if you can find a place for that body so it looks like an accident," Jim said quietly. He knelt down beside the tiny girl and gathered her in his arms. She was no more than five feet tall. He lifted her easily and carried her silently back to Cecilia.

Viper was still shocked. He was good, he knew he was good in the brush, but Jim Shepherd was a ghost! No one had ever approached him like that. After a hundred yards, he found a cliff that dropped about eighty feet. That would do to cover the broken neck. When he got back to the body, he found Scope, RC, and Bear waiting.

"Damn!" Scope said quietly when he arrived. "Shep walked right up to us! I ain't never seen anyone could move like that in the bush!"

"Nearly wet myself," RC said with a grin.

"I'll carry the body," Bear said. "Then I'll change my underwear." They all laughed quietly at that. Bear picked up the body and tossed it down the cliff when they arrived. For the men, it was an impressive sight, their huge friend lifting the body above his head and tossing it a few yards out to make it look like he was running when he went over. It took a few minutes for the men to manufacture evidence that looked like the soldier had run along the ledge until he stepped too far over and fell to his death. On the way back, Viper was careful to wipe out all sign of their presence. He took extra precautions to make sure the girl's trail was also obliterated.

Jim didn't like this complication, but there was little he could do about it. He asked Viper to continue on to their next chosen hiding place, where they would dig in for the day. Cecilia knew his feelings, but she was busy with the weeping girl. After a few minutes, she quieted and agreed to come with them. What she thought about the guns and military nature of the group remained unspoken. She had been praying frantically for help when help had literally risen from the ground behind her attacker and killed him. Somehow, though she couldn't quite understand it, she sensed she was completely safe with this group, despite the number of men.

In silence, they moved, and eventually Tiffany, the young girl they rescued, caught on. Her shoes were canvas, and she began placing them as carefully as everyone else. Soon she too was walking in near silence. *How did they manage to walk so quietly with boots on?*

Before dawn they reached the checkpoint on the map that marked the halfway point in their journey. Men began to dig holes, almost as quietly as they walked. Between some trees camouflage netting was tied to provide protection from anyone looking down upon them. Most of them made camp beneath the netting in small camouflage dome tents.

In the foxholes, two men kept watch. There were four foxholes, so that watch could be kept in every direction. None of the foxholes, she noted, were visible from the air, as small camouflage nets were set on sticks over the holes. She could see the men talking together, but she could not hear them. They were being very quiet. Soon the man in charge, she knew his name was Jim, came and sat outside the tent she shared with Cecilia.

"I'm sorry about your dad, Tiffany," he began. "Can you talk about it? You don't have to, if you want to wait," he added. But she wanted to tell this story, and so he and Cecilia listened in horror as she unfolded it.

Through her tears, she told the story of her father's work of five years among the people of this region. Her mother died two years after they arrived, but her father carried on. She came to stay with him a year after graduating from high school two years past. Caro had beaten her father several times and had personally beaten her about six months before this to try to stop him from his work. Both had agreed after that to take precautions, but to remain and minister as God intended. Jim thought her courage remarkable. Then, early yesterday, men had come to the house they lived in. She was returning from market when she heard the shots. She simply ran into the jungle and hid until nightfall.

"Was there a search party out looking for you?" Jim asked. This complicated things even further.

"No. Just a few men, I think," she replied after a moment of thought. "Just some of Caro's thugs. They knew I must have been at market when they shot my father." She began to cry again.

"What were you doing up so high on the mountain?" Jim asked.

"I was making my way to Caro's fortress to kill him!" she answered vehemently. "Isn't that what you're doing?" Her green eyes flashed with the rage she felt.

Jim looked over her head at Cecilia, his eyes filled with resolve, and she nodded without saying anything, her own eyes filled with deep sadness and compassion for this poor young woman. Turning back to Tiffany, he spoke.

"No. We're going to do something far worse than kill him," Jim replied, looking away. He brought his green eyes back to hers swiftly. "We're going to destroy his network, his power base, and his army. Then we're going to take him prisoner and take him to a country where he will be tried by a military tribunal and sentenced to life in solitary confinement. The prison he will be in will be filled with soldiers, and he will fear for his life every day he is there."

She leaned back from the intensity of his eyes. Cecilia put out a hand and laid it on his wrist, and he calmed immediately. Tiffany didn't miss the interchange between the pair, and she relaxed a little more. That intensity was not a threat to her, but she knew beyond a shadow of a doubt that it was a promise to do exactly what he said he would do.

"You can do that?" Tiffany's voice was choked with emotion and hope.

"I can do that," Jim replied evenly.

"I want to face him!" she said, her jaw suddenly set.

Again, Jim looked at Cecilia, and she looked back, her face now calm, understanding completely. Jim smiled wanly at his wife, knowing she was remembering facing Al'Loudi.

"You will." Jim nodded, saying nothing more. He could see that his acquiescence surprised her. Watching her think about his words, he waited patiently. Certain she hadn't thought clearly since her father was murdered, he watched her.

"Thank you," she said softly after a pause.

Jim alerted his men that a few might be out looking for Tiffany and to stay sharp. They weren't hooked up to the satellites yet, so they would have to depend on their skills in the brush. Sleeping deeply for a few hours, he awoke to see that the sun was high in the sky. His internal alarm had awakened him five minutes ahead of schedule. Sitting up, he stretched, then got up and made his way to the shower facility. Every one of the men knew the importance of staying clean. Body odor could give you away all too easily. In the jungle, one had to be very careful because breezes could change directions so quickly. He showered quickly, applied deodorant, shaved, and returned to dress for the day. For a few moments, he didn't feel the heat. That was the benefit of a shower.

When he emerged from his tent, he checked on Cecilia, who was asleep next to Tiffany. The rope burns and bruises on her arms, neck, and exposed shoulders reminded him of the violence of the men he was facing, and he hardened his resolve. Both of them slept soundly, so he left them alone and moved out to check the outposts. Bill Dodge was at the far perimeter, his binoculars pressed to his face, scanning the hillside up and down. David Carr was next to him, equally vigilant. Viper wasn't aware of Jim until the latter reached out and gently touched his shoulder. Jerking at the touch, he turned his head. DC looked up, startled.

"You part Indian or something?" he asked Jim with a grin. "That's the second time you appeared without a sound. Near messed my shorts last time."

"See anything?" Jim asked Viper with a grin for DC.

"Saw a few deer, a bobcat, and a coyote. No people. There are a few hawks out too." Dodge grinned. "A fair-sized patrol passed about two miles east of us two hours ago, heading down the hill. I think I counted fifty men."

"Looking for us?" Jim asked.

"Probably. We did disappear into the bush," Viper replied.

"Okay. Get some rest. I've got point for the next two hours," Jim said.

Dodge nodded, handed him the binoculars, and silently moved toward the camp, followed by DC. FM appeared and slid into the foxhole, and Jim put the glasses to his face and began a slow scan of the surrounding hillside. If Dodge was right, that patrol would be returning soon. That gave him pause for thought, and he pondered the situation for a moment. After a moment of thought, he pressed the talk button on his headgear.

"C. G. you up and around?" he asked quietly.

"Go, Shep," C.G. replied.

"Take a trip down the hill, angling a little to the east, no more than two miles. Viper mentioned a troop of fifty passing that way two hours ago. I don't want them accidentally walking into our camp," Jim said.

"On my way Shep," C. G. replied. Lifting the binoculars once again, Jim continued his survey of the area.

"You want any of us to go up the hill?" John's voice came over his headset.

"Probably wouldn't hurt," Jim agreed after a moment of thought. "Take the rest of your team and fan out. Keep us posted. Our mission is to stay hidden."

John passed him a few minutes later, grinned and waved, and set out uphill. Jim could see Wade about two hundred yards away, and beyond him, Vince. He swept his glasses downhill and saw C. G. disappear into some heavy brush. The next two hours passed without incident, and Zeke appeared to take his place. As usual, Zeke had a huge grin on his face, as though this were tremendous fun rather than the stressful reality. Jim smiled at him.

CHAPTER 14

"**S**outh post has movement about two miles downhill," C. G. announced. At that moment, C. G.'s voice came over the headsets.

"That group of fifty is spread out and moving up toward your position," C. G. said. "I'm going to draw the contingent that could get as far as camp to the east. Better get everybody ready to move, just in case. Over."

"Roger that, C. G. Don't get dead!" Jim replied. He and FM exchanged a look that said volumes about the danger they were facing.

Jim pressed his talk button. "Let's get the camp folded up and have everybody ready to move west. *Quiet* is the watchword. Staying hidden is the mission. Remember, we leave no evidence we were here, so work quick and work quiet. Let's disappear!"

Ten minutes later, the camp was folded, and five minutes after that, not a sign of their presence remained. Even the foxholes had been filled and smoothed over. Blue team was the last to leave the area, wiping out any sign of their passage. Even the best-trained eye would have difficulty determining that anyone had camped in that spot.

Jim climbed a tree, going very high, and when he secured his position, he used hastily cut branches to camouflage his figure. Confident he was safe from discovery, he watched the oncoming group of men. He could see some of them following C. G. They would miss the campsite by about fifty yards.

C. G. carefully moved around the men following him until he was behind them. They continued up the hill searching for the elusive figure, talking and gesturing, shouting to the other men, making a lot of noise. With seeming ease, Clancy made his way to the very tree in which Jim lay hidden. He pressed his headset talk button.

"Shep?" he asked.

A pinecone dropped on his head. He looked up and saw a hand move, then disappear. Grinning, he moved away, found a dense group of bushes, and crawled into them. From there he watched the group moving up.

"Shep, I have a group of about thirty, spread out, moving slowly downhill." That was John reporting. "I'm going to stay here until you bring the rest up to my position. I'm at checkpoint 10."

"Wade, Vince, where are you?" Jim asked quickly. He wanted to make sure his men were still safe from discovery.

"About two hundred yards from each other, Shep. We're going to wait until these bozos get out of the way and join JR," Wade replied.

"Roger that. Be advised there is a troop of fifty moving up the hill," Jim said.

From his perch, Jim could see the two groups. They met, talked, and turned around to head back up to the fortress. Everyone sighed. The enemy had not discovered the presence of the military *Bring It Up* force. MRE suppers were served just before dark. Jim climbed down from his tree and walked to the next camp with C. G.

"Buggers sure make enough noise," C. G. said conversationally as they walked. "Be easy to sneak up on 'em and take 'em down," he added.

"Don't start thinking this will be easy," Jim warned automatically. "We don't want to get careless."

C. G. received the rebuke without comment. He knew that a soldier who grew careless could easily end up dead or, worse, get someone else killed. Knowing that Jim agreed with him about his assessment, he said no more. Neither man had to prove anything to the other, and Jim appreciated his companion's assessment and silence at his rebuke. Never underestimate an enemy. That was the rule.

After their meal, they buried the evidence carefully and prepared to set out for checkpoint 10. Raider took the lead, with DC taking point. Once again, the group ghosted through the night, undetected by man. By early morning they would reach their objective. Everyone was wired for the upcoming encounter. Still, they moved with caution. About halfway up, they paused to let the fifty soldiers that had come up the hill return to wherever they were stationed.

John, Wade, and Vince were sitting at the base of a tree when they arrived at the checkpoint. All together once again, they set out for the next two checkpoints, making good time, traveling almost silently, cautious now even more than before, knowing that enemies surrounded them and could come upon them at any time. Tiffany noted that occasionally one of them would look back if she made a sound with her feet, and she tried even harder to walk quietly.

"Put your toes down first carefully." Cecilia whispered close to her ear.

"Thermal scan indicates a body of thirty men about half a mile from the fortress. They appear to be prone, pointing downhill," Zeke said over the headsets. "It seems they are expecting company, and I really don't want to disappoint them. Shall we drop in on them?"

Cecilia listened to the words and repeated them to Tiffany. Both girls shared a concerned look.

"Red team and Alpha team will take them," Jim said. "We'll hold at checkpoint 12. It's half a mile from that position. Zeke, you'll talk us in and lead us to our targets."

Zeke remained at checkpoint 12 while Pen, taking his place, traveled up the hill with Red Team and Alpha. Silencers and repressors were already attached to their weapons. They circled carefully around the unit and made the first ten kills without alerting anyone. A three-shot burst through the back of the head was sufficient to kill each target.

Pen marveled at the skill of these men. Jim was no more than six feet from his target when he made the kill. The enemy troops made the mistake of being far enough away from the next man for that person to miss the sound of the bullets punching through the skulls of their comrades. Moving back and to their left, they took out the next ten just as silently. Their enemies were concentrating on the hillside below them, never expecting death to come from behind, and they were boasting to each other loudly, because of the distance between them, which made it simple to cover other sounds. As they made their way to the left again, Zeke's voice came over the headsets.

"I've got one moving. Mark, he's your guy. He's moving off to the left, probably to relieve himself." His voice was calm as he gave the information.

Mark adjusted, wondering how Zeke knew he was the nearest, found his man with his night goggles, and followed him. As the man unzipped his pants, Mark dropped him with a three-shot burst. The other nine died silently as well.

"Someone is coming from the compound. He's alone. He may be coming to check on the troops," Zeke said.

"Got him!" Driver said. "Let's talk to this one," he added.

As the man passed his position, Jack rose up and clubbed him unconscious, catching his body before it hit the ground. Removing the weapons and disabling them, he hoisted the body on his shoulders and made his way back to the others. Jim's team collected all the weapons from the enemy troops and after disabling them, buried the evidence carefully.

"We'll take him back to the checkpoint," Jim said before he started collecting weapons. "Hobbs, you and your boys show this prisoner exactly what he needs to see!"

Hobbs looked at Jim for a moment in the darkness, and the two nodded. Smiling crookedly, Hobbs knew that tonight would be a bad night for this prisoner. He'd recognized him as Alfredo Munyez, security chief for Caro. He knew enough about Munyez to relish what was coming. Bear carried the heavy body all the way to the checkpoint, hardly showing the effort.

Security Chief Alfredo Munyez opened his eyes slowly. He felt strange and shook his head. That hurt, and he groaned through the gag that filled his mouth. Looking around, he could see only boots. He looked down and discovered that he was buried up to his neck in the dirt. He could feel that his hands and feet were bound tightly. *What is happening to me?*

"Freddy, old son, you're in a bit of trouble," a cultured English voice said from the darkness. He looked into the eyes of Calvin Weston and wished immediately that he had not. In the odd light surrounding him, Weston's eyes glowed red, looking almost insane. This effect was created with an infrared lens held where the prisoner could not see it.

Trying to talk with a gag in your mouth was impossible. Alfredo glared up at Weston in defiance. He had not been chosen head of security for nothing. *Whoever these men are, they have no idea what they are facing.*

Weston laughed at the look in his eyes. He leaned down so he was squatting before the captive. "You're in no position to be defiant, old bean," he spoke conversationally and pressed a button on a device he held in his hand.

Munyez opened his eyes wide and screamed into the gag, biting down hard on it in his pain. When they'd buried him, the men had placed three Tasers in strategic locations, one in each armpit and one against his groin. The dirt, packed in carefully, held him securely so he could not move away from the pain. Weston held the switch down for about six seconds before releasing it. From the wild shaking of the prisoner's head, it was obvious the pain was intense.

Alfredo panted, and tears flowed down his filthy cheeks. His teeth were still clenched in pain and agony. His head flailed for a few seconds before he finally grew still. The screams had been shrill and violent. Turning away, Hobbs found Tiffany looking down at the security chief with an expression of hatred. He understood. She, he was sure, had been personally assaulted by this monster. Nodding to her once, he waited before returning. Weston waited almost five minutes before squatting down again. Knowing the need for intimidation, he steeled himself for what he must do. In those five minutes, Tiffany quietly told him all he needed to do what he had to do.

"You really want to cooperate with us, you know, old son. The alternative is less than attractive. I'm going to remove the gag. If you try to yell out to your comrades, you'll just end up biting your tongue in half. I imagine that will hurt a bit, and it will certainly make understanding you even more difficult. Nod if you understand," he said.

Alfredo nodded. He was still panting. Weston removed the gag, and Alfredo immediately attempted to yell at the top of his lungs, trying to warn his troops. The yell never formed. Both armpits seemed to explode in pain and agony, and he did indeed bite his tongue nearly in half as his jaws clamped in the pain. The gag was roughly shoved back into his mouth, and he felt as if he were swallowing gallons of his own blood.

"Freddy, Freddy, Freddy!" Weston chastised in a soft voice, shaking his head. "You're not bright, are you?" He motioned to Tiffany, who appeared, and Munyez opened his eyes wide in recognition.

Before Alfredo could draw a breath, the pain exploded in his groin again. It lasted a long time. Somewhere after six seconds, he lost consciousness. When it came back, he could hear himself panting first, and then the pain hit. He moaned into the gag. Nothing had ever prepared him for this! He was helpless, and the pain was more than any one man could bear. He knew without a doubt that he was in the hands of men who would not hesitate to kill him. Cooperation was the only alternative.

"Now, we're going to try this again, lad. I'll remove the gag, and if you try to shout, you'll just bite off the rest of your tongue. Comprendé?"

Once again Alfredo nodded his head, and this time he did not try to shout. He wasn't even sure he could talk. His tongue felt too swollen.

"What do you want, Englishman?" he asked. It sounded more like, "Waf you wan Engwishma?" with his swollen tongue.

"How many troops do you have inside the compound?" Weston

asked. "How many men, soldiers, whatever you call these lazy bozos you hire?"

"There are over a hundred soldiers inside the compound, and Mr. Caro's personal guard of twenty," Alfredo managed. His tongue was getting worse.

"What do you read, Zeke?" Weston said over his shoulder.

A voice came out of the darkness.

"There are eighteen soldiers inside the compound, and twenty-five bodies around the Caro house. Caro has three men inside with him, and his family is upstairs." The voice seemed to come out of nowhere.

How do these men know this? The pain hit, and Alfredo bit the rest of his tongue off. He felt it separate and flop out of his mouth, but his teeth were clenched in pain. Again, he lost consciousness. Weston screwed the silencer on his pistol and shot him three times in the head before standing up. He heard Tiffany retching somewhere behind him.

"Sorry, miss," he said softly.

"He was one of the men who held me when Caro beat me six months ago. He liked when Caro hit my breasts." She was silent a few seconds. "I got sick because I wanted to hurt him as badly as you did. I never realized I could be so vindictive, want to hurt someone so badly! Sorry. Realizing I had that kind of anger inside of me turned my stomach."

"It ain't any easier for us, miss," he said with a sigh. She heard the truth in his voice, saw it in his eyes, and suddenly saw that this man had done something he never wanted to do to gain information the team needed. Comprehension of what that meant, the toll it took on him, caused her to reach out a hand and touch his gently. *Where did these men come from?* She rushed him and hugged him tightly, crying into his chest. He held her gently and waited, feeling the bile in his throat, holding it back, hating himself for what he'd just done to another human. Holding Tiffany helped him.

"Okay, troops. Let's move in and take the compound." Jim waited until Tiffany had cried herself out and locked eyes for a moment with Hobbs. The two nodded to each other, and Cecilia shivered at that look.

The men moved out, leaving Cecilia and Tiffany alone. Instinctively they moved away from the dead body and sat waiting for the outcome.

Jim and his men had a plan put together for the initial takedown. They all knew that in battle, the situation was always fluid, and they would have to adjust and adapt. Their plan worked well from the beginning and then fell apart as the twenty-five guards around the house spread out in the darkness. The one advantage Jim's men had was that all of them had night goggles. Sparks took care of the generator almost immediately, so the compound was bathed in darkness. As they suspected, Caro did not have emergency lighting!

Creeping silently into the house, Jim left the battle outside to his men. He made his way to the office where Caro and three guards were all gathered close together. Instead of trying to open the door, he knocked loudly and stepped back. As expected, a hail of bullets ripped through the door as he threw himself to the floor. Using his assault rifle, he blasted a hole in the door up high and lobbed a grenade through it immediately afterward. He listened as the explosive hit the floor and bounced, sliding to a stop somewhere near the desk. It needed to be close to the men in the room, and his aim was perfect.

It was a stun grenade, and seconds after it flashed, he was through the door. He dropped to one knee and took out all three guards, then shot the gun out of the hand of the man behind the desk. The resemblance was close, but Jim had an eye for detail. This was not Caro. He glanced under the desk and saw a man crouched there. Moving forward, he slammed his fist into the face of the man who had been standing behind the desk, then put three shots through his head.

Out of the corner of his eye, he saw the knife flashing for his groin. Dodging back, he kicked the arm holding the knife in the armpit, causing the hand to go limp. The knife flew away. Desperately he spun away as the man beneath the desk lifted his other hand and fired two shots, one going through Jim's left thigh, in and out, causing him to go off balance for a fraction of a second. That movement saved his life as the next bullet sped by his face. Silently breathing thanks to God, he went to the floor behind the man beneath the desk, denying him another shot, arms outstretched, rolling to his left until he had a clear sighting.

Bringing his H&K Mark 23 to bear on the back of the man's knee, he fired a quick shot. The high-pitched scream from beneath the desk let him know his shot had gone home, and the desk bounced up as the man's head connected. Leaping up, he threw the desk away from the man, not feeling the pain in his thigh at all, and put his gun to the back of his head.

"Drop it, now!" he commanded. The gun fell to the floor with a clatter, and Jim reached over and quickly grabbing it, hurled it away. Caro's knee was a mess. The bullet had gone in through the back and had literally torn the kneecap out on its exit. It was bleeding badly. Jim knocked the man out to silence his screams, then stood up to take stock.

He pulled a bandage from his backpack and wrapped it tightly around his leg after administering a disinfectant. Then he pressed the talk button on his headgear.

"Sean, how busy are you?" he asked tersely.

"You hit, boss?" Sean asked conversationally. On the battlefield, Sean would always be calm, talk conversationally, because he knew how stressed each man was during the battle. Jim appreciated that calm and began to breathe normally.

"In and out. Not serious. But Caro's in a bad way. I blew his kneecap out after he tried to knife me in the groin and then shot me in the leg. The coward was hiding underneath his desk," Jim said.

"I'll be there in about thirty seconds, boss," Sean said easily, grunting as he tightened a bandage on Lee Roy's ribs. Lee Roy had an in-and-out wound too, not serious, but it would hurt. The bullet had ricocheted off the ground and gone up under his vest, bouncing off a rib. At the moment, Lee Roy wasn't feeling anything as the adrenaline pumped through his body. Sean nodded to his friend.

"Don't get that bleeding again, mate, or I'll skin you alive," Sean said with a smile, patting his work. Lee Roy grimaced at him and then tested the bandage as Sean continued to speak. "Gotta go take care of the boss. Seems he kneecapped Caro. Poetic, don't you think?"

Without waiting for an answer, he headed into the main building and found Jim seated on the bottom of the desk, his gun still trained on Caro. Kneeling down, he roughly turned the unconscious man over and tore away the pants. He put his kit down beside him and went to work clamping off the artery that was bleeding and then took a look at the damage.

"Doc can probably repair this," he said conversationally, glancing up at Jim, who was still holding the gun steady on Caro. The look in his eyes was just a little bit wild. Guessing correctly that Jim had come close to death in this room, he continued to speak in a calm voice. He was pretty sure Jim wouldn't shoot an unarmed unconscious man, but he didn't want to take any chances. Caro had tried to kill him, and Jim was working through the moment.

"I'll give him a shot that will keep him out for a couple of hours. Then you can relax, boss. I'll look at that leg next, and no arguments." As the serum left the hypodermic needle, Jim relaxed slightly. When Caro's body went limp, he ejected his magazine, slid a full one in, and then put the gun back in his holster with a sigh. He certainly wasn't favoring that leg, but that was probably shock. Ox finished with the sedation and turned to Jim.

CHAPTER 15

Undoing the bandage, he saw that the antiseptic had already been administered. He ordered Jim to drop his pants, which the captain did without comment, allowing Ox to carefully apply glue and butterfly the wounds shut and then bandage them properly. He was just finishing up when John wandered into the room.

"You hit bad?" he asked Jim.

"Don't think so. In and out. Pretty routine," he answered cryptically.

John picked up the knife that had fallen from Caro's hand. He looked up at Jim with a strange light in his eye and then hurled the knife so it landed in the floor right next to Caro's ear. With a solid thunk, it sank at least half an inch into the wood. It quivered there for a few seconds.

"Gawd Almighty!" Ox swore softly. "Let's not go off the deep end here, mates!" He looked up and saw John's eyes change a little. Jim and John were brothers, and very close, almost like identical twins in some ways, and Sean understood the connection and the emotions. Nodding his head toward Jim, he smiled when John went to his brother.

John helped Jim up and waited to make sure Jim could walk on that leg. Wade came in, followed by Bear. Without saying a word,

Bear picked Caro up and slung him over his shoulders in a fireman's carry. Wade watched with a grin.

"Close, huh?" he asked.

"A little," Jim replied.

"Zeke says a contingency of soldiers is making their way up the hill. We should leave. It's probably Colonel Valdez or some of his men," Wade said.

"Any wounded?" Jim asked Ox as he walked out of the office.

"Lee Roy took a ricochet to a rib, but he's okay. Other than that, everyone is good to go," Ox replied.

"Right. Zulu, you have point," Jim said, putting a hand on John's shoulder. "I want to know if we can take these soldiers out on the way down. Don't try to take them all yourself, and don't get dead. Keep me posted," he added unnecessarily. For a moment, the two just looked at each other and then both snorted at the same time.

John nodded, tilted his head to let his men know it was time to follow, and the four of them took off with a mile-eating trot. Zeke would guide them around the oncoming body of soldiers, and Jim trusted John to assess the situation quickly and accurately. When he arrived back at camp, Cecilia was waiting next to Tiffany. His wife ran forward and threw herself into his arms, smothering him with kisses.

Jim laughed and hugged her tight, then put her down. "Now that's a proper homecoming, that is!" he said, holding her hand as they walked over to Tiffany.

"Do you have him?" she asked, craning to see.

"Bear is carrying him down," Jim said, and at the confused look, he smiled. "The big Englishman. We call him Bear. He's carrying Caro down. Caro is unconscious and will be for a while. Don't worry, you'll get your confrontation," he assured her.

"What happened?" she asked.

"He shot the captain in the leg, so the captain decided to show him how it was properly done, miss," Ox said lightly. "Blew his kneecap right out," he added with a grin. "It's going to hurt like a bugger when he comes to."

"I heard you were wounded," Cecilia said, moving in close to Jim and putting an arm around his waist. "How bad is it?"

"Not bad. In and out. I'll limp a bit for a few days, that's all," Jim replied. "Lunch Box took one in a rib, but it bounced off."

"Too blinkin' right, it did!" Lunch Box said, coming to sit down near Jim and the ladies. "Thought I'd come over here and get some feminine sympathy." He grinned wolfishly at Tiffany. "Me bein' wounded and all, maybe you could bat your eyelashes at me and smile that pretty smile."

In spite of her anger, she smiled at the Australian. She came over and planted herself in his lap and put her arms around his neck. "Does this help take your mind off it?" she asked, batting her eyelashes at him.

"Uh, I'm, ah, well, I, ah…" He couldn't find the words. Cecilia and Tiffany laughed at him as she bounced off his lap and touched his nose. His mates were laughing too. Sheepishly he lifted his arms. Tiffany had certainly unnerved him.

"Perhaps my Jim could give you lessons on how to properly impress a girl, Lunch Box," Cecilia said lightly.

"Like I was any better!" Jim said, his own face crimson. It felt good to laugh after their encounter, but the laughter didn't last long. There wasn't really time to rest or recover. Jim brought them all back to reality quickly.

"Let's get ready to move downhill. We have a group of soldiers moving this way, and we want to be ready for them," he said lightly.

An hour later, John reported in. "I have them in sight through binoculars," he reported. "Squad strength twenty men, two squads. They look like they belong to Valdez, and they're wearing military uniforms and carrying the usual weapons. Both squads are marching in uneven formation, spread out. I think they're looking for someone. Perhaps Tiffany," he added after a pause. "They certainly aren't expecting any kind of armed response."

"Is Valdez with them?" Jim asked.

"Negative, Shep. Highest-ranking officer looks like a captain. Each squad has two ranking officers."

"Can we take them at checkpoint 6?" Jim asked, searching his memory of their hike up the mountain.

"Easily," John replied.

"Concur, Shep," Wade said a moment later.

"We'll start digging in and getting ready. Watch your step coming in," John said a moment later.

Checkpoint 6 would give them a good field of fire downhill, and the climb up was steep. As they walked, Jim unfolded his plan. His troops would be divided into three groups, flanking and head-on. The group that was at the top of checkpoint 6 would open fire first, drawing the troops up. Groups 2 and 3 would then open fire in a deadly crossfire. Zulu would move uphill behind them and clean up any survivors.

Using claymores, John set traps well down the mountain, using trip wires. Wade devised a few nasty surprises from the trees. C. G. and Vince helped wherever they were needed. Since the four of them had worked together for so long, no one spoke. Simple gestures and nods got things done in an orderly fashion.

Jim moved his troops in place quickly. Lunch Box and Jim both helped dig the foxholes despite the growing pain from their wounds, neither making any indication of the pain they were feeling. As often happens, the group ended up waiting about ten minutes before the first traps were tripped.

The blast from the claymore was accompanied by screams. Seconds later, crackling from above heralded the arrival of a sharpened spike-studded log that killed two men and wounded another. Another claymore took out four more men. John, watching all this from behind the enemy, reported the losses.

It was a demoralized group that came out of the trees and straight into the fire from above. Jim's group strafed the line, taking the leaders first. The group melted into the trees to decide what to do. Guessing they would come charging up the hill, Jim prepared his troops for the attack. It came as expected. They had seen only four muzzle flashes, and they expected to overpower four men easily. Jim grimaced as he hunkered down.

The men sprinted up hill, only nine of them left, huddled together, firing blindly as they came. Two of their number dropped from friendly fire. Jim kept everyone's heads down and waited for the flanking groups to open fire. When they did, the seven remaining men melted to the ground, some dead, some dying, some badly wounded. Those still alive were screaming or moaning.

No one took any chances. The men moved in slowly, their guns at ready. If anyone raised a gun, he was immediately targeted and killed where he lay. Tiffany watched with a sense of shocked detachment as the men moved in, until she noticed Jim moving quickly and purposefully.

Finding two wounded men side by side was not difficult. Jim stepped over them and asked who sent them and what they were looking for. He spoke in idiomatic Spanish, just like a native of Colombia, to make sure they understood his request.

The one on the left spat at him, and Jim calmly put a bullet in his head. He turned the gun on the other man and asked the same question. The answer came pouring out of the man as he begged for mercy. They were indeed troops from Francisco Valdez, and they were looking for Tiffany.

"What were your orders when you found her?" Jim asked.

"We were supposed to kill her," the man admitted reluctantly. There was something in his face that told Jim there was more to those orders.

"You were supposed to rape her first and then kill her. Is this not true?" he asked.

"Yes! Yes! I was just obeying my orders. Please!" the man begged.

Jim shot him. He looked down at the body for a moment, the anger in him subsiding as quickly as it had risen. *You should have died slowly, you coward! Consider yourself lucky, filth!* He gave the terse order to terminate any survivors. He turned to find Cecilia and Tiffany behind him.

Cecilia's face was calm, and she searched her husband's eyes carefully. She still saw the sadness there. Tiffany was not calm. She was white and shaking. Suddenly she spat at the dead body and turned away and ran, sobbing. Cecilia sighed and turned to follow her but saw that Pen had stopped the girl. They looked at each other for a moment. Whatever passed between them, Cecilia left it with Pen.

"She's still very innocent," Cecilia said, turning back to Jim. "She hasn't been exposed to the evil of this world. Strange that her father was a missionary and she so naive."

"Captain, I have a man with a radio!" FM's voice suddenly sounded in their headsets. Jim sighed, smiled lopsidedly at his wife, and turned to assess this new bit of information. Together they walked away from the two dead bodies. He was walking toward FM when Zeke's voice interrupted him.

"Not to worry, Shep," Zeke's voice came over his headset. "I was jamming the transmission. I can give you the frequency, though."

"Yeah! This radio is encrypted. Can you give us the code?" FM asked sarcastically.

"Two niner four, six sixty-six," Zeke replied evenly. "Uncle Zeke is always watching."

"And how the hell do you know that?" FM spat as the two men came together with Jim. FM was still feeling the adrenaline rush from the battle. Zeke understood and took no offense at the accusatory tone.

"They were talking. He told one of the men he couldn't get through, and the other man asked him if he had the encryption code correct. They checked it together. Simplicity for a computer geek like myself, difficult to fathom for a computer illiterate like yourself," Zeke replied with a shrug.

"It was much more impressive without the explanation," Jim said with a grin.

"Geek!" FM shot.

"And proud of it!" Zeke replied.

"Did he happen to mention how often they were supposed to check in?" Jim asked.

"When they found her, not before," Zeke replied, looking over the radio carefully. "This is really a piece of junk!" he commented.

"Where do you suppose they got it?" Jim asked.

"Russian surplus," Zeke replied, dropping the radio next to the dead man.

"Maybe from Cuba, boss," FM said.

"Communist ties in South America! Shocking!" Jim said sarcastically. "One more nail in Valdez's coffin. From what I've seen, he's only interested in increasing his own personal wealth and standing and also gaining power any way he possibly can."

They moved off to join the rest of the men in erasing any evidence of their presence. It took hours, but Jim was taking no chances. Any patrols that came upon the scene would find little to tell them the story. Finally, near evening, they faded down the hill and into the shadows.

CHAPTER 16

Carefully moving along the trails, they passed through the night making their way to within a mile of Fundaciôn. At the lower altitude, the heat and humidity took its toll. Sean made his way through the camp, making sure everyone was drinking enough water and using their water purification tablets. Caro, he kept sedated, tending his wound to ensure against infection.

Jim's leg was bothering him some, but it was not impairing his mobility in any way. Lunch Box was struggling a little with his rib. Sean gave him some Tylenol for the pain and made sure there was no infection in the wound. Brown hadn't complained once during the trip. Jim made sure to stop by and talk to him. Lee Roy grinned and nodded at his bandaged leg.

"Didn't hear you complaining either, boss," he said when Jim thanked him for bearing up under the strain.

"Nobody listens anyway," Jim said with a grin. He shook Brown's hand and left to talk to the other men.

"Jim, can I see you a moment?" Zeke asked as he walked past. Jim paused and moved in closer. It was obvious Zeke wanted to talk quietly.

"What do you have?" he asked.

"Fate has placed both Marquez and Rivera in our hands, Shep,"

Zeke said with a wide grin. "They're both meeting at the largest processing plant we passed earlier. It's between Pivijay and El Piñón."

"When?" Jim asked tersely.

"Tomorrow. Both will have their personal security forces with them. They're a little worried that they can't reach Caro," Zeke replied. "They've also added an air patrol by helicopter and an outer patrol force numbering sixty."

"Is that all?" Jim asked sarcastically. "Fate isn't playing nice! That complicates things some!"

"Valdez is staying out of the area," Zeke said lightly. "That makes it easy."

"Oh sure! We just waltz in, take out a hundred-plus enemy troops, two cartel bosses, and then waltz out," Jim exclaimed, throwing up his hands.

"We could sashay," John said with a grin. "The steps are easier." He had arrived only seconds after Jim.

"What is it with the marines and thinking they're invincible?" Jim said with a grin. Never far from John, Wade stepped up with C. G. and Vince, the three of them striking a bodybuilder pose that showed off their upper body muscles.

"Because we are. Marines! Ooh Rah!" they said in chorus.

"I see the marines are flexing their muscles again," Pen said, stepping into the group with a laugh. "I always knew they thought with the hair on their chest, or elsewhere, depending on the situation."

"We step back deflated," John moaned theatrically, acting out his words. She laughed at his antics.

"So, Captain, do you think we can pull this off?" she asked Jim.

"Actually, I think it is to our advantage to pull this off," he said, looking at the topographical map of the site.

People began to gather around as they discussed the various scenarios of attack. Matthew Banks had a great idea, which he shared early on in the discussion.

"Why don't we take the helicopter before it takes off for the air patrol? That way we can use it to our advantage. They won't know we're up there in the bird, and when the time comes, we can do a lot of damage!"

"Bank Bond, triple zero at three-and-a-half percent makes an offer we can't refuse!" FM quipped from the back.

"I like it," Jim said when the chuckling died down. "Weston, Team Raider has that assignment. Make sure you look like you belong up there doing the reconnaissance, so nobody gets suspicious!"

Hobbs nodded. Discussion continued as they weighed the various suggestions for attack. Toward midmorning, Jim yawned, folded up the maps, and told everyone to get some rest.

Pen watched the men get up and wander off to rest and realized that she was mixed up with perhaps the deadliest force she had ever witnessed. Not only were they willing to take on difficult odds, but their plan almost ensured that they would pull it off without losing anyone! She'd seen them in action and knew that they were experts at being unseen in the field. It thrilled her to be working with such men. As the plan unfolded, she realized that strategizing such operations took great skill, and these men had the skills necessary for the job. Shaking her head, she got up and moved to her tent.

Cecilia was in the tent with Tiffany, but when Jim approached, she left the girl and came out to talk a few minutes. They sat in silence, holding hands, their thoughts turned inward. Tiffany watched them from within the tent. Jim Shepherd was a puzzle to her. She remembered the cold way in which he simply shot a man earlier. And yet each time he had spoken to her, his eyes had been gentle and his manner kindness itself.

After a time of silence, the two moved a little way away, and Jim pulled a Bible from his backpack. That surprised Tiffany even further. Her study of the two was interrupted as Wade approached the tent, squatted down, and smiled at her. She liked this tall man with gentle brown eyes. She smiled shyly back.

"You've been through a lot. Is there anything I can do for you?" he asked softly.

"Thank you. Not at the moment." Tears filled her eyes, and she sighed, feeling a great sadness. "Thank you, though," she replied. In her heart she felt the first stirrings of healing and smiled at Wade.

"If you'd like to take a walk or anything, I would be more than happy to escort you," Wade said with a nod. He rose and walked away. She admired that walk. He had been sincere, simply offering to be there if she needed someone. Shaking her head, she wiped away the tears and thought of her father's sacrifice to bring a message of peace and love to an enslaved and tortured people. It was worth it. Bowing her heart before the Lord, she asked Him for strength and forgiveness.

After about half an hour, Cecilia returned to the tent. Tiffany welcomed her with a tentative smile, and the two drifted off to sleep. Jim rolled out his blanket, plunked his body on it, and went to sleep immediately. Soldiers learn to sleep when they get the opportunity.

Near dark, the men began to wake and gather in clusters for an MRE and a canteen of water. Every canteen was emptied, refilled, and treated with a water purification tablet. No one really liked the flavor the tablet gave the water, but each one appreciated the purification. Dysentery was not something anyone wanted to contract.

Tiffany found herself next to Wade, who introduced her to the art of trading items from the MRE packets. Talking with him, she discovered his interest in engineering. Conversation after that became somewhat technical, but she made it fun by forcing him to explain in simple terms some of the concepts he was sharing. Somehow, making this big strong soldier so nervous made her feel stronger and filled her with warmth. His discomfort certainly was a source of amusement to his friends.

After dinner, the team gathered for a final briefing and prayer before executing their daring plan. Team Raider set off early to take the helicopter. The rest of them broke camp, cleaned all evidence of their presence carefully, and then melted into the darkness. Everyone wore night vision goggles, even Tiffany, and she found the greenish display eerie as she walked along. Careful to put her feet down where they would make the least noise, she was learning the rudiments of silence, and it surprised her how quickly she was making progress.

She was also curious at how slowly they moved. It took them three hours to cover the two-mile distance to their goal. Some of the men circled around and moved to the top of the hill, above the plant, avoiding detection as they penetrated the outer patrols. The helicopter arrived, having been taken without the enemy knowing, and per instructions, began illuminating the jungle around the plant. To those on the ground, the pilot looked very thorough, but he was, in fact, avoiding any of the positions of the team.

Two Barrett M82A1 sniper rifles at the top of the hill were now focused on the entrance to the manufacturing plant. It was there that Marquez and Rivera would appear. A third sniper rifle of the same make was pointing at the entrance from a tall tree, giving Chance a perfect trajectory. Scope was on one of the rifles on the hilltop, and RC on the other. Rifles had been checked, broken down, reassembled, and checked again, bullets loaded and ready, safety set to the on position for now.

The waiting game began. Men settled down to catch catnaps, trading with their partners, keeping sharp for the coming of the day. None of the outer patrols discovered the enemy force entrenched around the facility. One group passed within two feet of FM and Zeke and never saw them in their foxhole. Both men followed the group with their MP5s until they were out of range.

At first light, the helicopter returned to refuel. It was gone less than twenty minutes and returned to circle the facility. Three hours later, the helicopter went to refuel again. On the return trip, Hobbs radioed Jim that two H2s were on the way. Jim acknowledged by clicking twice, the signal he heard the transmission. The shared radio transmission alerted the men.

Marquez arrived first, and he exited from behind the steering wheel of his vehicle with a contingent of four men, who immediately took positions around him. Rivera was in the back seat of his H2. Each group came together so the two bosses could walk together to the facility.

"I have Marquez," Scopes said.

"I have Rivera," RC said a second later.

"Shooters are cleared to fire!" Jim ordered.

Both bosses seemed to suddenly jerk backward as the low-velocity bullets took them. A red mass exploded from the back of their heads, spraying the men behind them. In the second of shocked stillness that followed, FM, RC, and Scope took three of the security forces and then three more as they began to move. FM took the last two as they ran back toward the vehicles.

In the chaos that followed, troops inside the compound poured out of the facility, and the outer patrols converged toward those forces. As Jim suspected, they began firing at each other, cutting his work in half before they realized what was happening. Since the security team had been dropped, not a single shot had been fired by the unseen enemy within the compound.

The outer patrol and troops came together and paused to assess. It was then that Jim's teams opened fire. The helicopter came in, and the .50-caliber minigun spewed rounds into the packed group. Ten minutes later, the last man lay dying on the field. Hobbs landed the chopper expertly while the other teams cleaned up.

No fool, Hobbs landed the chopper so the minigun was leveled at the front entrance. At Jim's command, he fired a burst through the entrance, literally disintegrating the wooden gate. No answering fire was returned. Alpha and Blue teams approached the entrance from either side along a windowless wall.

Jim took a quick look inside and saw several workers standing with their hands on their heads. He guessed what might lie behind them. Looking back at his men, he pulled a stun grenade from his vest, armed it, and threw it deep into the facility. FM, Chance, and PU threw theirs at the same time, all in different directions. Tucking their chins down, they waited for the blast and then went in fast, separating to either side.

Staying low saved their lives. A dozen soldiers popped up from behind the workers and fired blindly, killing some of the workers too slow to hit the floor in time. Jim's team took them out swiftly. Even then Jim didn't relax his vigil, nor did his team members. None of them would be satisfied until they had personally cleared the building.

Moving through the facility, they flushed out another half dozen soldiers, who gave themselves up rather than die. From them Jim learned that they all belonged to Marquez and Rivera. Jim instructed his team to bind them and leave them in the center of the facility. Viper and RC were already planting charges. When they left, the half dozen soldiers were crying for mercy.

RC twisted the firing mechanism, and the facility disintegrated. Workers who survived gave a loud cheer as the facility went up in a blaze of amazing pyrotechnics. RC looked at Jim and surprised a look of sadness on his face. Covered in grime and sweat, RC grinned, his teeth white against his dirty face. He knew just how his boss felt. His own guts were twisted into a knot. Both were thinking about the men who had just perished inside and outside the facility, a literal slaughter.

"They showed no mercy, boss. Fitting that we shouldn't either. He who lives by the sword, dies by the sword. Nobody gets to choose when and how he dies," he philosophized. It was an old saying among soldiers, and Jim heard it often.

"I know," Jim replied quietly. "It was justice. I just hate the killing."

"Well, when you get to likin' it, you better get out of this business," RC replied with an emphatic nod. Jim smiled at him, clapped him on the shoulder, and went in search of John.

"Wow! Shep! We have major movement of a large force coming this way," Zeke confirmed, waving him over as he passed.

"Where are they coming from?" Jim asked, moving that way quickly.

"Barranquilla," Zeke replied.

"How large a force?" Jim asked.

"Three hundred, maybe more," Zeke answered. "It appears someone let the cat out of the bag."

"Good. We have plenty of time. Everyone, gather around," he commanded into his headset. The team quickly formed up around him.

"Valdez is sending three hundred or more men our way from Barranquilla. By the time they arrive, we'll be back on the boats.

We will probably be searched. That means Caro must be kept on ice, and Tiffany will have to do it." He looked at her and saw her nod in the affirmative.

"We can keep him sedated and offload them when the troops get close. After we've been searched, we'll leave and under cover of darkness, send a team back to pick them up. I'm sorry, Tiffany, but we're going to stick you with this duty. It won't be too difficult since he'll be sedated the entire time.

"We still have some sites to destroy. Stay sharp. We're going to pick up the pace a bit," he finished his speech, looked at the men, and nodded. They were in the zone, as a soldier says, and the mission was all that mattered at the moment. As quickly as possible, the area was policed, and they moved out at a quick march.

If Dorf or Bear minded carrying Caro, neither said anything. Nor did Jim complain of the quicker pace. Lunch Box, like his boss, pushed the pain into a far corner of his mind and moved with the rest.

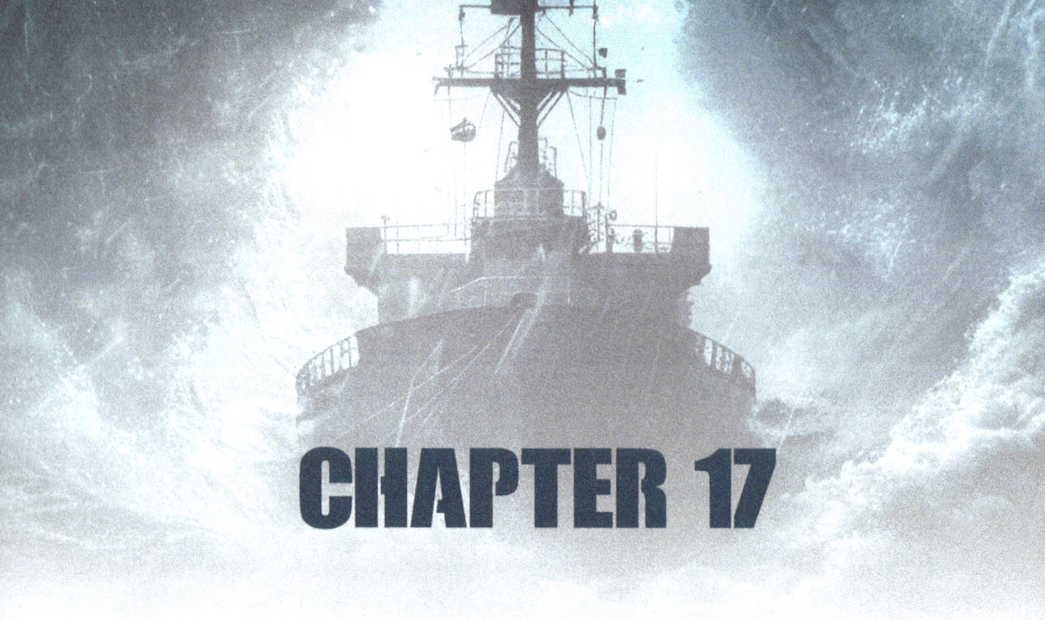

CHAPTER 17

Processing sites and facilities were all destroyed on their forced march back to the boats. Long years of no one bothering them had made the guards lazy and careless. Burying the bodies became the hardest part, and Jim shoveled along with the rest of the men. Workers were released, embarrassed by their enslavement to the bully drug lords, ashamed of their work in creating this product, and angry enough at their overlords to leave a few postmortem bruises as they passed bodies. Jim knew he was just one of many who wondered how quickly the plants would be rebuilt and restarted, probably with the same hapless men and women he'd just released into the jungle. The phrase "it is what it is" passed through his head.

Most of the last night of this part of their adventure was spent cleaning and storing the military gear. Dr. Persons spent that time on the computer, and long map pages began pouring out of the plotter. By early morning, the boats set off downriver. Caro remained sedated and well hidden. Zeke kept an eye on the troops moving toward them and gauged their meeting perfectly.

Valdez himself stepped to the shore and yelled for them to make fast to that side of the riverbank. Tiffany and Caro were already secure in a camouflage hideaway high in a large willow along the opposite bank. Jim gave the order, and the boats came to rest against the riverbank, where helpful soldiers tied them fast, taking up positions where the ropes were tied.

"You have been away a long time, Captain," Valdez accused stepping aboard the lead boat.

"Oh yes!" Dr. Persons spoke, poring over one of his latest maps. "We have done some fabulous studies of the course of this tributary. Did you know that this river once flowed past an opal and topaz deposit? There are untapped mines in those hills! Your government will be pleased with that information."

Colonel Valdez paged through the maps, his eyebrows climbing his forehead as he counted them and studied them. Careful measurements had to be taken to make these maps this detailed. He began to doubt his conviction that the military force that was operating in his country was this group of men. But he was not completely convinced. They made the hairs on the back of his head feel as if they were standing up, and he hated that feeling. "The untrustworthy are always untrusting," was a saying Jim was familiar with, and he read the mistrust in Valdez.

"Very interesting." It was obvious to Jim that Valdez was interested in that information, but not because he thought it benefited his government. It would personally benefit him! "Do you know the exact location of the mines?" he asked conversationally. Jim knew he was fishing, but he said nothing, allowing Dr. Persons to conduct the interview.

"Yes!" Dr. Persons began to page through the maps, found the one he wanted, and pulled it out. "They're right here and here," he stated, pointing to the markings on the map. Both mines were on Pico Christôbal Colôa, one very near Caro's fortress.

"Did you meet anyone up there?" Valdez asked.

"Just some thugs acting tough," Pen said, coming in with another map. Notations, in her neat handwriting, decorated the map. She almost ignored Valdez, coming to stop in front of Dr. Persons. "I've worked out where the old riverbed made the last change in the flood twelve years ago," she said. Valdez looked over her shoulder and recognized the changes he'd witnessed after that flood. Surely that kind of work took long hours of study.

"So you are a cartographer!" he stated.

"Duh!" she said sarcastically, slipping her map into the stack. "Sorry, the heat's getting to me," she said by way of apology. "That and one too many beers." She smiled and left.

"Do you mind if I search your boats again, Captain?" Valdez asked.

"Is this really necessary? We still have to travel up the Magdalena, and our funding will run out if we get stopped every time we meet you," Jim complained in an aggravated tone.

"You are independently wealthy, Captain!" Valdez said.

"You don't suppose I got that way spending my own money, do you?" Jim asked with some heat. "Damn it, Colonel, we were going to put in a few miles down this river, but now we'll have to spend the night here."

"I insist," Valdez said, his eyes growing hard.

"Fine. Insist. Do whatever you have to do! I'm making a formal complaint to your government, who gave us permission for this study as you know!" Jim stalked away muttering under his breath. Valdez watched him with a blank expression. Jim's ire had seemed quite real.

"It's the heat, Colonel," FM said laconically, sipping from a frosty bottle of Beck's Beer he'd just pulled from a cooler. He burped softly. "Just the heat," he repeated, moving away after Jim. Valdez watched him sardonically.

The search was thorough, as Jim expected. Valdez even checked through the bags of garbage. There were enough beer and soda bottles for a month to have passed, though he had no way of knowing that most of it had been dumped into the river the night before, to create the proper number of empty containers. He was looking for bandages, bloodied pads of any kind, and found nothing. That garbage was hidden away with the weapons in odor-controlling bags, just in case Valdez brought dogs along.

He checked the men, finding them sitting around drinking soda or beer, playing cards, looking rested and well fed. Some of them had scratches on their faces and arms from the hiking, but other than that, they were in excellent condition. They did not look like men who had fought hard battles. When he was finished, he was convinced that another group was somewhere in front of him.

"Did you meet any military forces on your trip inland?" he asked Jim.

"Just you and the thugs on the mountain," Jim replied ungraciously.

For a moment, he wondered if Jim considered him a thug. That he was one he knew, but he hated that anyone else dared point out that fact. "Bien! Señor, you may go." Valdez saluted and left the boat.

Jim decided to stay where he was for the night, leaving the boats tied up next to the soldiers' camp. He sent C. G. and Ox over to make sure Tiffany was secure and that Caro stayed sedated. Expecting another search of the boats, he urged the men to hurry back. They did, arriving long enough before the second search to be in their bunks feigning sleep. Both consummate actors, no one thought them anything but sleeping men.

Valdez made no apologies for his second search and seemed disappointed to find nothing had changed. He watched Jim the entire time the search went on. This captain had awakened the two women and brought them to sit with him while the search was conducted. Valdez knew why, but he didn't care. His men were notorious for rape and other atrocities.

Wondering vaguely if Jim could protect the women against his men, he decided after a few moments of studying the man that he probably could. He had no intention of losing a few good men in trying the American. Valdez saw Jim looking at him and nearly jumped when Jim smiled and nodded.

"You read minds, señor?" Valdez asked, irritated.

"I read men," Jim replied. "It's not worth it. I'll kill a lot of them, and then my crew will kill more, and you wouldn't like that."

"Jim, honey! Diplomacy!" Cecilia said, touching his arm.

"You are wise, señora," Valdez said, "to protect your husband." Her response surprised and irritated him at the same time.

"Oh no!" Cecilia laughed. "I am protecting you, colonel. You would be the first man he killed." Her feral smile surprised him, and he was suddenly aware that she was not afraid of him, nor was the other woman.

Valdez dropped his hand to his holster to unsnap the cover. But before he could even do that, Jim was beside him, holding that wrist in a vise-like grip. "Let's not be foolish, colonel. You don't want to die, and I don't want to kill you," Jim said quietly. Valdez realized not one of his men had reacted. It looked to them as if the captain was whispering in his ear. For perhaps the second time in his life, Valdez knew fear, but he forced it down.

"Perhaps not tonight, Captain," he said, relaxing his arm. Jim let go and returned to the women. *How did the man move so fast? He is indeed a deadly foe!*

"Come!" he snapped. "There is nothing to find here. We go!" His orders were followed, and the men slowly left the boat. Jim counted them as they stepped off and realized that two men had remained behind.

"Call your two men, Colonel, or you won't see them again," Jim said softly, just loud enough for Valdez to hear. Valdez turned to stare at him, one eyebrow raised.

"Manuello, Jorges, come!" he commanded. The two men came reluctantly, shooting hard looks at Jim as they passed. Both men thought about doing something, but they decided against it when their leader marginally shook his head.

"You are satisfied?" Valdez asked.

"Get off my boat," Jim said in a dangerous voice. Valdez complied.

When the camp had settled, Jim sent C. G., Vince, Ox, and PU to bring Tiffany and Caro back. As soon as the two were on board, the boats slipped quietly into the river and were away before the guards posted even knew they left. Jim thanked Calvin Beardsley silently for the stealth modes built into these amazing riverboats.

Red Eagle broke off from the group and headed back to *Bring It Up*. On his secure satellite phone, Dorf was already talking to a friend at a nearby naval station. His next call went to a Red Cross organizer. Everything had to be in place when Jim and the rest of the teams released the slaves in Cúcuta. None of the men wanted to leave the slaves to find their own way out, or to suffer even worse depravation than already suffered.

Jim knew they were running out of time, so they pushed the boats to their limit. At Magangué, they left the boats to a coast guard crew, who took them back to *Bring It Up Coral* without incident. They, at least, saw Omega Force fully armed for battle as they disappeared into the jungle. If the men were curious, none asked any questions.

Dorf met the team there with the CH-53D Sea Stallion. Thirty miles from Cúcuta, the chopper put down in a jungle clearing barely large enough to accommodate the seventy-nine-foot rotor span. A camouflage net was suspended above the craft to hide it from the air. More netting was hung from that to hide it from ground surveillance.

Caro, with Tiffany and Cecilia remaining to watch over him, would be kept sedated on the helicopter. Zeke and Smitty volunteered to stay and protect the women. Jim nodded his thanks and left with his troops. He assigned himself point and took off in the lead, with FM and Pen behind him. Chafing at the time it took to move through the jungle, he remained as cautious as ever. It was a frustration he had learned to live with. Careful men lived when careless men often died for no other reason than a snapped twig in the wrong place.

Ten cautious miles later, Zeke's voice came in over the headsets. "Hunker down. We have an air patrol coming this way. They may be trying to locate the chopper," Zeke said.

CHAPTER 18

Jim and his troops melted into the jungle, and the plane, passing overhead, continued. The lone pilot watching out his window saw nothing moving on the ground. In the jungle, it was hard to see anything, but movement always gave troops away. Most of the troops moving around down here thought the trees cover enough to continue moving. He radioed in after another thirty miles of flying that nothing was moving in the jungle and continued his run to Medellin.

Once the plane was gone, Jim moved out. He knew his troops would follow. Pen, who was following a hundred meters behind him, marveled that the man could pass through the jungle without leaving a trace of his presence. There were no broken branches, and he stepped where footprints left little impression. No noise came to her ears as she followed. She was no slouch when it came to combat tactics, so she recognized immediately the professionalism of this unit. In her own way, she exulted in being part of such a unit and realized she didn't want to leave. With these men, she could truly attain her utmost goals.

That thought gave her a moment of unease. She spent years working toward becoming the top agent in MI6, but working with *Bring It Up*, she realized they could do even more toward protecting the innocent from terrorist threats than any other entity. The freedom she had working with them was something that both frightened and thrilled her. Shaking her head at her conflicting thoughts, she kept her eyes and mind focused on moving through the jungle in silence.

With those conflicting thoughts raging in her head, she followed, her own skills tested to their limits as she passed like a shadow through the leafy greens and browns, the vibrant colors of amazing flowers, some of them deadly enemies to anything that touched them. She was constantly marveling at the complexity of the jungle, even though through it all, the oppressive heat and humidity beat at her without mercy. Drinking gallons of water, eating salt tablets, and having to pee often was a hassle, but it kept her strong.

They arrived at the perimeter of the mine complex six hours after leaving the chopper. Jim let everyone rest and eat an MRE while they waited for darkness. He and FM climbed to a high point and made a careful study of the complex and its security.

"Hey, boss, I see a weak point," FM said in a near whisper.

"Air shaft above the rail entrance?" Jim asked.

"Why don't you just shut up!" FM said with disgust. Jim hadn't been looking there, and FM was sure he'd missed it. He shook his head, grinning. "Should know you wouldn't miss something like that." He silently chided himself for thinking he might have noticed something Jim missed. He'd worked long enough with the man to know that the captain rarely missed anything. When Jim studied a situation like this, he was totally focused, missing nothing.

"Team Raider can take that one," Jim said. "Firefox can take the airshaft over on the far side of that derrick. Zulu will take down the gate guards and guard hut. Blue Team can take the north airshaft. We'll take the main control center with Red Team." Jim made the judgments as he studied the compound through his binoculars.

FM studied the compound again with Jim's plan in mind and nodded. Everything Jim suggested fit into his own assessment of the situation. "That'll work just fine. You given any thought to how we're going to play it when we get the slaves out?"

"The foreign slaves go in the chopper. The local slaves get set free with whatever they can take," Jim instructed.

"And us?" FM asked.

"We make for the border, like we're going to cross, then turn north and follow these mountains north to the coast. We're going to stay in higher elevations, where the cover will be good. We'll cross the border to the north when we hit the Serranta de Pertja range. They won't expect that. We can choose where we want to meet anyone following us," Jim answered.

"Would Valdez cross the border?" FM asked.

"In a heartbeat," Jim replied, still studying the compound. FM put his glasses back to his face and continued his own study.

"Full battle gear in this heat!" FM said, shaking his head. "Slave driver!"

Jim grinned, continuing his study of the compound. He knew FM was just kidding. They would all appreciate the armor when the firefights began. It could and had saved their lives several times. Hot and uncomfortable as it was, they would be wearing it from now on. It was just one of those things soldiers had to bear.

Back in camp, they drew accurate diagrams of the compound, and Jim explained his plan of action. This mine ran twenty-four hours a day, so there would be no relaxing of the guard at any time, though guards at night tended to be less attentive than those who served at daylight hours. They discussed the time it would take to get into position and decided on a deadline of three hundred hours. Jim lifted his watch.

"Twenty-one hundred hours in three, two, one, mark!" Everyone set his or her watch with his. "Any questions?" Jim asked.

"What do we do with Vásquez?" Dorf asked.

"Let the slaves decide his fate," Jim replied quickly.

"Sweet justice!" Ox said.

After their resting spot was carefully cleaned, they left to take up their positions. The compound basically was a ten-acre square with the mine itself near the northeast corner. Each team took great care in taking their position, avoiding detection more through care and experience than luck. Luck always played some part in a military operation. At three in the morning, the plan was executed.

Zulu made short work of the gate guards and proceeded to the guard shack. Red Team took the control center while Jim, Pen, and FM took the house where Gregorio Vásquez resided. Two guards were on duty outside the house, two more inside, and four slept in the house. Jim and FM took care of the guards while Pen made her way stealthily into the bedroom where Vásquez slept peacefully. Although she had prepared herself, the scene was more than obscene.

Vásquez woke to the touch of cold steel on his neck. Next to him, hands cruelly bound to the rails at the head of the bed, lay a girl—no, a child! Blood on the sheets and on her clothes told Pen the horror this child had suffered at the hands of this monster. She hoped Vásquez would try something the moment her gun touched his neck.

Vásquez opened his eyes when he felt the touch of the gun to his neck. His own hand closed around the pistol beneath his pillow. He pulled it quickly, and Pen shifted her own gun and shot his out of his hand. The blaze from her silenced muzzle blinded him for a moment, and Pen took advantage of that. She reversed the pistol and clubbed him between the legs hard enough to fold him in half, making him squeal in pain. Then she knocked him unconscious. Her rage was almost unchecked at that moment, almost, but her blow did not kill. That was for later!

Taking her time with the child, she untied the poor thing, and the girl began sobbing the moment she felt a touch on her. When the girl was released, Pen held her tightly as the child wept. Jim and FM came into the room, took in the scene, saw the blood, heard the ragged weeping of the child, and roughly dragged Vásquez out without looking her way again. Pen stuck her head out the door.

"Are there servants or slaves anywhere in the house?" she asked.

"I'll bring one of the women," Jim said quietly. He left on that errand, returning some eight minutes later with the child's frantic mother in tow. The girl fled into her mother's arms. One wept in horror and shame, the other with a mother's love. It was a scene Jim would remember for a long time, and he would use it to stoke the fires of his anger against men like Valdez and Vásquez. Jim knelt beside the woman.

"In a few minutes, all the slaves here will be free. Do not stay here. The military will come." The woman looked at him, blessed him, and nodded that she understood. He patted her and stood. His heart ached to do more, to see to the safety and security of these people, but he could not. With that thought still circulating in his mind, he turned his attention to the details that needed to be completed.

FM already had Vásquez on his shoulders in a fireman's carry. They walked downstairs and checked before exiting the house. The compound was plunged in darkness. All the tower guards were neutralized, and the search lamps were out. Slaves began to pour out of the mine and out of the prison cells where they were kept, having been released by a miracle, by men who appeared out of the shadows, silent and deadly, telling them they were free. The smell was the first thing Jim noticed, and then the emaciated figures, some barely able to stand. His teams assembled, and he made a mental count. Everyone was there, and he breathed his first sigh of relief. He knew the hard part was coming.

"All right. Let's sift out the Americans, English, and other foreign slaves," Jim ordered. "This needs to happen fast, folks!"

"All Americans, Canadians, and Western European people, over here with me!" Wade shouted. He repeated it in French, Italian, and German. Jim shouted the same order in Swedish.

"Any other foreign nationals who do not reside in South America, over here with me!" John shouted.

"Anyone who resides in Mexico, Central or South America, over here with me!" Mark shouted in Spanish and Portuguese.

John, as expected, had the smallest group. Two Greek women and their children huddled together near him. Wade had the next largest group and Mark the main group.

"Okay, Zeke, bring the chopper in," Jim said in his headset.

"Roger. On our way," Zeke said. "We're one minute out, repeat, one minute out."

"Roger that, Zeke. Ready in one," Jim said.

"Tell 'em the chopper coming is ours, so they don't panic," Jim instructed. His men relayed the message. The navy pilots set the chopper down easily and watched as the rescued slaves were herded on the chopper. Jim took some time to talk to Cecilia and was glad to see Tiffany circulating among the slaves, giving comfort.

"Honey, get these people sorted out for me. Tell Papa to weigh anchor and put out to international waters. Ask the navy team to pick us up when we radio for transport. I love you."

She was looking away from him, his lips close to her ear so she could hear above the chopper. At those last words, she turned to look at him with one of those looks that just melted his heart. He took her in his arms and kissed her with deep passion.

"Be careful. Don't wade in blood. I know this makes you very angry," she said in his ear. "I love you too." Then she was scrambling aboard the chopper as it lifted off. Zeke and Smitty were back with Jim and watched the chopper move off over the treetops.

"They'll fly under radar all the way to the ship, Shep," Zeke assured Jim. "The transponder will identify it as a private plane if any radar does pick them up. I made sure that the registration would be a legal one of a diplomat who often flies in this zone. Those pilots are as good as they come, and they know what to do if there's trouble," he assured Jim quietly.

"We have work to do," Jim announced, nodding so Zeke knew he understood. Reluctantly he turned back to a waking Vásquez. There were, Jim knew, evil men in the world, men who took what they wanted and did what they desired, seeming to think there would never be reckoning. "Tell them they can punish him as they see fit," Jim said, pointing to the prisoners that remained. "Remind them to leave before the military gets here. Tell them they have about two days and to post lookouts."

Mark relayed that message to the slaves, and Vásquez began to struggle. C. G. and Vince hauled him over to a whipping post and shackled his hands above his head with the same shackles he'd used on his slaves. They left him there, cursing them. It didn't take the slaves long to rip away his clothing, and then to grab some evil-looking whips and start working on him.

"Clean up all the brass and move out!" Jim gave the order. His men worked quickly. In less than an hour, with help from some of the healthier slaves, every piece of brass was gathered. Even the brass from the enemy troops was picked up. Using an acid mix found in the mine workshop, Wade melted all the brass into one pool of pure liquid. Nodding as the deed was done, the troops gathered into their separate units and prepared to move out.

"Wait!" one of the slaves croaked loudly. "What about the riches here?"

"Take them. But leave quickly," Jim replied with a smile.

"Via con Dios," the slave said.

"Team Raider, you have point," Jim said.

Calvin Weston nodded and led his men off at a trot. He assigned DC point as they trotted out of the compound. Tonight, they had to make time, putting as much distance between them and the mine, take a short rest, and get gone. They set a mile-eating pace, eager to get up into the higher elevations.

Later that day, in the higher elevations, they made camp above a small town where two rivers came together. They were far enough away that they doubted anyone but a shepherd might come across them.

"Where is Valdez, and how many troops does he have at the moment?" Jim asked Zeke, as he sat beside him.

"El Banco," Zeke replied, checking his satellite feeds. "He's got about two hundred men. Judging from the way they move, they're regulars with him."

"Let me know if they cross the border tomorrow," Jim said, patting Zeke on the shoulder as he stood up.

"How much water do you have in your canteen, Shep?" Ox asked.

Jim shook it. It was nearly empty. "Maybe a swallow," he answered.

"Good! Don't forget your purification tablets," Ox said passing on. Jim smiled. Military life was often interesting and sometimes downright exciting, but along with that, the mundane details were carefully watched. Ox would not allow any of them to become dehydrated. Those who had half a canteen left would be forced to drink the entire contents while he watched. Jim kept his eye on the man as he moved through and smiled when Ox finished. No one had forgotten.

Some of the men got Tylenol tablets for minor aches and pains. They dug in and slept most of the late morning and afternoon. From now on, they would travel under the cover of darkness. Late afternoon found them all awake and in a group. As the men waited for the evening meal, they checked their equipment.

Jim broke down his H&K Mark 23 and MP5SD. Everything was carefully wiped clean, oiled, and then quickly reassembled. When he was finished, he checked the batteries in his night vision goggles made by Celestron. Making sure his extra batteries were easily accessible from his pack, he put them back in the top pouch. Next, he checked his shoes. Everything was in good condition, but he carefully inspected the inside and the soles. A soldier's footwear was of paramount importance in the bush. These boots were the very best money could buy for the task they served, and he was satisfied.

All around him he could hear his men quietly going about their business, just as he was, because they were all professionals. He looked over at FM, who was just finishing tying his shoes. FM nodded, meaning everything was as it should be. Jim turned to look at Zeke and Smitty. Both men nodded. They were ready to go.

"Alpha has point," Jim said in a moderate tone, just loud enough for everyone to hear. "We make for checkpoint B after dinner."

He moved out as soon as they had eaten, taking point himself, using his Trimble Scout M+GPS to determine his first leg of the journey. They covered the ground quickly, avoiding any dwellings, moving ever higher into the terrain. When they reached checkpoint B, Jim stopped for a thirty-minute break. Within fifteen minutes, the entire team was there. Zeke walked up to him, squatted down beside him, opened his laptop, and turned it on, then drained his canteen while it booted up.

Satellite feeds flashed across the screen, and his fingers flew over the console. When he was done, he had a map showing Valdez and his troops already at the mine. To Jim's relief, no other bodies radiated heat at that site. Watching the recorded images, he saw the troops carefully inspecting the mine, a matter of three or four hours of searching. Then the troops moved toward the border.

"How long till they catch on to our ruse?" Smitty asked, coming to sit down beside them.

"They'll make camp at the border and then send patrols over the border at least half of tomorrow before they come back and pick up our trail," Jim said, after a moment of thought. "They'll come fast then."

"How much we gonna whittle 'em down, boss?" FM asked quietly.

"That will depend on how fast they catch up to us," Jim said.

"They got any satellite feeds of their own?" Smitty asked.

"Valdez could ask Cuba for help, I suppose," Zeke mused. "But they don't have our technology, so it would take days for somebody to point the satellite where they want it and then pore over the photographs to find us.

"So we're ghosts," Smitty said, nodding his head.

"More like shadows of ghosts," FM said in a low voice.

It began to rain, gently at first, and then in a steady downpour. Jim assigned Team Zulu point, and his team took the rear position. Their job was to make sure there was as little sign as possible of their passing. Rain helped. It also made footing treacherous and worked muscles to extremes, but not one man complained about that. It was part of the job.

CHAPTER 19

Valdez was furious. At the mine, he found the remains of his cousin, the man who had made him wealthy beyond his dreams. Vásquez had died hard, his face twisted in agony, his dead eyes staring out in horror. The mangled body was beyond description, and Valdez knew it had been the slaves that had perpetrated this horror, yet his fury was not aimed at them.

Somewhere out there was a phantom military force, moving through his country like a ghost, destroying everything that had taken years to develop. It was true, he thought, that he had enough to retire and live like a king for the remainder of his life, yet he could not until he had hunted down and destroyed this phantom force. That he had pledged to himself.

Convinced that they were Americans, he'd paid a large sum of money for information about the makeup and number of the force, only to be told it simply did not exist. The colonel he paid regularly for information about American law enforcement and troop movements had always given him accurate information. So who was in his country?

With harsh orders, he sent his men scurrying, some to track the military force and others to gather up whatever riches they could find. Since he had to wait for a report, especially if they crossed the border, he wanted to make sure he got his last ounce of payment out of the mines. Wisely he had told his men they could keep ninety percent of what they found, giving him just ten percent. Later, after dealing with this phantom force, he would have his own special forces kill the men and take the treasure for himself.

Using those men, his best-trained unit, he investigated what had happened at the mines. There should have been ejected shells to give him some indication of what type of weapons were used. None were found. Even the shells from the troops at the mine were picked up. Later the men found where the copper and brass had been melted down. He decided to have it tested to see if the grade of metal could tell him anything, though he doubted it. The acid saw to that.

Now, at least, he knew the military group working in his province was a covert group. They left nothing behind to give away who or how many they were. Not one of the prisoner slaves had been recovered yet. Perhaps one of them might tell him who and how many men there were. With freedom before them, they would melt into the bush, hiding as best they could, but at least one would be captured and brought back. The weakest and most frail would not get far in this jungle!

In the end, it was just one man, an elderly native of the area, too weak to run far. Valdez could tell he was near death, and so he was careful. What he gleaned didn't help him much. There were men among them who spoke the languages of all the captives. That made this unit an international team, perhaps a NATO force. One who gave medical aid spoke with an unusual accent in English. That didn't help either. He could have been from India or Africa, Australia, New Zealand, or a dozen other British-influenced colonies.

From the old man, he learned that there were no more than forty in the unit and that they were all men. That made them military and possibly foreign military. For a long time, Valdez pondered this. Never in recent history had a foreign military unit set foot on South American soil, apart from the British. Finally, he decided they were NATO forces, which made them less dangerous than a covert

American military force but not much. How had they known about the mine? His mind kept returning to Carastino.

Reports filtered in, and finally it was determined where the trail crossed the border. To make up for the lost time, he had his men flown to the border to pick up the trail and follow this troop and wipe it out. All his troops were too afraid of him to question the command to violate the border of a neighboring country. And so, the chase began.

CHAPTER 20

At checkpoint C, the elite *Bring It Up Omega Force* rested again, then pressed on to checkpoint D with Blue Team taking point. Checkpoint D had a cave. Chance had point, and he approached the checkpoint carefully. About to move forward, he spotted movement in the mouth of the cave. It was a puma. The big cat stood there for a moment sniffing the air, then turned and leaped up the mountain in an easy, graceful movement. Chance whistled silently. They would have to exercise caution here. He clicked his headset four times to signal danger.

Ox came up beside him, then Lunch Box and PU. "What do you have?" Ox asked, scanning the area carefully. Although he could see nothing, he trusted Chance not to warn of danger if there was none.

"Puma came out of the cave. Male, good-sized cat, went up the mountain." Chance pointed in the direction the cat left.

"We weren't going to stay in the cave anyway," Ox said.

"There could be a sheila in there with little ones," Chance warned quietly.

Ox nodded. "Best be careful then. Let's tell the others. Find a way to circle to the north and find us a good position to camp that won't threaten the cave," he ordered.

He pushed his talk button. "Captain, we're moving north of

the cave. Repeat, north of the cave. Possible animal threat. Repeat, possible animal threat. Over."

"Roger that, Ox. North it is," Jim replied a moment later. Ox appreciated the trust Jim showed in that simple statement. No questions, no doubts, simple acceptance that Ox knew what he was doing. He loved working with Jim Shepherd and found in him a leader who he respected more than any other he'd ever followed. He sent Chance off to find a better camp.

Chance was nearly two kilometers from the cave when he found the perfect spot for their day camp. Then he froze. Twelve feet from his position, the male cat moved out of the brush. Chance was downwind so the cat couldn't smell him, but it had heard him and was searching for him now. Slowly Chance stood up to his full height and brought his MP5SD around, flipping off the safety. The cat heard that. For a second, their eyes met.

Suddenly they were staring at each other. Chance decided on diplomacy. "Now then, I don't want to shoot you, and you don't want to be dead, so go hunt somewhere else," he said conversationally. "You've got better things to do than die today, cat. Get gone!"

The cat's ears went back, and it hissed at him, growling low, then turned and sprinted away. He watched it go with a prayer of thanksgiving and was about to move forward when another surprise came.

A hand descended on his shoulder, and Chance nearly jumped out of his skin. "You handled that well," Jim said, walking past him to check the new camping site. He wasn't aware that he had startled Chance so deeply and thought nothing of it as he moved through the area. It was actually better than the one they'd chosen earlier. Ox came up beside Chance.

"You okay, mate?" he asked.

"Why didn't you tell me he was coming?" Chance said.

"Who?" Ox asked, looking around.

"The bloody captain, that's who!" Chance snarled. "He nearly gave me a heart attack!"

Ox saw Jim at that moment, and his eyes got very big. "He's a quiet one, that one is. He's the real ghost among us. Never knew he was near us, mate. Sorry." Ox was shaken. He and his men were good in the bush. It had been years since he'd been surprised by the presence of another human being in his area. He punched Chance on the shoulder lightly. "We better learn fast or we're in barney!"

During the whole of that day, they rested as only soldiers expecting the worst can rest. The men fell asleep and stayed asleep, storing up for the nights and days to come. That evening everyone checked his weapons carefully. Everyone also washed carefully. Wet wipes were gathered, wrapped, and buried with equal care. They knew, better than anyone, that an enemy could be located by smell. That's why none of them smoked. A smoker could be detected easily.

"Oh, he's a cagey one, this Valdez!" Zeke said with a tight grin. The satellite feeds showed an enemy force almost equal to the one to the south coming down the border from the north.

"They're staying to the low ground, following the streams and rivers and roads," Zeke said.

"What bloody roads?" PU asked, coming up behind them. "What they call a road down here is two bloody ruts in the ground! Half the time it's just a trail through the bush wide enough for a donkey." He was in high good humor.

Jim looked at the two forces and thought for a few minutes. As the men gathered around, Zeke told them the news. Not one of them suggested running for the coast to avoid a confrontation. Looking up at the men, Jim spoke.

"We're vastly outnumbered, and that changes the odds," he said slowly. "I think I know a place where we can lure them in and wipe them out, but it's dangerous and any one of us could die here. So I'm going to ask you to determine if you want to continue or leave in a hurry. You decide."

"Best take care of them now, boss," FM said after a moment. "They may have superior numbers, but we've got something they don't have. We know where they are and what they're doing in real time. They don't know who we are, where we are, or what we're going to do. That gives us the edge. Besides, after seeing that slave mine and the condition of the slaves, I want to finish what we started here."

"What he said!" Wade agreed, nodding his head in the affirmative. Jim looked at each man and received a nod of agreement. His heart swelled with pride to lead such men.

"Let's move out men," Jim said after looking at the feeds. "Firefox, you have point," Jim said, nodding to Viper.

As before, they passed like ghosts through the sparse forest growth, leaving almost no trail. No one considered carrying on a conversation; they were too busy studying the ground, their surroundings, and looking for danger. Rain that night helped wipe away any prints they may have left, and Jim relaxed, knowing only the best of trackers could follow them. But in the morning, he discovered that they had one of the best of trackers. Their trail had been picked up to the point where the rain had washed it away the night before. As suspected, Valdez made for the cave.

"Hope the puma eats him," Jim grunted. "We move at sunset. Check your gear now before you go to sleep."

He needn't have given that last order. The men were already doing just that. With a smile of satisfaction, he sat down, checked his own gear, then stretched out. It felt odd not having Cecilia beside him. Smiling to himself, he closed his eyes and slept soundly.

Waking only for watch duty, each man slept well, coming to the evening meal refreshed and ready for another night of adventure. Jim was studying the terrain on a topographical map. After the men ate, he gathered them together.

"Teams Zulu and Blue will take this trail down to the stream and follow the stream for about seven kilometers. Find some rocky ground and head back up and wait for us. We're going to come slowly, making sure we leave no trail to follow. You can make good time splashing through the stream. Leave some tracks to follow!" He looked at the two teams selected for this duty.

"Roger that, Shep," John said lightly.

"Don't get dead!" Jim said with a grin.

John answered with a feral grin of his own. The two teams moved off down the hill. Jim nodded at the other men. "Red Team has point," he said. "Step lightly, guys," he added.

The men were careful. Even the best of trackers would find very little to signify their passing. JR and Ox, on the other hand, left a clear trail down to the stream and made sure a branch or two got broken as they walked through the shallows. Nature cooperated and gave them a perfect place to exit the stream. An old tree had fallen and lay half in the stream.

Now their steps were very careful as each one first got out of the water, wiping his boots dry before walking along the barkless trunk. Stepping on rocks and carefully wiping away any footprints left in dirt, they moved cautiously up the hill. This took longer than expected because of the extra care, and the two groups finally met at the top of the hill. No brush could be disturbed, no bark stripped, no branches left broken to tell the tale of their passing.

"Okay. Now we lead them where we want them," Jim said. "I want you to pair up and walk in each other's footprints. Whoever has the larger feet is behind. Their tracker is good and if he finds this spot, he will count the footprints to assess our size. Once we get over this knoll, we stop leaving prints."

"Diabolical!" Viper said with a grin. "Vásquez will think there's only twelve of us!"

"And he'll come faster than he should." Jim nodded.

It was a daring plan, but he needed a daring plan to fight a force as large as the one converging on him. Half an hour went by just climbing over the knoll, each man carefully stepping in the footprints of the man ahead of him. Once on the other side of the knoll, they pressed on, wiping away any signs, moving as quickly as the night and caution would allow. Jim had a spot in mind for the ambush. He led his men directly to that point, walking during daylight for two hours to reach it before allowing them to stop and rest.

He had the high ground and more. The hilltop he chose had huge rocks jutting out of the ground from some past earthquake activity. It was a warren filled with surprises. The men spent most of the day exploring and mapping it. By evening, they were very tired indeed.

After a meal, they rested for six hours before beginning preparations for the coming force.

"Zulu, you have the perimeter defenses. I want at least a third of that force killed by your outer defenses," Jim commanded tersely. John nodded. Like his brother, he hated the necessity of this action, but he certainly understood the need. It would be a grisly scene down there for those caught in the traps.

"I'll need a flash-bang and frag from everybody," John announced. The men began to unclip one of each to give to John and his team. "I'm also going to use a third of the claymores and about the same amount of PE4," he added, looking over his shoulder at Jim. Jim thought about it and nodded.

"Raider, you have the inner defenses. Wait until Zulu is done before you set them. I don't want to lose any of our people, especially my brother!" Jim grinned as he said that. "Make sure they are lethal and extremely difficult to find. I want a high body count," Jim said to Calvin Weston.

Weston grinned. "Can't be havin' any of our boys caught that way now, can we?" he said. "I want a flash-bang and frag from everybody too," Hobbs commanded loudly. The team unclipped one of each for him as his team went about collecting them. "Triggers will be set last, Shep. We'll plant everything now," Weston announced. Jim nodded.

"Okay. The rest of us map out positions. I want every position to have at least two escape routes. We want them good and mad and rushing up this hill to overcome us. What we don't want is to get caught with our pants down. Twelve Team 2 will have the highest ground. You're our defense against any planes or helicopters. Twelve Team 1 will take the low ground. Cover fire for movement and we'll leapfrog. Go to it!" Jim sent the rest of his men into the warren to map out their strategy.

"They bought it, Shep!" Zeke announced loudly later that morning. "They're coming hot and heavy, and the two forces have joined up."

"Roger that, Zeke. Keep your all-seeing eye on their progress. What's the ETA for them now?" Jim replied.

"They'll hit the outer defenses around three in the morning if they keep coming," Zeke said after a moment for calculations. "Judging from their recent movements, they aren't planning to stop until they catch us!" He grinned. "They'll be tired when they get here, and tired men make mistakes!"

"Roger. Keep me informed." Jim went back to searching the warren for good places to spring an ambush.

"So what if these bozos bring in air support?" FM asked, following Jim.

"We have four Stinger ATAS and two aerial pinches," Jim replied, looking into what appeared to be a cave, opening into the ground. He could hear water running below. Climbing carefully, he lowered himself about twenty-six feet to find a small waterfall and a pleasant pool. He circled around the waterfall, climbed back up, and cautiously peered over the rock formation. FM was directly below him. Jim dropped a small rock on his helmet.

"How the blazes did you get up there?" FM asked after collecting himself.

FM dropped into the hole, and he came up with Jim. He grinned. "Now this is nice. We get them sneaking up to the hole and then whamo! We got 'em!"

"Roger that!" Jim replied.

In the evening, the men pored over the maps of the area and memorized their dance of death. "Gonna be a storm, I think," FM said, looking up at the cloudy sky.

"A deadly storm, and we're it," Ox said softly, but everyone heard it.

Jim gathered the men after their meal for a circle of prayer. When that was completed, John took Twelve Team 2 to the high ground. He had Pen, Wade, Dorf, Mark, Lunch Box, PU, C. G., Vince, Viper, Bear, Scope, and DC on his team. Viper and Scope had the double duty of LAAD (low-altitude air defense) and sniper duty. Lunch Box and PU had the other two sniper positions and the opposite LAAD position.

Jim paired his Twelve Team. He and Driver took the left flank, while the Kline twins took the right flank. FM and Smitty paired up closest to Jim and Driver. Ox and Chance paired up and took the next position. Hobbs and Bond were next to them, and RC and .45 were closest to the Kline twins.

Some men chaffed at waiting. The professional soldier knew that waiting was part of the game. The men kept their focus by sighting down the hill and picking small targets, tightening their fingers on triggers but never firing a shot. Often, they checked their gear. Nothing was left to chance. Zeke kept them informed of the enemy's progress.

"They're moving in a large group, Shep," Zeke said near two in the morning. "Silly buggers don't have any point men out there," he added.

"All to our advantage," Jim replied. "Stay sharp, men," he cautioned.

At five minutes to three in the morning, the first booby trap was tripped, and at least a dozen men died in a fiery blast. Another, and then a third blast ripped through the night. Jim's team all waited patiently, not looking down the hill. They wanted good night vision. John, who was watching from above, reported in, keeping them appraised of the devastation.

"At least a dozen went down with each blast, Jim."

Jim heard the sadness in his brother's voice and recognized it for what it was. None of them liked killing, even when it was necessary. And John had planted those deadly traps. Yet killing was what every soldier was called upon to do in battle. Even these enemy troops had mothers, wives, and kids who would mourn their passing, and John knew it.

"Roger that," Jim said simply.

In a way, Valdez had chosen for him. He was going to have to wade in blood because of the size of this enemy force. Jim sighed and waited, listening. More blasts ripped through the night, and more screams were heard as the final three PE4 plastic explosive traps were triggered. Jim grimaced. The claymores would be next. Men often didn't die quickly in a claymore blast. The device hurled round shot outward, tearing through any bodies within twelve feet of the blast and wounding many more behind them.

CHAPTER 21

Dawn was just threatening when the troops encountered the inner defenses. John estimated that fully a third of them had been eliminated by the outer defenses. Now the carnage would infuriate them even more. They believed they were after just twelve men. As another third of them were killed by the blasts, Jim could hear the cursing. Firing blindly up the hill, they wasted a lot of ammunition. Finally, the last blast went off. It would be close-up killing now.

As one, Jim's team rose, aimed, and laid down a deadly storm of fire on the forces below. They melted before the barrage of bullets, some fortunate enough to take cover. Then Jim moved his men immediately. From the high ground, John's team provided cover fire for their retreat. His snipers were deadly, moving from target to target and dispassionately sending men to their graves. Cover fire in this instance was devastating to the enemy forces.

"Inbound chopper!" Zeke called from his position. "Coming in at two-oh-niner degrees," he added.

"Got it!" Viper zeroed in on the incoming chopper and blew it out of the sky.

"Two more, no three, coming in two-two degrees," Zeke radioed.

"Pinch released," Lunch Box said.

The aerial pinch was a new device, much like a nuclear missile, but without the nuclear explosion. Instead, it produced an electromagnetic pulse like that of a nuclear blast that destroyed electronic equipment. The men quickly turned off all their electronic equipment. Moments later the three choppers suddenly lost control and went down. There was no explosion to signify that they had been taken down, merely a thump in the sky.

On the ground, Valdez screamed in rage. He threw his radio to the ground. It no longer worked. He gave the order to charge the hill. There were only twelve men up there, and he wanted them. They had cost him dearly, and he meant for all of them to die, and at least one to die painfully.

"I want at least one of them alive!" he screamed.

Jim's team was already set in their second position. Their deadly fire sent the troops diving for cover and killed many of them in one short burst. Then he was moving again, his team splitting up in their pairs to ambush those who survived to come into the warren.

John's team provided cover fire again, so that it was with less than sixty men that Valdez arrived at the first position. His men rushed into the rocks, but Valdez remained just outside. He didn't like this. Only twelve men had killed most of his force. *What might they do inside those rocks?* He was about to order them out when his lieutenant's head exploded as his body flew backward. Without hesitation, he dove into the rocks.

In frustration and rage, he listened as his men died. The report of an AK-47 was unique, and it was not AK fire he heard time and again. He could hear the cursing and screaming as his men died, one after another, as he crouched where he was sure he was safe from enemy fire.

After about an hour, no more screams were heard. Valdez heard footsteps approaching and shot one of his own men backing around the corner, trying to escape the death that waited. His bullet severed the man's spine. Looking at one of his trusted lieutenants, Vásquez cursed. Then he froze as the hot muzzle of a recently fired pistol pressed against his head, searing and blistering the skin of his neck painfully.

"That was the last of them, Colonel. Don't you know it's not nice to kill your own men, even when you're a bloody coward?" Jim said quietly. He took the pistol from the colonel's unresisting hand. Valdez turned, his hands raised, and his eyebrows rose.

"You!" he exclaimed.

"Stakeout, boss?" FM asked, coming to stand beside Jim.

"How many live ones we got?" Jim asked.

"Seven, counting this refuse here," FM answered. "Only two down the hill are gonna live long enough to die in the stakeout."

Colonel Valdez found himself spread-eagled on the ground, naked, his arms and legs fastened to wooden stakes that had been driven into the ground. Dead bodies were piled up all around them, some lying across limbs. The stench was already bad. Only the faces and upper bodies of those still living were exposed when all the bodies were deposited. Weight pressing down cut off circulation to limbs, and cramps set in so that most of the living now groaned in pain. Jim's teams paid no heed to the pain evident in those cries.

"See, the ants and other insects are gonna come out to feast, along with buzzards and other carrion eaters," FM said conversationally, looking down at Valdez. "Since you won't be movin', they'll eat you too. Only you'll be alive to enjoy the grisly feast. Fitting!" he finished with a grin. His face disappeared.

Zeke was already making a radio call for the CH-53D to pick them up. Half an hour later, the chopper came into the green flares and hovered long enough to pick up all twenty-four men and Pippi. Breathing a prayer of thanks, he made sure everyone was on the chopper. Once safe on the chopper and feet wet, Jim pulled out his satellite phone and called Cecilia.

"Hello, my love," he said, choking back the tears that threatened. "Everyone safe and accounted for. See you shortly." He hit the off button to end the call.

At about the same moment, Colonel Valdez felt the first bite. He screamed and cursed as the pain mushroomed. Insects chewed in a feeding frenzy, sending him into spasms of pain, and the fresh blood seemed to deepen the frenzy. Then the vultures came. More and more vultures tore at his skin, and the bugs chewed in what seemed like a wild feeding frenzy. Between the vultures and the insects, it took a long time for him to die.

CHAPTER 22

On *Bring It Up Coral*, the men transferred their gear down to the war room, cleaned everything, checked everything, and stowed it properly. When they were finished, they headed for the showers. Jim noticed two of the men limping. He caught up to them. RC was scratching at his left leg, and .45 was merely limping. It was obvious that both were in pain and that walking in a normal way was impossible.

"What's up?" he asked the two.

"Heading to sick bay now, Shep," .45 said. "We both got bit by this spider." He produced a small glass specimen jar with a white spider in it. "Stung like a wasp, and both of us have some poison in our system."

"When did this happen?" Jim asked, concerned.

"Last stages of the battle," RC answered. "I think we'll be okay. Don't have any symptoms other than soreness and itching."

"Okay. Tell Doc to report directly to me," Jim replied, leaving them and heading to his own quarters to greet his wife.

Cecilia greeted him with all the fervor and passion he could ever wish for. He hugged her tightly. "I need a shower," he said when he let her go.

"Go ahead," she offered. He walked into the bathroom, disrobed, and showered quickly. After a shave, he felt much better. He brushed his teeth and cleaned up around the sink. Cecilia stayed close the entire time, and Jim understood why. He caught her up in another embrace and kissed her.

"How are the refugees?" he asked, as he began dressing in a clean uniform.

"They're on the British ship anchored off our stern. We bring them over here for meals, and Doc is helping with the treatments. It's all pretty awful. I never imagined." There were sudden tears in her eyes. Jim finished his uniform, checked in the mirror to be sure everything was as it should be, and led the way out of their cabin. It was time for breakfast and a debriefing. He paused by the door of the conference room.

"When did this happen?" he asked, a huge grin spreading over his face. The conference room was vastly changed.

"Calvin Beardsley brought his crew on board about three weeks ago to enlarge it," Cecilia admitted. "Abe doesn't mind the loss of his quarters for his crew. They're in larger quarters now one deck down. We lost some storage space, but we haven't used it yet, so Papa gave the go-ahead. I think this was all his plan."

Refugees began to filter into the dining room. Jim instructed his team to eat at the conference table to make room for them. After finishing his breakfast, he wandered around the tables talking to various refugees. All of them welcomed him with tears of gratitude. Some hugged him desperately, weeping and soaking his uniform shirt. His eyes sought Cecilia, and she nodded at him to encourage him to keep going.

Some of the women went over and hugged the men who had released them from their prison cells. Jim noted that for some of the men, this was a pleasant experience, and they returned the hugs with warmth. For others it was embarrassing, but nonetheless, they returned the hugs. Cecilia smiled when her husband lifted two little girls into his arms. Their mother was telling him her tale, and he was deeply moved by the depth of her despair and emotion. She hadn't really had time to mourn the death of her husband because in the mines, she'd had to struggle just to survive and protect her two little girls. Now, with her release and freedom, she was mourning deeply. His heart seemed to break as he held her while she wept for her loss.

He found he couldn't put the children down easily, because both were hugging his neck, their faces buried in his shoulder. Looking down at them with affection and tenderness, he smiled at their mother. Moving his head to signify she should follow him, he moved over to Cecilia. She took one of the girls, and they all stood talking for some time before the mother finally peeled her daughters away.

"Go ahead and announce the debriefing." Jim nodded to Zeke. It was time to assess what they had accomplished and how to move forward.

Quickly the conference room was cleaned up, and the men took their places at the table. The entire crew poured into the enlarged room, now comfortably large enough for all of them. Jim took his place at the head of the table.

"Dorf, why don't you open us with prayer and then we'll have the evaluations," Jim said when the men settled and quiet fell in the room. As he was standing, the men stood, each taking the hand of the man next to him. Jim found himself holding John and Wade's hands as he bowed his head. It was the first time the team had ever done this. As Dorf spoke, his words were words of praise for a mighty God who had given them a great victory, who had shown them great mercy and tenderness, protecting them from serious injury. It was, as Jim thought about it, exactly what prayer should be. Praise and adoration for a mighty God filled the room, and when Dorf finally said the "amen," every man echoed his final word together. They sat and were silent for a moment.

"Tactics were good, and the Twelve Teams worked well together," John said after a moment of silence. "We could have defended that position against a much larger force, as long as we didn't have to worry about heavier air support or running out of ammo."

"How large was the force Valdez brought against you?" Abe asked.

"Four hundred and twenty-six men, three helicopters, and a

partridge in a pear tree." Zeke's reply seemed flippant, at first, to many listening, but the men who had been there understood.

Cecilia caught her breath. She had no idea her husband had been in that kind of danger. She could feel her stomach sinking at the mere thought. Jim smiled at her, knowing what was going through her mind.

"And how many of them are left alive?" Papa asked softly.

"None."

Andrea looked into Jim's sad eyes as he spoke and nodded his head once. His nephew had been justified in killing that many, but Andrea knew he still hated the killing. It was an interesting ethical problem with moral implications that were important. That evil men would walk the earth all men knew, for all were evil, and every man in this room was capable of every evil, yet the blood of Christ had cleansed them of that, given them a new nature to do battle with that old sinful nature and that old deluder, Satan. As long as his nephews hated the killing, they were safe from becoming like the men they killed. He often wondered what God thought of it all.

There was a distraction that made them all pause and look for the cause. Outside the conference room, voices stirred as the refugees, listening from that position, began talking in excited whispers. That a mere twenty-four soldiers could accomplish such a thing produced in them an awe and respect for these heroes who had so valiantly risked life and limb to rescue them. However, the fact that they knew how many he'd faced posed a new problem. Jim addressed them directly.

"You may tell anyone you want that a force of twenty-four Americans, British, and Australian soldiers killed four hundred and twenty-six enemy troops in a battle. You may not tell anyone that that force came from this ship." He repeated his words in French, German, Greek, and Italian. The people outside the room nodded their heads. They would respect his wishes.

"RC and .45, how are you faring?" he asked.

"Doc identified the spider and figured if we weren't dead yet, we probably wouldn't die," Colt reported with a grin. Again, some of the women listening in reacted to the sarcasm of the answer and the almost callous report. "Of course, that made us feel much better," he added sarcastically. "Itches some and the muscles are really sore, Shep. Other than that, we're okay."

RC nodded his agreement.

"What spider?" Zeke asked. He hadn't known about the bites, and he looked at the two men curiously.

"From the genus *Nephila*," Doc said. "The venom is not deadly, but it can affect the muscles for a few days."

"You got bit by this spider?" Zeke asked RC.

"Seems we stepped on separate webs. The spiders got into our pants. I killed the one that bit me, but .45 thought we'd better save one of them alive," RC said.

"Wow!" Zeke said. "Good thinking on catching one of them. That's something I need to put in the report, so we know for next time."

"I thought Uncle Zeke saw everything!" FM piped up.

"I don't keep a camera up your pant leg!" Zeke retorted, coming back quickly. Everyone laughed. The comic relief eased the tension in the room and outside.

An hour of intense debriefing followed while the men reviewed and replayed the mission, analyzing it from every possible angle. Those listening were awed by the military precision that these men demonstrated and the prowess in battle they exhibited. When they were finished with that, Jim sat back. He looked at his team with pride.

"Okay, we accomplished that mission. Now we have a ship to find," he said. "Everyone has three days of R & R before we get back to work. We'll be anchored here, so enjoy the Caribbean, swim, dive, whatever. Abe and Sturdy, we meet in here for at least two hours each day, your choice of time. Only those on the mission will be allowed during those hours. Dismissed."

He closed his file, turned off his computer, and folded the cover down when it went dark. It had, he decided, turned out to be a very deadly storm on that hilltop. Adding up the numbers in his head, he realized he was leading a truly deadly unit of soldiers. He bowed his head and offered a prayer of thanks for divine protection.

Finn paused by the captain, one of the first to rise, eager to get back to his desk, no doubt. Jim looked up.

"You have some paperwork on your desk sir," he said.

"I have three days of R & R first, Lieutenant. I'll get to it then." Jim sighed, smiling at Cecilia. Finn sighed, frustrated. He saluted smartly and left.

"What's he been like since we've been gone?" Jim asked Andrea, as he walked beside him.

"Difficult," Andrea said with a grin. "We let Millie handle him," he added as Doc and Millie came up beside them.

Millie smiled. "I always find it amusing that brave men fear such foolish things."

"Yes, he is foolish," Doc echoed with some distaste.

"I don't think we'll keep him much longer," Jim said quietly. "If he can't unbend, he doesn't fit."

"Give him some time, Jim," Millie said. "He's coming along nicely."

He raised an eyebrow and decided to bow to her wisdom. Smiling, he answered her.

"If you think he needs a little more time, Aunt Millie, we'll give him that time." He hugged her, very uncharacteristically, and walked away.

Later that morning, Jim crossed over to the British naval vessel. Captain Jamison greeted him with a handshake and smile. Jamison was small, barely over five foot five, if he was that tall, and in good shape, despite his fifty-plus years. He had a habit rising up on his toes often, as if trying to grow taller. The way his men deferred to him told Jim he was a good leader.

"Let me introduce my team, Captain. This is a right mess you dumped in my lap!" he opened, introducing his other officers. Jim shook hands with each one, his eyes taking them in, assessing and finding them a very dedicated crew.

"Which one?" Jim asked, after repeating the last officer's name and shaking hands.

"Caro! Bloody creep!" Jamison said.

"Military trial set up yet?" Jim asked.

"We were waiting for you." Jamison smiled. Jim's eyebrows rose.

"You're going to hold the trial here?" he asked.

"Sir Edward is arriving later today. We'll hold the trial tomorrow, all legal, and then Sir Edward will take him back and lock him up," Jamison said.

"How's his knee?" Jim asked.

"Your work?" Jamison asked. Jim nodded. "He'll never walk normally on that leg again. He's crying lawsuit and wantin' his lawyer. In fact, the little bleeder has been obnoxious the entire time he's been conscious. Your doc came over and assisted ours in fixing that knee. Good man, that!"

Jim smiled at the captain's hasty explanation. He also understood the frustration of dealing with this kind of prisoner.

"Well done, sir," Jamison's XO said, nodding once. Jim smiled. "Wanted to shoot him myself after I talked to some of the refugees."

"Let's keep him healthy so he can enjoy a long life in solitary confinement," Jim replied.

"Aye, aye, sir!" the XO acquiesced, saluting him smartly.

"Now about these refugees!" Jamison said. "We've been able to identify all of them. Emergency visas are coming with Sir Edward. None of them have been allowed to talk to family yet. They have to wait until we get them on shore in Florida and debrief them."

"The British Navy invading an American harbor! What will be next?" Jim asked with a grin.

"Your boys can dust off the Merrimack and we can play bumper boats," Jamison said with a straight face. Jim burst out laughing.

"Quick repost." He laughed.

"We do have some information to share with you." Jamison became serious. "There's a Russian trawler supposedly fishing these waters. An Admiral Runion called me about it, wanted you to know all the facts. Sir Edward had a few things to add to the file on this bloke. The thing is, it belongs to a Russian named Rustin."

"Rustin the Mafia king?" Jim asked quickly.

"You're well informed!" Jamison said. He thought about that for a moment, remembering the dossier he'd read on Captain Shepherd and nodded. Not only was the man well informed, but he was also quite capable. He stopped worrying a little. "Admiral Runion asked us to pass the word along. It seems an American admiral was in contact with this Rustin chap and invited him over."

"Thanks for the warning," Jim said.

"We were wondering if you wanted some unofficial help," Jamison offered.

"Let's wait and see. Once you've dropped the refugees off, you might want to patrol these waters again, to let your men enjoy the Caribbean breezes," Jim suggested with a smile. "Everyone loves the deep blue Caribbean!"

"I might at that!" Jamison said. "I hear we're in for a hurricane. I'll probably ride that out off the coast of North Carolina."

"Just so we get these refugees feet dry before it hits," Jim said.

"Too bloody right!" Jamison said with some feeling. "Bloody civilians are always puking all over this vessel in heavy weather!"

Jim grinned, feeling much the same. Navy boats weren't always equipped with the latest in rough water handling and could be downright scary during a storm.

Jim followed the captain down to the makeshift refugee center. Cecilia was already there, and he saw Tiffany for the first time. The first thing he noticed was the smell of fear. Unaccustomed to it, he recognized it immediately, and he was troubled by its presence. He walked over to Cecilia, who was holding a child of about twelve on her lap. Jim was surprised to see a diaper on the child and a pacifier in the child's mouth.

As he drew nearer, the child cowered back into Cecilia, and she tightened her hold on the child. Jim smiled and squatted down. He reached out a hand and put it on Cecilia's hand, watching the child react. After a few moments, he put his hand on the child's hand, and she gripped his hand tightly. She relaxed then. Jim held her hand and kept his voice low.

"You can cut the atmosphere in here," Jim said softly. "They're still afraid."

"Tiffany, can you take her for a minute?" Cecilia requested, as Tiffany passed. Holding out her hands, Tiffany smiled, and the child leaned into them. It was touching and heart-wrenching at the same time. Jim didn't know what to think.

"Honey, they're on a ship filled with men for the most part. I doubt if any of them will ever be comfortable on the sea again. Then there's the coming storm, and they're afraid of that. Right now, all they really know is fear, especially the children," Cecilia said. "The children are the worst. This will leave permanent scars on their lives that will affect them forever." She was very sad as she said it.

"Isn't that girl a little old for diapers?" Jim asked, nodding at the child in Tiffany's arms.

"Regression is a natural result of PTSD in children," Cecilia said. "Millie can explain it better than I can. Just remember that PTSD is not rational. It's emotional for the most part. What they need more than anything else is patience and understanding."

A squeal of delight from several children made Jim turn. Abe and Sturdy came into the room, and the children swarmed them. Both men fell to the floor laughing and hugging children. Children were flung into the air and caught, giggling and laughing, even the twelve-year-old. Grinning, Jim watched as every child entered the fun. A moment ago, they had all been terrified. Now they seemed confident and at ease.

"How did they pull that off?" he asked. Suddenly Tiffany seemed to fly up to the ceiling and drop, screaming and laughing with the children, as Sturdy caught her gently and put her down. While the tossing went on, Cecilia smiled and answered.

"You are looking at the ogre and the giant," Cecilia said with a grin. "Prepare to be declared safe," she added.

CHAPTER 23

Abe had his head up and was sniffing the air. Suddenly he was on his feet and walking toward Jim, sniffing the air. He sniffed all over Jim and then smiled and shook his head in the affirmative. Sturdy walked around Jim, lifted him easily, and then dangled him by his ankle with one hand, seeming to weigh him. He too shook his head in the affirmative. The children laughed and clapped.

"Gonna drop ya, boss," Sturdy warned quietly. "Play along."

Jim hit the deck and lay on his shoulders, his body bent over with his toes pointing to the floor. Sturdy pretended that he had dropped Jim by accident, and his hands flew to his face in mock dismay. The ogre bellowed and lifted him by his ankle, looking at him and poking him.

"Ow!" Jim exclaimed. The kids all laughed, and Abe dropped him as soon as he spoke. "Hey! Ouch!" he said again, rolling to his knees this time. To his surprise, the kids mobbed him, and he found himself under a pile of bodies and laughing faces. He threw them around with Abe and Sturdy for a while. It was an effort with the older girl, but she loved it so much he was willing to tire himself out. Cecilia stood by watching with a smile on her face.

"Never thought I'd see that!" Doc said, coming into the room. Abe and Sturdy rolled to their feet and approached the Doc carefully.

Doc took Sturdy's hand and held it to his face, and Abe sniffed him, nodding the whole time. Sturdy nodded, and the children immediately relaxed.

"We used Sturdy and Abe to help the children feel more secure the first night. They were carefully guarded by an ogre and a giant! A few of the crew played along, getting tossed out, and the kids settled down right away," Doc explained to Jim while the ogre and giant returned to the floor to play with the kids. Jim watched them with a sad smile on his face and sighed. Victims really had no true justice, but if there were people who cared, a difference could be made. He was suddenly very proud of his crew.

"As soon as the trial is over tomorrow, I want these people moving toward Florida," Jim said quietly. "Is that possible?"

"Yes. They're anxious to get there," Doc admitted. "I'll miss them," he added with a sigh.

Jim watched him move through the refugees, touching a shoulder, bending down to talk, being the healer as he went. To Jim, it was obvious that the people in this room trusted Doc. Cecilia came over and took his hand. She looked up at him with a smile on her lips.

"He's a good man. All the refugees trust him. Ox didn't get such a reception, but then he wasn't here when they arrived," she said. "Most of them are fighting a plethora of ailments and illnesses, and we're doing everything we can to get them on the way to healing and health. For some, it will be months before they are well enough to begin coping with everything."

"Why do the children let us hold them on *Bring It Up Coral* but not on this vessel?" Jim asked.

"They trust that ship. It was their first haven after captivity. This one is different, and there are many more people on board this ship," Cecilia replied.

In the afternoon, most of the refugees ended up on Jim's ship, up on the observation deck in the sun or in the air-conditioned observation deck below. None of the crew minded giving up their space to the refugees. Some of them even allowed children to nap in their bunks.

Talking to many of them, he discovered that the wounds of losing husband and father were very raw, as if newly adopted. He wondered about that and sought out Doc and Millie. Doc was quick to explain.

"The horror of rape, degradation, enslavement all covered that loss because of the immediacy of the predicament. Now that they are finally safe and know they will live, they must face that loss anew, try to adjust, and many of them have no idea what they will do. They are, essentially, lost souls awash in the sea of humanity, and many will be unable to cope for some time. I hate what was done to them and for the first time in my life, wanted to be a part of punishing the men who did this. But after I calmed down, I realized that there is no fitting punishment. That, I will leave to the good Lord."

Jim nodded soberly.

For nearly an hour, Jim stood on the observation deck, hugging people who came to thank him, hugging children, seeing in their faces the reality of what they had to face and knowing that what he did was not enough. Yes, he punished those who committed heinous acts of slavery and cruelty, but now they had a life to face, as Cecilia had when she first came on board his ship. Bending his head, he offered up a simple prayer.

"Father, help me learn to think about the victims and to learn how to help them." He sighed.

A huge hand landed on his shoulder, and he looked over at Abe, who had a very sad expression on his face. It probably mirrored the look on his face, Jim thought. After a moment of silence, Abe spoke.

"We can only do what we can do. I want to help these people more, but I can't. I can pray for them, and I will, but in the future, I will plan to do more." His face was set as he spoke those words, and Jim knew that he meant the promise. He nodded, grasping hands with Abe, their muscles taut with emotion.

Later Jim watched Sir Edward's helicopter land on the British vessel from the bridge of his own ship. The seas were still calm, the deceptive calm before the storm. With a sigh, he headed down to put on his dress uniform.

An hour later, Sir Edward asked permission to come on board.

Dorf granted permission, and Sir Edward received a formal and dignified greeting, as was befitting his station. He smiled at the men in uniform who turned out for his visit. Walking right up to Jim, he shook hands vigorously. His eyes were relaxed and smiling for a change.

"Fine-looking crew!" he said. He looked at the newly designed insignia and grinned. "Very fitting." The eagle on Jim's collar was coming in for the kill, talons spread wide, a fierce burning glow in its eyes.

Jim took great pleasure in escorting Sir Edward through the ship. Sir Edward, taking it all in for the first time, was amazed at the condition of the ship. Everything gleamed with fresh paint, and every surface was clean. Every cabin was shipshape and would pass the most stringent of inspections. Even the engine room was clean. Master Chief Warner saluted from his station as the two officers passed through. The war room was a complete surprise. In fact, everything on this ship told him why Jim and his crew succeeded so often.

"Ingenious!" Sir Edward said as the bulkhead moved to open the war room. "Who designed this?"

"Wade Adams," Jim answered.

"Ah yes! The marine!" Sir Edward moved through the area looking at the lockers and weapons, inspecting some. "Most impressive!" he commented.

He paused to look over the full armor protection the team wore into battle. Some of it was familiar, but the Kevlar sleeves and leggings were new to him. Taking his time, he tried a full suit on, then looked up at Jim.

"Better you than me!" he admitted, beginning to peel it all off.

"If you were going into battle, it wouldn't seem like too much," Jim said prosaically.

"No, I suppose not," Sir Edward agreed. In companionable silence, they walked back up to the main deck. "You keep this ship in amazingly good condition," he complimented.

"The payoff is worth it," Jim stated. "When everything is in top condition, we know we can depend on him. The men and women of my crew know that."

"And now you're going after the *Estelle*," Sir Edward mused. "You know that Admiral Jacks asked Rustin to come out here and stop you?"

"No, I didn't know that. I did know Rustin was here," Jim said with a grim look.

"It would be interesting to know what's on that ship that Jacks and Rook don't want discovered," Sir Edward said. "I hope you find it," he added.

"Oh, I'll find her," Jim said with confidence.

"Rustin is serious competition," Sir Edward warned.

"He's a vicious creep!" Cecilia said, coming up to them as he spoke. "But we know how to deal with that kind, don't we?" she asked, smiling up at Jim.

"And what brings you looking for me?" Jim asked, kissing her lightly.

"Captain Jamison would like the two of you to join him on his vessel," she replied. "I imagine he's going to ask to move the trial up to this afternoon because of the coming storm. He seems to be concerned that the passengers might defile his pristine ship with vomit." She leaned up for another kiss from Jim before stepping back. Sir Edward watched without comment.

"It's picking up strength, then?" Jim asked as they made their way toward the stern and the gangplank to the British vessel.

"We should start feeling the oncoming wrath of nature before sunrise," Cecilia answered.

She was correct about Captain Jamison's wishes. Sir Edward was more than happy to go along. Jamison looked at Jim. "Could we borrow Lieutenant Weston and his team, Captain?"

Jim pressed the talk button on his headset and asked Weston to bring his team to the British vessel as quickly as possible in dress uniform. Calvin acknowledged with a simple, "On our way, Shep." Jim smiled.

Jamison led them to the room he used for military discipline. As captain of the ship, he took the place of chief justice. Jim, Sir Edward, and Tiffany were seated in the witness section of the room. Cecilia and a few others sat in the section designated for observers, a very rare occasion in a military tribunal.

Weston, Banks, Donnelly, and Carr were mixed in with eight other jurors and filed in, standing at attention before their chairs. The prisoner was wrestled into the room, fighting every step, cursing and spitting in rage. Jim was surprised at the violence of his actions.

"Mr. Caro!" Captain Jamison thundered. Caro paused in his struggles. "If you do not stop using that kind of language, I will have you gagged!" Caro ignored him, and Jamison nodded at one of the two MPs escorting him. The man whipped a bandanna from an inside pocket while the other wadded up a handkerchief, pushed it into Caro's mouth, while the other tied the bandana around to keep it there. Jim missed the paling of Caro's face as the chemical on the gag touched his tongue.

"I hope it was used," Jim whispered to Sir Edward, referring to the handkerchief now effectively muzzling Caro.

"Just treated with a drop of something to make him very sick," Sir Edward whispered back.

Sure enough, the prisoner began to heave, but the gag kept most of the vomit from exiting his mouth. He looked to be choking on his own vomit. The MP removed the bandana, and a crewman appeared as if by magic to clean up the floor. Caro was pale and gathered himself to begin a tirade when Captain Jamison looked at him.

"One word out of you, and another treated handkerchief goes in your mouth, and this time we'll let you choke in your own vomit!" he warned. There was in his eyes the promise that his word would be carried out to the letter.

Wisely, Caro remained silent. When he was in his place, behind his chair, everyone stood and faced the flag of Great Britain. The flag was saluted, the proper words repeated, and then the ship's chaplain led in a prayer. Caro watched with impatience through the formal ceremony. Not until Captain Jamison sat down did anyone else take his or her seats.

"This is a British war tribunal, held on British territory in international waters according to maritime law regarding military prisoners. The accused, Antonio Caro, declared war on the British Empire when he ordered the death by execution of our esteemed minister of finance, Sir Henry Crowell. He is charged with other war crimes in the murder of Mrs. Crowell and the other women on board the minister's yacht, not to mention the men. As a direct result of his actions, he is being tried as war criminal." Captain Jamison paused in his reading to look at Caro, who was still defiant.

"Any decision made here is final and will be carried out in accordance with our laws and traditions. Mr. Cummings, does the accused understand the charges against him?" Captain Jamison asked, looking at the officer chosen to defend Caro.

"The accused refuses to accept counsel," Mr. Cummings said, and sat down.

"Proceed," Captain Jamison ordered.

"Prosecution calls Esteban Lorenz to the stand," another officer said loudly.

Lorenz kept his one eye on the prosecutor and did not dare to look at Caro during the questioning. He described the attack of Juan Carastino on the Crowell vessel. His film was played with enhancement from Zeke identifying the pirate Carastino. Any comments he made were interpreted in English for those listening, and Lorenz was allowed to step down. He was escorted out of the room immediately. Captain Jamison made sure he would be transported to a new home in protective custody. Lorenz had agreed to this only when assured he would still be able to drink and fish, seemingly in that order.

"Prosecution calls Captain James Shepherd."

Jim stood up and walked to the stand. His testimony involved the attack and consequent capture of Carastino. Jim stated the facts simply. He explained how Carastino's confession was gathered. Every member of the jury looked at Weston and his team and nodded in approval.

"And what became of Juan Carastino?" the prosecutor asked.

"Alas, he learned he could not breathe beneath the surface of the ocean and drowned in the lesson," Jim replied. "I consider that my men showed great restraint in not skinning him alive and staking him out for the crabs to finish," he added.

"Ahem! Yes!" Captain Jamison said, trying to keep the smile from his face. "Thank you for your testimony, Captain."

"I do not care what happens to me, Captain Shepherd, but I promise you I will find a way to kill your entire family!" Caro threatened in a thundering voice.

Jim's move was so quick that even the MPs didn't have a chance to intervene. His left hand squeezed Caro's cheeks until his tongue protruded, and he stuck the point of his Mini Tac knife all the way through the tongue from the bottom to the top. Caro's blood poured down his chin and over Jim's hand. Through the pain, Caro could not take his eyes from Jim's.

"I pull this knife and you have a forked tongue. Fitting. You see how I'm shaking in my boots from your dire threats?" He pulled the knife, and blood poured out of Caro's mouth. Deliberately Jim wiped the blood from his knife on Caro's cheeks. Caro's eyes opened wide in fear as he stared into eyes that were like an open grave, his grave.

"I think perhaps a doctor should care for the accused," Captain Jamison suggested calmly from his seat. Ox appeared with a red-hot piece of iron, and Caro screamed as he cauterized the two pieces of tongue. The blood stopped, about the time Caro passed out from the pain. The MPs lowered him to his seat, one of them smiling, the other pale.

"I doubt we'll have any more outbursts from the accused." Captain Jamison's voice was calm, as if this was common. "Carry on."

"Prosecution calls Sir Edward Marsh."

Sir Edward confirmed the connection between Caro, Carastino, Vásquez, and Valdez. He produced a paper trail and evidence that might have shocked Caro, had he been awake to hear it. He did come around groggily toward the end of the evidence but was obviously in extreme pain. Eyes wild with pain and fear, he looked around him, aware that he was finally facing true justice and that he might not survive.

"Prosecution calls Ms. Tiffany Millstein."

Tiffany told her story of the murder of her father and the attempt to capture, rape, and kill her. When she stepped down, she paused a moment to look at Caro and shook her head sadly.

"You thought your power was absolute. Now you have no power at all." She slapped his face, hard, and walked back to the witness stand with her back ramrod stiff. She did not see the nods and smiles of appreciation from the jurors' box.

Caro ripped a sheet of paper from Mr. Cummings's legal pad and began to write furiously. Mr. Cummings watched with interest. When he was finished, Mr. Cummings read the paper.

"The accused, in his own defense, says that he did not personally attack any British forces, and that the killing of Sir Henry was carried out without his permission or knowledge. I'd like to add that the coward would claim anything to save his own skin."

Caro glared at Cummings.

"Prosecution calls Lieutenant Weston."

Calvin proceeded to describe the attack of the fortress and the subsequent battle. He produced evidence of communication between Caro and Valdez and described the consequent battle and the death of Valdez, the latter he recounted with great detail, dispassionately, as if reading a report. When he rejoined the jury, Caro sat stunned. Perhaps he was realizing that everything he had built was suddenly gone, useless, and that he was helpless. His empire, his friends…all were dead. His head reeled with the knowledge.

"Prosecution rests, sir," the officer said, sitting down. It was obvious that Hobbs's testimony had a profound effect on everyone. Caro's eyes were wild now as he looked around, desperate to find any way of escape, but there was none. All his wealth was gone, and now he was helpless and alone.

Captain Jamison explained the charges to the jury and the choices they had for punishment. The jury did not even leave the box. They stood as one when the captain finished. The jury foreman spoke clearly.

"We find the defendant guilty on all charges. It is the wish of this jury that the defendant be sentenced to life in a military prison in solitary confinement," he reported evenly.

"Very well. Sentence passed." Jamison dropped his gavel twice and put it down. "Remove the condemned."

CHAPTER 24

Jim stood on the stern of his ship, holding the rail lightly as the British vessel departed. The waves were already beginning to build, and the sky was a nasty color. Jim gave one last wave and with Cecilia and Tiffany, made his way into the ship. Five feet from the door, the clouds seemed to burst, and they laughed as they leaped the distance, avoiding getting soaked.

"We're in for it!" Smitty announced when Jim arrived in the CIC.

"What are we looking at?" Jim asked.

"Force 4, boss," Smitty answered. "Maybe we'll learn something about the *Estelle* from this one. It's following very similar lines."

"We seem to have a recurring theme of storms!" Cecilia laughed.

"Everything battened down and ready for the storm, Papa?" Jim asked, sticking his head into the bridge. Knowing the question was unnecessary, he asked it, nonetheless.

"We thought we'd wait for you to give the order," Andrea replied with a big grin.

"Well, then I want it done two hours ago!" Jim snapped in mock anger.

"All done then," Andrea said. Jim grinned at him and went back into the CIC to talk to Zeke.

"Keeping an eye on our Russian friend?" Jim asked when he entered.

"He's running for Cuba and cover," Zeke announced. "That trawler is not cut out to face this kind of weather. The Cuba connection could mean trouble. He could lure us into Cuban waters, and we could be in real danger!" Zeke looked up at him with a very serious look on his face, and Jim nodded in the affirmative.

"Noted. Let's concentrate on trying to figure out what happened to the *Estelle*. We should have enough information from her distress calls. If she started to drift and took on water, we should be able to come up with a successful grid pattern to search." Jim nodded. "See what you and Smitty can do, please," he added. "I know the two of you are eager to show us all how clever you are!"

"Can I get Bright Eyes up here to help?" Zeke said, as Cecilia came through the door.

"The great Uncle Zeke asking for help!" Cecilia said, stopping to give Jim a kiss.

"Is it proper ship etiquette for an ensign to kiss the captain?" Zeke asked in a pained voice.

"It's proper etiquette for a wife to kiss her husband, silly," Cecilia replied demurely, taking her seat behind a set of keyboards and monitors. "He is quite a good kisser. Perhaps you and some of the other men would like to have lessons?" Her look at Zeke said volumes, and he looked crestfallen.

"I retire worsted," he said at last, ducking his head and looking comically woebegone.

"I'll leave the two of you to your search," Jim said, leaving the CIC. He returned to the bridge and strapped his feet to the deck with Velcro straps provided for that purpose. The waves were building now, and the ship headed into the storm, climbing a wave and then slamming into the sea on the other side.

Bring It Up Coral was designed to take anything Mother Nature could dish out and tow the largest aircraft carrier ever built while doing it. Jim grinned at Andrea, both of them loving the sea even at its worst, thrilling to the battle they were about to fight. This would be an epic battle of man against nature. Jim knew his crew was ready for the challenge.

Every hour a new pair of hands took the wheel. Jim relieved Andrea, John relieved Jim, and Wade relieved John. Then they started all over again. At all times there were at least three people on the bridge capable of piloting the ship. Should anyone be injured, the ship would not be allowed to flounder.

Down in the engine room, Inchworm and TRT kept their eyes on all the systems while FM stood by to help if necessary. Sparks and Loony were on hand to repair any electrical failures or problems. Every other crew member knew his job for storm duty, and each performed it with the expertise Jim had come to expect from his men.

Dorf and Mark ran the crew in such a way that the men felt they were coming alongside to help, not being ordered to do something. Jim utilized the same leadership style and trusted them completely. Abe and Sturdy ran the kitchen crew with the same abilities. It was, he decided watching all the work go on with a sense of pride, the best and most effective and talented team he'd ever led.

For two days they battled the hurricane, and on the third day the bad weather passed, and the seas calmed. Jim followed the hurricane at a safe distance and dropped anchor east of Cat Island. For a day everybody rested. Doc and Sean treated all the bumps and bruises, cuts and scrapes, and a few broken fingers. Loony broke two fingers in a fall, and Inchworm broke his left index finger.

Everyone checked the ship thoroughly from top to bottom the following day, cleaning away the refuse and salt buildup, scraping, painting, and scrubbing until the ship was in pristine condition. At the end of that day, Jim announced that the following day would be a day of rest and recreation. He encouraged everyone to dive on the coral reefs or just swim in the sea. Making sure his crew knew he was proud of the way they handled the storm, he let them know they deserved the treat.

After spending a day diving on the coral reefs and swimming in the freshly cleaned Caribbean waters, the crew gathered in the dining room for a festive meal. Abe served steak, lobster, crab, and scallops in a buffet style with garlic mashed potatoes, roasted red potatoes, steamed vegetables, and a Shrimp Louie salad. Every crew member that wanted to was allowed to partake of a glass of Johannisberg Riesling from the V. Sattui Winery in St. Helena, California.

Jim enjoyed the wine much more than before, and he realized that he had acquired a taste for this particular 2004 Dry Johannisberg Riesling. It was a light, delicate, and slightly sweet wine, with a flower-scented bouquet, and peachy, even melon flavors, filled the mouth before its distinctive acidity took hold, finishing pure and smooth. He put his glass down with a sigh of pleasure.

When the meal was finished, Jim announced a briefing following breakfast the next morning. People filed out, but few went to bed quickly. Most of them took another dip in the waters, and some even went up to the observation deck and sat on deck chairs, talking quietly, watching the stars. Jim took full advantage of the stars and observation deck, finding a private corner to snuggle with Cecilia.

In the morning, the briefing defined their search. Some of the men groaned, because searches took time, and the monotony of the routine took its toll. However, when everyone knew what the plan was, the crew went to work with a will, and the search began.

Zeke and Cecilia were convinced the ship was somewhere east of the Bahamas, but close to the islands. There followed some pointed discussion on what such a vessel was doing in that particular location with an impending hurricane bearing down on them. Several reasons were proposed, but none seemed to satisfy the crew. Because they knew that Rook and Jacks were somehow involved, Jim was convinced the reason would not be discovered until they found the wreck. Even then they might never know the answers to those questions. He hoped sincerely that they would find the evidence they needed, but knew that sometimes, especially in shipwrecks, it just wasn't possible.

They began their search off the southern tip of Great Inagua and would later laugh about that decision. It would turn out that they placed the wreck in the exact center of their grid, in the last grid quadrant to be searched. They had no way of knowing other than to follow the plan, day after day, searching, finding sunken ships, checking them out, and moving on. Despite the constant drudgery and disappointment of such searches, the men maintained positive attitudes and high standards.

Dragging two underwater cameras, or HROVs, and a third device that could penetrate beneath the ocean floor, reading mineral deposits, they began the search, mowing the yard as they referred to the pattern followed. Often, they would stop and send divers down, or the submersible, to determine if the reading was indeed their ship. Time after time, they were disappointed after hours of work to uncover the name of another vessel. Even more frustrating was the fact that each of the vessels discovered was of little value other than accurately charting where they lay.

Sixty days passed without positive results. Daily the submersible went down to look at a ship, and twice they found historic relics at the bottom of the ocean, one with a rotted chest of gold. The gold would pay for the sixty days of finding nothing. On a ship those days could pass very slowly, except that this crew learned some secrets to keeping the doldrums at bay. There were always those who were adept at bringing laughter at just the right time, providing comic relief. Bible studies in the morning before getting to work and games in the evening made for interesting and exciting moments away from the daily grind. At no time did discipline slip, to Jim's satisfaction.

Two of the yachts they discovered at the bottom of the ocean rewarded them with safes. In one safe, they found nearly five thousand dollars in gold coin and in another, in a watertight container, a collection of stamps valued at nearly three hundred thousand dollars. There were jets, planes, naval vessels, and private vessels littering the bottom of the ocean. Each of these provided moments of exciting discovery, and one of the planes indicated that the pilot had crashed into a rogue wave, the only explanation for the state of the plane and cockpit.

Sixty days passed as they continued the routine of searching, and Jim was pleased to see that morale still ran high. Abe and Sturdy were experts in keeping the crew focused and happy. The crew was involved in a "Hearts" contest to see which team won the cup for having the best run of luck with the cards. Spades and a Rook tournament had already been decided. Jim and Cecilia won the Rook tournament while Millie and Sharky won the Spades contest.

Cuss and Windy won the Scrabble tournament. Jim was amazed at how Windy's influence on Cuss had changed the man. He was well on his way to finishing every book in the library, and under the guidance of his friends, had completed his GED and achieved an AA from an online college course. Physically he was stronger and faster than ever before, and Jim could tell the man was content and motivated. He had, in the time he spent on the ship, become an important member of the team, willing to turn his hand to anything.

Mark took the prize in the chess tournament, defeating Jim in a game that saw every piece taken off the board except for two. Mark had a knight and king, and Jim had a bishop and king, finally finding himself trapped in a checkmate. A good loser, Jim smiled at Mark, slapped his shoulder, and congratulated him. Most of the men on his team understood that in games there was always a winner and a loser. As long as they had fun, it didn't matter, and Jim had enjoyed the game and the challenge.

Every night there was something happening to keep everyone sharp. Along with those activities, the kitchen provided special treats, unusual and delicious. The drudgery of mowing the yard day after day faded in the evenings, and by morning everyone was in a better frame of mind to face the challenges of this new day. On the ocean, no two days were every the same, despite the repetition that came with the job of searching.

On the sixty-ninth day, they were half a mile from where they were first anchored when the search began and Zeke took a reading of two steel vessels in a narrow trench, one on top of the other. Had the third HROV not been in use, they would have missed the signature, because at that particular spot, part of the trench had caved in, leaving the ships in a tunnel. Jim ordered the anchor dropped and the submersible made ready for descent.

FM, Driver, and Sparks went through a complete check of the submersible before giving the signal that it could be lifted and dropped in the water. Dorf and Mark were in the water to receive the craft and make sure all the lines were properly attached before sending it down. Master Chief Warner was on the winch. In minutes the *Steel Crab* was in the water. Dorf and Mark checked the lines and waved the okay.

Cable played out as the craft sank beneath the surface. FM watched as they descended, amazed at the clarity of the waters here. Even in the trench they could see despite the overhanging rocks. He began to get excited. The outline of the ship beneath them matched that of the *Estelle*. Jack Boswell brought them right up to the bow, where they could read her name. FM used the mechanical arm to blow water against the side, uncovering the name, letter by letter. When he was finished, he sat back and began to chuckle.

"You ain't gonna believe this, boss!" he said into his headset. "We found her!"

"Can you believe we were almost sitting on top of her sixty-nine days ago?" Sparks commented. "She's sitting in the exact center of our grid search map! We found her!" He grinned and gave FM a high five.

"Well, your brother's gonna be harder to live with!" FM sighed. "He's the one who designed the search grid!"

"Uncle Zeke is watching!" Zeke said into his headset.

"We need an ignore button for certain personnel!" Driver said with a grin.

Dr. Persons, who had joined them once more at the beginning of the search, was ecstatic. Jim smiled as the man went through the various emotions of this type of discovery. He was hugged, slapped on the back, and then watched as tears ran down the good doctor's face.

"What kind of shape is she in?" Jim asked, handing Dr. Persons a Kleenex.

"Uh, boss, she went down with a submarine caught in her teeth!" FM announced, his voice suddenly tight.

"Say again!" Jim replied.

"It's a Russian diesel sub. I'm guessing they collided in the storm somehow, and when her seams burst, she floundered and went down in heavy seas. Two of her stacks are broken off, like she rolled under,"

Driver said, looking over the wreck with a critical eye. "The anchor from the ship is sitting on top of the escape hatch of the sub. I think the crew was trapped and couldn't escape. It's possible that a rogue wave took them both down, boss."

"If she was already heavy and rolled, no wonder nobody made it off the boat. She would have gone down fast!" FM said, studying the wreck.

"Roger that!" Jim said quickly. "We're going to register this as our find and claim the salvage rights. Bring the *Steel Crab* up for the *Diver's Can*," Jim ordered.

The *Diver's Can* was a diving chamber for saturation diving, allowing divers to work at depths for longer periods of time without decompressing. Jim pressed his speaker button again.

"John, I want your team in the can first, please," he commanded. "Be careful with that sub!"

"On it, Shep," John replied quickly. He'd been expecting the assignment and grinned at his brother before heading down to get ready.

The diving chamber was large enough to house six divers, but Jim had it modified for four to give the divers more room. At that depth, they would need plenty of rest and warmth before going out on dives again. From the bridge, Jim watched John, Wade, C. G., and Vince load their gear and then climb into the can and close the outer hatch. It would take twenty-four hours for the tank to pressurize for the depth and the mixture of air to adjust for the divers to survive. Master Chief Warner checked the hatch to be sure it was sealed properly before checking all the valves.

On the following day, RC was on the crane. Master Chief Warner claimed he was a natural at the controls. The chamber lifted gently, then swung over the side. RC seemed to love the work as he lowered the chamber into the water with hardly a splash. His hands moved over the controls with a deftness few men could master. Dorf and Mark were in the water to attach the lines to the chamber. Dorf attached them, and Mark checked them. It was routine, but Jim noted that each man took care in his work. The lives of their teammates depended on their ability to do it right. Again, attention to detail and daily practice showed results as the men worked through the familiar routine.

Dr. Persons now hovered over Zeke and Cecilia in the CIC, watching monitors that would show the work below. Zeke was thankful that the good doctor wasn't a pacer. He stood, or sat, watching, too excited to do anything else. Cecilia smiled at Zeke. They were excited too.

Searching for a lost vessel may take months of monotony and routine, but it was worth it. Finding a sunken ship was like stumbling upon a piece of history. An arrowhead in a field, a cannonball in the middle of the high desert, a ghost town hidden in a desolate, uninhabited place—these were pieces of history. Each of them told a story, and only those who saw the actual piece, in its place, could determine the facts accurately.

In the dive chamber, John, Wade, C. G., and Vince discussed what they might find. They were anxious to get on the ship and discover its secrets. The *Steel Crab* set up the cradle on the ocean floor and guided the chamber to rest securely. Once the divers were out, they attached heavy straps to keep the chamber in place. The current was slow here, but they took the precaution anyway.

On their first excursion to the ship and sub, they photographed everything for evidentiary purposes. While they rested and warmed up, FM manipulated the tools on the *Steel Crab* to cut an access through the stern of the ship and to open one of the central hatches. Using the high-pressure blower, he cleaned most of the debris off the deck around the hatch and off the stern section where an access had been opened.

The last thing the sub did was attach the cable from the crane on *Bring It Up Coral* to the heavy anchor. RC, at the controls of the crane, followed directions and lifted the anchor up, moved it over to the side, and then lowered it gently to the ocean floor. Tiffany wandered into the CIC and took a chair quietly off to one side. Wade was down there, and she considered him a good friend. As she had no other duties, she accepted Cecilia's invitation to the CIC. Cecilia glanced over at her and smiled a welcome, and Zeke nodded once to her. Pen came in a few minutes later. John too was down there. Smiling to herself, Cecilia went back to work on her console.

"Divers are coming out again, FM," Sparks said from his perch in the submersible.

CHAPTER 25

"**H**ey, JR, we got the anchor off the escape hatch of the sub, and we also got the top hatch of the *Estelle* cleaned off and an access in through the stern. If you can't get down to the lower parts of this wreck, you can use the stern access." FM let go of the talk button on his headset.

"Roger that, FM. We'll go in the sub first," John replied. "Once we've searched that, we'll go in the top hatch of the *Estelle* if we have any dive time left."

Driver kept the submersible hovering to provide light for the divers. They had powerful lights hanging from their utility belts, but they did not need them yet. He watched as John secured a lifeline and then seemed to dive into the open hatch area. Wade checked the knot before following. C. G. followed and then Vince. Each man checked that knot before going below. If anything happened, they could use the line to pull themselves out.

"Jarheads!" FM snorted. "You all have your fins on the wrong feet!" People listening on the ship laughed at the familiar joke.

"What's a jarhead?" Tiffany asked.

"A marine. It's the way they cut their hair," Zeke answered without looking up from his work.

"I thought you were all part of the navy," Tiffany said.

"We're the navy's chief weapons," Wade said into his mask mic. "The ducks you're with just waddle around and transport us where we need to go."

"When you get up here, I'll disabuse you of that notion," Mark said into his headset with a grin.

"Marines call navy men ducks?" Tiffany asked.

"We're always on the water. And we all walk different. Hence, the name!" Zeke answered. His hands were busy on a keyboard, enhancing the video feed coming back to the vessel. "If they want to be rude, they call us squids."

"Can you supply some power to us? I think we can clear this part of the sub. It's dry in the next chamber." John's voice came through with a tinny mechanical tone. He'd been tapping on the inner hatch with a wrench.

"We're dropping an auxiliary power line now," Jim replied as he watched a group of men open a locker, haul out the heavy rubber-coated extension cord. Two of the cords were attached and a rubber sleeve tightened to keep the connection from coming apart.

FM grabbed the line and fed it to Wade, who was now working at a panel outside the sub. Once he had the line connected, he entered the escape hatch again, pulled it closed, and latched it. Moments later, bubbles appeared as water was vented from chamber. Slowly, after a long time beneath the surface, the sub came to life as the auxiliary power brought the systems online. Vents came to life, but there was no oxygen in the tanks to provide oxygen for the sub. The divers removed their fins and looked at each other with sick expressions. Running out of oxygen was the last thing those men would register in the sub, if any were still alive.

"We've entered the sub," John's voice spoke, though everyone watching the video could see. It was a grisly scene. Mummified bodies lay in the bunks of the crew quarters, where men had chosen to die, lying in their beds. Some of them succumbed to starvation before the oxygen ran out. Either way, it was a horrible way to die. There was something macabre in the arrangement of the bodies and how the men chose to breathe their last.

In the captain's cabin, the captain died in a sitting position on his bunk. In his mummified hands lay the ship's log. John gently removed it, put it in a waterproof bag, and moved on.

"We're out of time and have to return to the *Can*. We're going out the main hatch," Wade said.

Those above who had been watching the video feed saw them climb carefully into the tower, close the hatch, and blow the air from the upper area, finally opening the hatch and making their way back to the *Can* after putting their fins on once more.

"What do you want us to do with the sub, boss?" FM asked as the divers entered the *Can*.

"We'll pull it free of the wreckage and flood it and leave it on the ocean floor," Jim said after a moment of thought. "I didn't include the sub in the salvage rights, and I don't think anyone knows it's there," he explained.

"Not likely. Did you notice that the communication antennae assembly is completely gone? That might explain how the *Estelle* ended up eating the sub," Driver said. "If they hit and the sub pushed her bows over, a good wave could have rolled them under!"

"We can find out some answers by reading this log," John said, as the men huddled around the table in thermal blankets eating a hot meal. "Zeke, can you use the *Can* cameras to zoom in on the pages?" He spread them out on a table, and his team gathered around him to read as he turned the pages. The writing was Russian, but John and Wade could both translate for the others.

"Set it in the center of your table," Zeke said, his fingers moving over the keyboard and then moving a stick that controlled the camera he was accessing. The pages of the log came into view and filled the screen. "I'll have the computer translate as we go, recording each page in two columns, one in Russian, one in English. We might have to get someone to translate the English," Zeke added with a grin.

"I can read American. I'm not sure about English," Dorf added to the fun.

"I'm recording. I'll let Jim tell us when to turn the pages," Zeke said, chuckling.

No one hurried through the reading, and Jim spoke to John directly when it was time to turn a page. John read the Russian text and translated for everyone listening. Cecilia read along with the men, even though she couldn't read Russian, following the tale, unraveling the mystery of why these two boats were tangled together and who was behind the tragedy. Two hours later, they turned the last page. In the CIC, there was a grim silence. Finally, Jim cleared his throat.

"John, please take your crew into the *Estelle*, get into that vault, and put everything in the smaller nets. We'll bring it up with the tanks and load everything on the chopper. The chopper will bury the evidence on our new property, replenish the tanks, and return. No one will be the wiser. Be careful!"

"Roger that, bro," John replied.

"'Bro'? Is that any way to address your captain?" FM's voice quipped.

"The brotha just tryin' to be like me!" Loony responded without hesitation. Everyone burst out laughing. Jim felt the tension leave the group and appreciated once more the apt humor and comedy relief his crewmen often provided. Laughing into his mask, John led his men to the upper hatch of the ship and down into the belly of the sunken vessel.

"We've reached the main passageway. We're going up to the bridge first," John said.

"Roger that," FM replied.

Everyone knew that inside a sunken ship there were dangers. The silence that followed as the four divers made their way to the bridge was almost palpable. Many watched as the cameras mounted on the divers' masks recorded their progress. When they reached the door to the bridge, it hung on one hinge, and huge pieces of the opposite wall had been torn out as the door slammed into that wall. It was mute testimony of a violent demise. Wade wrestled the door out of the wall and let it hang open.

Human bones were scattered on the floor, and Cecilia counted three skulls. They were close together, having rolled to the lowest point, two facing away, one facing in. John was brushing away silt, filling the air so that everything looked fuzzy in the picture. He lifted a book from the table.

"I have the log," he announced. "We're heading for the captain's cabin now."

"Hey, JR!" FM said suddenly. "You have three reef sharks coming in above you!"

Wade turned as the first shark pushed its way into the bridge through a broken window. He lifted his shark rod, but the fish merely circled above them. As they left the bridge, Wade wedged the door into the wall again so the sharks could not follow. Tiffany, who had been sitting on the edge of her chair, sighed and began breathing again. She had no way of knowing that sharks rarely attacked divers. To her, watching, the danger had seemed very real and very close. Dr. Persons noticed and talked to her about the instruments of the old ship, taking her mind off the danger.

In the captain's cabin, they gathered what they could and headed back to the *Can*. From the cameras in the diving bay, Cecilia could see the men clearly. None of them exhibited signs of being too cold. In swim shorts, they went through the hatch into the living quarters, and Zeke switched to those cameras. Only slightly blue lips spoke of the cold down there.

Behind a curtain, the men changed into dry, warm clothes and then began to go through the materials they took from the ship. This was done in saltwater tanks set up especially for the task. Pages were opened, photographed, and then turned. Zeke, working at his computer, was able to reproduce most of the pages in legible type, despite the faded print on the pages.

Dr. Persons and Jim pored over the pages like two boys who found what they thought was a real treasure map. Cecilia smiled watching them. This was the exciting part of salvaging a lost ship. Jim loved the discovery process and the history. Both men scribbled notes and compared their thoughts quietly as they read, shoulders touching, heads moving to read and write.

As the story unfolded, though, Cecilia took note of a subtle change in her husband. Without reading the text, she knew the story of the *Estelle* was an ugly one. Jim's eyes were stormy green now, like thunderclouds, threatening an eruption at any moment. Even Dr. Persons grew quiet as they read.

"I'm guessing from the silence up there we're on the same pages," John's voice came over the headsets. "Admiral Runion is going to come unglued with this one!" he added. "Rook was in on this from the beginning! So was Jacks!"

"I'd say he was just being a good Communist!" Vince snorted in anger. "He and his pal and a governor who later became president!"

"Hey! I'm a Democrat! I voted for the guy!" Master Chief Warner injected into the conversation.

"Not after you read this garbage, TRT," Vince said with confidence.

"Let's keep politics out of this and just stick to the facts. Not all Democrats are dedicated Communists. Apparently just the ones who made it into high office," Jim said cryptically. "I see now why Rook wanted this kept quiet! We're in real danger!" he added. His mind went to the danger, and he hoped that he and his men would be able to meet whatever danger came with honor. He sighed.

"Rook wants it kept quiet because it exposes one of our presidents in the worst possible light, not to mention himself!" Wade said. "We'd better prepare for the worst, Shep!" he added after a moment of silence.

"Noted," Jim replied. Being prepared for the worst didn't always mean things didn't get very bad. He sighed again.

John and his team returned to the ship for another sortie into its secrets. Driver and his team remained close in the submersible. Working together, they were able to clear away enough debris to allow the divers access to most of the ship. On the third day of diving, they reached the vault.

Using coretex and PE4 designed for underwater demolitions, they placed charges on the huge vault door and then ran the coretex up and out of the ship. Wade fastened the timer on the detonation cord, and the divers made their way into the can. Underwater blasts were very dangerous. The ship would cushion them from most of the energy from the blast.

Coretex burns at about 6,100 meters per second, or about 20,000 feet per second. When the timer went off and flashed, the explosion seemed simultaneous. Everyone heard the blast and the bang of the metal against metal as the door came away from its hinges. In the *Can*, the aftermath was a gentle shaking from the sound waves. Each of the divers had their ears carefully protected against the loud bang. In the *Steel Crab*, the men rode the sound waves for a moment like men on a bucking bronco. They also had their ears carefully protected. Sound, beneath the waves, could kill or maim, and they all knew it. Everyone breathed a little easier when the sound waves passed.

Driver moved closer once the silt began to settle and looked critically at the ship. Nothing appeared seriously damaged above the deck. He watched as John and his team exited the *Can* and swam steadily to the ship. Their powerful dive lights barely penetrated the cloud of silt when they went in.

On the surface, silence hung over the ship for nearly fifteen minutes before John's voice came over the headset. "The records didn't lie," John said clearly. "This vault is more of a gemstone showroom than a vault. We're transferring the stones to the nylon bags now, Shep. It will probably take us two or three dives to get them all. There's a fortune down here!"

Above the surface, all but one man cheered. On the observation deck, DC waited till the noise died down to make his report. "Captain, we have a new shadow."

"What heading?" Jim asked.

"East by south, about one hundred and four degrees," DC replied.

Jim ran up to the observation deck and took the glasses to look over the boat shadowing them. It was a luxury yacht. Two men sat on the rear deck with poles that looked like fishing poles but were actually listening devices. He could identify them clearly. When they saw Jim looking, they got up, put their poles on the deck, and went inside. It wasn't a very convincing act, and Jim didn't buy it. He began to play through his mind the various options open to him and settled for just keeping watch.

"Send the launch over to warn them to keep at least a thousand yards from our position. Explain that we have radar and sonar equipment that will tell us if they enter that area. If they do, we will consider them pirates seeking to steal our find. Mark, take Dorf, Bear, and Sturdy to make your point!" Jim smiled.

"Those devices won't work at a thousand yards," DC said. He had not missed the listening devices on the end of the fishing poles. "They probably have something in the water too. I imagine our bow thrusters are keeping that useless."

Mark was quick to get his three "goons" in the HSB. He was the only one wearing a uniform. Dorf, Bear, and Sturdy all wore jeans and a T-shirt, well stained by their work. As his boat pulled alongside, a Russian appeared. Mark recognized him immediately. It was Rustin's lieutenant. Knowing he was dealing with a professional, Mark began talking in English.

Although the man spoke English, he waved Mark off and spoke in Russian. He was surprised to hear Mark reply in that language. Even more so, Mark sounded like he came from Moscow, his accent perfect, and it made him pause for thought.

"You are trespassing on a salvage site. We have logged our find and registered it. Keep your boat a thousand yards distance or we will consider you a pirate threat and act accordingly!" Mark ordered.

Kovac looked at the three men in the boat, their arms folded in front of their massive chests, stained with sweat and dirt from their work. He smiled and nodded and apologized for getting close to their site and promised to keep his distance. Before he could give the orders to move the boat, Mark reached under the dash and pulled out a full bottle of vodka.

"We will drink to that agreement!" Mark said. He poured two shot glasses of vodka.

He took his glass and passed the other glass to Kovac, who raised his eyebrows and drank it in tandem with Mark. Mark put the cap back on the bottle, stowed it away under the dash, and reached out for the other glass. Kovac wiped it carefully with a kerchief he pulled from a pocket and handed it to Mark, wrapped in the kerchief. Mark nodded once to Kovac, pulling the HSB away and heading back to their ship.

"Thank you, Comrade Kovac," Mark said in Russian. Kovac scowled at the smile on Mark's face. He hadn't needed fingerprints to identify him! That made these men dangerous. Mark winked at him, deepening the scowl, and headed back to the tug.

Jim, who watched the entire episode from the observation deck, smiled. Russians who agreed always drank vodka to seal their agreement. Mark forced Kovac into keeping his boat a thousand yards away or losing face with another Russian. It was a brilliant performance, and Jim swelled with pride once more in leading such men.

"Smitty, if that boat comes within an inch of breaking the thousand yards, give him a blast of our air horns as a warning," Jim ordered.

"Roger that, Shep," Smitty replied.

Jim knew that it would only be a matter of time before the yacht was allowed to drift too close to the thousand-yard restraint. Ninety minutes later, the air horns startled everyone as they blasted out a three-time warning. From inside the bridge, where he could not be observed, Jim chuckled as Kovac stomped across the deck, cursing and waving his fists, but the yacht backed away.

"Shep," Smitty was speaking. "We have another hurricane building in the south."

"Yo-ho-ho! Around again we go!" Andrea said. His face was alight with anticipation, and Jim grinned at him in response.

"Will we have time to bring the dive chamber and submersible up before it gets rough?" Jim asked, smiling at Andrea's quip.

"It'll be close, but we should be able to. It depends on how quick those lazy so-and-so divers get the job done!" Smitty replied.

There was the sound of a loud snore in the headsets. Jim laughed.

Two days later, in the early morning, the bags were attached to a line and hauled to the surface. This was done on the opposite side of the ship, away from the shadowing yacht, and with absolutely no fanfare. One man operated the winch, and the other lifted the bags to the dive platform. They were carefully settled in a steel cage full of used nitrogen and oxygen tanks. This was lifted and loaded into the helicopter. It was normal procedure for refilling used tanks for the dive and other jobs.

Kovac watched the cage being lifted into the helicopter and saw what it contained. He looked at his men. "They're sending the chopper for more nitrogen and oxygen. They must be planning on staying down longer."

Zeke listened to his voice as he spoke. Unknown to those on the yacht, listening devices had been placed in strategic locations on the boat during the first night it rested at anchor. Phones were also easily accessed by Zeke's equipment, especially at sea. A conversation with Rustin told them much. Jim was able to plan accordingly because of that information, and he once again thought of how valuable Zeke and his equipment was to the mission.

Mark, Dorf, Pen, and the Dodge team flew the chopper away. First, the chopper landed on the island property now owned by Jim and Cecilia near Rum Cay Island. Carefully and as quickly as possible, they buried six large steel boxes containing the gemstones and other evidence. Using the helicopter as a crane, they lifted a huge boulder over the treasure. Then they flew on to New Bight to meet the British destroyer and exchange tanks, dropping Pen on the destroyer to make her way to England and oversee working through the Russian connection evidence.

Kovac expected them to fly all the way to Nassau. They wanted to make sure he didn't suspect that anything else took place on that trip. Timing it carefully, Dorf returned the chopper to the ship. Kovac, aware of the flight and landing, checked his watch and nodded. So far nothing had come up from the ship, but the storm meant he could not stay and watch further.

With the threat of the oncoming hurricane, the luxury yacht pulled anchor and made for safe port. Jim watched it move away. It wouldn't be divers from that boat that would try to sneak on board and steal the documents and gems. Sighing, he moved to help his crew get ready for the storm.

CHAPTER 26

John and his team needed forty-eight hours to decompress, which would bring them up just before the storm. Master Chief Warner brought the *Can* up in stages until on the second day, as the sky began building toward the storm, activity on the ship became evident. The *Diver's Can* was lifted on board first and then the submersible. These were lashed down in preparation for the storm. Everyone worked together to dismantle the crane and derrick and stow everything properly.

As they finished the last task, the storm broke in fury around them. Jim, Dorf, and Mark were the last three to stagger into the wet room. Laughing together, they moved to their lockers, stripped off their waterproof gear, and hung it to dry. As they headed into the interior of the ship, Jim pressed his talk button.

"Who's got the helm?" he asked.

"Beer Bottle has it," John's voice came back.

"Oh boy! We're in trouble. Got a jarhead at the helm!" FM quipped.

"Hang on, boys! This is gonna be fun!" Wade said into his headset. He gave a rebel yell, and Jim almost fell as the ship turned a little faster than normal. "We take the waves sideways, right, Shep?" Wade added. Jim could hear the laughter in his voice.

At that moment, the boat heeled sharply, then righted. "Oops! Guess not!" Wade said.

Jim knew he was turning the ship into the storm and smiled as the banter continued for a few minutes. Moving with the ship, he made his way to his office. Sharky had everything ready for the storm. He was locking the last drawer on his own desk when Jim came in.

"Good work, Lieutenant," Jim said with a smile and a wave. He headed up toward the CIC. Cecilia was strapped into her seat across the room from Zeke. Jim kissed her, clapped Zeke on the shoulder, and went into the compass bridge. Smitty was there, his feet firmly planted, plotting the course of the storm. Jim marveled at the information available to his crew as he came to a stop.

"How long before they make the call?" he said into his headset when Jim entered.

"Shouldn't be long. They'll wait a bit, let the storm get past," Jim replied.

"Distress call!" Zeke's voice came in urgently. "Small cruise ship east of Mayaguana Island. One stabilizer damaged, listing heavily, taking on water. Two hundred and ninety people on board, including crew."

"ETA!" Jim said into his headset. Smitty grinned at him, beginning the calculations. Jim watched his face and read the answer.

"Seven, eight hours, Shep," Smitty said.

"What's the heading, Zeke?" Jim asked.

"159.37 degrees south by southeast," Zeke replied.

"Roger that. Wade, turn to 123.75 degrees southeast by east. Master Chief, give me everything this baby has!" Jim said.

"Turning to 123.75 degrees southeast by east, Captain," Wade replied.

"Full power, boss," Master Chief Warner added.

"That's a dangerous course, Jim," Smitty said, looking at his charts. "We're going to quarter the worst of this storm until we intercept the cruise liner."

"It will also get us to her fastest," he replied. "Warn the crew," he added unnecessarily as Smitty was already pushing the Klaxon one long and two short blasts. The crew knew what that meant. Everyone prepared to be tossed around, despite their best efforts to protect themselves.

After an hour, Wade handed the helm over to John, staggered outside the bridge into the storm on the leeward side, and vomited. He was soaked before he turned around to come back in. Wiping his mouth, he nodded to everyone and headed down to check on Tiffany. She would be terrified in this weather.

He found her in the observation room, strapped into a seat, her face set. She wasn't even seasick! Rosa sat next to her with Cecilia on the other side. Just then the ship rolled, and Wade's feet slipped out from beneath him, and he slid down. He caught himself on the leg of a chair and held on, then righted himself and strapped himself in. Tiffany was laughing at him. Blushing, he finished that task and looked at the three women.

"Why are you so wet?" Rosa asked.

"Lost breakfast," he admitted. "Right after I handed over the wheel."

"It's the helm, jarhead!" FM said with a nasty grin. He was seated in a chair near the door. "Who is at the helm now?" he added.

"JR has the helm," Wade said, reclining his chair with a weary sigh. Just at that moment, John's voice came over the headsets.

"So…uh…where are the turn signals again?" he quipped.

The hours passed quickly as the crew fought the storm. Jim had the helm for his second turn when the cruise ship appeared on their radar. Regular ten-minute updates came in, and the crew and passengers on the damaged ship were becoming desperate. Jim breathed a sigh of relief. It had been a close race against time, and once again God had provided the time necessary to come to the aid of others.

"Rescue crews at the ready!" he ordered. "She's listing starboard, so we're going to hook up on that side and use chutes to evacuate. Dorf, watch the timing on the drops."

They were well through the worst of the storm, but the water was still roiling from the storm. Jim maneuvered his ship expertly alongside the cruise ship, and his crew quickly attached lines to the crippled vessel. Chutes were deployed, much like the emergency chutes from an airliner, and people slid down to the deck of *Bring It Up Coral* into the arms of waiting crew members. With the rough waves, it was a tricky maneuver, but no one was tossed over the side between the ships.

The injured came first, and these were gently led or carried into the sick bay. Doc and Ox were ready to receive them. Others were taken up to the observation deck, now empty of all crew members, or down to the dining room. Crowding into the rooms, the two hundred and ninety passengers and crew made the best of the accommodations.

Pumps from *Bring It Up Coral* soon turned the tide, and a temporary repair was done on the seam that was leaking. Towing the cruise ship through the first six hours was tricky in the aftermath of the storm. Those at the helm fought unusual currents and sudden wind shifts as the two boats made their way to New Bight on Cat Island. Twelve hours later, in calm seas and sunshine, *Bring It Up Coral* towed the damaged cruise liner into the harbor while the crew and passengers cheered from the observation deck and rear deck. Jim was sure some of them were cheering because they would finally have their feet on dry ground and no longer be sick.

Jim watched Lieutenant Finn conduct the insurance agent from Lloyds on deck and down to the office. With a sigh, he headed down to sign papers. The money for the rescue and salvage would be automatically deposited in their bank in London. Because they were in port, everyone wore their dress uniforms, and Jim smiled as he walked through the ship. His men looked impressive.

Rosa was walking down the corridor to join Andrea, and Jim hugged her as they passed in the corridor outside his office. It was good to have her on board again, and he knew Andrea had missed his friend and possible fiancée in the past days. He hoped that soon the two would be married.

Eventually the festivities came to an end, and they put out to sea again and began the arduous task of making everything shipshape. Purposely Jim brought them to anchor beside the Dominion Venture, where students from Old Dominion Center for Coastal Physical Oceanography continued their studies on the reef. Their shadow was back, keeping its distance.

All day men went back and forth. Some returned and headed down into the war room. By the end of the day, Teams Red, Blue, and Zulu were in the war room with Rosa, Tiffany, Cecilia, Doc, and Millie. Risky the plan might be, but it was sure to succeed, even though it left the crew shorthanded. Slowly activity stopped, and the men in the yacht watched the final crew members of *Bring It Up Coral* return. When all was ready, Jim took the ship back toward the site of the *Estelle*.

An hour later, the call came. A ship was in distress near Cuban waters and adrift. Jim responded, and Andrea took the helm. No sooner had they entered Cuban national waters than three Cuban destroyers bore down on them. Sirens sounded, and horns blew. Andrea drew the ship to a stop and dropped anchor. The trap had been sprung, and they were now in great danger. Jim sighed heavily, squared his shoulders, and prepared for the worst.

Twenty Cuban soldiers poured onto *Bring It Up Coral*, rounded everyone up, and then kept them under guard on the inside observation deck while they searched the vessel. Once they were satisfied no one else was on board and there were no weapons available to the crew, they departed. The next group to arrive was Rustin's crew.

Rustin had half a dozen men in the room with him, all armed and pointing their guns, and he walked up to Captain Shepherd with a smile on his face. Jim studied the man as he approached, and he decided that whenever Rustin thought he had the upper hand, he would be smiling.

Rustin was tall, two or three inches taller than Jim, and in excellent physical condition. His eyes were hard agates in his face, devoid of emotion, empty and void. They were the eyes of a man who no longer believed in any law but his own. He was a killer.

In this man, there was only cruelty and the lust for power, and Jim knew immediately that he would never be satiated, never realize satisfaction, for he wanted the power of a god, and his mortality would always limit him. That made him doubly dangerous. Pondering the sociopathic disease of such men, Jim merely watched and waited. This would have to play out moment by moment, until the time came for Jim to act. Steeling himself for anything to come, he waited.

Rustin, on his part, studied the crew as he approached. There were twenty-three. He'd been told there were more but was assured all had been gathered. There needed to be an object lesson to show that he was in charge. Rustin chose Windy as he approached. The man was older, not in as good physical condition as the three men standing around him, and he was looking at Rustin as if he knew every shortcoming in the Russian's life.

"I was told you had forty aboard your boat, some of them women," he said in excellent English as he came to a stop in front of Jim. Looking at Jim for only a moment, he moved over to where he could grasp Windy.

"Half my crew is on leave at the moment," Jim lied easily. "They stayed on the *Dominion Venture* to enjoy some reef diving."

Rustin thought about that and decided it must be true. He smiled. "My men are searching your vessel now for the gems and papers you removed from the *Estelle*." He watched Jim closely. Jim's face was impossible to read, but Rustin was positive there was a smile behind those green eyes somewhere. It made him very nervous, though he refused to believe that of himself. Reminding himself that he was in control and he had the guns only intensified his unease. The Russian would never admit that there was an aura of danger emanating from the captain.

"You're a little ahead of the game," Jim said. "We found the *Estelle*, but the storm came up before we could lift the vault free of the wreckage."

"Why didn't you just blow the vault?" Rustin asked.

"We blew a lot of stuff down there getting to the vault, but the superstructure was damaged, and some beams fell in front of the door. We decided to pull the whole vault to expedite things. Then the storm came up," Jim replied. As an explanation, it was feasible.

Rustin's lieutenant had not reported that anything was recovered from the wreck.

"We shall see," Rustin said. He took a chair and waited. After an hour, he became impatient and used his radio to contact his searchers. After two hours, he became angry when the men reported they could find nothing. It was time for action.

He rose and suddenly grasped Windy, hauling him away from his friends, no one daring to move because two other guards had their guns pointed at the group. Bob Stankus was having none of that. He moved fast, hitting Rustin's arm so that Rustin was forced to drop his hold on Windy.

In that moment of time, Jim saw what was happening and realized with a sinking feeling that there was nothing he could do, no action that would be quick enough to save his friend, no words that would be sage enough to turn Rustin from his purpose. Jim was both proud of Bob, and frustrated that he'd moved too soon, that he didn't have the experience to know when to wait. But Windy was his friend, and Jim understood completely. Bob Stankus had purpose in his movements, and deep courage.

Everyone on the crew remained still, powerless to stop the inevitable, aware of the horror that was about to take place, and many of them breathed a prayer. They watched the gun move, saw in Rustin's eyes the decision, witnessed the coldhearted monster that rose to the surface, the pure joy in killing as he pulled the trigger. Yet even as he did so, Rustin realized that something had suddenly gone wrong, and he felt the second stirrings of unease.

A shot rang out, and Bob reeled back, fell, and died. There was, as always in situations like this, a moment when time seemed to stop. Seconds seemed to pass as the stunned silence settled over the room like an invisible blanket. Rustin felt the change of atmosphere in the room, and for the first time in his life, he felt the stirrings of something deep within, something alien, and fear mushroomed into a tangible thing. He couldn't understand why, and it frustrated him.

"God no!" Windy cried, crawling to his friend. "Oh God no!"

Abe and Sturdy knelt beside them, weeping. Gently Windy put

Bob's head in his lap and smoothed the hair from his forehead. Sturdy closed his eyes, his giant body racked with sobbing. Windy looked up through his tears and saw Jim looking down at the body of his fallen friend. What he saw in Jim's eyes told him that this death would not go unpunished. In that instant of time, he could almost smell fresh dirt beside an empty grave, dark and cold. He bowed his head and wept for his friend. Rustin felt it too, saw the resolve in the captain's eyes, and didn't like it.

"Congratulations, Rustin. You just shot a cook. I guess shooting unarmed, defenseless people is always fun for a coward like you," Jim said. With deceptive ease, he moved until he was between Rustin and any of his crew. "He was a good man and my friend. For that crime, I will personally kill you. Know this." There was no mistaking the implacable determination of those words.

Rustin almost recoiled from those stormy green eyes but recovered quickly. After all, he had the guns. He felt the fear rising again, and it made him angry.

"Perhaps. Everyone dies. But I do not think it will be you who kills me. Now tell me where you hid the gems and logbooks, or I will kill another."

"Better start with me," Jim said softly. "If you don't, I'll kill you before you shoot anyone else."

There was in that voice a resolve so strong, so sure, that it rose up like a wall of impenetrable steel. Rustin knew that Captain Shepherd was not bluffing. His face clouded. He knew the reputation of this man. Admitting to himself that he was afraid of this man was not easy. Bravado came back quickly, and with it shame and anger.

"Enough of this!" Rustin snapped. "Lock them all in the center hold!"

Jim remained close enough to kill Rustin while his crew passed. Sturdy had Bob's limp body in his arms, still weeping. The look he gave Rustin made the Russian shudder. And Rustin knew why Jim stayed so close. Keeping his gun trained on Jim didn't seem to faze the captain of *Bring It Up Coral*.

"Remember. I *will* kill you. Today is a good day for you to die,"

Jim promised when the crew had passed. His voice was even, no emotion allowed to enter that statement, only resolve. "You should kill me now." He paused at the hatch to give Rustin the chance, but Rustin wasn't ready for that yet. Angrily he motioned for Jim to proceed, fighting against the fear that rose up inside, ashamed and confused at the same time. There was no fear in Shepherd's eyes, nor in the eyes of the others, despite the guns pointed at them. He didn't like it at all.

Putting them in the center hold was a mistake. Rustin didn't know that. As the hatch was closed and locked down, RC and Bill Dodge pounded on the steel to cover the sound of the war room door opening. It was quiet enough it wouldn't be heard above that. They could hear the men above laughing.

"Keep laughing, punks! I'm coming for you!" Dodge whispered under his breath as he climbed down after RC.

Jim stood with the crew looking at him, waiting. There were things to do, and he was a man of action. He didn't wait.

"I want this man prepared for burial at sea. He will have full honors, and a 21-gun salute for his bravery and service," Jim said, wiping tears from his eyes as he gently touched Bob's cold dead hand. Suddenly his eyes grew hard and cold. "Gear up!" he ordered. "We're taking back our ship!"

Cecilia grabbed Jim's hand as he turned away, and he paused to look down at her. Her own eyes filled with tears quickly, and she held his hand tightly. He gently gathered her into his arms, stroked her back, and kissed her hair.

"I know what's in your heart, my love. Don't let your rage cloud your thinking!" she said through her sobbing.

Letting her go was hard. He tore himself away and suited up, checking his weapons. For the first time ever, the war room was silent as the men prepared to take back their ship. Jim knew why. There was killing to be done, and every member of Rustin's crew would be marked for instant death. One of their own had fallen at the hands of a coward, a noncombatant, and there would be hell to pay. When Jim was ready, he stood and made a circular motion with his finger so the men would know to gather around. Everyone gathered around, even those who were not part of this fighting unit.

"One of our own has been shot and killed. The unimaginable has happened. Bob was one of us, a true soldier at heart, and he was unarmed, protecting his friend. The man who shot him commands the crew that holds our ship. What say you to his sentence? What say you to the sentence of the other men of his crew?"

"Death!" every voice shouted as one.

Tiffany spoke with them, as did Rosa, their voices full of anger for such a heinous act.

"Anyone disagree?" Jim asked, waiting for a full thirty seconds until he knew there would be only silence. For once he felt no sadness at the sentence.

"Fall out and follow the plan!" Jim replied. He nodded once, checked his weapon one more time, and led his men through the hold to an emergency hatch that could not be seen from the bridge. "Close the war room!" he ordered.

CHAPTER 27

Above on the deck, the men heard the slight rumbling of the wheels as the door closed. Curious, they opened the hatch, as Jim knew they would. Wade was coiled like a spring and thrust the hatch up, standing straight on the last rung of the ladder, thrusting the men up and back while Jim slipped out of the emergency hatch and shot both guards with his silenced weapon.

Leaping out, Wade, John, C. G., and Vince crouched in the darkness, slipping their night vision gear down. Jim spotted another guard near the stern and dropped him silently, watching the body drop off the stern and listening for the splash. Zeke, FM, and Smitty leaped out of the hold, followed by the rest of the team. The hatch couldn't be seen from the bridge, all to their advantage, and as the deck lights were off, the main hatch was invisible too. Like shadows, they faded from view, spreading out as they moved through the superstructure of the ship. Unlike their enemies, they knew every inch of the ship.

Moving in the shadows like ghosts, they took each level, appearing out of the shadows to kill, disappearing again just as quickly and silently. When they had control of the CIC, Zeke talked the teams through the ship to take out the rest of Rustin's crew. It was a grisly scene as bodies fell to silenced automatics and knives. Not one sound alerted the leader of this cutthroat crew. While Zeke watched, he sent an email to Captain Jamison and one to Admiral Runion.

Rustin was seated at Sharky's desk, going through papers. So far, he had been completely frustrated in his search, and he felt he knew less about this crew than before. Jim nodded once to his team after a quick look. Zeke watched with a sense of satisfaction as the men came together.

They joined up with Zulu. John put his hand on Jim's shoulder once, and they moved down together. Jim explained his plan in whispers outside the offices. It was a daring plan, and fitting. Captain Shepherd's men nodded. Smitty moved off and at Jim's signal. banged the wall to Rustin's left. Rustin turned his head to the wall at the sound. When he looked back, five men in special forces gear stood in his office doorway, their guns pointed at him.

Slowly Rustin stood, his hands raised. "You move very quietly," he admitted. "What is an American SEAL team doing in Cuban waters?" He knew his radio was on and his crew would hear him. The fact that his crew may already be dead never entered his mind. Thinking perhaps they were a SEAL team that somehow slipped past the Cubans, he waited for his men to respond. Several seconds passed.

"More quietly than you think!" Jim said softly from behind Rustin. Blood drained from Rustin's face, and he looked over his shoulder into stormy green eyes hardened with resolve and saw there his impending death. It was like looking into an open grave, and he swore he could feel the cold penetrate his skin. "You killed my friend. He was unarmed. I made a promise. Today you die!"

Rustin turned all the way around, playing his last card. "You cannot shoot me! We are in enemy waters. If I do not report, the ships out there will blow your boat out of the water!" he spat.

Jim's shot took him low, in the belly, and for a moment Rustin stared with shock as he doubled over, his hands immediately covering the wound, warm blood spreading quickly. Slowly he sank to his knees and then with a groan, fell to his back, knees folded under him, his hands pressing tightly against the wound. Jim waited for several minutes for the shock to wear off and the pain to begin, and when it did, Rustin sucked in his breath and cried out. His hands shook, and he panted with the pain.

He looked up at the men gathered around them, all of them watching as if waiting. *What are they waiting for? Why don't they help me?* A scream of pain ripped from his lungs, and he begged for help. Shame mushroomed inside him as he felt the fear blossom, fear of death and over all that the mind-numbing pain! If anything, the hardness in the eyes of the men watching intensified as they watched.

I had control of this ship! I had the guns! How is this happening? What are they waiting for? Breathing became difficult, and then after a long time, impossible still to the Russian, slowly and painfully he died. Around his dead body, the men looked at one another and then turned away. Without looking back, Jim walked around the body and headed up to the bridge. When he arrived, Zeke was already talking to Captain Jamison.

"Roger that Captain, and thanks," Zeke said as Jim stepped into the CIC.

"What's going on?" Jim asked.

Zeke grinned. "Listen," he said. A horn blasted, and the whoop of a siren could be heard. Jim moved out of the CIC to look at the British destroyer and two other ships moving in at flank speed. One was an American aircraft carrier, and every jet was being scrambled into the air. Then the voice of Captain Jamison came over the radio.

"This is the British nuclear-powered guided missile cruiser *Bristol*. You have exactly ten minutes to move your ships away from the American vessel *Bring It Up Coral*. Failure to do so will be considered an act of piracy and dealt with summarily. Countdown begins now."

Jim looked out the window to see Jamison's vessel positioned so that her guns could be trained on all three Cuban destroyers. Then another whooping siren sounded, and he watched the two American ships, one a cruiser, the other the carrier, flanking the British ship. Both identified themselves and gave similar warnings. Within five minutes, the Cuban ships were departing.

"Take us out to international waters," Jim said.

"I have the helm," John replied. As the ship moved away from

Cuban waters, Jim went down and opened the war room. Abe, Sturdy, and Windy had prepared Bob's body for a burial at sea. Without comment, Jim removed his fighting gear, broke down and checked each weapon before putting it away, and put on his uniform. *I lost a man, a good man, one of my own! God help me.*

Cecilia waited until he was finished and taking his hand, walked toward the ladder. She climbed first, and when she stepped out of the hatch, she saw bodies being carried to the stern. There was blood on the deck under her feet. She turned and held out her hand for Jim, and together they went up to the bridge.

"Captain has the helm," Jim said, entering.

John nodded, turned over the wheel, and headed down to change. Jim picked up the radio microphone, adjusted the frequency, and contacted Captain Jamison.

"*Bristol One*, this is *Bring It Up SAR One*. Do you copy?" he said.

"Go ahead, Captain Shepherd. This is Captain Jamison." Jamison's voice sounded tinny coming out of the radio.

"Thank you for your assistance, Captain," Jim said. "We took one casualty. We will be burying him at sea at sunrise. Your crew is invited to see him off. Over."

"Who was your casualty, Captain? Over," Jamison asked quickly.

"Seaman Robert James Stankus. He was killed in the line of duty. His sacrifice saved the life of a friend. He acquitted himself with honor. Over," Jim replied.

"Who shot this seaman? Over," Captain Jamison asked quickly.

"Rustin. Rustin and his men are all dead. Over," Jim replied.

Jamison swore under his breath and shook his head. "We would be honored to attend his burial. Captain Jamison out," Jamison replied.

Jim called upon the two US ships and offered the same invitation. Both captains accepted. With a sigh, he put the microphone down. Cecilia stood behind him with her arms wrapped around his chest. He patted her hands gently. They stood that way until Andrea came to relieve Jim.

CHAPTER 28

At 6:58 in the morning, Robert James Stankus, lovingly known as Cuss by his mates, was commended to the deep, just as the sun rose above the horizon. Abe read the service. Captain Jamison provided a band and a bugler to blow taps. Following the 21-gun salute, taps was played and the litter was released, carrying the remains of a good friend to the bottom of the sea. Windy wept openly for his friend, and he was not alone.

In Washington, Admiral Runion sat before a television, receiving the live signal from *Bring It Up Coral*. Sitting beside him, stiff and silent, was Admiral Rook. When the service was completed and the body slid beneath the waves, Admiral Runion turned to Rook. His blue eyes were hard as steel, and Rook almost recoiled from that look. He tried to cover his fear with bluster, but it came off badly. Worse, he knew somehow that Jim Shepherd had once again defeated him.

"Today your career in the navy ends," Admiral Runion said quietly. "I will have your resignation on my desk in thirty minutes or you will lose not only your position but your freedom. That man is dead because of you!"

"You have no proof of anything!" Rook blustered. "Rustin searched the ship and found no documents!" Too late Rook realized his mistake and closed his mouth.

With a malicious smile, Runion produced a folder of the ship's log. Rook looked at it, the blood draining from his face. It was all there—his involvement with Russia, the money, the information he passed to the Red Army Faction members, all of it. He had risen to the rank of captain at that time, but he wanted more, and it was promised with his cooperation. Riding the wave of help that came his way, he rose through the ranks, and now it was all over.

"How long have you had this?" he asked, his voice barely above a whisper.

"Since before the hurricane," Runion replied.

"Jim Shepherd asked me to deliver a message," Admiral Runion added after a significant pause. He was looking at Rook, enjoying every reaction. The man was badly rattled.

"What message?" Rook asked, a quiver of fear in his voice.

"If you contact any of your old friends or get involved in anything else criminal, it will be your last act," Runion said.

"I have friends in high places!" Rook sputtered. "How dare you threaten me!"

"I gather that for Captain Shepherd, that is not a threat but a promise. If I were you, I'd keep away from my friends in high places. You might just look up one night and find yourself staring down the barrel of Jim Shepherd's, or more probably, John Shepherd's gun. It's just a suggestion, of course. Personally, I hope you do go to your old friends. This world will be a better place when you leave it," Runion spoke evenly, relaxed in his chair, not even looking at Rook. He could sense Rook's fear.

"What if I go to the joint chiefs?" Rook asked after a pause. "Scrambling those jets over Cuban air space could have been interpreted as an act of war!" he sputtered.

"Oh, I wouldn't do that if I were you. Captain Shepherd might consider one of them an old friend." Runion smiled, but Rook noted that the smile never reached his eyes. Some called what Runion was doing shooting in the dark, but he guessed correctly, and Rook's reaction justified the gamble. Admiral Rook was shaken to the core.

"So you know it all." Rook sagged. Gambling in a last-ditch effort to save his position he'd lost. The look of satisfaction on Runion's face irritated him. Angrily he picked up the pen in front of him and wrote his resignation. Runion watched, seething within. Three men whom he now identified as the Washington Triad wormed their way into the upper echelons of government with the sole purpose of pulling it down from within. They were anarchists with a veneer of sophistication and social standing. Abraham Lincoln had been correct when he said that if America fell, it would be from enemies within.

Eventually the triad realized that the American people were much too strong and communism too weak, but they continued their work, even after the fall of communism. Runion suspected one of the joint chiefs was among this nefarious group, and Rook had just confirmed it. His next task would be to find and eliminate that threat. Jacks and Rook were finished. Rook finished writing, and Admiral Runion leaned forward. Stretching out his hand, he took the first leg of the triad out.

"I'm not sorry," Rook snarled, standing up. His bluster died as Runion raised an eyebrow. For the first time, he saw the gun in Runion's steady hand.

"Go take that uniform off. You're a disgrace to what it stands for. The only reason you're still alive is I made a promise to John Shepherd," Runion said, the steel back in his voice. As Rook turned away from his desk, Admiral Runion pushed a button, and Captain Shepherd's voice came clearly from the next room.

"Stay away from your friends, Rook."

Once more the blood drained from Rook's face, and he darted for the door and practically ran out of the building, feeling sick and afraid. Runion grunted in satisfaction. He picked up a phone and dialed a number.

"He's just leaving," he said simply, and he hung up the line.

Jim called his unit to order, and they divided up into their individual teams of four. Standing at attention, he marched to the center and saluted the three ships standing by. His men followed suit. Horns whooped and whistled as the ships began to pull away. The crew from each ship, designated for the honor, saluted back. On board *Bring It Up Coral*, a camera recorded the entire funeral and departure.

As Jim turned away to dismiss his troops, his face was grim. He saluted them, and they saluted back. This was a moment for formality, not only for Bob's sake but for the sake of the men and women on board the ship. Feeling the loss, all of them felt he understood the need. They needed a strong captain now, and he squared his shoulders with resolve. He addressed them.

"Today we sent home a true soldier, a friend, a man of honor. He became a true soldier through the help of his friends and mentors, and he served this ship with distinction. His death will not be forgotten, nor was it meaningless. In the case of his murderer, justice has been served. Soon we will deal with the one who sent that criminal against us. Until then we will honor Bob's memory best by continuing to serve as we have, unwavering and undaunted. Dismissed!" he said.

After a moment, he continued, "Dorf, please get the chopper ready for a flight to Miami. Lieutenant, please arrange for a private jet to fly us to Sandusky, Ohio. Contact all of Bob's family and have them arrange a meeting. Then call Ken Worthington and have him meet us at Reagan International. Ask him to have a cashier's check in the amount of Bob's portion to give to the family. Papa, will you and Rosa come with us please? Commander, you have the ship." For a moment, Jim had to breathe evenly to keep the emotions he felt at bay.

John nodded, sensing his brother's deep emotions, turned to the crew, and ordered them to get into their work clothes. He would take the ship to the island where the treasure was buried and retrieve all of it. Jim and Cecilia hurried down to their cabin to pack for the trip and change into travel clothing. As they entered their quarters, Jim looked at the plastic display case Abe, Sturdy, Windy, and Bull made for Bob's family. Hot tears stung his eyes, and he blinked them away, embarrassed.

Cecilia reached up and touched his face, then drew him down until he knelt before her, and held him while he wept for the loss of his friend. Instinctively she had known he would cry for his friend, but always in private. At least now he no longer had to do so alone, as he surely would have. After a few minutes, he regained control and stood, gathered Cecilia into his arms, and hugged her tightly. Then he let her go, and they prepared for their trip. With a sigh, she went about her task, wishing her husband would learn to open up even more. Her own eyes were puffy and red from weeping.

"Why are we traveling with you?" Andrea asked, once he was seated and had his headgear on for the flight.

"Mom's getting married to Alistair Gregg!" Jim announced, and grinned at the openmouthed expressions on his family. "She wanted you and Rosa to be the first to know, and she's meeting you at Reagan International. I'll pick you up on the way back," Jim added.

Mark looked at Dorf and winked. Dorf understood. Mrs. Shepherd was going to talk to her brother about getting married to Rosa. Grinning, Dorf turned his attention back to the instruments. Driver and FM exchanged looks as well at their positions at radio and navigation. Andrea saw the exchanged looks and guessed what might lie in store and had a secret smile on his face.

They landed near a Mitsubishi jet, walked across the tarmac to the jet, and climbed on board. A pretty stewardess ushered them in, closed the door, and the captain and copilot turned around to greet them. FM and Driver followed, loading the luggage into the compartment. Two ground crew maintenance workers closed the luggage compartment, and one signaled the pilot that he was good to go. They were in the air in minutes.

Talk about the upcoming wedding filled the hours to Washington. Toward the end of the flight, Jim leaned forward in his seat, his hand entwined in Cecilia's, and he looked Andrea in the eyes. "It would be nice if it was a double wedding," he said emphatically. Andrea had a strange expression on his face when he replied.

"I will tell you when the wedding between Rosa and myself will take place!" Andrea said, waving his finger in the air just as emphatically. There was a twinkle in his eye as he said it, though. He winked at Cecilia. Then he looked at Rosa. "She is a beautiful woman and worthy to receive the most proper proposal of marriage."

"Just make sure you get around to it soon, Papa!" Cecilia said with a smile. Then she leaned over and whispered in her husband's ear, "Take a look at the ring on the fourth finger of her left hand, sweetie!"

Jim grabbed her hand and looked at the diamond ring sitting there for everyone to see. Papa began laughing, and Rosa joined him with Cecilia. Red in the face, Jim sat back with a silly grin on his face. He thought that perhaps it was Bob's death that made him miss the obvious. That ring was huge, obvious, and he'd missed it completely. Shaking his head, he smiled at his uncle and new aunt.

Rosa signaled the stewardess, who came forward with four wineglasses and a delicious red wine. They toasted Rosa and Andrea formally and then sat back to discuss the possibility of a double wedding. Before they were prepared, the jet was landing in Washington.

Much stood at the rear door of the Rolls Royce, opening it for Gwyneth to emerge. She greeted them all with joyful cries. Jim didn't know how he felt about his mother getting married yet, but when he saw her joy, he smiled. She hugged him tightly. For a few minutes, they stood on the tarmac talking, then Ken Worthington arrived in a taxi. Jim said his goodbyes and with Cecilia and Ken, walked back to the jet.

Ken booked them into the Embassy Suites hotel in Sandusky, where they would be meeting the Stankus family the following day. Jim and Cecilia spent most of the day with him discussing various business ventures and one very important one. Jim was planning on buying a second ship with the proceeds from their latest conquest. The money from that venture would surely be put to good use, and the plan he had would further add to their cover. What lay in store promised to be a great adventure. After an excellent dinner at a nearby steak house, they retired for the evening.

CHAPTER 29

In the morning, Jim and Cecilia put on their dress uniforms. It wasn't so much to impress the Stankus family as to honor their fallen friend. Ken knocked on their door at the appointed time with a package in his hands. He handed it to Jim. It was addressed to him at the hotel. Jim raised his eyebrows and opened the package.

Inside was a navy Medal of Honor and a letter from the president and from Admiral Runion. The Medal of Honor was for Robert James Stankus. Jim sighed deeply. He'd asked for it, not really believing it would be approved. The current navy Medal of Honor is a five-pointed bronze star, tipped with trefoils containing a crown of laurel and oak. In the center is Minerva, personifying the United States, standing with her left hand resting on a bundle of rods called fasces and her right hand holding a shield blazoned with the shield from the coat of arms of the United States. She repulses Discord, represented by snakes. The medal is suspended from the flukes of an anchor.

With reverence, Jim pinned the ocean-blue pin with five white stars above the left pocket of Robert's uniform. When he was satisfied that it was properly placed, he folded the shirt again and put it in the clear plastic bag, returning it to the plastic memory case Sturdy, Windy, and Abe had so carefully packed.

After breakfast, they waited in the lobby for the Stankus family to arrive. Ken had booked a limousine service to collect them all. They arrived a few minutes ahead of time. Two of the brothers looked enough like Bob to bring a lump to Jim's throat. He stepped forward and introduced himself after saluting Mr. and Mrs. Stankus.

They met in a conference room decorated with comfortable chairs for the adults and with toys for small children in one corner. The family gathered around and introduced themselves. Jim listened for a while to the stories about Bob as a boy and how he had become lost to them. Finally, he cleared his throat, stood, and everyone grew quiet.

"I am honored to meet the family of my friend and valiant crew member Robert James Stankus," Jim said formally. "We called him Cuss," he added with a smile. "He was an equal partner in our venture, and his share goes to his family. His last will and testament is inside this envelope, and a copy was registered. His personal share in our company came to just a little over eight million dollars. Some of that he invested wisely, so his actual holdings are closer to twelve million now. All the details are in this folder."

Jim handed the folder to a stunned David Stankus, Bob's father. "Also, and more important is this." That got everyone's attention. "The president of the United States and Admiral Runion of the United States Navy have awarded the navy Medal of Honor to your son. It is arranged in this display case with the letters from the president and Admiral Runion." Jim handed the case over.

"Last, here is Bob's dress uniform, with the Medal of Honor pin attached. He was a seaman on my vessel, a respected and loved member of our crew. We will all miss him terribly. In the last few years, you would have been proud of your son, Mr. and Mrs. Stankus. He was a brave and honorable man." Jim paused for a moment. "And here is the traditional flag that is given to those who remain in honor of our fallen soldiers." Jim handed the flag over, stood at attention, and saluted the parents.

"I have something for you as well," Cecilia said, standing beside her husband. "This is a photo album full of pictures of Bob and a DVD of the funeral at sea. I know you didn't get to see him much after he began working for us, but he wanted you to have this to remember him by. His friends on the crew helped gather and create the book for you."

David and Norma opened the album, put it on a table in the middle, and the whole family gathered around to look through it. Cecilia explained some of them, but the rest were self-explanatory. Various family members pointed at pictures with interest. At one point, one of the older boys pointed at a picture of his uncle practicing martial arts.

"Uncle Bob knew martial arts?" he exclaimed.

"Yes, and he was very good," Jim said with a smile.

"He was so different when he came to visit us a few months ago. He said it was because of you, Captain Shepherd. You, Abe, Sturdy, and his friend Windy. We want to thank you for rescuing our son," Mrs. Stankus said with tears in her eyes.

They enjoyed a meal together in the hotel, paid for by *Bring It Up*, and took their leave after lunch. Everyone stood for a moment contemplating the life lost. The Stankus family left to grieve as a family for one lost and later to enjoy their new wealth, and Jim and Cecilia to return to Washington. That emotional meeting became the catalyst that pushed Jim Shepherd to make another decision.

It was time to do something positive about the oceans upon which he traveled, the oceans that he loved. Many countries treated the ocean as a garbage and sewage disposal. His own nation dumped toxic chemicals into the deepest parts of the ocean. Part of the impetus for this train of thought was the ship he came across, full of students studying oceanography under the tutelage of a dedicated professor. Hank had spoken with passion about how the coral reefs were being destroyed. The other part was the battle he'd fought with overwhelming numbers against him. As his thoughts came together, he sought the counsel of his dear wife.

Jim spoke of his plans to expand his company. Cecilia listened and nodded her approval. What he proposed was not only brilliant, but it would add layers of security to what he did for the world against anarchy and terror. Occasionally she asked a question. Her eyes shone with pride as she listened to her husband's plans. Many changes would come, but she knew they would be changes for the best. At one point, Jim stopped and looked down at her.

"Do you believe in what we're doing?" he asked suddenly.

"You mean a paramilitary force fighting against terrorism?" she asked with a smile. He nodded in the affirmative. "Your solution is the only possible solution with terrorists," she said slowly. "Few people understand that today's terrorists are much worse than yesterday's anarchists. They have no value for human life, even their own, and that makes them doubly dangerous. Annihilation is the only answer. They can't be reasoned with. They will respect no treaty. I believe they are so sold to evil that their souls swim in the darkness of hell itself. Yes! I believe in what you are doing. And I think your ideas on research merit full trust as well!"

Jim listened to her in silence. Then he gathered her into his arms and hugged her. "I love you!" he said huskily. She beamed. "God has been helping me become a better man. Somehow you too have helped me to change into a better person, a better man, and though it still confuses me at times, I just wanted you to know that I appreciate it."

"That was a pretty little speech!" she said with a small smile, and she kissed him.

CHAPTER 30

Bring It Up SAR enjoyed another month in news, maritime, and science magazines. Finding the wreck and recovering the treasure proved once again that Jim's crew was at the top of the game. Two-hundred and sixty-five million dollars in gems, precious stones, uncut diamonds, and jewelry from the vault went into the bank to further the operations of *Bring It Up SAR*. Dr. Persons enjoyed further kudos from his faculty colleagues and students, especially when a major portion of his share of the treasure was donated to the archaeology department of the school. For a short period of time, he was allowed to speak freely, often mentioning his personal faith, his dedication to Christianity and to his country, and to his college. He also made sure the funds were going to be used to further archaeological studies of merit.

Jim's mother was married to Dr. Gregg, and Andrea was married to Rosa. Each took a month-long honeymoon. To Jim and John, the new addition to their family proved to be a welcome one. Dr. Gregg obviously doted on their mother, and she glowed with joy in his presence. That they were deeply in love was obvious. Both men knew that was what mattered most. They also agreed that their father would have liked Dr. Gregg very much and would approve of the union.

Parting on a high note, the pair left their mother in good hands, knowing that soon Mr. and Mrs. Gregg would be joining them once again. Sighing at the added responsibility that would bring, Jim looked at John and grinned. Both men knew the risks, and yet each accepted them without hesitation. Shoulder to shoulder they made their way back to the ship. Jim and his crew made their way to England after the weddings and dry-docked at Calvin Beardsley's yard.

Calvin closed his yard for the winter months, something he did every year. If he was a little early, no one said anything. He'd been very fortunate that year, and his business was flourishing. Jim, his crew, and Beardsley's crew worked long hours every day for the next six months retrofitting a new ship for the fleet, making changes to their original vessel.

The new ship was another sign of added responsibility. Jim and his crew realized that without research, the oceans of the world were in jeopardy. Long discussions during the recovery and sale of the treasures ended with a unanimous decision to add another ship, a science vessel, and bring on board the top minds in oceanic and archeological research. *Bring It Up*, as a corporation, intended for their research ship to be the best-equipped ship on the ocean. Research done from that ship would make a difference in an indifferent world. That his crew would make this decision further impressed Jim that he led the very best in the world.

Wade, of course, was in his element. He and Calvin Beardsley worked side by side on the designs for retrofitting the two vessels. Their genius did not go unnoticed. Both men were somewhat embarrassed by the accolades accorded them during the process. Smitty, Sparks, and Zeke soared as well, providing technology and designs that would put them at the top of their class in searching for lost artifacts beneath the ocean. In fact, every member of the crew participated in the design and reconfiguration of the ships, which Jim knew would make caring for these vessels a top priority.

Coral and *Pearl*, now registered out of Norfolk, Virginia, were the names the crew chose for their vessels. *Pearl* was a research ship purchased from the US Navy. Built in 2016, her length was three hundred and thirty-six feet and her beam sixty-six feet. Maximum draft was seventeen feet and gross tonnage was 3,600 long tons. Displacement was 3,900 long tons.Originally the ship carried a crew of 28 and scientific berthing for 36. It was streamlined with plush accommodations for a crew of 24 and scientific berthing for 18. Crew quarters were mostly set up for four to a room with their own bathroom including two urinals in the men's section, two stalls, and four showers. In the women's section, the showers were larger, and there were only two stalls. Scientific berthing was divided into four and two bed cabins and two single cabins for married scientists.

Beneath the deck, the *Pearl* was driven by two GM EMD 20-645F7B diesels modified to produce 4,000 horsepower each. Each engine could sustain 5.73 MW of power. She was outfitted with cp props, 300 horsepower bow thrusters, and Z-Drive Lips propulsion.

Aboard the *Pearl*, 4,000 sq. ft. of laboratory space was available and almost 5,000 sq. ft. of working area on the main deck. Around 1,400 sq. ft. of the laboratory space was wet lab and the rest dry lab area. Scientific equipment included Multibeam EM120 at 12 kHz, Sub-bottom profilers, Knudsen 320 B models at 3.5/12 kHz, ODEC Bathy 2000 at 3.5/12 kHz, magnetometer from Geometrics, the G-886 model, a Sippican MK 12 XBT, and ADCP RDI Narrowband and RDI Broadband at 150 kHz. There was also Hydrographic Doppler Sonar at 50/140 kHz profiling to depths of 1,000 meters with 15-meter depth resolution. The Underway Data System was a state-of-the-art meteorological and sea surface mapping system.

Within the ship was a communications/data network with Ethernet, audiovisual in labs and staterooms. F/O and copper links were used to ensure top quality. Zeke modified two SUN Enterprise 450 servers and hooked them to MAC workstations throughout the labs and ship. The system included 600 gigabyte disks: CD-ROM, DAT and Exabyte Tapes. Each workstation had its own Epson laser or inkjet printer. Two plotters were added to the system to complete it and make it the most advanced and capable system on the ocean in its day.

Included was the latest in INMARSAT satellite voice and data communications providing excellent ship phones and faxes. VHF, HF radio, SSB voice, and TELEX were also available for communications. Area codes differed depending on the location of the ship.

Smitty made sure the navigational capabilities of both ships included GPS Trimble Tansmon P-Code and GPS Trimble NT 200 DGPS systems. Sperry radar, an ADU GPS Ashtech Attitude-sensing System, and Acoustic Positioning System Nautronix 916 SBL/LBL were included in the array of equipment. He also included a Furuno FV 700 50 kHz Fathometer, an ODEC 200 kHz Doppler Speed Log and an EDO 600kHz Doppler Speed Log, Robertson Dynamic Positioning, SIMRAD Taiyo ADF, and two Sperry MK 37 Gyro units.

Jim and Cecilia visited Admiral Runion during a whirlwind three-day trip to Washington. It fell to them to gather the science crew, and they kept busy interviewing candidates Admiral Runion recommended, and people they already knew or knew about. Keeping in contact with the crew during the process, the two produced an outstanding science crew. Both found the task rewarding and sighed with relief when the last contract was signed.

Looking at each other across the table they were using as a makeshift desk, each smiled with satisfaction. Jim gathered his contracts carefully, placing each one in the proper file, and when he was finished stacking them, he slid them into a leather satchel. Cecilia moved around to stand behind him and gently massage his shoulders and back. She ran her delicate hand up over his short haircut and playfully rubbed the top of his head.

"You do realize that your men are going to be impressed with our science crew, don't you?" Her voice was soft, and she rested her head on top of his for a moment, letting her arms drape over his chest, feeling again those supple muscles beneath the skin. Jim was a powerful man in every way. It thrilled her to be this close to him physically, and he reached up and took both her hands gently in his, leaning back into her.

"It will certainly be interesting to see how the two teams react to each other when they first meet!" Jim laughed easily. "I wonder how John is doing," he mused. His brother, he knew, had a special mission all his own.

In London, with some trepidation, John visited Sir Edward, giving himself a mission that only Jim knew about. It took him most of the day to find her in the labyrinth of offices where she was working, after his visit with Sir Edward, but he finally tracked her down. She was seated at her desk, working diligently on a report, the office chatter and movement blanked out for the moment, so she was unaware of him until he opened her door.

Pen looked up from her desk as John entered the office, sprang up from her chair, and leaped into his arms, kissing him soundly. John was just as passionate, and in another instant, they parted, both confused and surprised. John smiled.

"I suppose that now I have to marry you," he said. "I've kissed you."

"You're joking, of course!" Pen said, breathing heavily.

"Actually, no. I love you." He paused, swallowing hard and finding the resolve to continue. After clearing his throat, he continued, "I came to offer you two things. Will you allow me to communicate those offers?" He took her hand as she sat heavily in her chair, and he knelt before her.

"Oh! Must you?" she said, a catch in her voice. She wasn't ready for this.

"I must," John said. "Penelope Peril, I offer you my undying love for as long as we both shall live. And with that offer, I believe you and I have similar interests and that our lives were destined to be brought together. Therefore, I offer you the opportunity to use your talents and abilities at my side."

"Yes! Well done, old chap. Well done!" Sir Edward approved, stepping into the room. Pen looked over John and saw some of her colleagues smiling at her. Her face turned red. "I had something similar in mind. Sort of a permanent loan," Sir Edward mentioned. "Unofficially, of course," he added, clearing his throat. He smiled, not feeling at all like an interloper. This was unexpected but welcome!

Sir Edward closed the door and turned to face them. As usual his face was devoid of expression. He looked at them both and then spoke again. "With the Shepherds, you can do more for England than you can in my organization, Pen. You're the best agent I have, and I'm loath to let you go, but I do believe it is for the best. Provided, of course, that you love this churlish American and wish to marry him." He smiled as he added the last.

"He is not at all churlish!" she said hotly in John's defense, then blushed again as Sir Edward grinned at her. Someone had finally cracked that shell, winning her heart. He was secretly pleased.

"Well, I believe she does love you, old chap," he said to John with a wink.

"Yes, I do," she said, looking at John and smiling.

"I'll leave the two of you to make all the arrangements, then. You have my blessing. You still work for me, Ms. Peril, and for England," Sir Edward reminded her. He stepped back through the door and closed it behind him.

"What happens now?" Pen asked when she could regain her breath. John had snatched her up and kissed her again, twirling her around.

"We go back together and make plans," John said.

"Just like that?" she asked, her eyebrows raised.

"Just like that!" John replied. She laughed as he shoved all the paperwork on her desk into a drawer and slammed it shut. "See! There's nothing left to do!"

"I'll meet you tomorrow afternoon at Beardsley's Shipyard," she said, getting the papers out of the drawer. "Now go and let me finish so I can pack and leave," she added, pulling him down for a kiss. Pulling the stack of papers out of the drawer, she smiled and tried to work, but it was no use. All she could think about was the feel of his lips on hers, his arms around her. *I really do love that man!*

John walked through the crowded office, receiving congratulations, beaming, and practically walking on air. Pen tried to concentrate but gave it up after only a few minutes and ran after him. She caught him at the front door of the building, and together they rushed out into the rain. Hand in hand, they ran down the street to John's hired car. Sliding to a stop, he opened the door and motioned for her to enter.

She did, and he followed her. So excited was she that she didn't even notice there was a driver in the front of the limousine.

"Why were you here to see Sir Edward?" she asked once they dried themselves off as best as they could.

"I came to ask for your hand in marriage!" he said, sliding a glance at the driver. Pen understood. He didn't want to be connected with Sir Edward in an official capacity. She chided herself for being so obtuse and smiled lopsidedly at the man who had so rattled her.

"Perhaps you should have asked my father!" Pen said with a twinkle in her eye. She looked again at the huge diamond now residing on her left hand.

"Your father said I had to ask your mother. She said it was fine with her and told him to say yes," John replied without missing a beat. It sounded so much like her parents she raised her eyebrows again.

"You already spoke with them!" she asked.

"Of course!" John replied. "Your mother said it was about time you stopped trying to compete with men and realized women were superior in every way and get on with life," he added.

"Oh heavens! You did talk to them!" she said, her face flushed.

"Yes. Six women sitting with her in the atrium nodded emphatically. I'm sure I'm doing the right thing," John said. Pen broke into laughter.

"I'm doomed, then!" she said tragically.

"Yes. Sad, isn't it?" John said, throwing up his hands. "Takes all the romance out of the thing to be told to marry," he added.

The two of them engaged in some kissing and hugging, which took them some time. The car coming to a stop startled them. John laughed, tipped the driver generously, and dragged Pen out onto the runway to the plane that waited to fly them both to the coast.

Jim and Cecilia met them at the airport, but they didn't discuss any business until they were inside the security of the shipyard. Ships, their new high-speed boats, new Rigid Raiders, and equipment now crowded the huge building. The smell of fresh paint and the special coating on the hulls filled the building with a thick heavy scent. Pen paused in front of the new research ship.

"What's this for?" she asked.

"It's a research ship. The Old Dominion research ship gave us the idea," Jim said. "Some of her crew will be new team members. Our last battle decided that for me. The rest will be true scientists who lead in their fields," he added.

"And will she do actual research?" Pen asked. She was quite impressed and interested in the concept.

"Absolutely. Cecilia and I have gathered an amazing team of scientists ready to go when she sails. You and John will be on *Coral*. He has command of that ship. I have command of the *Pearl*," Jim explained.

"And how many teams will you add?" Pen asked.

"Three," Jim replied. "Another twelve team will be perfect."

"And what will your scientists know about all this?" she queried, very curious now.

"Everything, just like the crew," Jim answered without pause. When Pen raised her eyebrows, he continued, "I've asked Admiral Runion to scour the navy for the very best. They will enjoy joint ownership of the company along with everyone else and an equal share in all recovered treasures, scientific discoveries, publication royalties, etc."

"You know scientists are a different breed?" Cecilia asked, looking up at her husband with a knowing smile. "They can be difficult. Many of them tend to live in a very different world!"

"We'll learn," Jim said easily.

"When do we meet everybody?" Pen asked.

"We're all going to Hawaii to get acquainted," Jim said with a grin. "Some lovesick sailor has requested a honeymoon on the beach!" He winked at Pen as he said it, and she blushed. "Calvin is going to finish the *Pearl* this afternoon. We sail tomorrow for Norfolk. The scientists will meet us there. Our new recruits are already here."

Pipi didn't have to look long to pick out the new recruits. There were four from the SAS. They were talking to Weston and his team and the Australians. From the United States, Admiral Runion provided four SEAL team members and four from marine force recon. When Jim entered the room, the men came to attention.

Pen stood back and observed as Jim walked among them. They were all of a kind, regardless of their difference in size and weight. Each man moved with a deadly grace, and she decided that thirty-six men like these could seem like a thousand in a battle. John saw her watching him and winked at her, and she smiled.

When Jim and John met everyone, John announced his engagement to Pipi, and she was pleased and teary-eyed as the men cheered. That they were truly happy to have her join the crew in this manner was evident. Those who knew her well welcomed her in a way that told her she was part of the team. It warmed her heart that her husband led such men as this.

Once the introductions and congratulations were finished, Jim and John divided their crews and put them to work. Both crews knew that the captains would work shoulder to shoulder with them, not command and supervise as many did. Both men were as sweat-stained and dirty at the end of the day as the rest of the men, pleased by the progress and completed tasks.

The day passed quickly while the crew and Beardsley's unit finished the two ships. *Bring It Up SAR* was painted on the stern and bows of each boat, with the name of the boat beneath, followed by their harbor of registry. USA, with an American flag, was painted in one corner, with the *Bring It Up* Eagle mascot painted in the opposite corner on the stern.

Pearl white, burgundy, and sky-blue paint glistened in the sun as the two ships were wheeled into the water on their giant cradles. Another day passed as they loaded supplies and tested systems before the two ships left their berths and headed out into the channel.

John Shepherd had command of the *Coral* and her crew. Pen was one of two new members to that crew. She was given the rank of lieutenant and registered as chief research specialist, historian, and forensics expert. She was also a certified meteorologist and cartographer. The other new crew member was the replacement for Bob Stankus. He was short, thin, and seedy looking. Abe assured her that he was on the road to recovery from drug and alcohol abuse and introduced him as Ned Vintner.

Jim Shepherd had command of the *Pearl* and her crew. He had all twelve of the new team, his own squad, and all the new crew members. Andrea had been promoted by unanimous vote to lieutenant commander. It would be his capable mind and hands that would support Jim and his crew.

In the sick bay Dr. Will Penny and his charming wife, Donna Jane, had command. Both were commissioned lieutenant and were given the designation chief medical officer and chief nurse. With his name, Will was quickly christened Cowboy by the rest of the crew, and Dr. Penny didn't seem to mind. He was a small man, five foot six, and weighed 150 pounds, carrying most of the weight proportionately. His wife was two inches taller and two years younger, thin, and very sweet.

Lieutenant Junior Grade Tom Ives was the new ship's clerk and executive assistant to the captain. As far as Jim was concerned, Tom was a great addition to the crew. He might be a bean counter like Marvin Finn, but he was much more easygoing.

Uncle Zeke was along as the computer and communications expert. Bob Neff served with Cecilia as a research specialist, historian, meteorologist, and forensics expert. Jim lured him away from the FBI. Richard Nelson was another computer expert that Zeke had somehow enticed away from navy intelligence. He didn't like being called Ricky, so the crew nicknamed him Rock 'n' Roll. At five feet eight inches and only 145 pounds, he was a very handsome young man with dark curly hair and blue eyes. When he wanted to, he could look and act the part of a rock star. Cecilia and Smitty were the other two ensigns on board the crew.

Master Chief Petty Officer Zeke Good was the chief mechanic. Much younger than Master Chief Warner, he differed to Chief Warner in a winsome way, and the two became close friends almost instantly. Warner thought him extremely competent. His assistant was PO3 Mike Romentowski, whom everyone called Wrench.In the kitchen, a jolly man named James Earl James ran the show. He was a heavyset cook with a beaming smile, and everyone called JimJim. Given the rank master chief petty officer, he seemed amused at his role. Bob

Hinkle and Frank Lafayette, who bore the nicknames Winky and Frenchy, also served in the kitchen. Both were seamen. JimJim's second in command was PO1 P. J. Jennings. Jennings towered over the other kitchen help at six foot four and was a powerfully built and funny addition to the team.

PO3 Sam Hammer was the chief electrician on board. He could easily have been one of the team. He was an expert marksman and a champion boxer. At six three and two hundred twenty-five pounds, he was impressive, with his flattened nose and large ears.

Both ships, as expected, performed to expectations on the journey across the Atlantic. Buying the second ship was a major step for the company. Both crews worked hard to outdo the other in keeping their vessel in top condition. Jim and John worked beside them with pride. By the time they reached Norfolk, the twelve new men were settling into their new routine and catching up.

CHAPTER 31

Jim met his science team in a conference room of the Embassy Suites Hotel in Norfolk, where they were eagerly waiting after two days of inactivity. Though the hotel was very nice, they were anxious to be on the ocean, and especially to see their new home on the water. Cecilia and Bob Neff accompanied Jim to the meeting, all wearing their new dress uniforms. In honor of the meeting, the science team also wore their unique dress uniforms.

Fifteen of the eighteen scientists were women. Jim looked them over with interest, noting again that the younger women were not just pretty, they were lovely in a way that drew every male eye in the establishment. Pondering this, he thought that perhaps it had something to do with the fact that they were all believers, women who followed Jesus. Cecilia had that same quality about her, a beauty from within that was like an aura. Even the older women had a beauty about them that was more than skin deep. As he looked at them, his mind ran over the problems that could erupt with shipboard romances. It was a problem he'd already discussed long and hard with Dr. Will and Donna Penny.

Leading the marine biologists were Dr. John and Dr. Alice Dinsmore. They were in their early fifties and looked like they'd spent most of their lives on the sea. Dr. Iris Copeland, Dr. Carol

Lowe, Dr. Michael Putnam, and Dr. Angela Rysdale were the marine biology team. These came from the navy's top researchers and from universities that worked closely with the navy. That they had been stolen away was still a secret. Jim could read in their body language and words excitement for this new avenue of research with seemingly unlimited funds.

Dr. Alistair Gregg led the archaeology team. Dr. Lisle Mirelle was on board as a marine archaeologist, and Dr. Heidi Van Haaten was the other archaeologist. Mary Anne Lewis and Barbara Stafford were administrative assistants. Jim knew them all, and his team had selected them personally.

Rachael Hague, René Millstein, Tiffany Millstein, Elizabeth Minor, Stephanie Morris, and Lynn Ross were lab technicians, along with Jim's newlywed mother, Gwyneth. René and Tiffany were identical twins, and Tiffany greeted Cecilia with an enthusiastic hug. She and her sister seemed pleased to be invited to serve as lab technicians on board the *Pearl*. Cecilia had recommended them, and Sir Edward had cursed when Jim asked if he could have them. Both worked in the forensic labs at MI6 and were accounted the best in their respective fields.

Once introductions were finished, Jim invited them to come and see their new ship and they left the conference room in a group. A hired tour bus ferried them to the dock and deposited them at the gangplank. On the ship, he listened to the expressions of delight and amazement as the scientists toured their facilities and living quarters. Not only were they impressed with the facilities, but they were also thrilled with the potential. Talking more about the latter pleased Jim, because it told him they were truly interested in their research, not on a free semester at sea. After the tour, he brought them to the ship's conference room for a very private chat.

It was there many of them learned for the first time the true nature of the company. Admiral Ashley and Sir Edward had not disappointed Jim in handpicking the very best and most honorable men and women for the job. Many of them served in the navy, and all of them were thrilled not only with their mission but the mission of the team for which they now served as cover. When they learned that they were also part owners of the company and shared in all the profits, they were ecstatic. Profound gratitude was expressed, and Jim found himself liking all these new friends.

It surprised him a little to think of them as friends so soon, but there was a bond, something special in all of them. Again, he thought perhaps it was the bond of Christianity, the answer to Jesus's prayer in John 17 that all believers would be one, as He and the Father were one. For Jim that meant a great deal and told him he was partnered with people who shared his faith and vision. That last had been the most important criteria for choosing each individual. He or she had to be a professing Christian.

"What's our first assignment?" Alice Dinsmore asked briskly. Jim decided it would always be business first for Alice.

"We have been awarded a grant to study the volcanic activity off of Hawaii and its effects on the ocean temperatures and currents," Jim informed her with a smile. "When certain organizations learned you were leading this group, they insisted you take the study."

"How much of a grant?" John Dinsmore asked, his eyebrows raised.

"Two hundred fifty thousand dollars plus all royalties. Study nodes and equipment included!" Jim replied. "Pictures, published works, everything that goes with it!" he added.

"We could easily turn that into nearly a million dollars!" Dr. Copeland exclaimed, her hand over her mouth.

"Nonsense!" Dr. Gregg spoke up. "Triple that sum!" he announced, winking at Jim. "That kind of upheaval is bound to uncover lost ships," he added.

"Wow!" René Millstein said. Her voice sounded almost breathless with excitement. "When do we leave?"

"Tomorrow morning, early, if all goes well. Breakfast is served buffet style from 0430 to 0630 hours. This conference room is available to you as well as your lab and office space. Tonight, we're having a special dinner on board the *Coral* to welcome all our new crew and staff. Dinner is at 1800 hours, dress uniform preferred," Jim said.

"Not ordered, Captain?" John Dinsmore asked with a smile.

"In this company, John, rank doesn't mean we give orders. We will give orders from time to time, of course, but I want this understood. Rank defines responsibilities. I know it is different in the navy, but we make an effort to ask rather than order, and everyone pulls his or her own weight. When I state a preference, it doesn't mean you'll be in trouble if you come in shorts and a Hawaiian shirt. I have discovered that dress uniforms create an atmosphere of being part of a team effort and also an atmosphere of decorum. That was the reason for my request, nothing more." Jim smiled at him.

"I heard that about you, Shep," Dr. Dinsmore replied with a big grin. "Now I see that it's certainly true." Slowly everyone stood and walked past Jim and Cecilia, shaking hands, sharing a hug, thanking them both for this exciting new adventure.

Dr. Gregg and his new bride stepped up to Jim after the others filed out. Alistair touched his epaulets with a smile. "Very impressive!" he said with a grin. He wore an ensign epaulet with one gold stripe at the bottom. Above the stripe was the Greek omega symbol with the eagle plunging in the center. Above that the words *Science Officer* were embroidered in gold lettering, and above that four icons outlined in gold. The icons represented molecular biology, marine biology, general science, and DNA research.

Lab technicians wore a black patch on their sleeves with three yellow horizontal stripes, the words *Lab Technician* embroidered above the stripes, and the omega symbol with the eagle in the left at the top and a lab technician icon outlined in gold. Uniforms were tan, military style, and designed for their purpose. Jim liked them very much, and he was pleased that his crew also appreciated them. As he looked at his new stepfather, he smiled in appreciation. He and his wife looked like they belonged on this crew, and he felt already a deep affection for Alistair.

"You look like you belong in that uniform, Alistair," Jim said, hugging him.

"Our quarters are magnificent, honey!" Gwyneth said, hugging her son in turn.

"I'll have to be on my best behavior with my wife and mother on board!" Jim said with laughter in his eyes.

"I'll see that when I believe it!" Cecilia quipped.

"Captain to the CIC, please," a voice sounded over the intercom.

"Duty calls," Jim said with a sigh. He left them and hurried up to the computer intelligence center of the ship.

"Hey, Shep. You got a call from Admiral Runion!" Richard Nelson said as Jim entered.

"Sir!" Jim said, picking up the phone.

"When are you going through the Panama Canal?" Admiral Runion asked without a greeting.

"Nice to hear your voice too, Admiral!" Jim said sarcastically. "All the way from Greece too! I heard you were there."

"Belay that, you pirate!" Runion chuckled down the line. "Pay attention. We have intel that says the cartel is going to hit your ships when you go through," he added seriously.

"Which cartel?" Jim asked.

"We don't know for certain, but we believe that the Medellin Cartel is behind it. It appears that Edwardo Munez is behind the whole thing. We intercepted a call from an American citizen to that number giving him the information about your boats," Runion added.

"That citizen better not be who I think it is!" Jim said with steel in his voice.

"He's offered to lead the raid personally." Admiral Runion chuckled. "None of us would miss him if he never came back," he added. "That's an official sanction, by the way."

"He won't!" Jim replied softly.

"Well, get there fast, so he doesn't have time to plan anything elaborate!" Runion snapped.

"Sir!" Jim replied, his thoughts racing.

"Don't get dead!" Admiral Runion said. "Give that wife of yours a kiss from me, you pirate," he added and hung up.

Jim put the phone down and quickly picked up the intercom microphone. "All hands on deck! Immediate departure! All hands on deck!"

"Call John and tell him what's happening," Jim said to Nelson as he put the microphone down.

"Who is the citizen, sir?" Nelson asked as he picked up the phone.

"Lyle Rook," Jim replied, his eyes suddenly hard. "A disgrace to the United States Navy."

"Damn!" Nelson said, an evil grin on his face. "About time somebody took that REMF out!" He made the call. Jim winced at the acronym and realized some of the men would have to learn to moderate their language.

At 1800, they dropped anchor and met on the *Coral* as planned. Adding to Jim's pride in the crew, the appearance of thirteen unmarried and beautiful female crew members did not bring the expected catcalls and whistles. Every man on board either vessel was an honorable man that believed in purity and knew how to treat a lady. Polite introductions flowed, and chivalry abounded. Gwyneth raised her eyebrows at her son and smiled.

"I don't know what I expected from a ship full of men, but it wasn't this!" she said, putting a hand on Jim's arm and smiling up into his eyes.

"Some of them are still a little rough around the edges when it comes to language, the newer members of the crew, but you'll see that change quickly," Cecilia said, joining them. "Our Bible studies and the example of others will fix that little problem."

After a feast, Jim explained the situation to everyone. He was pleased to note that among the science staff, no one seemed overly concerned except his mother. Smiling at her to reassure her, he asked the team to gather in the conference room. There were thirty-six seats around the table in the conference room.

"Okay, gentlemen. We have a tight schedule here. I need to know everything we have on Munez, his operation, his fortress, his military forces, bodyguards, family, the works! We need eyes on Rook before morning. We will convene a joint task force meeting tomorrow at 1100. By then I want ideas on how to take the fortress and good ideas on how we repel boarders in the canal. Get cracking!" Jim looked around the room as the men leaped to their feet.

"Zeke, Rock 'n' Roll, get us up and running and synched and make sure nobody has itchy ears," Jim said as the two men passed him.

When the men were gone, Jim joined his mother and wife and sat down again. "We have about fifteen minutes before we have to go back to our ship," he said, picking up a glass of wine. "Until then, let's enjoy the moment!" He held up his glass. "May the winds be kind, the ocean peaceful, and our eyes fixed upon the beauty of the Creator's hand and upon His countenance," he said solemnly.

In the conference room of the *Pearl*, Jim gathered the four teams he had aboard. Norm Geissler, whom the men called Counselor because his father was a famous attorney in London sat with his three former SAS compatriots. Lee Ainsworth was compactly built at five foot six and one hundred and seventy-five pounds. He seemed to have picked up the name Lord Lee for some reason. Lloyd Brookstone was five inches taller and only ten pounds heavier than Ainsworth, lean and tough. Everyone called him Rock. Earl Duncan sat next to him, five ten, one hundred and ninety pounds of bull muscle who bore the unlikely moniker of Donut.Terrance Red Claw had been named Chief, and it stuck. He was pure-bred Blackfoot and proud of it. His marines sat next to him. Gene Hardesty was six five and built along the same lines as Wade, though twenty pounds lighter. His friends all called him Hayseed, and he really did look like a farm kid. Not surprisingly, he was a Pennsylvania farm boy. Neil Meyers sat next to Hayseed, six feet, two hundred pounds of hard marine muscle. And Mel Pierson, an inch shorter and built like Meyers, sat glowering at his computer readout. Jim allowed the teams to pick their own name, and he was not surprised that they chose Bulldog for their team designation.

The SAS team had chosen Sniper for their designation. They were, for the most part, smaller in build than the marines but equally tough. For a soldier, size didn't always matter. Strength was important, but skill and intelligence often trumped strength and size, and every soldier knew it. Quickness and superior weapon power always gave one the winning edge.

Four ex-SEAL team members sat together next to Jim's team.

Tom Izbicki was a brick at six feet and two hundred and five pounds. Steve Coleman was six four and weighed in at two twenty-five. The men called him Santa, which he didn't seem to mind. Bernie Finlay looked like an accountant, wearing round wire-rimmed glasses and an owl-like expression. He was five foot nine and weighed in at 165. Because of his looks and name, he'd been dubbed Fingers. Dick Kagan was two inches shorter had been instantly nicknamed Fagan because of his seedy appearance and long face. It seemed to amuse him.

Zeke, FM, and Smitty sat with Jim. Information began to pour in, and Jim saw many men making notes as he too took notes down on a legal pad next to his computer. Two hours passed with little in the way of conversation. At last, however, there was a break in the flow, and the men sat back. Red Claw looked across at Jim.

"There ain't no REMFs lookin' over our shoulder on this one, right?" he asked.

Jim smiled and shook his head in the negative.

"Just how serious we gonna be in the canal?" Red Claw followed quickly.

"We will repel boarders with extreme prejudice, certainly, but more likely we will take the high ground and engage the enemy away from the ships if possible," Jim replied quietly. "And please moderate your language, gentlemen." He got some odd looks at that. "We believe in the lesson of Ephesians 4:29, not letting any unwholesome words come out of our mouths. I know you're not used to that, but it will come in time. Just try to be careful, please."

"And we're really going take this Munez character in his fortress?" That was Ainsworth asking in his cultured British accent.

"We're going to eliminate that part of the cartel," Jim said flatly.

"Hot damn!" Red Claw said, slapping the table. "'Bout time somebody took those clowns on!"

"We will apply the military solution on both these missions, gentlemen," Jim said quietly. "I want the name Munez to mean nothing by the time we're through. I want his assets, and I want to destroy his pipeline to the rest of the world!"

"What are we gonna do with his assets?" Pierson asked.

"Absorb them into our company," Jim said quietly.

"We could bring a shit storm down on us, Shep!" FM said softly.

"We don't exist, FM. We're ghosts. Whom will they come after?" Jim asked with a grin.

"God! And he used proper English. Bein' married is ruinin' you, boss!" FM replied. That got a laugh from the men, and on that note, Jim closed the meeting.

"Since you invoked the name of God, FM, perhaps you'd like to lead us in prayer for this mission," Jim suggested with a grin. FM gave him a quick grin, and the men bowed their heads and prayed as FM led them.

Both vessels pushed for the Panama Canal while the teams worked out the logistics and strategy for both missions. Intel came in hot and heavy. Admiral Runion dropped a few hints to some friends in the DEA, got some great information, and a promise to keep away from Munez. He had to promise them the pipeline, but Jim didn't mind giving that up. His team certainly had no interest in a pipeline for distribution of illegal substances.

Pen flew to Miami in the chopper and made her way to Panama to keep eyes on Lyle Rook. Her cover was good. She posed as a graduate student working on her doctoral thesis, and her subject was the building of the canal and its early history. Demonstrating her expertise in the field of espionage, she uncovered Rook's money source within days of her arrival and was able to send valuable information to the team. She'd worried about being married taking her edge, but instead she felt a new sense of pride in her work. That made her feel good about her future.

Like all the other ships passing from the Atlantic to the Pacific, documentation was checked, and a cursory inspection followed by Panama officials. One of the officials, an undercover agent for naval intelligence, slipped a piece of paper into Jim's hand as they greeted one another. Jim deftly slid the paper up his sleeve before shaking hands with the next official, doing it so adroitly that no one noticed.

When he read the missive, he smiled. Once the officials were gone, he pressed the talk button on his headset, connecting him to both ships and all crew members.

"Queen's knight takes rook," he said cryptically. "Fourth move in the game."

His team understood that Rook's attack would come during their rise to the fourth level. Checking his watch, Jim guessed they had about eight hours to prepare. Rook was waiting for the cover of darkness.

"Captain Shepherd, please report to the command intelligence center," Zeke's voice came over the speaker system in the ship. Jim left the deck and climbed the steps to the CIC quickly. Zeke looked up as he came in.

"Second terminal," he said, his eyes going back to his monitors.

Jim sat down at the second terminal next to Ensign Nelson. On the monitor in front of him, Pen's coded message seemed to melt and become readable text. Committing the text to memory, he read it quickly, stood up, nodded once to Zeke, and headed for the conference room. The message disappeared as quickly as he did. Nelson watched the entire scene with interest. This captain fascinated him, and the mission appealed to his nature. He grinned at Zeke.

After researching the company and its amazing successes over the past two years, he was anxious to take part in an actual treasure hunt. But more than that, he knew the reputation of Captain Shepherd, and now that he was part of the organization, he also knew what they had accomplished. Pride filled him as he thought about being a part of that aspect of the company.

The conference room was, according to Zeke, impregnable to outsiders. What was said in there, once the doors were closed and the airlock sealed, could not be heard by even the most advanced listening devices. In twos and threes, the fifteen men of his team entered the conference room. Zeke was the last to enter, sealing the doors behind him.

"How is it that a defeated enemy like the Nazis can still influence the terrorists of our world?" Zeke asked, sitting down in his seat and plugging in his laptop.

"Because the bloody Russians picked up where the Nazis left off and made the bloody terrorists sophisticated warriors," Lloyd Brookstone said. "Training camps for anarchists and terrorists, come one, come all!" he added with derision. "They never seemed to realize that terrorists and anarchists can't be part of society."

"And now drugs and their money!" Hayseed said, throwing his long arms out and nearly unseating Neil Meyers.

"Yes," Jim said slowly. "It seems to me an international group driven by one twisted mastermind is behind that. Somehow that doesn't really surprise me. The question is, who is that mastermind?"

"Maybe what we do in the next couple of days will flush him out of the shadows," Red Claw said gruffly.

"One thing at a time," Jim said, sitting forward. "Let's get everyone up to speed."

"Sorry we're late, Jim. Everybody's here," John's voice came out of the voice boxes in front of every team member. "What did we miss?"

"Hayseed clothes-lined Neil, and we've decided to go back in time and nuke the Nazis and Russians," FM quipped. Everyone laughed.

"Best get Zeke and Sparks working on a design for a time machine, then," Wade said with a straight face. "I'll start drawing up the plans." Everyone laughed again. The men could not only hear each other, but they could see each other as well. Each computer had a mini-cam recorder, and whoever spoke was featured on the computer screen of all the others. Wade made his statement with a deadpan expression of seriousness that made his announcement even more hilarious.

"We're going to work in teams of twelve tonight," Jim said quietly. "Alpha, Delta, and Sniper have the south side. Zulu, Knife, and Bulldog have the north side. Firefox, Raider, and Nightfall have the ships. As soon as it's dark, I want the teams in position with the high ground if possible. Standard central group with two support groups will be our tactics tonight. Watch your arcs of fire!" He looked around the room at his group and then into the camera and continued, "Remember! We're ghosts. When the officials arrive, I want everybody back on deck and winning Oscars for their performance in innocence!"

"We'll have to hide Fingers and Fagan, then!" Tom Izbicki piped up. "No one's gonna believe those two are innocent!" The men laughed again. Bernie Finlay was affectionately called Fingers by his team and mates because he looked exactly like you'd expect a CPA running numbers behind the scenes to look. Fagan, of course, just looked the part. He had quickly adopted a habit of rubbing his hands and looking as if he was about to steal anything he could.

Bernie removed his round spectacles and set his face in a mockery of innocence, and the men laughed again when he cleared his throat to bring his picture on screen. Jim didn't mind the interchange. In the serious business of death, any laughter was deeply appreciated. Fingers grinned and put his glasses on again. Fagan rubbed his chin after Bernie's act.

"I'm reviewing the situation!" he sang the line of the famous Broadway number. More laughter erupted. When the laughter calmed, Jim continued, "An old friend is going to land his chopper near here, wait for half an hour, and take off again, giving us an alibi. Gear up!"

When the water rose in the second lock, no one noticed twenty-four men clad in digital design black, gray, brown and green night gear slip away. This was possible because a dozen very attractive women were having a party on the upper observation deck of the science ship, lights ablaze, music playing loudly, and all of them decked out in bikini swimwear. Most of the men wore grins as they melted into the night. The song the girls were playing was the popular "I Need a Hero."

Lyle Rook made it easy. That wasn't his plan, but in his rush, he had to hire mercenary troops that were undisciplined and overconfident at best. Jim looked over a small bush and saw twenty men huddled behind a container waiting for the water to rise in the lock. The two officials on that side of the lock were tied and gagged and hidden in the weeds growing on the hillside.

On the other side, John peered down at his hated enemy. Rook had the main group of thirty men on that side, divided into groups of six. John watched as he slipped into one of the containers when it was time for the attack to begin. It would be his last cowardly act.

At Jim's command, the lights on both ships went dark. The men on either side of the lock, preparing to fire, were suddenly night blind.

Slipping his night vision goggles over his eyes, Jim sighted down the barrel of his H&K MP5SD. Most of the mercenary force went down in the first barrage of fire. The rest went down when they wheeled to fire uphill and the men on the two ships opened fire. Perfectly positioned, the enemy was caught in a deadly crossfire.

The firing ceased. Jim's teams used silenced weapons and fired three rounds into each target. When Rook heard the chatter of machine gun fire cease, he peeked out of his container and found himself looking down the smoking barrel of an H&K Mark 23 complete with silencer. His face drained of all color when he saw that the man who held the weapon was John Shepherd. Looking into those blue eyes, he saw a resolve that sent a shiver of fear down his spine.

"You can't just shoot me!" he sputtered. "That would make you a murderer!" He smiled triumphantly, thinking he had gained an advantage, but the look in John's eyes did not change.

"You're sanctioned," he said simply. Flame spat from the barrel, and Rook died instantly and horribly. John brought his weapon up and watched the traitor fall backward into the container. "That was for my men, their families, and my country!" John said fiercely, feeling the satisfaction and accepting it for what it was.

Men stooped, picked up their empty shell casings, counting as they went, making sure they left nothing behind. This was done silently. Within nine minutes of the ceasefire, every man was back on board. The lights came back on, and both ships were illuminated, further confusing witnesses. Ten minutes later, the men who had participated in the takedown were lined up at the railings or at their posts. It took the officials and police nearly an hour to board either vessel.

This time the officials were not friendly. They did ask permission to board the ships and then produced search warrants issued by a local judge. Jim and John issued orders to their crews that every service was to be rendered to the local officials, which seemed to appease them only a little. The colonel in charge did not search the boats personally, but he walked among the crew talking to various individuals.

Colonel Francisco Valdez and a large contingent of Colombian soldiers disappeared while chasing a ghost force through the mountains of Colombia. Colonel Villa remembered reading that Valdez had been suspicious of this company. He also remembered reading that Valdez had written them off as legitimate. There was something about many of the crew that raised his hackles, so to speak.

He waited expectantly for his search party to find a cache of weapons. At the end of three hours, they returned and reported. Only two weapons had been found. A shotgun in a waterproof gun safe on the bridge and an antique pistol in a plastic display case in Dr. Wozniac's quarters did not seem threatening. The rack of spear guns in the dive ready room didn't interest him either. On the tug, only a shotgun was found, also in a waterproof safe on the bridge. Not one other weapon, other than typical work knives, was evident. He listened as his men explained that they had been allowed to search unhindered wherever they wished.

"Your crew! Many of them are military, Is this not so?" Villa interrogated Jim, his eyes filled with suspicion.

"Almost all of them are ex-military," Jim replied. "The kind of work we do requires the highest discipline, and I've found that military men and women already possess that quality. Only a small portion of the crew is not military, and all of them are on this ship, except for two men in the kitchen crew of the *Coral*."

"All Americans?" Villa asked.

"British, Australian, Italian, French, Dutch, American Indian, and American," Jim corrected. "The best crew you'll find anywhere in the world," he added with some pride. "An international crew like this opens doors for us when it comes to research, which is an important part of what we do. Also, our scientific research is such that an international crew works best."

"Si," Villa agreed. "And why did the lights go out on your boat just before the firing began?" Villa added. He had waited to pose this question, hoping for an advantage.

Jim was prepared with an answer for that one. "One of my sentries scanning the skyline and lock saw men with guns. He radioed his warning, and I ordered the lights turned off immediately. I didn't want any of my crew being easy targets."

"And why did you have sentries posted?" Villa asked after a pause.

"I always have sentries posted," Jim replied. He pointed up, and Villa noticed for the first time a single man on the upper observation deck looking through binoculars. He looked across at the *Coral* and saw the same thing. "So far this year I've been attacked by pirates and whoever was out there tonight. We are famous for being treasure hunters, and very successful. Do you know what they wanted?"

"No. They are all dead, including the man who apparently hired them. They were mercenaries from Colombia, according to their passports," Villa shared, watching Jim closely.

"Colombia!" Jim exclaimed, his eyebrows raised. "Well, then they didn't want anything with us," he said after a moment of thought.

"The man who hired them was American," Villa said, looking away and then quickly back.

"Who was he?" Jim asked.

"He was traveling under the name of Ben Jones. I do not believe that was his real name. We have sent his fingerprints to the Americans and Interpol," Villa replied. He watched Jim as he gave this information, but the man seemed simply interested, not surprised or overly curious. For a moment, the two men simply stared off into the darkness. Jim broke the silence.

"Good thinking. If he's a criminal, his prints will be on file," Jim said, nodding in approval.

"If he is military, his prints will be on file too," Villa said.

"Or any other government job," Jim replied, nodding.

Villa sighed. The man just wasn't acting guilty. This was, to him unsatisfactory, and he knew he had nothing. Saying his goodbyes, he turned and left the ship. News of a helicopter lifting off near the area sent him running for his transportation.

"Thanks, Stick!" Jim whispered under his breath. Part of the ruse was leaving room for doubt. Stick would fly under radar and escape easily, Jim knew. Villa would be sure an outside source was responsible, and Munez would have his doubts set to rest when Jim and his crew continued to Hawaii. Jim smiled.

CHAPTER 32

Balmy skies, gentle ocean breezes, and tropical paradise beckoned as they dropped anchor off the island of Molokai. Reaching the Hawaiian Islands gave the men and women that were new to the company an opportunity to experience the subtle differences of serving under the Shepherds. It was not all sun and roses, but for the most part the lessons were acceptable.

With anticipation for their work, they waited patiently while the coast guard checked all the medical records and did some random drug testing. This was standard, and the crew accepted it. As part of their contract, they were tested regularly on the ship anyway. To work on a ship, one needed a seaman's card, and to keep that card, one had to pass regular and random drug tests.

"Who's the Colombian?" Jim asked the captain of the coast guard cutter as they stood on the observation deck talking together.

"How did you know he's Colombian?" Captain Richards asked.

"His shoes are only made in Colombia. The cut of his shirt and those pants are a dead giveaway," Jim replied easily.

"You have sharp eyes!" the captain replied with a rueful grin. "He's some diplomatic attaché to the Colombian Coast Guard who wants to study how we do things. Hasn't lifted a finger to help or asked a single question until today. Today the secretive little toad wants to know exactly how many crew members are on board both these ships, how many of them have seaman's cards, and how many have military identification."

"Eighty-one crew members, eighteen of those are scientists or lab technicians. Eighty-one crew members carry a current seaman's card, and none of us carry current military identification other than our Veteran's cards. We're all tested for drugs on a random basis, no exceptions. That includes me. All of us signed a waiver allowing our rooms and personal belongings to be searched at any time. Almost all but a handful of the crew are veterans. I've found that veterans have the discipline necessary to success in a venture such as ours," Jim replied, looking toward the island.

"And do you want him to have that information?" Captain Richards asked quietly.

Jim turned to him and grinned. "Let the bugger have it all. Yes, he's here to spy on us. He works for a drug lord named Munez."

Tom Richards didn't show any emotion as he stared back at Jim, but he had guessed. The Colombian just didn't seem legitimate, and Richards had been on the sea long enough to know that criminals had long arms and friends in high places. Jim's crew bore the mark of soldiers of the highest training and abilities. He made a lightening decision.

"Should you and some of your crew be off on a scientific expedition somewhere, sort of TDY, I could keep a couple of cruisers close to your boats. Bit of a storm brewing to the east. Might end up being a deadly storm," he offered.

"That storm should arrive here in two days. I'd sure appreciate your cruisers in the area for the next couple of days after that," Jim replied, holding out his hand. They shook hands solemnly.

"Best cooperation we've had in a long time, Captain!" Lieutenant Junior Grade Paul Meyers reported with a smart salute for his captain. "This is also the cleanest and best kept pair of ships we've seen in a long time, outside of ours, of course," Meyers added.

"Thanks, Lieutenant," Jim said, saluting the young man. "Can

I invite your crew to a fantastic dinner?" Jim asked, turning to Richardson.

"Sadly, Jim, I must decline. I have an observer who needs to be on shore to catch a flight this evening."

Jim didn't miss the snort from the lieutenant. Obviously, the man didn't like or trust the Colombian, and he was wise not to trust him.

"Perhaps seven days from now, then?" Jim asked.

"Perfect," Richards answered Jim's grin.

Jim allowed the crew to visit the island after dinner, but he kept the teams on board. They had a mission to plan. Pen sat next to John in his conference room, and Cecilia sat beside Jim in his, sharing the end of the table. As the men gathered to their seats, their computer monitors showed the acronym SMESSCS set perpendicularly on the left side of the screen. The letters stood for *Situation*, *Mission*, *Equipment*, *Service*, *Support*, *Communication*, and *Signal*.

Along with their usual chores on board, the men worked hard at planning this mission, and Jim thought they were ready. He clicked each heading and read the information attached, frowning when he came to support. The truth was they had no support of any kind once they were in Colombia. They would be on their own. But that was the very nature of their existence. At least they had some air support that no one knew about.

"Dang, boss!" That was Chief speaking. "He may think he's got protection up there all alone, but help is a long way away, especially on the ground! He's not going to realize that, silly bugger!" Red Claw was correct, and the men nodded.

"Pippi and Rock 'n' Roll, you've got our backs," Jim said, referring to the air support.

"The AH-1W Super Cobra will be armed and ready when we get there, Jim," Pen said. "I've arranged for it to be TDY for several days. The crew for the CH-53D is ready too." Her voice was steady, and Jim smiled at John's sudden smile of pride in his new wife.

"Okay. As soon as this storm rolls in, we leave. Gear up," Jim commanded.

In the war rooms, each man double-checked his weapons to

be sure they were operating properly and used a written checklist. Their packs would touch on seventy-five pounds with food and ammunition, medical supplies, and everything else. Everything was loaded onto the CH-53D Sea Stallion under cover of darkness, and when the storm hit, the chopper lifted off. The flight to the aircraft carrier cruising off the coast of Colombia was quiet, for the men slept as much as they could, knowing that once in country sleep might not come easily.

Captain Robert Morton was one year from retirement, and he was enjoying his last tour of duty in the navy. He greeted Captain Shepherd with a hearty handshake and escorted him to the admiral. They knew each other slightly, and Morton had been briefed in part of what was going on. Jim filled him in on the rest. Jim was never one to keep information back when he knew he could trust a man.

Admiral Samuel Flint was also one year from retirement, enjoying a chance to get away from his desk and out to sea for a change. This mission was one he approved of completely. He smiled and shook hands with Jim, and the three of them sat down.

"This room is secure," Admiral Flint said by way of beginning.

Jim leaned forward and began to fill in the admiral. Five minutes later, he sat back and watched the two men. Flint was a small man, still trim, with red hair streaked with gray and pale blue eyes. His nose was long and aquiline, and he had a habit of tugging on it while thinking. Morton reminded Jim of Andrea, buff, almost larger than life, a man of the sea. His brown eyes were thoughtful, and his face gave nothing away.

"If Admiral Runion hadn't talked to me, I'd have you thrown in the brig!" Flint said with a grin. "Imagine! A small force of mercenaries invading a sovereign country with the sole purpose of killing one of its citizens! About bloody time we did something that made sense!" he added.

Jim decided that the admiral was being frank with him.

"You're taking six of my men into this. You'd better bring them back!" Morton said emphatically. It was his crew that would man the CH-53D Sea Stallion in the attack. Although their job was delivering the teams, they would be in harm's way the entire time they went feet dry over South American soil. Jim understood his concern. Every commander of men understood the weight of looking after the welfare of soldiers on duty. Appreciating the situation, he smiled at the captain and nodded.

"Not so long ago, a large force of Colombian military under Francisco Valdez went after an invading force, Captain. Do you remember hearing anything about that?"

"Jesus, Mary, and Joseph!" Morton whispered. "Four hundred and twenty-six men were found in the hills. Valdez was at the bottom of the pile of bones and rags. That's all that was left of them."

"I had twenty-four with me on that mission. Imagine what I can do with thirty-six. Valdez was convinced it was a NATO force he was chasing, not my group. I'll get your men back," Jim stated, his eyes suddenly stormy green. "That's a promise!"

"Ensign Ramirez, bring me the report on Colonel Valdez!" Admiral Flint said into a phone.

While they waited, Jim was silent. Ramirez came to attention and saluted smartly, handing over the file and leaving immediately. Flint opened it. He began reading aloud.

"The skeletal remains of Colonel Vásquez and the troops he led against an unknown force were found early this morning by a shepherd. Animals, birds, and insects had stripped the bones clean of all flesh. Authorities believe that Colonel Valdez may have been alive when the insects began eating him." Flint paused and looked up at Jim, who nodded in the affirmative.

"Evidence of a heavy firefight was discovered in the area, along with four crashed helicopters," Flint continued. "Whatever or whoever the troops were fighting remains a mystery. No footprints other than those of the Colombian soldiers were found. No spent shells from any guns other than the guns fired by Colombian troops were found. All efforts to find some hint of this unknown force proved frustrating to local law enforcement and military experts. Vásquez believed it to be a NATO force."

"And we let you go?" Flint asked, leaning forward so that the four stars on his epaulets flashed under the overhead lights.

"Not entirely, sir," Jim replied with a grin. "I do report to Admiral Runion and the president."

"So they told me!" Flint said, sitting back. "And for that reason, I'm going to tell you something else," he added.

"My nephew is a DEA agent. I use the present tense because I can't bear to think of him as anything else. He was following up some leads on Munez when Munez was warned. True to character, Munez kept Donald floating around Cali, Cartagena, Medellin, Bogotá, and his home near Yarumal. While Donald was busy there, Munez sent agents to kill his entire family. His wife, two small children, and her parents were all to be brutally murdered. Somehow Donald found out and got them out. Donald disappeared shortly thereafter. Rumor has it that Munez is keeping him prisoner." Flint's face was almost gray as he remembered the details.

"How long ago did this happen?" Jim asked. His face was suddenly grim, his eyes focused.

"Two weeks ago, yesterday." Flint sighed. "Now comes the good part!" he said, leaning forward again and sliding a photo of Donald over. "I'm scheduled to fly three F-117A fighters over Colombia tomorrow night. We're testing a new satellite tracking system. The brother of my nephew's bride is one of my pilots. The other two have different assignments, but he has the sole assignment of providing aerial support for your mission and protecting both of your choppers. His orders are clear, and he agrees to them."

"You could get into a lot of trouble for this, Admiral, if you don't mind my saying so," Jim warned.

"Just bring my nephew home," Flint said flatly. "Captain Morton is with me on this," he added, waving at the silent captain.

"If he's able, I'll let him take care of Munez," Jim said quietly after a pause.

"Use your skills, Captain. Make it happen!" Morton ordered with emphasis on the last word. To honor the two men, Jim stood and saluted them both. He was not surprised when they stood to return the salute and shake his hand.

After Captain Shepherd left the room under the care of a lieutenant junior grade, Morton stared at Admiral Flint with a feral grin. "Hot damn, Sam! That is one dangerous soldier!" he said. "Four hundred and twenty-six enemy soldiers with just twenty-four men!"

"Nearer seven hundred if you count the drug lords and their troops," Flint reminded him, tugging at his nose. "Four helicopters too! Shame we can't ever talk about it," he said. He winked at his friend.

Jim watched as his men dismantled the outer plates of the CH-53D Sea Stallion. Beneath the thin brightly painted plates was a camouflage skin of digital design. When the blades were folded, the top blade was painted the same way. They could set this bird down on the ground and be virtually invisible from the air. With the camouflage netting, someone would have to stumble over it to see it on the ground.

A mast-mounted sight was fastened above the blades and two .20 mm automatic Gatling guns were mounted on either side. The Super Cobra already had a mast-mounted sight and automatic guns mounted. Side by side on the deck, the AH-1W was dwarfed by the huge Sea Stallion.

Jim grinned when he heard John chanting in a singsong voice to Pen, "Mine is bigger than yours!"

"Men!" Pen snorted in mock despair. "Just keep that hulking junkyard out of my way."

"Junkyard!" John whined. "That's a state-of-the-art piece of machinery you're insulting, I'll have you know!" he responded.

"Mine is faster," Pen interjected with a small smile. For a moment, John didn't know what to say, and everyone laughed.

"Say your goodbyes," Jim said loud enough for everyone to hear. "We mount up in ten."

Jim introduced himself to the six crew members from the aircraft carrier. All of them had high security clearances and were among the best of chopper crews that could be found. Briefed already on their responsibilities, they turned back to the controls, getting ready to lift off.

Lieutenant Briggs, communications officer on the flight, watched the men as they climbed on board. He'd been around soldiers most of his adult life, and at fifty-five, he knew a thing or two about them. These were the cream of the crop. They moved with the deadly grace of a stalking tiger. Whatever unit this was, they were loaded for bear.

Flying within a hundred feet of the ground at night required special skills, and Captain Edwards had those skills. His helmet was connected to the mast-mounted sight. One eye saw a digital readout of upcoming changes in the topography and the other eye saw the whole view through night vision technology.

Lifting over the Cordillera Occidental mountain range, they crossed the Cauca River, between Medellin and Yarumal and turned north. He pulled the nose up and hovered for about eighteen seconds over a flat spot while the men pushed their gear out and then zip-lined to the ground. At Captain Shepherd's signal, he eased the stick forward, dropping the nose level, and then sped off.

To those in the Munez fortress, the faint sound of the helicopter gave no indication that a major force had just been put on the ground. They relaxed again when they heard it continue north along the river. Not one even had the slightest inkling that death stalked their mountain fortress.

At the first checkpoint, Jim gathered the men around him. Slipping his night goggles up on top of his forehead, he sighed and squatted down. Some of the men squatted with him, some stood, and some sat on the ground. None seemed to be struggling with the altitude or rigors of the march in darkness.

"Every one of you knows the plan, but remember, in battle plans have to be fluid and adaptable. Stay in touch. Our next checkpoint puts us less than three hundred yards from the fortress. We'll assess at that point." Some of the men nodded.

"Uh, Shep!" Zeke was looking at his laptop. "We have a major enemy force camped about eight miles from the fortress to the south.

Platoon strength or more with vehicles. I'd say the camp was recently occupied and not permanent."

"What! You decide we haven't got enough excitement going here, boss?" Chief said with a grin. "Need a little challenge?"

Jim grinned at Red Claw. His language had cleaned up significantly in the months they'd spent together. The captain knew he was just making a joke to ease the sudden tension in the group and was glad for the diversion.

"Okay. Who invited these guys?" Jim asked, looking around. "Do we know who they are, Zeke?" he added after the chuckling died down.

"Colonel Valdez has a replacement. He's promoted himself to general. His name is Neils Brimmer. He's a German mercenary with a violent nature and a real lust for blood. He's got at least fifty mercenaries in his own personal force and is commanding a small army, all paid for by Munez. Looks like Munez is still nervous," Zeke replied quietly.

"How long will it take his force to arrive at the compound?" Wade asked.

"Thirty minutes on these roads by vehicle. An hour with the men on foot," Zeke replied after a moment.

"Plans are fluid for sure!" FM commented. "Ours just got flushed!"

"No. Our timetable just got advanced," Jim said after a moment's pause. "If we take the fortress, Brimmer is going to hotfoot it up to the fortress. He's going to know the fortress is a tough nut to crack, so he'll come slowly. By the time he arrives, we'll be long gone. We'll take care of him after Munez."

"The river?" John asked, looking at a map.

"It offers many possibilities for ambush. My guess is Brimmer isn't equipped to move at night, at least not with the whole force," Jim replied.

"I concur," Wade said, nodding. He'd been studying some intel on Zeke's computer.

"Timing will be critical. We have to have him angry enough to pursue us after dark once we reach the river," Jim urged.

"Just taking out Munez will do that!" Zeke said with a laugh. "Munez is his money source!"

"Bulldog, you have point!" Jim said, clapping Red Claw on the shoulder.

Terrance Red Claw was a full-blooded Blackfoot Indian and proud of his heritage. Attending the tribal gatherings was important to him, though for the past eight years he'd missed several in the service of his country. He considered himself an American first and knew his family was proud of him.

Growing up in the Rockies gave him the advantage of rough terrain and opportunities to learn hunting and tracking skills. When he first joined the Unites States Marine Corps, he had dreams of returning and becoming a hunting and fishing guide. Two years in Iraq and several other missions taught him there was better hunting. Terrorists and anarchists were his game now, and he led his men through the brush with that in mind. He was on the hunt for a man who trafficked in misery and slavery. For the first time in his career, he knew that this hunt would end bagging the prey and then stuffing and mounting it for display. Smiling grimly, he made his way.

Jim was no fool. Taking the fortress could only be done under cover of darkness. They had the high ground, and that gave the enemy an advantage. He had surprise, and that evened the playing floor. Once everyone was in position, the men turned off all their electrical equipment. Sid Barrett lit up the generator with a laser, and Sam Colt pushed the remote that would fire the pinch missile from the landing site.

The pinch was the latest in EMP technology. Made of paper, it was almost impossible to track by radar. Everyone on Jim's squad hunkered down and kept their eyes on the ground while the missile flew over to protect their night vision. It exploded above the compound, taking out everything electric with a powerful electromagnetic pulse.

Plunged in sudden darkness, the compound became a place of bedlam. Soldiers fired at movement, shooting down their own men. By the time order was restored, all nine teams under Jim's command were inside the walls at their prescribed positions. Darkness was their territory, many claiming they owned the shadows, and indeed, not one person witnessed their insertion within the walls. With their night vision technology, they swept through the compound like a pestilence.

That didn't mean there wasn't danger. Bullets were flying everywhere. Several of the men were hit with debris, but their armored suits protected them. Jim had a bullet glance off his helmet, and Hayseed found a knife sticking out of his bulletproof vest. Every team member had a mark all the way around his helmet that the others could see so they wouldn't shoot each other. Still, there was great danger.

Jim watched Mark Drumheiser rise from a shadow and kill a man with a single knife thrust. Another man ran at is back, but Dorf was there, as silent as his partner, breaking his enemy's neck with an easy, almost casual movement.

Lee Roy Brown was near enough for Jim to watch in motion. The man moved with a deadly grace using his silenced MP5-SD with uncanny skill. Chance appeared, silently stalking an enemy soldier who died without making a sound. Never knowing what had come from the shadows, the soldier lay with eyes wide in surprise and terror. Many of the dead in the compound would wear that death mask.

Jim emptied his clip in three-round bursts, taking men down as he saw them, each burst centered on a face that appeared out of the darkness and went down instantly. Protecting his own team was foremost in his mind. The battle was short and deadly.

Once the soldiers outside the main house were dead, the teams converged on the house, coordinating an attack that took all three floors at once. Flash grenades were tossed through windows, and specters of death followed. Blinded by the stun grenades, men and women saw only ghostly figures pouring through the windows and doors. Only women and children were spared.

Munez sat behind his desk blinking after the flash grenade momentarily blinded him. He heard the bodies of his men fall to the floor and waited for the bullet that would take his life. When it didn't come and his vision finally cleared, he looked around, his ears still ringing. One man stood in the doorway in full body armor, his MP5-SD steady in his hand. Munez looked down at the laser dot on his chest and slowly dropped his weapon and raised his hands. The unimaginable had happened!

Three men slid into the room behind the man with the H&K. One checked Munez for weapons and removed all of them, then stripped every bit of clothing off the prisoner. Naked, with his arms raised, Munez faced his captors with confusion. *Am I now to be kidnapped? Who are these soldiers? What do they want?* He felt the prick of a needle in his arm. That came as a terrifying surprise.

"What did you just give me?" he said, looking at the man with the empty syringe standing next to him.

"Frank, do you have the antidote?" Smitty asked, tossing the empty syringe into the wastebasket.

"Got it!" FM answered.

"What did you give me?" Munez repeated, his voice rising.

"Snake venom," Smitty said easily, pushing Munez into his chair. Munez looked at his arm and saw it turning black and swelling. He swallowed, and when he spoke, his voice cracked with tension.

"What kind of venom?" he squawked. Stretched wide in terror, he watched the blackness spread down his arm.

"Death adder," Smitty said quietly. "You have about fifteen seconds to answer our questions. Where's Donald Flint?"

"Basement! There's a tunnel behind the tool bench!" Munez said frantically.

"Give me the combination of all your safes and instructions on how to open them," Smitty ordered, holding up a recorder and switching it on. Sweating profusely, Munez complied. "Now give me the passwords to your computers," Smitty added. Munez was weeping in fear as he gave them.

FM stepped forward and stuck a needle in the drug lord's arm. "This is just enough to keep the venom from killing you in the next hour," he said conversationally. "It won't ease the pain much, though."

Munez closed his eyes and passed out.

"Snake venom?" FM commented, looking at Smitty.

"Seemed like a good idea at the time," Smitty said with a grin.

Half an hour later, Wade ushered Donald Flint into the room. Flint was bone thin, filthy, and had open sores on his body. He'd been beaten many times and starved. Jim looked into his eyes and saw that they were still clear and steady. Flint smiled weakly and spoke in a hoarse voice, badly damaged from screams during his long hours of torture.

"You the one I'm supposed to thank for this?" he asked, coughing and spitting blood.

"Your Uncle Sam said if I didn't bring you home, not to bother coming myself." Jim grinned. "I figured I'd better comply, or I'd be cleaning the inside of toilets with my tongue for the next year." Without further comment, he handed his H&K Mark 23 to Flint. "There's already one chambered," he said.

FM stuck a needle in Munez, and in seconds, he came around. He looked up and saw Donald Flint holding the Mark 23 steady in his hand. The gun lowered, and Flint fired five bullets into the prisoner's abdomen. With each bullet, he said a name, beginning with his wife and children and ending with his in-laws.

Munez screamed in pain and slid to the floor, his hands covering his abdomen, trying to stem the blood. Then he screamed as the pain mushroomed.

"Think on them as you die!" Flint snarled, tears streaming down his face.

It took Munez several minutes to die, every one of them filled with pain beyond belief. On their way out of the compound, Bear and Hobbs tied Munez to the gate, spread eagle.

"How much did we get from the safes?" Jim asked as he trotted beside Zeke.

"About a hundred and sixty-five million," Zeke reported, looking over with a grin. "We also got deeds for properties, bearer bonds, and some communication codes. If I'm not mistaken, we may also have a lead on our Nazi!"

Bear, Dorf, Wade, and Hayseed trotted along easily with Donald

Flint on a stretcher between them. He kept trying to apologize for his weakness. Dorf looked down at him finally with a huge grin.

"I'd let you run with us, but we have an army chasing us, and your uncle would skin me alive if you didn't make it back," he said.

"An army? Brimmer?" Donald asked.

"The man himself," Wade replied.

"He's a maniac!" Donald said.

"Not for long," Bear said from the foot of the stretcher.

Through the daylight hours they pressed on, different men taking the stretcher every twenty minutes, tirelessly moving toward the river. Donald marveled at their agility and strength. Each man who took a handle of the stretcher introduced himself. Flint wondered who these men were. None of them wore military insignia to identify what branch or group they were with. Eventually he decided it was an international unit because of the British and Australian accents. Whoever they were, he was glad someone sent them.

"How much of a lead do we have?" Jim asked Zeke when they reached the river.

"Two and a half, maybe three hours," Zeke figured, looking at the satellite feed.

"Firefox, Raider, and Nightfall, you have the west side of the river. Dig in in twos and make sure you have at least three safe attack points each. The trail on this side follows the river, so we'll have high ground on both sides. We want to turn him upriver, and we want him madder than a wet hen when he comes," Jim ordered.

"He will be!" Dorf said. "My team will backtrack a hundred yards and leave some surprises," he added, nodding his head. Driver, Mark, and Sparks followed him at an easy lope.

"With three teams, we can keep them pinned down and leapfrog up the river," Tom Izbicki pointed out. "Last one across takes first position!" he challenged, plunging into the river. Jim watched the mad dash across with a smile. Bear was first to step on dry land. Bill Dodge was last, Jim suspected purposely, and the men laughed and began to move uphill.

In ten minutes, Jim had to look hard to find them, and he could only find them because he'd watched them take up their positions.

"Delta, Zulu, and Bulldog have first ambush. I want you to find your second and third ambush positions and mark them on this map for me. Alpha, Sniper, and Knife will supply cover fire for your movements," Jim ordered.

"Dorf, Chief, with me!" John said, waving his arm. The three set off upriver and did not return for half an hour. When they did, they were sweating, filthy, and soaked to the waist. John handed the map to his brother with a grin. "These guys are going to think they walked into hell," he said simply.

"Don't get dead," Jim said quietly. John nodded.

"Knife has first position, boss," Ox said quietly. He nodded once and led his men uphill.

"Sniper, you take second position," Jim ordered. Norm Geissler nodded and waved an arm at his men.

"Let's go!" Jim said to his team, and they set off, climbing to the high ground and working their way along the upper ridges to the third position. Jim paired with FM, and Zeke and Smitty moved a little higher for their three positions. This time they didn't have long to wait.

Brimmer stopped his troops and organized them some distance from the river. He sent a contingent of thirty men to move forward and see if the enemy had boats waiting. While he made plans for the rest of his men, a sudden explosion rocked the ground, and he looked up in surprise as the screams reached his ears. All thirty men were down, most of them dead. He cursed, but he cared little for the deaths of his men. They would be avenged, though. That he swore.

Dorf set up a large circle of mortars with the tripwire in the center of the circle. The six mortars shredded the thirty men instantly. Brimmer halted his men and carefully moved toward the death scene. If these were newer mortars, he knew he had American or European forces on the ground. Examining them he grunted. They were older, one from as far back as the Vietnam era. He was certain it wasn't the Americans.

Choosing thirty more men, he cautioned them to watch the ground and sent them toward the river. Dorf's second surprise was simplicity itself. As soon as the men entered the area, he pressed a detonator, and they were buried under an avalanche. Brimmer swore profusely. Sixty men lost in seconds. Now he would have to send one of his own to lead the next group, or the men would lose heart.

"Murdock! Take thirty men and get to that river!" he commanded. Murdock nodded, knowing why he was going and routed the men together with curses and shoves and then led them down to the river. Murdock was the first to die. A sniper's bullet took him, spraying several men behind him with bone and brain matter as his body hurled backward in the loose display of an already dead body in motion.

Three more men went down. Then six dropped. The men broke and began to run back, but none made it. Brimmer couldn't believe it. Ninety men were dead, and he had yet to see, let alone engage the enemy! He'd watched the firing carefully and saw flashes from only three positions. He guessed there couldn't be more than a dozen men up there. It gave him courage.

"Okay!" he said decisively. "They have a rear guard. They are across the river. That means that the main force is on this side of the river and heading north. Hans! Give us cover fire on that position! The rest of you come with me!"

Hans set up the SAW and began to fire at the location of the snipers. He had no way of knowing they were long gone, but the constant barrage of fire gave the other men a sense of protection as they followed Brimmer down to the river trail and north. As Hans was packing up the SAW, a single bullet dropped him. Three men trotted out of the darkness to retrieve the SAW, reloaded it, and followed Brimmer's troops. There were grim smiles as the men thought of Brimmer's men facing his own SAW.

With the men spread out on the narrow trail, they were exposed and easily taken down. Crossfire from both sides of the river and the high ground sent his men into a panic. Brimmer screamed for

Hans and the SAW only to see it open up on his own men. Then he screamed for his helicopters.

Two Aérospatiale/Westland Gazelle SA 341s came over the ridge. He looked up in horror as the two choppers exploded into flames and dropped from the sky. Half a second later, Penn flew over in the AH-1W Super Cobra and began to circle. All firing ceased, and Brimmer rose from his hiding place as two powerful spotlights lit him up.

"Hello, Neils," a soft voice said behind him as the cold steel barrel of a pistol pressed against the back of his neck. He dropped his own pistol and said nothing. His hands were tied behind him with plastic restraint ties commonly used by law enforcement while another man searched him for weapons. They missed nothing, including the small pistol he kept between his legs in his underwear. No one had ever searched him thoroughly enough to find that one.

After taking all his weapons, they stripped him, bound his feet, and left him on the ground. Eventually, just before dawn, four men came for him. He was shivering and cold. In the cold gray light of early morning, he saw that his men had been moved into a huge circle where they first gathered before the attack. Although they were dead, all of them were sitting up. Then he saw the sharpened stake in the center.

He began to struggle, but the four men held him tightly. They took him to the stake, and the big man moved behind him, holding him in a sitting position, and they shoved his body down on the stake. His screams were horrifying, and the heels of his feet scraped uselessly at the ground until they bled. It took him a several minutes to die.

When it was over, Terrance Red Claw untied his feet and hands and dropped the marker he'd made. His face was grim as he stood up and faced the rest of the men. The CH-53 appeared, and the men quickly tossed their gear on board and followed it. As they began to head toward the coast, Penn radioed.

"I have two bogeys heading this way from Bogotá," she said calmly.

"Give me a minute." That was Flint's cousin, Maverick 1, speaking. Smiling, he came around behind the two jets and lit them up. The pilots were alarmed and looked around. He pushed the throttles to fly directly above them. "Tag, you're it!" He chortled into his radio, then banked away.

They tried to chase him, but their antique A-10s were no match for the stealth fighter. He kept them busy until the choppers were over the water and then disappeared. Pen set the AH-1W on deck while the CH-53D hovered with Donald Flint watching with a tired smile about thirty meters from the ship. Then the navy pilots put the helicopter down on the deck.

CHAPTER 33

Twenty minutes later, the regular identification plates were back on the Sea Stallion. Jim sat in a lounge with Admiral Flint and his nephew, wrapped in blankets, listening to the younger man recount his capture and imprisonment. Then Jim recounted his report. When he was done, Admiral Flint looked at him silently for a long time.

"You've made friends here, Captain Shepherd. You can call on my family any time," he promised finally, shaking hands.

Jim was the last to board the CH-53D Sea Stallion. When they were in the air, Dorf turned the nose back toward Hawaii. Counting to make sure everyone was on board, Jim finally relaxed. Once again, his men had proved they were the best of the best. There was just one more thing he needed to clear up, and for a moment, he thought about the scene. He turned and looked at Chief and pressed his talk button on his headgear.

"Chief, what did you drop beside Brimmer's body at the end?" he asked.

"An old Apache marker. I picked it up when we walked through the burial ground. Local people may know something of the Apache and what that marker means," Chief replied.

"What exactly did it mean to the Apache?" Jim asked, curious.

"That anyone who desecrated that particular holy grave would be pursued by spirit warriors and destroyed," Red Claw said with a grin. "I figured we fit the bill."

"The Apache didn't really use that method for killing anyone, though," Jim pointed out.

"No. But the hairs I left scattered around that I gathered in the burial ground will help everyone think they all came back from the dead to wreak revenge," Chief replied.

"You took hairs from the dead bodies in the burial ground?" Mark asked from the copilot's seat.

"They weren't using them," Red Claw said.

"What if their spirits come after you?" Wade asked with a big grin.

"Ain't an Apache alive or dead can take a Blackfoot," Red Claw said. Pen was sitting across from them, listening to the banter, and for a while she looked inward. Finally, she spoke.

"That was a horrible way to kill someone," she said quietly into her headset. "But Brimmer was an animal, and he deserved a horrible death."

"You saw it from the air. Some of us lost our supper over that one," Counselor said with a straight face.

"It will leave a message that will not be forgotten quickly," Chief intoned, his own face set like stone. "I hate killing," he added. "Maybe for a while our enemies will ponder their own mortality."

"Some won't," Jim said. "That's the trouble with terrorists. They don't even respect their own lives. Nothing matters to them but their twisted belief in an ideal. It can be religious, financial, political, even a personal fantasy. Whatever it is, that is all that matters. Once the world realizes we are not dealing with sane people, things might change. Until then we are the final solution.

"Our teams did well together in a very tough first test. Let's hope we don't have to go into anything like this again for a while. In the meantime, we keep our edge razor sharp, we train, go over the basics again and again until they become habit.

"Now let's put this behind us and move forward. Ladies and gentlemen, we have a job to do and a grant to fulfill. Let's get back to work!" Jim turned forward and rested in his seat, taking Cecilia's hand. She smiled encouragingly at him.

Even though he had not expected to test his new teams so quickly, he was proud to lead them and felt very confident of their future. But he obeyed his own command and put that all behind him, concentrating on the soft hand holding his, and looked into a pair of hazel eyes, more green than blue today, and decided that a man could drown in a woman's eyes.

His head bent down, and he stole a brief kiss, and Cecilia had that special smile she reserved for those moments on her lips. Jim didn't remember much about landing, putting things away, and getting to their quarters, so lost in her presence, but he did remember their moments together before sleep took them both.

www.ingramcontent.com/pod-product-compliance
Lightning Source LLC
Chambersburg PA
CBHW041044310726
48978CB00011BA/420